Saint Gabriel's Return

A Stephen Saint Gabriel Mystery

✠

J. L. Harber

St. Gabriel's Return

ISBN 978-1-62880-121-7

DEDICATION

To Two Women Who Made A Difference

Ellen Prewitt was the first person to read my very first attempt at novel writing. A successful author, and gracious woman, she was generous in giving me encouragement and guidance on developing *Saint Gabriel's Gospel*. Had she not seen something in those early efforts, I might have not written another word.

Donna Casey is the graphic artist who created all the covers for my first seven novels, five Saint Gabriel and two Patrick Orion's. We've never met. All our work was done through emails. Her hard work made the books look attractive and even intriguing.In the process, I have come to think of her as a friend and collaborator. During the course of our work, Donna has had to battle a life-threatening disease. Sadly Donna succumbed in October 2016. I will miss her.

It is to Donna and Ellen that I dedicate this sixth book in the Saint Gabriel series and I do so with profound appreciation.

ALSO BY JERRY L. HARBER

The Stephen Saint Gabriel Series

Saint Gabriel's Gospel

Saint Gabriel's Passion

Saint Gabriel's Revenge

Saint Gabriel's Apocalypse

Saint Gabriel's Resurrection

The Patrick Orion Mystery Series

The Priest's Dead Wife

The Mama's Boy Murders

The Beale Street Murders

1

HAIFA, ISRAEL

The doors between the waiting room and the surgery suite flew open. He wore blue scrubs;she was in white scrubs. Without hesitation, the two walked into the waiting area in which three apprehensive souls quietly held vigil. Waiting for this moment Nicki Gabriel, Valerie McMurphy, and Trevor Wiley sprang to their feet, faces a mixture of fear and hope. "Nicki," the woman in white scrubs—a nurse named Hammadi—said, "this is Dr. Greenberg. Doctor, Nicki Gabriel." Hammadi's face was passive and gray. Greenberg offered his hand, and Nicki eagerly grasped it.

"Mrs. Gabriel, I'm the trauma surgeon who operated on your husband this time. Please sit," he said, gesturing toward a chair. "I'm afraid the news isn't good. I'm so sorry."

A gunman hired by an ultra-Orthodox Jewish group had attempted to assassinate Nicki's husband, Biblical archeologist Stephen Saint Gabriel only a day before. Gabriel and his team, including Valerie and Trevor, had been exploring in the hills surrounding Nazareth, seeking a tomb believed to hold the bones of Jesus' mother, Mary.

Trevor was a former graduate student who completed his Ph.D. in archeology under Gabriel. Even before he graduated, he was an important part of Gabriel's team, including being the photographer on the *Mary's Gospel* codex. After a stint as curator for a cache of uncataloged finds amassed by a nineteenth century Episcopal bishop and stored for years in their original shipping crates, Trevor joined the Gabriels' firm, Archeological Research Associates. Trevor had suggested the use of modified satellite imaging to help their search. His suggestion led to finding Jesus' mother's tomb.

A radical group of Orthodox Jews objected vigorously to ARA's search for tombs, but was overruled by the Israel Antiquities Authority. A few of the most radical decided to stop the dig by any means possible. Their solution was to engage an assassin, a former Israeli Army sniper, a mercenary, but also a man somewhat sympathetic to their cause. His shot was almost the perfect kill shot, but only almost. Gravely wounded, the original surgery on Gabriel had appeared successful, but when he began to bleed internally and neared death again, he was rushed back into the trauma's center's operating suite. Hours had elapsed, and now the surgery was over, and Nicki was about to hear the result.

"Is he alive, Doctor?" Nicki asked.

"Yes. That's the good news. But there is bad news as well. As you know, because of the amount of blood loss prior to the original surgery and the trauma his system endured, we feared there might be cognitive loss if he recovered at all. We'd had him in a medically induced coma to give his body time to heal with as little other trauma as possible. When we reopened his chest, we were startled at the amount of blood from a leak in the repair. Our fear, all along, has been the consequences of reduced oxygen to his brain and other organs. My repair this time was extensive; effectively I redid the entire surgery. We almost exchanged his entire blood volume before we could get the repair to hold. His oxygen saturation is in the lowest acceptable range. So once again, we just can't be sure of his overall condition. I think the next twenty-four to forty-eight hours is critical. If all goes well, we will bring him out of the coma during that time. Then we can access his overall functioning, including his cognitive abilities."

"So he might recover without a problem?" Valerie asked.

"Frankly, based on my experience, I'd say he has, at the very best, less than a fifty-fifty chance of complete recovery. I'm sorry."

"Dr. Greenberg, I'm sure you've done your best and the ICU team will continue to do their best," Nicki offered. "Gabby is strong-willed and very determined. We have a lot of life left together and he won't let a bullet take that from us. Thank you for meeting with us." Nicki offered her hand and Greenberg took it in his.

"That will be my prayer, Mrs. Gabriel," he said, looking deeply into her eyes.

"I'm calling the Cardinal," Valerie said. The Cardinal she referred toisAlessandro Greganti, Gabriel's friend and her contact at the Vatican. At the Cardinal's request prior to the dig's start, Valerie, a devout Catholic, was added to the archeological team for the project. Her youth and pious spirit had commended her to the Church as their representative on the team. Depending on the outcome of the work, the news could have a significant impact on the Church. Having a "good Catholic" on the team would only help legitimize whatever was found. "He'll say a mass and I bet Pope Boniface will as well."

"I'm sure he will, Valerie. Gabby will need all our prayers." Turning back to Greenberg, Nicki asked, "May I see him?"

"Yes. He's in recovery and still sedated, but I think it will be fine. Speak to him as if he were alert. Many of us believe those in comas hear what is said even though they can't respond. Nurse Hammadi, will you take her back, please?"

"Trevor, you and Valerie wait here, please. I won't be long."

"Sure," Trevor said. "We'll be right here."

Trevor and Valerie had become something more than work colleagues in the last few weeks, but there was not yet what might be characterized as a full-blown romance. However, it was clear it would only be a matter of time.

"I'm ready," Nicki said to the nurse and the two of them headed to the ICU.

✠

The beeping monitors that Gabriel was hooked kept a steady, but subdued tempo. The room lights were dim; illumination from monitor readouts pulsed and flashed vital signs like a cheap neon display in a bar window. He had been intubated and was on a ventilatorto assist his breathing and to assure his blood oxygen level stayed high. His face was colorless; his lips parched. Nicki stood at the foot of his bed, composing herself before moving nearer. She touched his forehead, gently caressed it, and then took his hand.

"Gabby, we've got to stop meeting like this," she said, as cheerfully as she could muster. "I'm ready to get back to Memphis, or maybe our little place in England."

Nicki was an immensely wealthy woman, having inherited considerable money from her deceased first husband. As a part of that wealth, she maintained a home in England as well as their primary residence in Memphis, Tennessee. She graduated from the University of Memphis with a master's in Egyptian archeology after marrying Gabriel. And their firm, Archeology Research Associates, was based there in their home. Nicki didn't flaunt her wealth. She was, however, very generous to others.

"We healed in England once before, and I think a month there would be wonderful. But, you've got to get out of this place to pull off that plan. So get to work on that!" She leaned down and kissed him tenderly on the mouth. "I love you, Gabby. We all miss you. Get some rest and I'll see you later."

With that, she patted his hand, and left the room. Her deep sadness and fear began to flow down her cheeks, dripping from her chin onto her blouse. She didn't bother to wipe them away. She had no strength for that.

2

Haifa, Israel

Gabriel's vitals slowly improved as the hours ticked by; the repairs were holding. Almost forty-eight hours after Nicki's first ICU visit, Dr. Greenberg gave the order to bring Gabriel out of his medically induced coma and replace the ventilator with a nasal cannula. Nicki was at his beside when his eyes first fluttered open.

"Hey, Sweetie," she cooed. "Welcome back to the land of the living."

Gabriel blinked several times, his eyes swiftly shifting from right to left and back again. He tried to speak, but a parched throat stymied his efforts. He managed to rasp out a single word: "Water."

Nicki retrieved a cup from a bedside table, poured water from a pitcher, inserted a straw, and brought it his lips. Gabriel closed his eyes and sipped the tepid water from the cup. When he was finished, he turned his head slightly dislodging the straw and Nicki moved the cup. His eyes darted around the small ICU room. "Where am I?"

"You're in the hospital in Haifa."

"Why?"

"You were shot at the airport just before you were to fly to Rome with the bones."

"Who shot me?"

"Someone who took exception to our digging up old tombs, a hired assassin, Dov Turkovich."

"I want to go home."

"And I want you home. Would you like to go to our place in England?"

"No. Let's all go home."

The nurse who had been standing just behind Nicki spoke, "Let me get the doctor and then Dr. Gabriel needs his rest.

"No. Nicki stays."

"But Dr. Gabriel," she began, but didn't finish her sentence before Gabby interrupted. "No. She stays. I need her."

✠

Three weeks later, the team touched down at Memphis International Airport. A car was waiting at the private aviation terminal to drive them home to The Gardens in Midtown Memphis. Valerie, as the newest employee of Archeological Research Associates, had traveled with them, as had Trevor. Trevor had an apartment near the Gabriels' home that included a spare bedroom, but propriety suggested Valerie would be more comfortable—at least for the time being—in the guest room of the Gabriels' spacious old home and headquarters located in the upscale Chickasaw Gardens in Memphis, Tennessee.

Mandy, Nicki's long time assistant, was waiting when the limo pulled to a stop in the rear of their home, and when Gabriel emerged, she threw her arms around his neck and began to cry. "I was so afraid for you," she said when she pulled back.

"Thank you, Mandy. I assume you've held things together here?" Gabby asked, though he was moved by her obvious affection and genuine concern for him. The guesthouse behind the main house was her office and residence. Attempts to get her a more suitable place to live had not been well received. "I need to be near you two," was her line of reasoning. Mandy eventually wore them down.

"I need to rest," Gabby announced once the troop was in the house. "And to be able to do that in my own bed sounds like heaven.

Nicki, can we order some dinner for everybody for later. We can eat and talk a little strategy." Gabby was still clearly feeling the effects of his weeks in the ICU in Haifa. His khaki pants were bunched at his sides where his belt was pulling them tightly to try to close the inches between his waist and the pants waist size. The oxford cloth blue dress shirt he wore was hanging limply at his shoulders. As pronounced as these changes seemed, the gray in his salt and pepper hair was now the dominant hue as it framed his gaunt face.

"I'll take care of it. Do you have a preference?" Mandy asked.

"As a matter of fact, I do. How about A-Tan's?" A-Tan's was their favorite Chinese restaurant and was only minutes away.

"The usual?"

"I'm very predictable," he said. Gabriel wondered if he could actually eat something, which tended to be spicy after the relatively bland hospital fare, but he was certainly going to try.

"Do you need any help with the stairs?"

"I'll take it slow. I don't have much strength or endurance, but at the hospital they told me to work on my stamina."

"We should have stayed longer in Haifa and let you recover more fully," Nicki said.

"Probably. But we didn't, did we?" he smiled as he spoke to her.

"No, hardhead, we didn't. Go to bed. I'll get Valerie settled in and I'll wake you for dinner." She kissed him lightly on the mouth. "I am so glad to have you here in one piece."

"That makes two of us."

Nicki glanced at Trevor and Trevor took the hint. "Gabby, I'll just walk upstairs with you to make sure you get settled in okay."

"I don't need help climbing stairs."

"I know. I'm not helping—just accompanying."

"Just this one time, okay?" Secretly Gabby was thankful for the "accompanying" since he felt very tired and unsteady. He hadn't slept much on the flight home.

"Hell, yeah. I'm not some private duty nurse. Just today."

"I can tell you this: if I had a nurse, she'd be a she and a hell of lot better looking than you! C'mon. Let's get this over with." Both men laughed and headed toward the stairs.

✠

After Gabriel's nap, one that lasted several hours more than he'd planned, they gathered in the kitchen to eat. Dinner was essentially a social affair. There was no talk of Israel, Gabriel's recovery, or of business of any kind—until the dishes were cleared.

"Guys," Gabby said, "I want you all to know a few things. First, I have some memory problems. For example, I can remember parts of our previous digs, but then I draw a blank about some details. Try as I will, I can't get anything to come up. I think it's improving, but I'm not positive. Second, sometimes I struggle for the right word or phrase. It's very annoying. Sometimes it's worse than others. Third, I don't much want to undertake a new project, and even if I could be persuaded, I'm pretty much done with Israel and the mid-east, at least for now. I think we could concentrate on working on things we've already discovered. Trevor, Valerie, I want you to know that there will be no hard feelings if you want to go dig in the dirt with someone else."

"Hell, Gabby, I can't speak for Valerie, but I'm okay with a break, too. Besides, I'm not interested in working for someone else, and I know I'm not ready to strike out on my own."

Valerie spoke up quickly. "Exactly. What he said." She smiled. "I can learn a lot right here with you guys."

"Thank you both. If you change your mind, let me know."

Nicki joined in. "Gabby, maybe after some time off, you'll feel differently. I have to be honest, I trained for Egypt and I'd like to get there sometime in the not too distant future. But I'm okay with waiting a bit to go anywhere. I'm pretty fed up with people trying to kill us." Nicki's own life had been in jeopardy more than once as they worked in the field. She smiled and reached out to pat his arm. "If any killing is to be done, I have other plans about how to do it where you're concerned, but you need to be stronger."

"Nicki! Not in front of the 'children'!"

Laughter rocked around the table. Then Mandy spoke. "Maybe tomorrow you can start your next phase of convalescence by reading the mail that stacked up for you. And don't worry;there are no bills in the stacks. I've handled all that. And I haven't touched your email at all. You probably have a ton of messages."

"Right now, reading letters and emails is about my speed. As for Egypt, Nicki, there's no reason for you not to see what you could put together. I can go with you without really being involved in the work. I'll just keep you company at night when you come to our tent."

"Hmm. I like the sound of finding you in our tent, but I'm not so sure about working without you."

Trevor took a sip of his wine and said, "You guys apparently have a lot of 'catching up' to do. Personally, I'm starting to squirm a little. What about you Valerie?"

"Uh, I hear there's a lake within walking distance. Why don't we take a stroll and let these two have some time together."

"Oh, Gabby, we've scandalized the 'kids'" Nicki said with a look of mock horror on her face.

"And not for the last time, I hope," Gabby replied, reaching for her hand, while knowing he could likely do little more than hold hands.

3

Memphis, Tennessee

The Gabriels' Home and
Headquarters of Their Company

After the breakfast dishes were cleared the next morning, Nicki, Trevor, and Valerie headed to the living room to talk. They planned to kick around some ideas about what projects at the lab they could undertake. Nicki also wanted to do some follow up on Gabriel's idea about Egypt. In a sense an archeological dig is an archeological dig, but both Trevor and Nicki had cut their teeth on Gabriel's specialty, biblical archeology. Valerie was the least experienced team member, but her work had also taken place in the Holy Land. Egypt didn't offer much, well, really anything, in that regard. Nicki didn't want to consider dragging the others there if it held no appeal for them.

While the three talked in the living room, Gabriel headed upstairs to his office. He climbed the stairs slowly, like an old man, he thought. But his energy still wasn't back. He was breathing heavily when he circled his desk and dropped into his office chair. Mandy had placed a huge stack of mail in the middle of his blotter and he settled in to attack it.

Flipping through the stack, he saw journals, a couple of large envelopes, likely containing articles somebody wanted him to read and comment on, and a number of letter-sized envelopes. He recognized some return addresses, but there were some completely unfamiliar. He didn't feel ready to tackle any of it.

Shifting the stack aside, he centered his laptop on his desk and turned it on. He first called up his email program, only to discover his Inbox was overflowing with messages. He hadn't been at his desk five minutes and already felt tired physically. Worse he felt emotionally fragile. He really didn't want to read any of the mail, electronic or otherwise.

For Nicki's sake, Gabriel was trying to put on a brave face during his recovery. But he didn't feel very brave. In fact, he wasn't sure he wanted to be in the field ever again. Clearly, he thought, people have gone nuts. Disagreements about most anything seemed to require physical force at a level and of a kind that seemed foreign to his values. In all likelihood, if he continued in the field of biblical archeology, no matter what he might discover, someone would be offended. And these days, that kind of offense seemed to spawn violence, not just controversy. The latest episode was the third time his life had been threatened, and clearly the most nearly lethal. He'd decided he didn't want to put himself in a position for there to be a fourth time.

Gabriel spent the next few hours looking at journals and magazines. He wasn't eager to open any of the other mail, even from people whose name he recognized. He was taking a break from reading and just looking out his window when Nicki knocked softly on the open door.

"Relaxing a bit?" she asked.

"Yeah. Resting my eyes and my feeble brain."

"Anything interesting?" Nicki asked as she crossed the room and sat on the edge of his desk near his chair. She ignored the 'feeble brain' comment. She felt sure Gabriel wasn't being entirely honest about his mental functioning, but she wasn't going to confront him about it. If he were having problems, he'd tell her in time.

"Not really. I'd probably care more if I were still in a classroom where the latest journal article might be important, but not so much now. Hey, that's an idea. Maybe the University of Memphis would let me teach for them, at least as an adjunct."

"They would be lucky to have you in any capacity, but is that really what you want?"

"Less likely to be shot in a classroom. That appeals to me."

"Oh, honey." She leaned over to hug him, but the position was awkward. Nicki decided to just sit in his lap and wrap her arms around his neck. "I don't know what to say."

He kissed her. "You don't have to say anything. I'm just being a baby. I'm don't feel ready to go back in the field. Give me some time and I'll be fine." He said that with a conviction he didn't feel.

"There's no rush. The others and I thought it might be fun to go to Oxyrhynchus. I read recently there are still acres of dumps that have never been explored. Digging up ancient papyrus isn't going to bother anybody. I was thinking about contacting the Egyptian Ministry of State for Antiquities to see if we can get a permit. Or we can try to join the team already working there, but none of us could remember what university is running the show. I'll have to look it up. Our third idea was to see if Doogie needed help in Pella."

Doogie is Dr. Douglas Howard, a classmate of Gabriel's from their graduate school days. Gabriel had consulted with Doogie on a dig that discovered the tomb of Mary Magdalene under the ruins of a fifth-century Byzantine church in Pella, Jordan. Nicki had also provided financial support for equipment Doogie needed to work the site. He was likely still at work on exposing the entire church.

"That could be good solid 'work in the dirt' for all of you. I could give him a call if you like," Gabby offered.

"Not yet. We're still kicking around ideas. Who knows, maybe your stack of mail will give us a direction. Remember that's how Baruti contacted us."

Baruti Boutros was an Egyptian merchant, who was also a member of a secret organization that supported various Christian ministries around the world, but principally in the Levant, Greece, and Egypt. His specific work was with an isolated, and all but forgotten, desert monastery that housed a priceless library of first century Christian manuscripts. The expedition had turned out badly for everyone through no fault of Gabriel's team. The manuscripts, along with the monks, now lay under a small mountain of stone that had collapsed, sealing them in the caves where the manuscripts were stored.

"Not sure I'd want to go through anything like that again," Gabby said. "I still have bad dreams about those dead monks."

"Me too. But maybe there is something less dangerous in those letters. You never know. It could also just be a bunch of requests for funding."

"I'm going to rest a little, maybe take a little snooze, then I'll attack the stack."

"I'm so tempted to join you in bed, but you really do need to rest. I'll call you for lunch."

They both stood and embraced. "I love you, Nicki Gabriel."

"Not as much as I love you Gabby Gabriel. Get stronger. I'm having trouble not jumping your bones."

The rest would help restore his energy. He would soon need all he could muster.

4

MEMPHIS

Gabriel was back at his desk following a nap and light lunch. He was feeling a little more like his old self, perhaps if for no other reason than that he was back at home. Gabriel was troubled by his diminished cognitive abilities, troubled much more than he was sharing with the others. Still postponing delving into the stack of snail mail, he started work on his email. In less than an hour, he was up-to-date. Most called for little more than a one or two sentence reply, or a simple delete action. Now, like it or not, he needed to start ripping open envelopes.

With letter opener in hand, Gabriel began with the business-sized envelopes in the order they appeared in the stack. Most items required little or no response and could be easily handled by Mandy. He scribbled a note on those and set them aside for her. But one caught his attention.

Gabriel didn't recognize the return address—some attorney in Baltimore. When he saw that, he wondered what the heck it could be. He'd had no business in Baltimore and didn't know anyone there. He slit open the envelope, noted the date was shortly before he left the hospital in Haifa, and began to read.

Dear Dr. Gabriel,

I represent an organization, which at this time wishes to remain anonymous. It also wishes to engage you in a project in which we have an interest. Our project is set in Turkey, the portion that was once a part of Syria. As you know, ISIS is wreaking havoc in northern Syria, including the destruction of millennia old monuments. We fear that pattern may extend over the border into Turkey and threaten antiquities in that region.

Our organization is in possession of extensive archives of great historical interest, but for certain reasons, these materials are not available to the public. In fear of the possible ISIS intrusion into Turkey, we have been searching our files frantically for clues as to what historical treasures might be in the potentially threatened zone. Our search has recently uncovered information about artifacts that may exist in Turkey. If this material actually exists, we believe it to be of significant interest to world religions, especially Christianity and Judaism.

We are turning to you with our concerns because of your recent work in Israel and the impact your discoveries have had on extending the world's knowledge of the Christian Gospels and the early Church. We are aware that the controversial nature of some of your discoveries has resulted in, as is sometimes said, mixed reviews, for your work. Nevertheless, we believe that new light on old matters, especially of faith, is ultimately good for everyone.

That said, on behalf of our organization, I would very much like to have a meeting with you to discuss the proposed project we wish you to undertake on our behalf. At that meeting, after we execute a Non-Disclosure Agreement, a slightly redacted copy of which is enclosed, we can be more specific about the artifacts we believe exist, as well as more about who we are. Once that formality is out of the way, we hope you will agree to undertake an expedition.

We are very well aware of the most recent misadventure you experienced and have tried to stay abreast of your condition. All of our members are delighted you are recovering well, and hope a new project will be of interest to you. We sincerely believe this work is very much in line with your professional interests. We think, as you, that the more knowledge we have about the Christian Faith, the better it is for all, not just Christians.

Please call me at your earliest convenience to discuss your possible involvement in what we hope will be a mutually beneficial relationship. I will gladly come to Memphis for such a meeting, and at any time you deem acceptable. At this time, nothing is more important to us.

With the greatest regard for you and your work,

Jonathan Samuel Gulliver, Esq.

Gabriel reread the letter. He felt an odd tingle he'd experienced before when being enticed by something. He read the attached Non-Disclosure Agreement. The redactions appeared to have removed the name of the organization and certain other material that was likely specific to the proposed project. Otherwise it was a pretty standard agreement the like of which he'd used and he'd signed in the past. No red flags there.

He opened Google and called up a map of Syria, and the surrounding region. He wondered what place that was not currently experiencing war might be threatened by what was happening in Syria. He looked at the Turkey/Syria border area first. In a moment he saw the most significant city in Turkey near Syria: Antioch, now known as Antakya. Gabriel sat back and tried to remember what he could about Antioch from the Christian scriptures. He remembered something from the *Acts of the Apostles* that left the impression that Antioch was a hotbed of early Christian activity. He needed something more reliable than his memory.

A Google search for Antioch provided a nice summary. Among other things, St. Paul was said to have spent a year or so there with the followers of Jesus before setting out on his missionary work. A little more research produced an article describing a confrontation between Paul and Peter that took place in Antioch and referenced Paul's account of it in his Letter to the Galatians. They were squabbling over the importance of following Jewish law and customs in order to become a follower of Jesus. Peter was for it, Paul against.

As he continued his research, Gabriel learned that the Jewish historian, Josephus, wrote that the city was one of the largest cities in the empire. A few more clicks and he discovered that some New Testament historians believed the Gospels of Matthew and Luke might have been written there. Then another revelation: it had long been believed by scholars that Mark's Gospel was written in Rome, but more modern scholars were arguing for a Roman audience, but a birthplace of the Gospel in Syria, and if in Syria, that probably meant Antioch.

Antioch clearly had once been a major center of Christianity, Gabriel thought. *This was where Jesus' followers were first called Christians according to* Acts. *Could Gulliver's group, have knowledge about that mid-to-late first century period? And if they did, what artifacts could they be concerned about?* He leaned back from his keyboard and reclined his chair slightly. He pivoted to look out the window, and then closed his eyes. Nothing came to mind that might be in Antioch that could have the importance Gulliver's group was suggesting. Maybe he was wrong about the city. But then, he didn't really trust his reasoning ability yet.

Gabriel did a little more web surfing and confirmed what he vaguely remembered. Paul spent a year in Antioch not long after his conversion. The disagreement between Paul and Peter seemed never to have been settled in any official way, though apparently Paul's position prevailed since those who wish to become Christian aren't required to follow any Jewish practices.

Might there be some semi-official record of the Peter/Paul dustup in some forgotten archive? Gabriel asked himself. As fascinating as such a document would be, he thought that unlikely. He couldn't imagine a Jesus related artifact that would have made its way to Antioch from Jerusalem. It's true that scholars believe that an influx of Jesus' followers fled to Antioch from Jerusalem during the Jewish revolt in the late 60s C.E. They could have brought something—but what? And after all, there's no record of relics being important in the Church until the fourth century when Constantine's mother, Helena, made her famous visit to Jerusalem looking for important sites. Historians generally believe that the Christians there told her what she needed to hear, rather than pointed out places they'd venerated for centuries.

Still debating with himself, he remembered that Mary Magdalene had kept the Cup that Jesus used from what became known as the Last Supper. And apparently Jesus' mother had kept the shroud in which Jesus' body had been wrapped. So maybe there were other physical objects that had been protected in similar ways. His problem was, he just couldn't imagine what they might be. Maybe something belonging to Peter wound up there. The Cave Church of St. Peter in Antioch is said to be from that time. Could there be a relationship?

Gabriel realized he was getting nowhere in trying to guess what the lawyer had referenced. Did he want to pursue this? At least it wasn't in Israel, but it *was* near a war zone. And while modern Christians had been tolerated in Turkey, they were a tiny minority, making up maybe ten percent. The dominant brand, if you will, of Christians there are from the Eastern branch of the Church, rather than the Latin, or Roman Church. He'd done no work with them and wasn't sure how to even go about it, or if it were even necessary. Gabriel decided to stop speculating and talk it over with Nicki. With that, he turned back to his stack of mail. None of it offered any other opportunities or problems. That was a relief.

5

MEMPHIS

Nicki tapped lightly on the open door of Gabby's office. "Ready for lunch?" she asked.

"Wow. Where'd the morning go? Sure." Gabby rose and headed toward Nicki. The two embraced, quickly and gently, then holding hands, headed down the hall and downstairs toward the kitchen.

"Find anything interesting in your mail?" Nicki asked.

"Maybe. Puzzling if not interesting."

"Oh?"

Gabriel began to summarize the attorney's letter and his own research on Antioch. He was in the midst of the story when they arrived in the kitchen to find Trevor, Valarie, and Mandy sitting at the table. "Start over, honey," Nicki said. "I think they'll want to hear this, too."

As Nicki brought the sandwich ingredients to the table and everyone began crafting their own version of Dagwood Bumstead's creations, Gabriel began again. They all listened, exchanged a few glances with each other, and began to eat.

When he wrapped up his report, Trevor said, "So, what'd you think? Gonna talk to the guy?"

"I don't know."

"Talking never hurts, Gabby," Valerie offered. "You don't have to commit to anything if you don't like what you're hearing."

"She's right, Gabby," Nicki said. "He's willing to come to us, so there's not even any cost involved; just a little time."

"All true, guys. I think we need some information. Mandy, would you please find out what's involved in doing archeological work in Antakya? Who do we have to deal with, how difficult are they to deal with, that sort of thing? I'd also like to know what role the Orthodox Church might play in digging for religious artifacts."

"I'll get started after lunch, though the time differential may require spilling over to tomorrow if I have to make some phone calls to Turkey."

"No rush. I noticed Mr. Gulliver had an email address on his letterhead. I'll email him to let him know I received the letter and that we're thinking about it. Now, what have you guys been up to this morning? Give me an alternative to Turkey."

Valerie spoke up. "I did some research on Oxyrhynchus. Bottom line is this: though some archeological work continues there, the focus of the project now is studying and publishing the volumes and volumes of papyri already unearthed. For example, they anticipate publishing another forty volumes of material related to Christianity alone. So while we could likely be given permission to dig, anything we found would apparently be placed in their queue and might not see the light of day in our life time."

"Sounds a bit bleak," Gabby volunteered.

"Yeah," Trevor said. "So we moved on to something else. You know Sarah Parcak of UAB has done pioneering work with satellite archeology in Egypt and elsewhere. You remember we used her methods, modified for an aircraft, for our search in Nazareth." Gabby nodded. "She has identified seventeen possible pyramids, somewhere around three thousand settlements, and maybe a thousand tomb sites. Using satellite imagery has made finding sites relatively easy, but they still need people on the ground moving sand. We might be able to partner with her or with Egypt in some way and select a site to work on. If it worked out, we'd likely spend a large part of our professional lives in Egypt on that single site."

"They shoot at people in Egypt?" Gabby asked, only half jokingly.

"Probably not, though in your case they might make an exception."

"Thanks for that encouragement. Anything else come up?"

"Nope," Trevor answered. "But we've got other possibilities to explore."

"Okay. I'll email Mr. Gulliver, and you guys keep searching for a direction."

The remainder of the luncheon conversation was talk of inconsequential matters. Gabriel finished up his sandwich and iced tea, and took his plate and knife to the sink. "I'll stick it in the dishwasher, sweetie," Nicki said. "Go send that email."

Gabriel kissed her cheek. "Thanks, babe. Then I'm going to take a short nap. I still don't have squat for energy."

"Hey, I don't care how many naps you take. I just want you to get your health back."

At his desk, Gabriel clicked on his email program and then keyed the "compose" icon. He typed in Gulliver's email address and tabbed down to the subject line where he typed, "Your request." One more tab and he was ready to write the email.

Mr. Gulliver: read with interest your letter. Not ready to make a commitment, but didn't want to leave you hanging. My team and I will think about it and let you know something soon.

Gabriel reread what he'd written. He hit the send icon and heard the telltale swish of the message heading to Baltimore. With that done, he picked up his last magazine from his earlier stack. Five minutes later, his phone rang.

"What's up Mandy?"

"You have a call from your mysterious lawyer. Want me to take a message?"

"What the hell? I just sent him an email telling him we'd think about it."

"Evidently, he thinks you're a fast thinker."

"Damn. Put him on."

As soon as he identified himself, Gabby heard, "Dr. Gabriel, this is Jon Gulliver. I received your email and hoped we might chat. Perhaps I can give you some additional information to assist you in your decision."

"You haven't provided us much time for reflection, Mr. Gulliver."

"I'm sorry Doctor. It's just that we are so eager."

Gabby sighed. "Okay. I'm listening."

"Is this a bad time, Doctor?" He had picked up on Gabby's irritated tone of voice.

"No. Now's fine." Not exactly the truth, but a polite answer.

"Splendid. I am sorry for the intrusion, but I think what I have to say might be helpful."

"Please go ahead. Sorry for my gruffness." He almost meant it.

"I understand. I don't mean to bring pressure. Well, let me just get to it. The organization I represent has existed in one form or another for quite a long time. It is no exaggeration to say centuries. Along the way, it has created and/or added to quite an extensive collection of material. Some simply document the life of the organization, our history, if you will. But at various times, the collections of other groups was made available and incorporated."

"May I ask how that occurred?"

"Yes, well, by various means. For example, there came a time when one of the members was a high ranking religious official. In that position, he had access to extensive, one might say, important records associated with his religion. I'm sorry I can't be more specific about what religion. In time, I can perhaps tell you more. At any rate, he had some documents copied, other he simply stole. All became the property of our group, or rather the group I represent."

"So not all acquisitions were above board?"

"That's correct. Regrettable, but each time something such as this occurred, it was believed that a greater good was served."

"Well, isn't that often the rationale for such actions," Gabby said, his sarcasm barely veiled.

"Yes. Yes, of course you're right. But from what I know, I have confidence in these cases, at least the vast majority of cases, it actually was served."

Gabby sighed. *A true believer. Oh, Jesus.* "Please, go on," he said.

"Thank you, but do feel free to interrupt with any questions. We're eager to enlist you and want to help you decide to help in any way we can."

"Okay."

"Well, as I was saying, the collection is large, if not vast. We have several full time archivists/librarians at present, but until the last decade or so had only one or two. Consequently, the collection is not well organized. There has been a growing sense of urgency in the last years to more fully determine what we have which is the reason for hiring additional staff. And may I say here, that a good bit of our material is historical in nature. For example, we have a number of personal journals and diaries. We have correspondence between important historical personages. So it's not that we possess many actual, physical artifacts, such as, sword or shield, but we have a great deal of written material."

"I'm with you. You're more a library than a museum," Gabby offered.

"Exactly! A good description. Well, Doctor, as the war in Syria took the turn it has taken, as well as elsewhere in the region, we've tried to concentrate our efforts on discovering what we have that relates to that part of the world. What I'm getting at is this: we were looking for historical accounts of important events, materials, and the like related to Syria, Iraq and nearby countries. We needed to know to what did our material sometimes point, and whether or not whatever it pointed to is important enough to warrant some attempt at recovery, even at this late date."

"Hold just a second," Gabby said, "let me see if I'm following you. Let's say you were reading the personal journal of Dwight Eisenhower. He might mention that at the end of the war, he came into possession of Hitler's sidearm. You'd read that and ask yourself if trying to locate that sidearm was a worthwhile venture."

"Precisely, except we were most interested in the history of the present war-torn area and its ancient monuments or other significant material," Gulliver explained. "We aren't just looking for curiosities; we're looking for noteworthy items or buildings that preserve or explain history."

"Okay. I think I'm following you," Gabby said. "Go ahead."

"Thank you. It was during this new emphasis that we discovered certain documents that point toward the artifacts, for lack of a better description, about which I wrote to you. We were taken by how, in your last project, it all began with a personal journal entry of a long dead bishop. We have similar, entries, if you will, that point toward something that needs to be located, if the material still exists, and if they need to be protected, and perhaps shared with the world."

"Mr. Gulliver..."

Gulliver interrupted. "Please call me Jon."

"Okay. Jon, this is interesting, but it's really not much more than you wrote about. I still feel pretty much in the dark."

"Of course. I see that. Give me a moment. Perhaps there is more I can tell you." He paused, then in a moment exclaimed, "Yes. Yes." Gulliver's speech betrayed his excitement. "The documents we are finding point to the very earliest of important sites—the absolute very earliest. The site is in a region that was instrumental in the early growth of Christianity. The artifacts are associated with this site. We think. And they may still exist at that site or nearby."

Gabby remembered the morning's research. "I'm going out on a limb, Jon. I think you're talking about ancient Antioch, modern Antakya. It was in Syria until 1939 when Turkey annexed the area. If I'm right about that, then this project may have something to do with what is likely to be the oldest worship site in the area if not in the history of Christianity. If that's true, then the likely target is a church commonly called the Cave Church of Saint Peter. How'm I doing?"

"I can only say it is deductions and instincts such as this that commend you to us."

"Okay, I'm gonna take that as a 'yes'."

"I'm sorry. I can't comment further."

"I'm willing to meet you face to face and execute the Non-Disclosure Agreement. No promises beyond that."

"I can be in Memphis tonight."

"Let's make it tomorrow."

"I'll text you my ETA as soon as I know it and then again when I arrive."

"We can meet your plane."

"No, thank you. I'll rent a car. I can use MapQuest to find directions. Dr. Gabriel, I can't begin to thank you for seeing me. You won't be sorry."

I hope to God you're right, Gabby thought. "As my young associates reminded me this morning, it doesn't hurt to talk."

6

Memphis

Gabriel hung up the phone and headed downstairs to tell the rest of the team about his conversation with Mr. Gulliver. He found them huddled around the table in the kitchen, each with an open laptop.

"Hey, guys. Got a minute?"

"How'd the phone call go?" Nicki asked.

"That's what I wanted to tell you. Gulliver is coming tomorrow. I told him we'd sign the Non-Disclosure Agreement, hear his story, but no promises beyond that."

"How'd he take it?" Valerie asked.

"He was ready to fly down immediately."

"Oh, wow. Guess he was excited."

"Yeah. We fenced a little before I told him to come on down. My guesses about the area he's interested in seemed on target. He wouldn't confirm it, but he as much as agreed we were talking about something related to ancient Antioch, modern Antakya, Turkey."

"What's there?"

"That's the big question. History tells us it was a major Christian center in the first century and St. Peter's Church, a cave church, located there is reputed to be the oldest known place of Christian worship in the world. I think it may be connected to that in some way, but just how is the open question."

Mandy spoke up. "I did the research about archeology in Turkey. I haven't heard directly from Turkey yet, but my other sources tell me it's tough to get permission to work there. They are currently not very keen on Americans in general, and especially Americans who have an interest in Christianity. The Christian communities in Turkey are just barely holding on. Though there is no official persecution, there seems to be plenty of unofficial unhappiness with all non-Muslims right now. There have been a few instances of Christian churches being firebombed and a few isolated murders of Christians."

"That could make Mr. Gulliver's trip a complete waste of time as far as I'm concerned," Gabby offered. "I don't want to be where people are trying to hurt each other. But it's his time and his dime, and I'm curious now."

✠

Gabriel received an email from Gulliver later in the evening indicating his flight would touch down at the private aviation terminal of Memphis International around 8:00 a.m. He relayed the message to the others as Trevor was about to head to his apartment for the evening. Valerie was ready to head to the guest room—perhaps because Trevor was leaving.

"I imagine since he's flying private, he'll have a car waiting. That would put him here by 8:30ish. Let's all gather at 8:00 and be ready for him. Okay?" Gabby asked. All agreed that would work well.

"I'll have a light breakfast and coffee," Nicki said, "if you want to come a little earlier." And that was the way it was left. Gabby and Nicki headed to their bedroom.

"Are you excited, honey?" she asked.

"Not as much as I was before I found out the natives are hostile toward Christians in general and Americans in particular."

"Perhaps if we try to operate under the radar we'll be left alone."

"We can hope. Or maybe if we get the Church hierarchy involved they can tamp down any heat."

"I wish it was the Roman Church where we already have friends," Nicki said.

"Maybe the Pope can put in a good word for us with the leaders of the Church in Turkey."

"Who knows?"

✠

The team, except for Mandy, gathered the next morning. She was researching the situation for doing archeology in Turkey and expected some returned calls from the previous day's efforts. Nicki had prepared a French toast dish that involved thickly sliced French bread, eggs, butter, cinnamon, brown sugar, and time in the oven. A warm carafe of maple syrup sat on the center of the table. Coffee steamed on the countertop nearby. By 7:45 they were all scooping the dish from their plates to their mouths and remarking on how good it was. When 8:00 a.m. arrived, Gabriel expected a text with an updated ETA from Gulliver. None came.

No message had arrived at 8:30 or 8:45. Mandy had joined the group for coffee and to meet the mysterious Mr. Gulliver. At 9:00 when there was no message, Gabriel asked her to call the private aviation terminal at Memphis International for an update.

"Good morning," the team heard her say. "This is Dr. Stephen Gabriel's office calling. My name is Mandy. We were expecting a plane from Baltimore this morning with a Mr. Jon Gulliver on the manifest. Can you check that for me please?"

"Hold a moment, please." Thirty seconds later, everyone heard, "I'm sorry. We don't have a record of any inbound flights from Baltimore today."

"Maybe we got the day wrong. Can you check what might be arriving tomorrow?"

"Yep. Hold please." And then, "No, no flights from Baltimore are scheduled to arrive tomorrow either."

"Thank you," Mandy said and disconnected.

"That's strange. Mandy, give Mr. Gulliver's office a call, please."

Mandy keyed in the number. After a few rings, the line was answered. "Walker, Walker, and Donaldson Law Office. How may I direct your call?"

Gabby took the phone from Mandy and said, "This is Dr. Stephen Gabriel in Memphis. We were expecting Mr. Jon Gulliver to fly in early this morning, but haven't heard from him. Has he been delayed in Baltimore?"

"Did you say Mr. Gulliver?"

"Yes. Jon Gulliver."

"I'm sorry, Dr. Gabriel. We don't have anyone by that name associated with our firm."

"Odd. I have a letter from him on your letterhead, and I spoke with him at this number yesterday."

"I'm mystified, Doctor. We only have the three principals along with six associates. None are named Gulliver. Could someone have been playing a prank?"

"Thank you for your time. Sorry to have bothered you."

"That's quite alright, Doctor. Have a nice day."

Gabby disconnected. "What the hell is going on?"

7

MEMPHIS

I went on line while you were on the phone and checked out the Bar Association in Maryland. Gulliver is a member of the bar, admitted, let me see," Mandy scrolled through the website. "Yeah. Admitted in 1985. His office number is the one we just called."

"See if the firm has a website," Trevor suggested.

Mandy typed in the law firm name on her browser and clicked Enter. The program was searching. A minute went by. "It says it's under construction."

"Some IT dude is scrubbing Gulliver's name off the site," Valerie said. "This is creepy."

"Creepy doesn't begin to describe it," Nicki said. "I'm thinking the group Gulliver represented either had a change of heart, or never authorized his contacting us to start with."

"I don't like this," Gabby injected. His iPad pinged, indicating a message. "Hold on a second." Gabby clicked on the message icon and then retrieved the message. He read it aloud. "Mr. Gulliver made a mistake. Please drop the matter."

Gabby typed in a reply. "Who are you?" He hit Send.

Almost instantly a reply showed up. "A private group that wishes to remain private."

"Hey, Mandy, do a reverse lookup on this number, please."

Gabriel read the number from which the message originated. Mandy typed in the reverse lookup website to which the company had a subscription and then typed in the number. She read from the screen. "It shows as a private number in the Baltimore area."

"Can we find out more?" Nicki asked.

"I can check with Patrick Orion. You remember him from church? He's also the investigator we almost called in when we were being harassed by that crazy, rogue priest, Donovan." The Gabriels and Orion all attended St. Mary Magdalene Episcopal Cathedral. After Gabriel and Nicki first visited the Cathedral, Gabriel had been pulled in by the Dean of the Cathedral to help with a project of stored, but unpacked artifacts accumulated by the first bishop assigned to the church.

"Yeah. He and I were on some committee together. As I remember, he was good guy. See what he can scare up. Meanwhile, I'm a little pissed off and I'm thinking we need some more info about working in Turkey. I don't like being yanked around," Gabby growled.

"Whoa, cowboy," Nicki said. "If somebody wants to wave us off and we plow ahead anyway, isn't that a recipe for trouble? I thought we wanted a break from the drama of the last few years."

Trevor and Valerie were looking on, a little hesitant to join the conversation. Mandy didn't feel that constraint. "Nicki's right, Gabby. Go dig in the sand and find some papyrus. Or excavate a temple or a church."

Trevor decided to join in. "Look, I spent a year opening crates and cataloging someone else's finds. It had its moments, but I can tell you, it doesn't compare to discovering something on your own. If we do the satellite archeology thing and go dig up a temple in Egypt, we'll be at that the rest of our professional lives. It will take us away from our roots of biblical archeology. I don't want to give up on that."

"Okay, everybody. Nicki, Mandy, I get there could be some risk involved, and just yesterday I said I was tired of getting shot at. I meant that. I get Trevor's point, too. I'll rein in my state of high pissivity and we'll do more research on who Gulliver might have been working with. We'll learn more about Turkey—Antioch in particular—and then we'll talk again. I'm willing to let it be decided by a vote. Just because I'm used to running things doesn't mean I need to keep doing that. How's that sound?"

The team essentially agreed that gathering information was a low risk activity, and that it would help them make a better decision. Then Trevor said, "I'm absolutely willing for you to make the final decision, but I really appreciate the thought."

"That goes for me, too," Valerie added.

"Goes without saying that I don't need to vote, but thanks," Mandy chimed in.

"Thanks, guys, but I still want to vote. Frankly, I don't trust my judgment a hundred percent. So, let's do our info gathering and we'll talk more. How about each morning, we get together for an update?"

Everyone voiced their agreement and began to stand up. Mandy headed to her office to contact Orion and continue researching work in Turkey. Trevor and Valerie indicated they were going to continue brainstorming what finds stored in the lab they might study. ARA used a few graduate students to do much of the work of cleaning and reassembly. Marge Thrasher, Gabriel's long time lab director, oversaw the students on a day-by-day basis. Marge was physically located in Washington, D.C. where she worked on the *Mary's Gospel* project.She used FaceTime every day and visited Memphis every couple of weeks or as needed. Trevor and Valerie headed out. They would call Marge for input as they drove. That left Nicki and Gabriel alone.

"Nicki, I don't like being yanked around."

"I know Gabby, but this isn't a battle you have to fight. Whatever's going on doesn't have to affect us. We can simply go back to where we were before Gulliver contacted us. No harm, no foul."

Gaby looked at her periwinkle blue eyes. He could see the worry she was experiencing, and he could see her love and concern. "You're right, of course. If Gulliver hadn't contacted us we'd be deciding to do something else that doesn't include Turkey. I know I can be pig-headed, but I promise to rein in my need to deal with this. We'll get some info, and then we'll vote."

"Thank you, Gabby." Nicki leaned toward him and gave him a little kiss. "For my part, I'll try to keep an open mind." An open mind is usually a good thing. Would it be this time?

8

MEMPHIS

The rest of the day passed uneventfully. Patrick Orion had agreed to do some poking around for ARA. He had a couple of contacts in Baltimore from his days in the Naval Criminal Investigative Service or NCIS. They might have access to resources he could use to speed things up. He'd told Mandy he'd call in a few days with an update.

Mandy began to receive answers to her queries in Turkey, and they were surprisingly positive once Gabriel's name was mentioned. She also learned an interesting fact about St. Peter's in Antioch that could benefit the team should they decide to head in that direction. She decided not to wait until the next day's morning meeting to tell Gabriel. She called him to see if he could meet.

"Sure. I'm shuffling papers and answering emails while slowly losing my mind. Come on over. I'll get Nicki. Come to my office. Wait. On second thought, let's meet in the kitchen. I want a Coke and some cookies."

"Be right there, and I'll get out the cookies," Mandy said, cheerfully.

Gabriel walked the few steps to Nicki's office and told her about Mandy's request to meet. "I wanted a break from the tedium, anyway."

"Let me wrap up this email and I'll be right there. A graduate student I met at U of M has gone on for a doctorate and is requesting a research grant from the Foundation." To give Nicki something meaningful to do once they were married, her first husband, Roger, asked her to oversee a well-funded charitable foundation he had personally established. He changed the name of the Foundation to The Nicole and Roger Taylor Foundation after they married. Nicki plunged into the work. She hired Mandy as her personal assistant, and Mandy had become devoted to her. While Nicki was no longer involved in daily operations, she was still chair of the Foundation's board and of the grants committee. Several hours a week were required, with several extra days on a quarterly basis for a Board meeting. Along with Nicki's personal fortune that resulted from Roger's death and the subsequent sale of her portion of the VC company stock to the other investors, Nicki's access to the Foundation's funds enabled her to positively impact hundreds of lives.

"Gonna say yes?" Gabby asked.

"I'm directing him to the Foundation for a formal application. I think his project is worthwhile, so if they turn him down, I'll probably fund it. Not gonna tell him that, though."

"Doesn't it bother you that a friend is hitting you up for money?"

"You know, it doesn't. I—we—have more than we'll ever need and more money coming in from investments all the time, so why not give the surplus away?"

"You're special; you know that?"

"No I'm not, but thanks for thinking I am."

Gabby threw her a kiss, and said, "We'll wait for you." She nodded and he headed downstairs. Mandy was waiting, and true to her promise, cookies were piled on a plate on the counter.

Gabby grabbed two of the Oreos and a napkin. "You not going to have any?" he asked.

"I ate a couple before I made the plate," Mandy said. "Couldn't resist."

"What's the news?"

"Is Nicki coming?" Mandy asked as Nicki entered the kitchen. "Oh, there you are. Well, I've had a productive day. The Ministry for Culture and Tourism is the granting authority for archeological investigation in Turkey. I spoke to an Assistant Director General, Ahmed Tabak, who seems to head up the division that oversees archeology. As soon as I mentioned your name, Gabby, he shifted from bored reluctant dispenser of information to very interested. To say he gushed when I said you were considering a project there wouldn't be overstating his reaction."

Mandy picked up another cookie and began to pull it apart as she continued. "It seems he's a Christian and has followed your work over the last few years very closely. He thinks you are hot stuff and to have you in Turkey would be nothing short of wonderful. He asked what project we are considering and I said we had something in mind in Antakya, but I couldn't be more specific just yet. We needed to know more about the application process, dig guidelines, and the like."

Mandy scrapped the creamy white Oreo filling from the cookie with her front teeth and continued. "The short version of what he said is he will FedEx everything we need right away. Even better, he will intercede on our behalf with Dr.," she looked at her notes, "Tutku Sadik, who is the Director General for Cultural Heritage and Museums and the final decision maker." Mandy looked up again. "He said, with the turmoil in the region and Turkey's own internal problems, our work there would have important ramifications, both financially and in terms of public image. When I asked what he meant by the latter, he said it would bring positive publicity to the country at a time when they most need it. And then later, depending on the outcome of our work, tourists—and though he didn't say it—and their money." Mandy popped the rest of the cookie into her mouth.

"Well, that is interesting," Nicki said.

"Yeah," Gabby agreed. "First, we need to find out if we can even work in and around St. Peter's. Then, I guess we need to find out all we can about the church—what's been done there already, who controls it, what the lay of the land is like—literally. Third, we need to know where we can set up our camp and where we can have a warehouse/lab. And finally, we may need locals to assist with whatever we are going to be doing, so the question is where do we find them."

Mandy was writing down everything he said. "I have a question."

"Shoot."

"Two really. First, what are we looking for, and second, how do we know St. Peter's has anything to do with it?"

Gabby laughed. "Excellent questions, Mandy. I wish I had excellent answers, but I'm clueless. Well, not quite clueless. Our Mr. Gulliver praised me when I guessed Antioch and pointed out St. Peter's was a significant place. Beyond that, I'd say we're just going fishing."

"You know," Nicki interjected, "no other archeologist would undertake something like this with as little as we have to go on."

"Yeah. It's not terribly rational. Probably a bad business decision, too. Nobody would fund it."

"Nice to know we don't need anybody's money," Nicki said with a smile. "I think it's a wonderful adventure." What she left unsaid was it might help get the events of the past truly behind them. " I say we go for it."

Mandy spoke up. "I wonder if we should start with number two on your list. I'd say we need to know all that before we can to even see if going there is a viable possibility."

"Hmm. Good point. If you'll contact your new friend in Turkey, I'll chat with him and see what I can find out. Let's make it a conference call and include you and Nicki."

"How about right now? He might still be in his office."

"Yeah, let's do it," Nicki said. "I want to hear it first hand."

Mandy placed the call and was pleased to learn Mr. Tabak had not left for the day. "Sir, Dr. Gabriel would like to speak with you for a few minutes. Is this a good time?"

"Yes. Yes! It would be an honor."

"Here is Dr. Gabriel, sir."

"Mr. Tabak," Gabby said, "thank you for speaking with me. I just have a few questions."

"Anything Dr. Gabriel. I'll be as helpful as I can."

"In confidence, I want to ask you about the Cave Church of St. Peter. We have reason to believe there may be some items of importance that are in someway associated with the church. I wish I could be more specific, but our source was vague, and has since been inaccessible. Is it possible to do some exploratory work there and in the area surrounding the church?"

"I believe that can be arranged. In 2013 the church was scheduled to undergo some restorations, but circumstances have resulted in a postponement. Consequently, the church is as it has been since the nineteenth-century restoration undertaken by Pope Pius IX and Napoleon Bonaparte. As you may know it is only used for religious purposes once a year."

"I believe that is 29 June for the feast day of Sts. Peter and Paul?"

"Yes, exactly."

"You said Pius IX undertook the restoration. Is the church associated with the Romans? I was under the impression it belonged to the Eastern Church."

"The church was associated with the Syriac Catholic Church. The Syriac Church is a semi-autonomous Church which has given its allegiance to the Roman Pope since the seventeenth-century."

"So," Gabby asked, "do we need permission from Rome or from the Syriac Church to do work there?"

"It is a very odd situation, Dr. Gabriel. Turkey, and not Syria, since the annexation in 1939 is responsible for the site, under broad permissions from Rome. Consequently, you need only state permission to work at the site."

"That will simplify things, I think," Gabby remarked.

"Yes. May I ask, Doctor, have you surveyed the site using Google Earth or some satellite view?"

Damn, Gabby thought, *I should have thought of that. I'm slipping.* "Not yet. I wanted to talk with you first," Gabby lied.

"When you do, you will find the church is located at the foot of Mount Staurin. The surrounding slopes are dotted with caves and rock bas-reliefs, most of which are damaged or eroded. The entire mountain is considered church property, so when you make your formal application, be sure to include the entire site. Though it has all been explored many times, it has never been systematically examined, to my knowledge. There may be something you seek outside the cave proper."

"Thank you for pointing that out. What little I know about the church itself would seem to suggest there is basically just one room, the cave. Apparently the crusaders added a narthex or entrance area when they closed off the cave. Is that correct?"

"Exactly so."

"Mr. Tabak, you've been most helpful. My team will make a formal request to work the area, and in the meanwhile, perhaps we can come to Turkey and walk the Mount Staurin to get a better feel for where we might wish to concentrate our efforts. Would that be possible?"

"I'm confident it can be arranged. I'll discuss your proposal with Dr. Tutku Sadik, our Director General. I will update you after I've spoken with him. May I suggest you make a formal request for the necessary visas in the meanwhile? I will alert our State Department of your wishes and our concurrence to speed things along."

"Thank you, sir. We appreciate your help and support. I look forward to our continued association."

"You're very welcome, Doctor. Goodbye and good hunting."

"Thank you."

The men disconnected. Because he had placed the phone on speaker, Nicki and Mandy had heard the conversation. "Mandy, will you get to work on our visas, please? I think we're going to Turkey."

"Right away. Will you want to fly commercial or private?" she asked.

Nicki spoke up. "Let's fly commercial for this exploratory trip. Do the usual logistical prep for an expedition, Mandy, but we'll hold off on executing it and on our final travel plans until we get the actual okay from Turkey, but if you can get everything lined up and ready to go, that would be great. That okay, Gabby?"

"Oh. Yeah. Sure. We don't want to get ahead of ourselves. Uh, I'll contact Trevor and brief Valerie and him. I'm sure he'll have ideas about what kind of survey equipment we need. Mandy, I'll tell him to coordinate that with you. But I would like to get over there as soon as feasible for our walk around."

"Sounds good, Gabby."

Mandy chimed in, "I'll take care of everything."

"I'm still kind of wobbly," Gabby said. "I think I'll rest for half an hour."

✠

BALTIMORE

"Do you think he'll drop the matter?"

"I doubt it. My sources tell me he can be very persistent. But, he has nothing much to go on. He knows only that Gulliver intimated the objects are in Turkey—at least that's what Gulliver told me."

"Is he likely to narrow it down to ancient Antioch?"

"Possibly. I'm sure he's smart enough to know Antioch was a major center of first-century Christianity, but it wasn't the only place in Syria. On top of that, he knows only that the objects are ancient, not necessarily first-century."

"We need to stay up-to-date on his plans."

"It's not a problem. Ever since we discovered Gulliver contacted him, we've had access to his archeological company email server. That gives us access to the entire group's emails."

"What about his phones?"

"We haven't broken the encryption on his, his wife's, or the company cellphones. We have managed to get access to the company landlines, so we have some information. But ever since that unpleasant experience with that priest Donovan, they use only the best encryption on their cellphones. Money's no object with them."

"Do we have anyone who's qualified to be on their team? Having someone on the inside would make it much easier to monitor and control what Gabriel's people are doing. I'm working on a way we can get into their offices to see what we can gather."

"Good. And I'm sure if he goes to Turkey, he will need locals to help with the work, whatever it is. We should be able to get someone who'll do what we need. As it turns out, money is no object for us either."

"On another topic, have the Elders decided what to do with Gulliver?"

"Yes."

9

MEMPHIS

ORION'S OFFICE

Shortly after talking with Mandy, Patrick "Paddy" Orion called his contactin Baltimore, Robert Parker. As soon as the call ended, Parker began to make inquiries about Jonathan Gulliver. A few days later when Samantha, Paddy's assistant, buzzed him telling him Parker was on the line, Orion was eager to hear his news about the vanished attorney.

"Hey, Bob. Thanks for getting back to me so quickly. What'd you have?"

"Morning, Paddy. As we suspected, Gulliver is an attorney here and until a few days ago, he was associated with Walker, Walker, and Donaldson. He's a long time member of the local Baltimore Bar Association. I checked with a random sample of his fellow Bar members. He's well liked, well thought of as an attorney, and involved in community affairs. At one time he ran for a local political office, almost ousting the incumbent."

"Sounds like a stand up guy, not someone who would just vanish," Orion replied.

"Yeah. I checked with a couple of the associates at his law firm. They claim to never have heard of him. That is so far-fetched as to be completely unbelievable. I checked a few county legal filings on cases on which he was the attorney. He's listed on W, W, and D's letterhead on those filings as recently as last month.

"I made an appointment to see the senior partner of the firm on a made-up matter. That was a truly bizarre conversation. When I asked about Gulliver, he started in with the denial that's become the party line there. When I confronted him with copies of the filings I mentioned, he flushed and then got all conspiratorial on me. You should have seen it. He leaned forward, lowered his voice almost to a whisper, and told me, and I quote: 'Jon has asked us to handle his departure in this unusual manner. He told us he needed to leave the country to attend to a private matter, and was unsure if he would be able to return.' So, Paddy, looks like bullshit to me."

"That is just beyond clumsy as a story."

"I know. I found out where Gulliver lives and went to his home. It's pretty much what you'd expect for a successful, older attorney. Probably built in the 1930's and kept pristine, at least on the outside."

"You couldn't get in?"

"Nope. Blinds all drawn, and a Realtor's sign in the yard."

"What about a wife or other family?"

"Never married. Friends in the Bar tell me he's devoted to his work, not all of which is the practice of law. He travels a fair amount to various European destinations, but never talks about the reasons or what he does. He dodges any questions by saying he just needs to get away now and then, or passes it off as a little business trip."

"Odd."

"Yeah. It get's better. I used the Homeland Security network at the office to see if I could trace some of his travels. And I could. About once every quarter, sometime more often, he travels to major cities in Europe and Asia. He's gone for about a week each time. His most recent trip was to London and that was about a week before he contacted you."

"Do you know who he saw or what he did there?" Paddy asked.

"Sort of. According to the concierge at his hotel, who happens to be on Homeland's payroll when it's convenient, he checked in, stayed one night, then hired a car for the next day and left the city. I tracked down the car service. The records indicate he drove to a private estate north of London. I contacted the driver who told me that when they arrived, he noticed limos from several foreign countries, like France and Belgium parked in front of the mansion. Those folks could have taken the Channel Tunnel very easily."

"Hmm. Sounds like some wealthy friends getting together for a few days. Maybe they went hunting."

"No evidence of that. I did find out something about the estate. It's owned by a trust called Real Estate Holding Trust of England. That was a black box. I couldn't find out a damn thing about the Trust. The Trustees are in the public record, but they are just law firms, so obviously someone wants to remain anonymous."

"This is fascinating, Bob. Gabriel's assistant mentioned when she engaged me, that Gulliver said he represented some group. I'm thinking it's obviously some secret group and that the gathering in London was a meeting of some of the members."

"Could be," Parker said. "Maybe a committee or board or some other kind of leadership group."

"Anything else?"

"That's what I've got so far."

"I've done some poking around, too," Paddy said. "We think we know some of his credit card numbers and, apparently, none have been used in a week or so. Wherever Mr. Gulliver is, he doesn't need money."

"What now, Paddy? Need anything else?"

"I'd like to know more about this group he met with. I bet we'd find every one of his trips is like this one. Fly into a major city, drive to a nearby private place, and meet with limo passengers."

"I can see if I could turn up anything on another trip he took. Might have to bribe someone because Homeland doesn't have assets at every hotel in Europe."

"If the bribe isn't too large, my client can cover it. See if you can track one more trip. Two isn't a very big sample, but if it turns out like this trip, I'd say we have a pattern."

"I'll get back to you."

"Thanks, buddy. Give my regards to Gayle and tell her I said you were a lucky guy."

"She'll think I made up that last part, but thanks."

With another two or three light-hearted comments, the call ended. Paddy leaned back in his chair. *What has Gabriel gotten himself into this time?* He wondered.

10

MEMPHIS

Gabby," Mandy said, "Paddy has some information on Gulliver. He's going to email you a preliminary report, then he'd like to come by to discuss it."

"Great! Tell him to come by anytime. Just let me know when."

"You want to talk with him? He's on line one."

"Sure. Thanks." Gabby punched the button on his desk phone for line one. "Paddy? This is Gabby. Hear you have some news."

"Hey, Gabby. Yeah. Interesting stuff. I've emailed it, but I'd like to talk about some of the implications and about how much further you'd like me to go."

Gabby clicked open his email and saw Orion's message. "I'll go ahead and read it right now. Come whenever you want."

"Now?"

"Sure. Since we don't have anything going on, I have what I like to call 'schedule flexibility' which is code for 'not doing anything.'"

Orion laughed. "I'll be over in half an hour."

"Great. I'll let Nicki and Mandy know; the four of us can have some coffee."

"See you then."

✠

BALTIMORE

"Sir, we have email activity on Gabriel's account."

"What is it?"

"Somebody named Orion has sent him an attachment."

"Let's see it."

✠

MEMPHIS

Gabriel forwarded Paddy's email to Nicki and Mandy and let them know Orion would be dropping by. He then opened the attachment and read the report. A couple of minutes later, Nicki stepped into his office.

"Pretty strange stuff, don't you think?" she asked. "By the way, Mandy can't join us."

"I'm no investigator, but I'd say he's flitting off now and then to meet with members of his group. Then after the last meeting he contacted us. And it now appears, against their wishes."

"I think you're right. Gabby, these must be some formidable people to make one of their own 'disappear', as it were, into thin air. You sure it's a good idea to keep pursuing this Turkey thing?"

"Truthfully? No. I sense drama about to rain down on us and I've had all the drama I want for my lifetime."

"So we're going to drop it?" The look of hopefulness lit up Nicki's face.

"Probably not. My rational self says we should. My enlightened self-interest, which is on high alert, says we should, but my curiosity, stubbornness, and deep-seated need to discover stuff keeps pushing me toward Turkey."

"I don't want to go. I don't want you to go. If we never make another discovery of any kind, never mind huge ones like the past, your place in history is assured. If you want to find stuff, let's go somewhere safe. Let's go back to Egypt and spend a bunch of money to dig away that huge pile of stone that trapped the monks. The odds are the manuscripts they guarded are still buried there. We'd satisfy our need to discover and, at the same time, deal with our unresolved grief over their deaths."

Nicki's face looked pained and Gabriel saw it. She seemed sure this Gulliver business would end in no good for anyone. He knew she'd been traumatized as he when he was shot in Israel on the last project they worked on. She loved him and he knew it. More important, he loved her and wanted to do nothing to hurt her. But he couldn't promise he'd drop the idea of going to ancient Antioch.

"Nicki, baby, I know it makes no sense to keep pursuing this thing. But I don't think I can let go. If you want me to, if you're really afraid for me—for us—I'll try to pull back, but I just don't know. I realize I'm being an irrational, selfish bastard about it, and I'm truly sorry."

"I don't think I can insist, Gabby. I'm afraid you'll resent me. But I'm very apprehensive. Can we at least slow down? Let's talk to Paddy. Let's do some more preliminary investigation. Let's see if we get any more strange emails from unknown sources. Can we do that? Can we slow down?"

"Yes." Gabby rose from his chair and moved to Nicki who was still standing in the doorway of his office. He reached for her, and she moved quickly into his arms. He felt her body heave slightly and knew there were tears welling up. He felt like the worst kind of husband. "I'm sorry, Nicki. I'll try to be more rational, I promise. We'll get more information. Maybe that will settle it for both of us, one way or another." He pulled back from the embrace just enough to kiss her. He wiped a tear away with his thumb. "I'm sorry, honey. I'm sorry."

11

MEMPHIS

Gabriel's intercom interrupted the pair. "Gabby, Paddy's here. Shall I send him up, or do you want to meet in the kitchen?" Mandy asked.

Gabriel disentangled himself from Nicki, and walked the few steps to his desk. Pressing the intercom button on his desk phone, he instructed her to send Orion to the kitchen. Then to Nicki, "Let's go see what the man thinks." They walked hand in hand down the stairs and headed to the kitchen where Orion waited with coffee in hand; Mandy had excused herself to go back to her office. The three exchanged cordial greetings, Paddy pecked Nicki on the cheek, and then the three sat.

"Thanks for coming over," Gabby started. "We've both read your report. The whole situation seems very strange."

"My thoughts exactly," Paddy replied. "I can find out a bit more from here in the states, but it'd be great to be on the ground in one of the cities where Gulliver attended a meeting. And preferably the last one outside London."

"Can you go?"

"Not officially. My PI license is useless outside of Tennessee, but I can snoop around unofficially," Paddy said. "I've got my passport. Donna can cover what I have going on now." Donna was Donna Miles, Orion's business partner and perhaps a little more. At least, each of them flirted with the idea and did go out occasionally on the pretext of a professional meeting. Both were hesitant for their relationship to evolve into anything more for a lot of reasons. But there was a certain attraction there that they couldn't deny.

"That's good. Gabby," Nicki interjected with some excitement. "I think I know who we can contact to help us. If we're dealing with some big, international group, wouldn't it be nice to have a different big, international group on our side?"

"Absolutely."

"You guys have contacts in a group like that?" Paddy asked.

"Well, we know a Cardinal and a Pope," Gabby said. "Think that would count?"

Before Paddy could answer, Nicki said, "That's not who I was thinking about, though they could be of help."

"Okay. I give up."

"Remember Egypt?" she asked.

"Oh, my God! The Order of Christ! Sal!"

"Yes!" Nicki exclaimed.

"Who are you guys talking about," Paddy asked, thoroughly confused.

Gabriel picked up the conversation. "You remember our little Egyptian misadventure a few years ago? I think we shared the highlights with you and Donna over coffee and dessert one night."

"You mean that business about an ancient monastery getting blown up and buried by an ISIS group?"

"Yep. We had help in the fight, as we told you, but we just didn't tell you everything. You've heard of the Knights Templar I'm sure."

"Yeah. Officially out of business centuries ago, but rumors persist about some continuation of the group," Orion volunteered.

"They actually never were completely suppressed. A remnant of the group escaped to Portugal and reformed themselves into the Order of Christ. Today they hide that identity from the public by functioning as—of all things—a 'consulting' business. The Cardinal we spoke of put them into the game to help us. They remain dedicated to the cause of the Church, and more than that, to the cause of Christ. I'm betting if we or the Cardinal asked, they'd help us."

"So how do you go about it?"

"Well their cover, actually a real business, is called Worldwide Strategics, that much we know. They should have a website. I say we call up Salvador Aurélio—the Sal I mentioned—who led the guys on the ground that helped us, and ask for help," Gabby said.

"I'd rather contact the Cardinal and have him make the contact," Nicki injected. "After all, the site we're thinking about is associated with the Roman Church."

"Really?" Orion asked. "I thought all the Christians in that part of the world were some branch or something of the Eastern Orthodox Church."

"Generally true," Nicki said, "but in this case, that particular group of Christians, the Syriac Catholic Church, is amenable to the Pope."

"Ah. So what're you thinking? You enlist the Templars, and then I go to England and work with them?" Orion asked.

"Something like that," Gabby said. "There's another reason to try to involve them. We may need protection—if we actually go, that is." He glanced at Nicki. "It's still something of an open question as to whether or not we take this on."

"You might not go to Turkey?" Orion queried.

"Might not. We need a lot more information before deciding. I'm thinking we might ask Trevor—you know Trevor, right? —and Valerie—she's our newest team member—to head up an exploratory team in ancient Antioch, as a part of our fact gathering."

"I feel much better with this approach, Gabby, especially with Paddy in England poking around. I want to know what wemay be getting ourselves into before we commit," Nicki said.

"Do you guys have any idea what it is you're looking for," Orion asked.

"Nope. Just that it's ancient and important to Christianity."

✠

BALTIMORE

"The email attachment is a preliminary report from a PI in Memphis. He's been asking questions about Gulliver."

"What's he turned up?"

"He says Gulliver goes to meetings out of the country on a regular basis, and he indicates he has some ideas about what the trips might be for."

"This isn't good. We've got to get Gabriel to drop this thing. Now."

"What would our organization have to do? May I ask, Sir?"

"Certainly; that's how one learns. As for what we might do, I know what someone tried in Israel."

"You mean kill him?" The troubled, puzzled look on the face of the IT person was raw and uncontrolled.

"An assassination, or maybe a tragic accident, might be called for."

12

BALTIMORE

"It seems scary to me to be talking of eliminating someone." The IT tech looked and sounded rattled. "I guess I didn't know we did such things. May I ask why Gulliver contacted Gabriel in the first place and why such an action on The Enlightened Ones' part might be required?"

"I'm happy to enlighten you. You have a lot to learn about our calling. I asked Gulliver that. It took some effort, but he was eventually forthcoming. It seems he has become increasingly concerned about our group's work in the field of religion. From what I gathered, his Catholic faith has gotten the better of his judgment. He's been convinced by Pope Boniface's new policy of transparency—I hate that word and the concept it represents—to 'share' our resources. He's come to believe it would be a good thing to give people information and let them make their own decisions. Given Gabriel's previous discoveries, especially Mary Magdalene's damn codex, he thought Gabriel would be a natural to find some of the items our archives tell us exist that would be helpful to religion."

"Why haven't we tried to find the things ourselves?"

"Well, until Gabriel and his ilk started digging up these kinds of things, we thought their existence was safely unavailable—if they actually existed at all. Controlling information flow is essential in managing people and policy. We think we're on the right track without adding anything to the body of knowledge about

Christianity. The discovery of the Nag Hammadi gnostic documents in the 1940s helped raise questions about what Christianity was actually like in the early years. That kind of confusion is helpful; it creates an environment in which people can be more easily influenced.But, in this case, we can't be sure what Gabriel might find. The Mary codex, the Cup of the Last Supper, those kinds of artifacts have created some difficulty for us. There is a movement toward taking Christianity more seriously and this is the very time we don't need that."

"Why do we even care about that stuff? I thought controlling public policy through legally elected politicians was our focus."

"Influencing religion was not The Enlightened Ones' original focus. We came into existence to influence powerful people who could control the masses. Controlling religion became one means of control to do that. We've been very influential over the centuries in making sure certain men were elected Pope, archbishop, or cardinal. Even outside the Catholic Church, we've had influence. There was a movement begun in the 70s called COCU, which stood for Consultation on Church Union. It was composed of ten of the largest Christian denominations that were seeking organic union. We had to be sure that failed. And it did. It got watered down to Churches Uniting in Christ. Basically, the new group pledged to work together while maintaining their separate identities. It does very little, and in fact, several of the original denominations have withdrawn.

"We don't always succeed, at least not immediately. You're too young to remember, but in the 1960's there was a big theological debate—even made the cover of TIME—about God being dead. It was one of our attempts to undercut a growing sense among world religions that unity and cooperation was a good thing, even God's will. We wanted to elevate the level of controversy about what constituted true religion to help put the brakes on that notion."

"But it didn't work, did it?"

"Not immediately. But look at the demographic data for the U.S. One of the largest groups today are called the Nones. These are those who say they are spiritual, but not religious. They hold organized religion in disdain and we want to keep it that way. I think they are the progeny of our efforts in the sixties. They are the social media generation, who can easily be swayed by tweets, Facebook posts, and the like. This makes our work so much easier. That's one of the reasons we support efforts to extend the Internet and wi-fi to undeveloped areas. It's about planning for future ways to influence people.

"A part of the reason we support these theologically strange Islamic fringe movements, such as ISIS and Boko Haram, is the tension and confusion it causes between Muslims and non-Muslims. We flirted with trying to promote a single worldwide religion back in the Middle Ages and it was just too difficult. It's easier to create division and confusion. That way, people turn from religion to something else. And we can offer influence and directionat times of confusion very easily."

"But wouldn't things be better if everyone could learn tolerance and mutual respect?"

"That borders on heresy, my young acolyte. If there aren't wars, there is no money to be made from supplying arms. If there is no unrest to test the markets, there is less room for profit from the predictable swings we push along. Without money, we lose our influence. Have you ever noticed how well off retired politicians are? We assure their financial security in ways that can't be traced. All they have to do is vote this way or that at a particular time, or tie up some piece of legislation we don't like."

"I'm sorry. I don't mean to question our brothers agenda or methods."

"You're fairly new; you have a lot to learn. But your cyber knowledge is going to be very, very useful to us. You bring the latest knowledge and skills in this increasingly important area.Noticing the importance of this apparently innocent email exchange between Gabriel and his PI is just an example. Your future can be especially secure. Just follow the lead of your superiors. You'll eventually come to understand completely."

"Yes sir. Thank you. I only want to serve."

"Good. That's exactly the spirit we need. Gulliver decided he wanted to take things into his own hands. That's not service. Obedience is essential. As you move up in the ranks, your value will increase even more. Mark my word. Now I need to go talk to some of the other Elders about what we are going to do."

13

MEMPHIS

Orion left with assurances that as soon as the Cardinal had been contacted, he would be informed so he could make his plans accordingly. "I hope to God none of us regret this, guys," were his last words to Nicki and Gabby.

As the door closed, Nicki turned to Gabby and said, "I echo that sentiment and then some."

"Don't worry babe. We're going to go slowly and we all need to remember that working in Turkey isn't an assured outcome."

"I'm holding you to that."

"I guess we need to get Trevor and Valerie up to speed and get a call in to the Cardinal. How about you clue them in, including their being our advanced guard, as it were, and I'll start trying to contact Alessandro?" Gabby said.

"Good plan." Nicki kissed him quickly, and said, "I know this approach is a little hard for you, and I want you to know how much I appreciate the effort you're making. I'm going to step over to Mandy's to take care of a few items, then I'll contact the others."

"Let's see. It's a little after 9:00 here, so it must be... about...4:00ish in the afternoon at the Vatican. I'm going to give it a try right now. See you later."

Gabriel headed upstairs to make his call. His contact list contained the Cardinal's office number and his private quarters. He tried the office first. After wading through several functionaries whose principal job was to protect the Cardinal, he was connected.

"*Buon pomeriggion, mio amico*! Have you a few minutes for me?" Gabby asked.

"*Sempre il, mio amico*! Always! How are you, Gabby? Have you recovered completely? The last time we spoke you were heading home from Haifa." Alessandro Cardinal Greganti had been instrumental in the last two adventures involving Gabriel. They had grown close, partly because they shared the same basic belief that the truth, while not always what one wanted to hear, always made for better decisions. He also had the ear of Pope Boniface X who, in the spirit of Pope John XXIII, was doing his best to throw open the windows of the Church. In that endeavor, His Holiness was opposed by hardline Vatican insiders, but was making progress, nonetheless.

"I'm probably about seventy or eighty percent. I tell Nicki it's better than that, but I think she sees right through me."

"I'm sure she does. But, my friend, even seventy percent is a vast improvement from when I was preparing to say a requiem mass for you."

"It sure is! In fact, I'm well enough to be considering a new undertaking, and since the outcome may have some impact on Christianity, I think you can be of assistance, that is, if you're still willing to work with anaccident prone archeologist."

"Gabby, I would hardly call your brushes with death accidents. Demented persons planned to bring you harm because your discoveries threatened their narrow worldview. So of course, if we can work together again I would consider it an honor."

"You are kind, Alessandro, excessively kind. If you have a few minutes, I can give you the background for my request."

"I am happily at your disposal."

Gabriel sketched the events that led up to the phone call, and where he could, answered questions asked by his friend.

"Gabby, this organization of which the lawyer spoke, do you have any more information about it other than what you've shared?"

"That's the basic reason I called you. Patrick Orion, who I mentioned a moment ago, wants to go to England to have feet on the ground and see what he can learn about the most recent meeting Gulliver attended. His problem is he can't do anything officially since he's only licensed in Tennessee as an investigator. Additionally, we have some concerns for his safety if his poking around stirs up trouble. We wondered if this might be something our friends who helped us in Egypt could help us with? We gather they are far-reaching in their organization and we hoped they might have a presence in England. That would allow Orion to work with them."

"I gather you would like me to contact them on your behalf, put in a good word, as you Americans say."

"I know it may be presumptuous of me to ask, but yes."

"It is not presumptuous at all. I will happily make contact and, I will attempt to do so today. Either one of their representatives or I will let you know the outcome of the conversation."

"That's very gracious, Alessandro. And while I have you persuaded to help us, we may need assistance if we go to Antioch. We're not certain, as I said, for what we are searching, but if we're poking around an ancient church, you can be sure something we find could be volatile. Others may want to keep us away, or they may want to take from us whatever we find."

"Again, as you Americans say, you need some muscle. Is that correct?"

Gabby laughed. "Yes, my friend. We need some muscle."

"I will let the Knights know. I also happen to know they have a few archeologists among their number. Perhaps they can lend a hand as well. I will raise the issue with the Grand Master."

"Nicki and I knew you would understand and help. I'll wait by the phone for the call. Please give my deepest regards to the Holy Father. His prayers for us were a comfort to Nicki and me."

"You are important to us, Gabby, both as a human being, and as a fellow seeker of Truth. May God bless you with protection and success. All the best to Nicki, and as you like to put it, to the gang. I will increase my prayers for all you."

"Thank you, Alessandro. Not to be flippant about it, but I feel more comfortable knowing you're doing that. God must listen to a man as good as you."

"Ah, Gabby, God listens to even the most hateful of us. He just listens differently, hoping to hear contrition."

"Given the state of the world, I expect God is often disappointed in that regard."

14

MEMPHIS

"Dr. Gabriel? Cardinal Greganti gave me your private number. This is James Desterro, Grand Master of the Order of Christ, and also CEO of Worldwide Strategics. I believe you wanted to talk with us about several matters."Desterro's excellentEnglish was colored with the tintof someone who spoke Portuguese as his native language rather than English.

"Thank you for calling Grand Master."

"Please call me James."

"Sure. I answer readily to Gabby."

"Our mutual friend has sketched out your situation, Gabby. May I review it with you to be sure I understand what prompted your call?"

"Or I can just tell the story myself; whichever seems best to you."

"Please do. I would always rather hear about situations from those directly involved."

Gabriel spent the next several minutes sharing all that had happened from the original email from Gulliver up to the report provided by Orion. "That's the whole story. We don't know what the artifacts might be. We're not positive they are in Antioch, or that they are associated with the Cave Church of St. Peter. To be candid, we're not even sure they exist. Plus, we have no idea what organization Gulliver was purportedly representing. Gulliver's strange disappearance gives us pause about plunging ahead with a project in Antioch. We hope your organization can help with Orion's work in England, and then, if our information suggests we should pursue Antioch, we have significant safety concerns. We're hoping, given the nature of the project, your Order would be willing to help."

"Thank you, Gabby. That is very useful. We will absolutely provide help in England. One of our major offices is located there, and our resources are extensive in Great Britain. We would like to deal with Orion directly, but of course, keep you informed of what is learned. As to protection for you in Turkey, my Council would like to see what Orion and we turn up in England, though I can tell you, they are inclined to become as involved as you might permit. Frankly, we have some suspicion as to who the group might be based on other situations we've dealt with, but we can't be sure. In fact, we're not certain we know whom we confronted in the past. Everything is so secretive and multi-layered, but we have some slowly growing clarity about it."

"Is there anything you can share with me regarding your suspicions?"

"Ordinarily, I wouldn't but because of the Cardinal's involvement, I believe you can be trusted. I must ask your word as a Christian that you will share what I'm about to say with no one."

"Not even my wife?"

"Perhaps that is permissible, but do so cautiously."

"She can be trusted completely."

"We hope that is true. Sadly, we have been disappointed many times over the centuries by people we trusted completely. We prefer to err on the side of the angels, but there is often the devil to pay for doing so."

"You needn't fear her—or me; we'll keep whatever you tell us to ourselves. None of the other team members will be informed."

"Thank you, Gabby. In that case, let me provide you with the roughest of sketches. We think the name of the organization is The

Order of the Enlightened or, perhaps, simply, The Enlightened Ones. In any event, the organization has ancient roots. Exactly how far back it goes is unclear, but we know it was very strong and very active in the Late Middle Ages. Consequently, it existed from at least somewhere around the eleventh century. Our research points to a possible earlier date, but there is no proof.

"The organization or Order exists to control as much of the world as possible, but only as indirectly as they can. For example, they have clearly influenced the election of several Popes, Medieval monarchs, and in modern times, Presidents, CEO's and others across Europe and the Western World. As well as we can determine, the highest ranks care only for the money that can be made from conflict and chaos. Their members, all persons of substantial power of varying kindsare all committed to the idea that they will be improving the all of society by exerting their influence.

"How many people are involved is anybody's guess, though we think the leadership group is fairly small, and even the so-called second tier constitute a relatively small, but influential number. These are estimates, barely more than guesses, if you will, because the organization is like smoke, wispy, elusive, and dark."

"James, forgive me, but this sounds like the biggest conspiracy theory I've ever heard."

"I agree, Gabby. Sadly, I can document everything I've told you. If Gulliver has vanished, the odds are he is dead already or will soon be dead. Every trace of him will soon disappear. They have that kind of power and ability. In some cases, even the person's national identity number, such as the U.S. Social Security number, vanishes. It truly becomes as if the person never existed."

Gabby responded, "This business of Enlightened Ones sounds like the Illuminati, at least the myth of what the Illuminati is said to be."

"We have investigated the Illuminati through the years. Frankly we think its reputationis undeserved and overblown,and that some of The Enlightened Ones' work has been attributed to the Illuminati by them to cover their own tracks," the Grand Master replied. "The present day Illuminati is little more than a secret fraternal society. It controls nothing we can detect. The other group—that's a different story."

"James, the more I learn, the less interested I am in going to Antioch. As you may know, I've already had more attempts made on my life than anyone should have to face. The potential of another attemptin my pursuit of some real or imagined artifact is more price than I think I'm willing to pay."

"I believe I understand that, Gabby. I've been at risk myself, but not because of who I am, but just in the course of trying to serve a higher good. I don't think one ever gets used to that; I know I don't. I don't want to place undue pressure on you, but if you continue— with our involvement and support, of course—it may help us in ferreting out more about this diabolical group. The more we know, the better we may be able to counter or contain it."

"James, I get that. I'm just not sure I can do it. I'm not sure Nicki, my wife, would support me in something like a crusade. Can we see what turns up in England? Plus, two members of our company are going to Turkey next week to do some preliminary on-the-ground surveying. What we find there may not be promising at all."

"As I said earlier, we will absolutely support the England operation. I believe I can assure you of support for your advanced team in Turkey as well. I think we are agreed that a final decision will wait to see what those two missions turn up."

The call ended with Gabriel supplying Desterro with Orion's contact information, along with the information needed to contact Trevor. Gabriel had decided early that Trevor, who was more experienced than Valerie, needed to lead the initial survey. Trevor had also had experience in setting up a working headquarters, a warehouse, and any equipment needed to work a site. Valarie was not completely inexperienced in such matters, but Gabriel preferred her in a support role until she had been a part of the team longer. The fact was, while he was certain of Trevor's commitment to him, he had yet to arrive there with Valerie.

With that taken care of, Gabriel went in search of Nicki. He had a lot to tell her.

15

MEMPHIS

Nicki had contacted Trevor and asked him to come back to the office and to bring Valerie. They were on the way as Gabby filled her inon what he'd learned.

"Oh, my God, Gabby. This is starting to get out of hand," she said in response to his story.

"With the Templars involved, I feel pretty good about our safety. But don't get me wrong; I still want to take it slowly. We won't know if they'll help us in Antioch until we hear back from Orion in England. And, sweetie, I'll be honest: I'm wavering."

"An international conspiracy is not something we need to be involved with. You know that."

"Yeah, I do. But if we can help the Templars, it seems the least we can do after they saved our bacon in Egypt. And if this 'evil empire' thing is real, they might be able to cripple it—or more."

"I understand that, but I don't like it any better. But we'll wait and see. Right?"

"Absolutely. I promise."

"Good enough for me." She leaned toward him to give him a kiss that was interrupted by the arrival of Trevor and Valerie. Gabby greeted them, and then excused himself to return to his study. Nicki briefed them on their next assignment.

"When do we leave," Trevor asked.

"We expect the visas any time now," Nicki replied. "Get Mandy to make hotel reservations at some nice nearby hotel. That will be our temporary base. Our first priority is to get whatever surveying equipment you need from the warehouse to the terminal we use at the airport. We want it to be shipped to you after you've made a preliminary review of the area. I think we're interested not only in the church itself, but the surrounding area. You've seen the Google Earth pictures. You know about the tombs and caves. There may be more. You'll know what to use beside GPR; we may want to do an aerial survey like we did in Nazareth, so check into that before you go, if possible. Otherwise take care of it once you're there."

Nicki continued, "I'd like to do digital imagining of the exterior and interior of the church. We'll walk it, of course, but being able to get dimensions, look at it from different vantage points, etcetera, may give us clues we can't get another way. We need every advantage we can get sincewe don't know what we're looking for. The church is just a narthex and nave, but there may be openings in the cave walls that have been covered over. Maybe the digital stuff will help us see them. Beyond this, you map out a plan for us.One other thing. We may not work there. Our situation is getting more and more complicated."

Valerie spoke up, "What'd you mean?"

"Guys, I hate to sound so mysterious, but I can't tell you. I don't think you'll be in any particular danger on this initial visit, but if we decide to undertake the project, we think we'll need protection. We're working on it. But until we get some additional information from Orion, we're not committing."

"You know, Nicki," Valerie said, "I was sure signing on with you guys would be an adventure. This is almost more than I bargained for." She laughed. "Put's Indiana Jones to shame, I'll tell you that."

"Valerie, you don't have to be a part of this project. Really. And 'no harm; no foul' if you want to wait this one out. We've got plenty for you to do."

"Oh, Nicki. I wouldn't miss this for the world."

Nicki's cell alerted her to a call. It was Mandy. "Nicki, Gabby's not answering, and Mr. Tabak from Turkey is calling. Can you take it in your office?"

"Yes. Ask him to hold. I'll head there now. Give me a minute."

In less time than that, she was speaking with the Assistant Director of the Ministry of Culture and Tourism. "Mr. Tabak, this is Nicole Gabriel. My husband is indisposed. May I help you?"

"Mrs. Gabriel. It is good to speak with you. I wanted to let you know that your application for visas for your team is approved. You will get them within twenty-four hours. We have a small embassy in Nashville, Tennessee that will get them to you."

"That's good news, sir. I wanted to let you know that we are sending an advanced team to do some preliminary investigation before we commit to a full-scale expedition. Dr. Trevor Wiley and Dr. Valerie Murphy will arrive within a few days. Is there someone with whom they need to coordinate? It would seem unlikely we could just show up and start taking pictures and measurements."

"Yes. In fact, I will need to be present when they arrive. I will make all the necessary contacts to smooth their way, and then make the introductions when they are in Antakya. Let me know when they are arriving and where they will be staying and I can meet them at their hotel."

"I'll have them contact you with that information as soon as we have it. We're excited about our preliminary work. I just wish I could assure you it will lead to a full blown dig."

"We will be terribly disappointed if it does not, but we also understand these things. Mounting a project such as this is expensive and you must watch your purse."

"That is certainly part of the equation, Mr. Tabak, but there are other considerations. To be candid, we think there are those who don't want us there."

"Oh, my dear! That can't be! Our Dr. Tutku Sadik is enthusiastic about your coming. As I mentioned previously to your husband, to have someone of his renown working here will help our economy at a time when we need it the most."

"Those who seem to want to keep us away are not from Turkey, as far as we can tell. They are outside influences. But we just want to get more information. We hope for the best. The project is intriguing."

"I'm so relieved you don't think we are not one-hundred percent supportive. As to the outsiders, tell me who they are and the government will deal with them, I assure you."

"I'm afraid I can't because, at this point, we don't actually know. But let's not worry about such things now. We'll move forward; just more slowly than we usually do."

The assurances seemed to mollify the Assistant Director and the call ended with the usual pleasantries. Nicki wasn't terribly comforted, but she was glad they were going to be able to take this first step soon. She was ready to decide go or not to go and put this indecision behind them.

16

LONDON, ENGLAND

The next day, Orion's plane touched down at Heathrow in London. As he made his way to baggage claim, he saw a casually dressed young man holding a sign that said, "Mr. Hunter." There were also three stars arranged in a slightly off-center way. He understood immediately: the belt of the constellation Orion, the Hunter. He made his way toward the sign-holder.

"I believe you're waiting for me. I'm Patrick."

"Yes, yes I am. I'm glad you got the little coded message. Frankly, I thought it was a little over the top, but I follow orders. I'm Oakley. I'll take you to your hotel where Sal will meet you for dinner at 7:00, if that's okay with you." Oakley looked about thirty or so. His complexion showed an even tan; his dark brown hair was clipped close to his scalp, but was long enough to have a messy little part on the left side. He was close to six feet tall and clearly buff as evidenced by a light blue golf shirt stretched tightly over his pectorals and accenting his small waist. His speech pattern suggested he was reared in or near London. Orion wouldn't have known that, nor would it have mattered to him.

Orion glanced at his watch. It was 5:30. "Sounds good. I assume you know where I'm staying."

"More than that Patrick; I know the room number." Oakley chuckled. "Is that a little cheeky?"

Orion chuckled, too. "Maybe. A little."

As the two men walked to the car park, they chatted about the flight, the weather, and finally Oakley asked about Graceland, Elvis Presley's home in Memphis.

Orion laughed. "To tell you the truth, Oakley, I've never visited it. All I know is what I see on TV or read in the paper."

"I'm coming there one day, mate," Oakley replied. "I'm a big Elvis fan. My mum loved him and played his records almost every day. I guess I just soaked up her affection for him."

"Let me know when you're coming, and we can go together."

"Brilliant! Ah, here we are. Let me open the boot for you." Oakley thumbed his key remote and what Orion would call the trunk opened as the door locks released. "Just toss your bag in the boot, and we'll be on our way."

In a moment the car was merging into the airport traffic making its way toward the city streets. Standing in the lot near where Oakley had parked, a non-descript man pulled his cell from his pocket and thumbed in a number. After a few rings, he heard, "Jack, here."

"The PI from America just drove off with some bloke who was waiting for him. I got the number plate as they were pulling away."

"Give it to me." As soon as the tag number was relayed, the call ended.

✠

ENGLAND, NORTH OF LONDON

Jack was John Reynolds-Smythe. He took the call sitting in his office located in a medieval Tudor style home north of London. The place had thirty or so rooms, about half of which had been converted from their original purposes to office space for the Great Britain contingent of The Enlightened Ones. The estate adjoined an Abbey, but was physically separate from it. He put down his cellphone and punched a button on his desk phone.

"Yes, sir?"

"Lance, run this number plate, please, and get back to me." He read thenumber he'd been given.

"Right away, sir."

Reynolds-Smythe was a wealthy man, whose fortune had been handed to him by his father and grandfather, neatly, but illegally, bypassing the inheritance laws of England. He was on the Board of several international companies, but had stepped down from his former position as head of The Bank of Southern England to devote full time to the work of The Enlightened Ones or TEO. His principal task was to plan and execute the wishes of the Council of Elders, the ruling group, as it were, of TEO. His focus was their operations in Great Britain, though he often coordinated his work with the tasks assigned to his counterparts in other sectors. After all, when one was attempting to influence or control world events, there was often international overlap.

Reynolds-Smythe had been present at the meeting Gulliver attended only a few weeks previously. Gulliver was not a Council member, but was there as a trusted advisor. Many believed he could be moving up in the ranks soon,though there were those who had nagging concerns. His advice and legal direction had improved a number of schemes the Council considered.He had an excellent strategic mind that often proved useful in guiding discussions. At the meeting, the Council had received a report from their archivists that items of great historical value, particularly to Christianity, might exist in Antakya, but they could not narrow the location. The evidence was sketchy, but if the items did exist, the archivists believed they could be in jeopardy. If the civil war in Syria should expand into Turkey the items could be lost forever.

Additionally, there was apprehension that an expansion of the war was entirely possible. In 1939, Turkey annexed the city of Antakya and the surrounding area.Bashar al-Assad, the Syrian president and unpredictable leader, might decide to take it back, especially since his regime was receiving military support from Russian president Vladimir Putin.

The exact nature of the items reported on by the archivists was somewhat muddied because ancient lists held in the archives did not always agree. On one list, the *Titulus Crucis,* "Title" as it was sometimes known, was mentioned, but not on another. The *Titulus* was widely understood to be the plaque the Gospels say was placed on the cross with Jesus. The message announced in three languages that his crime was claiming to be King of the Jews. How it might have gotten to Antioch in the days after Jesus' death was not described. And Reynolds-Smythe doubted it was actually there.

Why did he doubt? There is a church called*Santa Croce in Gerusalemme*, or Holy Cross of Jerusalem, located in Rome,that has long claimed to have the small piece of wood that was claimed as a part of the *Titulus.* In 1997, a team of experts in Hebrew, Greek, and Latin—the three languages on the *Titulus*—studied the artifact and concluded there was no indication of it being a later forgery. They all dated it between the first and third centuries based largely on graphological evidence, that is, a study of the characteristics and patterns of the writing. A majority of the experts opted for the earlier date. However, radio carbon dating done on the wood in 2002 suggested a date between 980 and 1146 CE. An attempt to reconcile the two studies suggested it was a copy of the original.

So was the original *Titulus* hidden away in ancient Antioch? Perhaps it was the missing piece of the Titulus in the Roman church. The records weren't clear. However, the uncertainty seemed to argue for trying to find it. If it was real, it was priceless proof of Jesus' crucifixion. But the Council was divided. Unfortunately, it was the long-standing practice in Council matters to require a strong consensus for any decision, so the matter was shelved. The lack of action was seen by a few as explaining Gulliver's decision to involve Gabriel.

Among the other items the archivists suggested might be endangered were written documents. They found several references to a cache of documents that purported to be from the very earliest days of the Christian movement. One list described manuscripts that recorded decisions made by the rulers of the Antioch Church in its earliest days when Christianity was in its infancy and still developing.The biblical book of *The Acts of the Apostles* and some reference in Paul's letters describe tensions between Paul and others, including Peter that emerged in Antioch. There was a written notation on the list that hinted the documents might be a record of that controversy and its outcome. Finding something that was truly unbiased and contemporary with the events could have a major impact on the history of Christianity, including its practice today. The New Testament accounts had some element of conflict in the outcome of the dispute. Perhaps Gulliver decided it was time to settle the disagreement since the Council wasn't willing to act. Still another document the scholars had reported mentioned the word "tablets" without explaining what they were or exactly where they were.

Preserving these items would be important simply because TEO needed to know if they actually existed, and exactly what they were or contained. It might be best if they were lost to history, but there was no way to know that with the present level of information about them. On the other hand, their release could be an excellent disruption to further shake the roots of the Catholic Church, and by extension, reduce its influence. Knowledge was needed to develop a course of action.

Gulliver had apparently left the meeting determined to take matters into his own hands. One of the concerns of the Council that had kept him from rising to the role of Elder was that he was seen as too involved in the Christian faith. He didn't make a secret that he was a practicing Catholic, a fact that set him apart from other Elders who were, at best, agnostic. Some privately worried he might let his faith overrule some of the decisions that had to be made that would bring harm to thousands, but enrich The Enlightened Ones and their secret supporters. Apparently, that worry was well placed.

All this information skipped through Reynolds-Smythe's mind as he waited for the report on the license. As he drew his musing to a close, his phone rang.

"Yes, Lance."

"It's a rental car. I was able to hack into to the place from which it was rented. It was rented to Grand Central Optics, and paid for in advance in cash. I checked for information about Grand Central Optics. It doesn't exist."

"Is that so? Very interesting. See what you can find out beyond what you've told me. I'm afraid this may be our nemesis joining forces with the investigator. We can't have that."

17

MEMPHIS

As Valerie and Trevor made their preparations to fly to Turkey, Gabby realized he had to go to Turkey with them. Finally concluding he had to tell Nicki what he was thinking, he stepped across the hall of their home and tapped on her open office door.

"Hey, sweetie. Got a minute?" he asked.

"For you? Always. What's up?"

Gabby walked in and took a chair opposite Nicki's desk. She swiveled away from facing her computer to look directly at him.

"I...um...I've been, um...thinking."

"Oh, no. You're about to do something crazy, aren't you?" she asked.

"No. Not without talking it over with you first." His smile betrayed a hint of guilt. "That's why I'm sitting here now."

"Gabby, I've come to understand that 'talking it over with me' often means informing me of what you've decided. You've decided something about Turkey, haven't you?"

"Well, kind of. Kind of decided. But not if you don't agree," he quickly added. "A promise is a promise and I promised I'd slow down any action."

Nicki's concern was written all over her face. Her periwinkle blue eyes didn't seem to have their usual sparkle. There was a crease on her forehead that only appeared when she was feeling tense. She feared what she was about to hear. "You want to go, too, don't you?"

"I need to be on the ground. It's not a commitment to undertake the project. Hell, I'm still not sure what the project actually is. I just think I need to see the situation first hand." He wanted to be stern. He thought about pleading. Instead he tried to modulate his stance so Nicki wouldn't feel pressured.

"Gabby, they can send us video updates. We can do FaceTime and see first hand what they're seeing in real time. They can send us data to review. We really don't *need* to be there. You know that, don't you, honey?"

"Yeah. Yeah." The guilty look grew. "It's just I've never had someone do my scouting for me before. I'm not sure how good my intuition is when I'm looking at stuff kind of second hand. You know?"

"I know you've never tried it this way before. That's all I really know. Well, I know you still have the tendency to plunge into things and this approach is hard for you. But what I don't know is why you won't try this. If it's unsatisfactory, we can go later—and I say 'we' because you sure as hell aren't going without me."

"Nicki, honey, I know I should give this approach a chance. If we're going to grow this business, I've got to trust others more in site selection and stuff like that. But, can't I learn that on the next project? I'm going nuts sitting around here pretending to work."

The sound of a vacuum running in the hallway was growing louder. Today was the regular day for their cleaning service. Mandy had reminded them earlier there would be people underfoot all morning. Gabby raised his voice a little to be heard over the vacuum.

"I get why you don't want me to go. I really do. It's a dangerous part of the world, we don't have enough information, I'd said I'd wait for Paddy, and I'm not fully recovered. But, I can take it easy over there. I just need to be in Antioch. Physically present."

"Can I at least think about it?" Nicki asked. "I don't want to keep reacting to my fears, but I also don't want to say 'yes' just because waiting is hard for you."

"That's fair. We already have visas in anticipation that we'd be going, so all I need to do is get airline and hotel reservations. I want to be with Trevor and Valerie when they leave. Which, is tomorrow."

The vacuuming sounds had stopped in mid-conversation, and Nicki noticed the cleaner walk by her door with cord in hand. Evidently he was moving from one outlet to another to continue. He glanced in and smiled. She realized later she didn't recognize him as a member of the usual crew that had been doing their work for years.

"I'll let you know later today. I need to be honest, Gabby, I'm not happy about this. I feel pressured and I've never experienced that from you before. So, if you don't mind, I need to get this email done and do some thinking."

"I'm sorry, Nicki. God, I'm sorry. I know I'm being an ass. I'm sorry."

"I'll get over it, but let me be alone with my thoughts for a bit."

Gabriel started to speak, decided he'd said enough, and rose from his chair. "I'll see you downstairs at lunchtime?"

"Probably."

With that, he walked back to his office. The vacuum was running again and someone else was dusting furniture that sat in the eight foot wide hallway. He was oblivious to the action around him. He'd hurt Nicki for the first time in their relationship and he felt terrible about it.

✠

Nicki was hurt, and she was angry. She was also smart enough to realize she couldn't let either one of those emotions enter into the decision she was being asked to make. She turned her attention back to her unfinished email—something about the Foundation's business. She'd lost her train of thought, so she reread what she'd already written. A few deep breaths helped calm her enough to resume her reply.

The email took close to ten minutes to complete, revise, and proof. When she hit Send, she was much calmer than when she'd been talking to Gabriel. Nicki pulled a small bound notebook from her desk, turned to a clean page, and picked up a pen. This particular notebook was reserved for her preliminary work on decisions. A number of pages were filled with Pro/Con diagrams with each item given a weight from one to ten. The final sums informed her decision. Nicki didn't let the diagram dictate her final decision; the process was just that, a part of the process of deciding.

As she started to write the Pro/Con column headings, she stopped. She didn't need this device. She knew her decision. Lunch was still an hour away. She'd let the matter steep for that hour and then, if she was still as certain, she'd tell her husband.

18

LONDON

O akley pulled up in front of the Holiday Inn-Kensington Forum in London's South Kensington area. The high-rise hotel was of contemporary design both inside and out. Mandy had booked a suite for Orion believing he'd need some room to meet with the people with whom he'd be working.

"Everything is arranged at the front desk," he said to Orion. "Settle in and then come down to dinner to meet Sal. He's seen a photo or two of you, so you don't need to worry about finding him; he'll find you. I may see you again as the project unfolds. Good hunting, mate!"

"Thanks, Oakley. I appreciate you picking me up."

Orion and Oakley moved to the rear of the car, and Oakley said, "Let me pop the boot for you." Each man reached for a bag, but Oakley snagged the larger roll-on. "Here you are, mate," he said, as he sat it on the sidewalk.

"Thanks again, Oakley."

"Nothing of it, Paddy." The two men shook hands and Orion headed inside toward the front desk trailing the roll-on and carrying the smaller carry on bag by its shoulder strap.

The reception area was quite large with the fifty foot long front desk on one side and a cocktail lounge on the other. A marble floor glistened ahead of him as he entered the lobby. Orion stopped at the first of three distinct counters areas and was warmly greeted with, "Checking in, sir?"

"Yes. Patrick Orion." He pulled his wallet and began to remove his credit card.

"Oh, yes, Mr. Orion. We've been expecting you. I won't need your credit card. Archeological Research Associates has an account here and your stay is guaranteed." After typing a few other items into her computer, the clerk, whose nametag read Jennifer Huffman, handed him a small envelope with his key card. "Your room number is shown on the envelope. We have your stay as open-ended. We would appreciate it if, as your plans firm up, you could let us know your approximate check out date. Do you need assistance with your bags?"

"No, I'm fine, thanks."

"A dinner reservation has been made for you at 7:00 this evening in the Hotel Pub. I believe you'll be meeting someone. You'll find your room on the tenth floor. Thelifts are just across the reception area," she gestured in the direction he needed to walk, "then turn right. You'll be in the liftreceptionarea. All lifts serve each floor. If you're interested, our fully equipped exercise room in located one level down from where we are now. Just press LL1."

"Thank you, Jennifer. I'm assuming dress for the Pub is casual."

"Business casual, yes. The lobby bar allows for even more casual dress. They also serve a wide selection of sandwiches. And of course, fish and chips. Breakfast is available in the Pub, the Reception Area bar, and the Consortia Restaurant on this floor. Enjoy your stay, Mr. Orion. Should you require anything, please call the front desk."

"I will. Thank you."

Orion glanced at the small envelope and saw he was on the fourteenth floor. He made his way to the elevators and waited only a moment. One of the four elevators opened and he entered. He pressed fourteen and was on his way. He found his suite easily. The door opened onto the living room which was furnished with a sofa, two arm chairs, a television and small minibar set in a cabinet on which there was a coffee maker and ice bucket with four glasses. To his left was the bedroom furnished with a king size bed and the usual furnishings, including a second television. He had just time enough to put away his things, shower away the fog in his head from the trip across the Atlantic, and change for dinner.

A little before 7:00, Orion headed to the Pub. When he entered, the hostess greeted him by name. "Mr. Orion?"

"Yes."

"Welcome. Your party is waiting. Please come with me." The room was large with a mixture of wooden tables for two, four, or six, each with the appropriate number of captain's chairs. All the wood was darkly stained oak. The walls were richly paneled in the same wood. All in all, the room looked like an Americanized version of a traditional English pub. The hostess took him to a table for two that sat nestled in a small partitioned area with head high walls on two sides, offering some privacy. The chairs were comfortable looking upholstered chairs. A well built man rose from one of the two chairs and extended his hand.

"Patrick, I'm Sal. Very nice to meet you. Please sit," he said, motioning to the empty chair opposite. Once the hostess left, he leaned forward and handed Orion his business card that identified him as Salvador Aurélio. "I understand you are investigating a matter in which you believe our group can be helpful."

"Right." Orion sketched the background information he had on Gulliver, and then continued. "We thought perhaps your organization could help us hit the ground running. You know, point us in the right direction to pare some time off this investigation."

Salvador Aurélio was a native of Spain, having been born in Rota, on the Atlantic coast near Gibraltar. His olive complexion and dark hair was what you might expect. His dark eyes, however, pierced you, even in casual conversation. A few laugh lines near his eyes, and a crease here and there pointed to his being in his early forties. He carried his two hundred pounds of muscle well on his six-foot frame. His English was colored by his native tongue in a charming way. Orion immediately felt comfortable with him. He was sure Salvador could turn the head of any woman in the world. But as a Knight, it was unlikely he would even try to do so.

"As you already know," Aurélio replied, "we think we know something about who you're dealing with. This group that we think is The Enlightened Ones, based on what little about them that we are sure is true, is power hungry and ruthless. Frankly, if Gulliver has disappeared, it is almost certain he's already dead. His body will never be found, and within a few months all traces of him will disappear. Well, making him vanish was easier in the past. Social media seems to last forever, so if he had emails or Facebook or the like, there will be traces, but they will be hard to discover and likely will lead nowhere.

"That you've been able to trace them to England is a plus for us. We know they are in the States, and we were sure they were here in Great Britain somewhere, but we have very little about them to prove that. Perhaps by tracing Gulliver's travels here, we can discover their meeting place, if not their headquarters."

19

MEMPHIS

Gabby was dreading lunchtime. Nicki wasn't happy with him, and he felt especially bad about that, given what he'd already put her through. He couldn't remember a tiff between them in all the time they'd been together. He was worried he was being too inflexible about needing to be on the ground in Turkey. There was a big cost if it meant emotional distance between them. He didn't want to have to pay that.

He was in the kitchen when Nicki came down. She saw the ingredients for their usual lunch of sandwiches already laid out. "You've been busy," she said in a somewhat neutral voice.

"I had a little time," he said lamely. "Uh, look, Nicki, I'm rethinking this going to Turkey thing. I need to let Trevor and Valerie go ahead and do their thing. Sorry I brought it up, really."

"Gabby, I believe you and I wish I could be sure you were comfortable with not going. But I don't think you can. I think you'll be miserable. I'm not going to be your warden and keep you locked away from what you believe you have to do. I can't honestly bless what you want to do, but I won't try to stop you, and more important, I won't hold it against you."

"No, Nicki, I really mean it. I'll let them do the preliminary work. If they turn up something, well, then we can talk about my going then."

"Gabby, you're restless. You're tired of shuffling papers and reading novels about which you care nothing. Go. Go to Turkey. Your going will be better for both of us."

"What about you? Are you coming?"

"Not now. I'll come when there is something concrete to look at or talk about."

"I want you to be there, Nicki. We're a team." Gabriel realized he was pleading.

"I think what would be more useful for us is for me to go to Rome. I've emailed the Cardinal about coming. I want to talk with him and with the Vatican archivist about any information they may have about Antioch that's never been published. Some dusty old something stuck on a forgotten shelf might give us useful information. Who knows? It can't hurt to look."

"I don't know what to say, Nicki. That sounds like a good idea, but couldn't we have Valerie go? You come to Turkey and let her deal with Rome. After all, the Vatican is the reason she's with us now." Valerie, a devout Catholic, had been selected by Rome to represent the Church on the last dig the team went on that resulted in the finding of Mary's tomb and the Shroud. The thinking was that having a Catholic on the team would offer some "extra" legitimacy to whatever was found. She'd turned out to be a valuable asset.

"We could do it that way, but I'd rather go to Rome. Valerie can use the field experience and you and Trevor will be good teachers."

Gabriel looked perplexed. "Your mind's made up?"

"Pretty much. Go to Turkey. Don't feel guilty. I knew who you were when I married you. It's not my job to change you, and even if it were, I wouldn't try."

The cleaning crew had been busy dusting the furniture in the living and dining rooms while the Gabriels talked. They tended to start on the second floor and work their way down. Nicki had been told they liked to dust last, because even though the vacuums had great filters on them, some dust always got exhausted as the vacuum worked.

"Look, Gabby, honey, let's just eat. We can talk more later if you'd like, but I'd say go ahead and let Trevor and Mandy know what you're going to do. Mandy will need to make reservations for you with the airline and hotel. I'll tell you what: if the Cardinal hesitates to let me come to Rome, I'll go with you. How's that?"

"Okay. I guess. I'll...uh...let them know after lunch." Gabby didn't really feel better, but he knew Nicki could be resolute once her mind was made up. He'd have to make the best of it.

✠

ENGLAND, NORTH OF LONDON

Later that same day, in the TEO offices, a technician tapped on Reynolds-Smythe's open door.

"Sir, I just received a report about Gabriel. Our source thinks Gabriel and others are going to Antakya soon to do some preliminary surveying. And his wife is thinking about going to Rome to poke around in the archives. Apparently there is some tension between him and his wife about this, but it looks decided."

"And we know this how?" asked Reynolds-Smythe.

"Our Baltimore office managed to arrange for a person to join the crew they hire to clean their offices. He overheard a couple of discussions between the two earlier today. A real stroke of luck. We thought the crew would be there at night and our bloke could rummage through the trash bin and the like. But because the Gabriels live where they work, they want the crew to come in the daytime. He just happened to be in the right place at just the right moment. Not just once, but twice."

"If I were religious, I'd call this a sign. Thank you, Lance. Gabriel is beginning to annoy me and I think we may need to take some action. Turkey would be a good place to end this. It's lawless there anyway; nobody will even investigate very closely."

20

LONDON

After dinner was concluded, Orion and Aurélio firmed up the plan they'd been discussing to guide the investigation into Gulliver and The Enlightened Ones. When they met the next morning, Aurélio already had a report to share. Overnight some of his men had been tracking Gulliver's movements during his last visit. Over breakfast, he shared it with Orion.

"My men did some checking overnight and learned the name of the place from which Gulliver rents his limo. Turns out, he uses the same one each time he's here and, just to make it easy for us, he always requests the same driver. One of our team is staking out his house as we speak. I think this could be our first stop today."

"You work fast. Let's skip breakfast and get going."

"There's no rush. If he leaves home, he'll be followed. We'll know where he is at all times. We—well I, anyway—need some food."

The two men took their plates from the buffet line, and each filled it with breakfast common to his particular background. Orion chose sausage, scrambled eggs, and buttered toast. He skipped the grilled tomatoes and mushrooms common in England. Aurélio, tried to replicate a common Portuguese breakfast, but given the dearth of choices, he had to make do. He selected toast, butter, jam, and a bowl of corn flakes. Both men had coffee. The meal was over quickly.

"The driver lives about twenty minutes away. Let's go have a talk."

"I'm more than ready."

With Aurélio driving, the trip didn't quite take twenty minutes. "Hope I didn't scare you," he said to Orion.

"Honestly? I didn't even want to have my eyes open. Driving on the left side of the road is a new experience for me. And the roundabouts aren't very common in the States. But I've been more frightened." He chuckled. "Still, I'm not ready to drive myself, yet."

"Here we are, Paddy," Aurélio said, as they came to a stop in front of a block of flats. His phone chimed before they could make a move to exit the car. "Ah. Our 'eyes' say the driver is still inside."

"What's his name?"

"Rodney Hightower. He's been driving for the same company for about fifteen years."

A moment later, Aurélio knocked on the door. "Follow my lead, Paddy."

"Who's there?" they heard a voice answer from behind the closed door.

"Scotland Yard, Mr. Hightower. We'd like to ask you a few questions about the accident you witnessed two days ago," Aurélio responded. "Please open the door."

"I never reported no accident," Hightower said, but they heard the chain rattle and the deadbolt turn. The door opened. "I think you got the wrong Hightower, mate."

"Are you Rodney Hightower and do you work for Imperial Transportation?"

"'At's me, all right. But I never saw no accident nor made a report."

"May we come in? We can clear this up in a flash."

Hightower was slim, but braces were holding up his trousers over a wife beater undershirt. He stepped back. "I guess it'd be okay. C'mon in."

Orion and Aurélio stepped into a small entry hall and moved to allow Hightower to close the front door of his flat. "What'd you say your names wuz?" he asked.

"Can we sit down to chat?" Aurélio asked, moving from the entry to what appeared to be a small, but neatly kept living room. A cup of tea and a teapot covered with a cozy sat on a small table next to a well used side chair facing the television. A newspaper lay beside the chair.

"Sure. Sure. Just sit there on the sofa." He motioned them toward the small sofa and reoccupied his chair. "I still didn't catch your names."

"Mr. Hightower, a few weeks ago, you drove a gentleman, Mr. Jon Gulliver by name, did you not?"

"Aye. But I didn't see no accident."

"We want to know where you took him. It seems the address you logged in at work for the destination doesn't exist." This was news to Orion—if it were even true. Orion smiled inwardly.

"'Ere now. What you accusing me of?"

"Making a false entry in your log book. You should know here in England, such an act is investigated by MI5 because it could be a cover for a terrorist act."

"I never done that. Memate who books the rides enters the destination in the computer. I don't have nothin' to do with 'at. Look, I remember where we went because Mr. Gulliver always goes to the same place. If there is something wrong with the log, then the bloke who typed it in the computer is the bloke you need to be talkin' to."

"And where did you take him?" Orion asked.

"Hey, you ain't English! You're an American bloke."

"Correct. I'm with U.S. Homeland Security. We're working with MI5 on this and similar crimes." Aurélio didn't even blink when Orion joined in the fabrication.

"I done nothing wrong! I'll tell you where we went. We always go to Elon Abbey up in Hertfordshire, toward Cambridge. And we ain't never alone there either. There's always more limos in the car park. I drop off the Mister, and I drive back here and pick him up when 'e tells me to. It's usually four or five days. I don't know what goes on there."

"We know that much, Mr. Hightower," Aurélio continued with the bluff. "What we want to know is what you know about who else is there and why Mr. Gulliver goes there. We're sure you've overheard phone conversations or chatted with him on the drive."

"I never done! He's a nice enough bloke, I mean gentleman. He always gives me a very nice tip. I reports it on me taxes, too! But he wants me to keep the glass up between 'im and me."

Aurélio stood and Orion joined him. "Very well, Mr. Hightower. We'll be going now. Thank you for your cooperation." Both men moved toward the door. "We'll let ourselves out."

"Well, that was fun," Orion said. "What happens if we get caught impersonating federal officers?"

"I'd say Mr. Hightower must have misunderstood what we said when we introduced ourselves," Aurélio answered. "Heck, he can't even prove we were here."

"True. I noticed how you never told him our names. Neat. Now what?" Orion asked as they climbed back in Aurélio's car. "Are we heading out to Elon Abbey?"

"I'm up for it. But first, let me make a phone call." Aurélio pulled out his cell and punched in a number. "Hey, man. I need whatever you can get me on Elon Abbey. Who owns it? What's it used for? Stuff like that." He listened. "When do I need it? We'll be at the Abbey in forty-five or so minutes. Is that enough time?" He held the phone from his ear and Orion could hear a string of invectives. "Great! Thanks." He punched End and slipped the phone back in his pocket.

"He always says things like that, but he also always delivers. He'll give us enough to get us started, at least."

21

MEMPHIS

Nicki headed to her office to contact the Cardinal. She called his private residence in the Vatican and he answered on the fourth ring.

"*Pronto. Questo è* Greganti."

"Cardinal, this is Nicki Gabriel. Have I called at an inconvenient time?"

"Nicki! *Buonasera*! No, no, this is a perfect time. I'm just relaxing from my day with a little wine from my hometown of Pescara. It's a red called *Montepulciano d'Abruzzo*. But that's not important. How are you? Is everything all right with Gabby?"

"Gabby's fine. Hardheaded, but fine. I'm well, too. And you, how are you Alessandro? Well, I hope."

"My age is creeping up on me, but nothing serious troubles me. But you didn't call to inquire of my health. How may I help you, Nicki? Is it something about your latest project?"

"It is. Gabby is determined to go to the site with our advanced team. Nothing I say will change that. I'm resigned to his going, as ill-advised as I think it is. We are not even sure what we'll be looking for and most important for me, I'm not sure he's fully recovered. But I'm not going to fight him over it. I believe I have to help in some way. Which bring me to the reason I called. Internet resources about The Cave Church of St. Peter's in Antioch don't reveal much that will help us. Would there be material—ideally first century or so—in the Vatican Archives that might be helpful? Have you any idea?"

"I don't, Nicki, but there is far too much material in the Archives for me to even hazard a guess about what is and is not there. The Librarian would know more and I can arrange for him to help you in your quest."

"That would be wonderful. I'd like to come to Rome and meet with him, if that's possible rather than try this long distance. Plus, I would love to see you as well."

"Tell me when and I'll make the arrangements. Of course you'll stay in the guest room in my quarters."

"I don't want to impose, Alessandro. I can stay in a hotel."

"I won't hear of it. The room is ready for you. Just tell me when."

"I'd like to come tomorrow. I have to arrange for a flight, and I can let you know the particulars as soon as I have them."

"Splendid. Let me know when and where you'll arrive and I'll have a car waiting for you. It will speed things up considerably to have a Vatican auto available, along with someone to speed you through customs."

"You're so very kind, Alessandro. I look forward to seeing you."

With a few more pleasantries between them, they ended the call. Nicki buzzed Mandy and asked for her to arrange a charter flight to Rome at the earliest possible time the next day.

"What about Gabby? Is he going, too?" Mandy asked.

"No. He'll be going with Trevor and Valerie to Turkey. I'm going alone to do some research at the Vatican archives. I'll be staying with the Cardinal and he's having someone meet me, so I just need a plane."

"I'll let you know as soon as it's arranged."

Within the hour, Mandy called Nicki to tell her the arrangements were made. Her charter would leave Memphis at 7:00 a.m. with about a ten-hour flight time to Rome. Nicki informed Gabriel and began to pack for the trip. There was emotional distance between the two, something they'd never had to contend with previously. Nicki tried to find comfort by telling herself that some time apart would give her an opportunity to deal with her unhappiness with him. Gabriel simply felt miserably guilty. Within twenty-four hours Mandy was alone at ARA offices with Nicki in Rome and the others settling in in Turkey.

22

ANTAKYA, TURKEY

The flight to Turkey had been tiresome, but uneventful. Gabriel, Trevor, and Valerie put their bags in their respective rooms and headed to the hotel restaurant for a late meal. Thehotel was the historic Liwan Hotel located a short drive or a long walk from St. Peter's. The architecture was decidedly old world, but very well maintained. The spacious rooms, though modernized, preserved the ambiance of an older building with furniture pieces styled to reflect the best European style of a previous century. Each room had wi-fi access and a modern TV. There was no mini-bar given the religious sensibilities of the country. The restaurant on the main level was only an hour or so away from closing for the evening when they were seated.

"Even though the church is close,"Trevor mentioned, "I've ordered a rental car which will be delivered tomorrow. I thought we might want take it easy the first day, so the car will be here at 10:00 a.m. That leaves us time to sleep a little later, and then have breakfast before we head out. Dr. Tabak will meet us at the church to introduce us to the people at the site. He'll be able to show us where we can set up our site headquarters while we're working there, too."

"That sound fine, Trevor," Gabriel replied. Fatigue grayed his face

"Gabby, I'm wondering how you're doing? That was a long flight even for me," Valerie said, noticing for the first time that his salt and pepper hair was now almost exclusively gray.

"I'm tired, but I'm okay. I'm going light on dinner because I want to get right to bed. Thanks for asking, but so you guys don't spend time worrying about how I'm doing, I promise to let you know if I need us to slow things down. Okay?"

Both his colleagues quickly agreed that approach would be best. "We don't want to be bugging you all the time," Valarie added, "but we also don't want to overtax you."

"I appreciate it. Trevor, what are your ideas for tomorrow once we're at the site?"

"I thought we'd see the church and walk Mount Staurin. According to a topographical map I scored, it's really more of a big hill with fairly gentle slopes than a mountain. I've scanned it and uploaded it to iPads that each of us will use for the project; I'll hand those out in the morning. We'll be able to make notes directly on the map of anything we're interested in examining further. A few days of that, and I'll get Mandy to expedite the equipment we need to begin an electronic examination of the site.

"Everything I think we might need is waiting at the airport in Memphis and can be here within twenty-four hours after I tell Mandy what to have shipped. Air transport has been arranged. I've rented a warehouse about a thirty minute drive from the hotel where we'll store the equipment. When we know where on the site we can set up, we can have what we need moved to the mountain, assuming we can secure it. We may need armed guards; I just don't know yet. The exception is the equipment we need to do an interior and exterior scan of the church, or for that matter, anything else we want to scan. It's already here at the warehouse because I thought we could start that while waiting for other stuff to arrive."

"Sounds good," Gabriel told him. "You seem to have everything covered."

"Don't know about that, but I think I've done enough to get us going."

After they ate, they each headed to theirindividual rooms for the night. Gabriel thought about calling Nicki, but decided against it. He thought it would be best to compare notes after they each had a day or so at their tasks. However, just before he brushed his teeth prior to changing for bed, he sent her a text. "Made trip fine. Will report in tomorrow night after site tour. Miss you and love you." She hadn't replied by the time he turned out the light and closed his eyes.

BALTIMORE
TEO HEADQUARTERS

"Just got a text from our contact in Turkey office of Culture and Tourism. Gabriel and two others checked in to the Liwan Hotel this evening their time. They're meeting an official at the Cave Church of St. Peter tomorrow. So obviously the artifacts must be in the church."

"I'm not sure how Gulliver would have known exactly where they are. The archivists could only say they were somewhere in Turkey, maybe in Antioch. Find out what's special about that church. Gabriel has to have a good reason to be going there. Notify Reynolds-Smythe."

23

ROME, ITALY

Nicki had been met at the Fiumicino Airport, also known as the Leonardo da Vinci, at Terminal C, the transatlantic terminal. The airport islocated about sixteen miles southwest of Rome. Trains serve it, but the Cardinal wouldn't hear of Nicki having to deal with that. A man in clerical garb was standing inside the customs area with a sign bearing her name.

"*Buongiono,*" she said, extending her hand. "I'm Nicki Gabriel."

"*Buongiono, signora*! Welcome to the Eternal City. I'm Father Paul Cavallo. I'm an aide to the Cardinal. Your bags are being collected from baggage claim. If you'll come with me, we'll use the Vatican's pull to speed you and your bags through customs. May I have your passport?"

She handed over her passport and took his measure. Cavallo looked to be in his forties, fit, tanned and standing somewhere around six feet. He was handsome by any standard, and Nicki found herself thinking that his celibacy was a waste. She quickly chastised herself, remembering that the Father's sexuality was none of her business.

Cavallo walked to a small desk sitting to the side of the other customs lines and handed the passport to a clerk. A rapid Italian language exchange between the two men followed, and in less than a minute, the clerk stamped the first blank page he could find in the well-traveled document. Cavallo took the passport from the clerk and handed it to Nicki.

"We'll get your bags now," he said. "They will have been cleared by the time we arrive at the baggage claim area."

"Father, I could get used to this kind of treatment."

"Please call me Paul. Any time you come to visit his Eminence you may expect this. He regards you and your husband very highly. The Cardinal was traumatized by the recent attack on Dr. Gabriel."

"We love Cardinal Greganti. He has been so kind and so very helpful in our work. And, while we're dealing with names, I'm Nicki and my husband is Gabby."

"As you wish, signora," the priest said smiling broadly, his perfect white teeth gleaming. "Ah, here we are," he said as they arrived at the baggage claim area. He walked directly to a man dressed in the black livery of a driver and spoke rapidly to him, then turned to Nicki. "The bags are on this cart. Did we collect everything?"

"Yes, you have all three."

"Excellent. Let us proceed to the car. It's waiting at the curb just outside those doors."

In moments, the three were in a late model Mercedes sedan with Vatican flags flying from each front fender.Immediately, the car pulled into traffic. Nicki had the rear seat to herself; Cavallo occupied the front passenger seat, but was turned slightly to allow eye contact with Nicki during their conversation on the thirty or so minute drive. The priest made superficial conversation, for the most part, but did query Nicki about her interest in the Secret Archives. She essentially said she had some research on an ancient city to do and the topic changed to something else. Thirty-five minutes later, the car pulled through the Vatican gate. A short drive into the complex found them stopping in front of a pair of doors on an unassuming brick building.

"Here we are, Nicki," the priest said as they walked inside. "His Eminence knows you are on site and is waiting for you in his office.

Your bags will be taken to his quarters and placed in the guest room."

"Thank you, Paul. You've been very gracious."

"It is my pleasure, *signora*."

A quick elevator ride to the fourth floor, and a short walk down a rather plain hallway led them to the Cardinal's office. Cavallo opened the outer door and ushered her into the reception area of the Cardinal's small suite of offices. Greganti was waiting for her.

"My dear, Nicki. How good to see you again. I trust you were well cared for by Paul."

Nicki wanted to give the Cardinal a hug, but restrained herself from doing so. Instead they shook hands, each using both hands to provide a warm greeting. "He was as gracious as you, Alessandro. I told him I could become accustomed to such treatment."

"Wonderful! Thank you, Paul."

"It was my pleasure and honor, Eminence." Cavallo bowed with a small nod of his head and continued. "I have a few things to which to attend, Eminence. Do you require anything else before I head out?"

"No. If something comes up, I'll call."

Turning toward Nicki and bowing slightly, the priest said, "*Signora*, it is a pleasure to meet you. I wish you well in your project."

Greganti ushered Nicki into his private office. The space was several centuries old, but it had been well cared for. Marble floors gleamed and roughly plastered walls were painted in a soft cream color. Twenty feet overhead, a coffered ceiling showed the recently restored scenes from the New Testament in each coffer. Less visible was the most modern technology that had been installed. The only obvious example was the twenty-inch computer monitor sitting on the return on his desk and a very modern looking phone with an array of buttons. Even less obvious was the level of encryption to both computer and phone that protected the Vatican. The Cardinal showed Nicki to a chair and then settled himself into one opposite.

"Nicki, I have spoken to the Librarian, Father Arturo. He has begun a search for anything on ancient Antioch. He didn't seem daunted, as I would have expected. Instead, he took my request in stride. If you'd like to freshen up, I can have someone take you to my quarters. Afterwards, a bit of dinner, if you please, before we do anything else."

"That all sounds wonderful. Flying privately is not nearly so exhausting as flying commercial, but I would like to freshen up, as you put it. I always feel better if I can put things away when I'm going to be somewhere for a few days. Then dinner would be fine."

The Cardinal smiled broadly. "Good. That will be our plan. Let me send for someone to escort you. May I order for us, or do you have a preference?"

"Anything you decide will be fine, I'm sure," Nicki said.

Greganti stood and walked to his desk. He removed the handset from his desk phone, punched one of the buttons and spoke rapid Italian. He turned to Nicki. "Sister Mary Bernice is on the way. She'll take you to my quarters and assist you in anyway you might need while you're here." He looked at his watch. "It's a little before five now; would 6:30 be good for dinner?"

"Perfect." Nicki replied.

"I'll join you in my quarters at 6:30 and we'll eat there." A soft knock sounded on the office door. "*Entrare!*"

The door swung open and a woman in a simple habit stepped into the office. "Eminence?"

"Sister, come meet your new charge. Nicki Gabriel, this is Sister Mary Bernice. Sister, our good friend, Nicki Gabriel." As the women shook hands, the Cardinal continued. "Sister Mary Bernice is from the States, Boston to be precise. I thought it would be nice if you had someone from home to assist you."

"It's a pleasure, Sister. Please call me Nicki."

The nun was dressed in a simple gray skirt that ended several inches below her knees. Her blouse was white, starched, and plain. Over her shoulders was a gray sweater in a color complementing her skirt. A wooden crucifix hung around her neck on a cord. She worn tan stockings that ended in black lace up shoes with thick rubber soles. The most striking article of clothing was a short white veil, or headdress, that covered much of her hair and draped down to her shoulders in the back. It was the non-traditional garb favored by many nuns since Vatican II.

"I'm looking forward to helping you, Nicki. The Cardinal thinks it will be easier on you if you have an 'official' representative with you during your days here. I'm pleased he's chosen me."

The Cardinal said, "Sister, if you will take Nicki to my quarters, and please plan to join us there for dinner at 6:30. It will give you two a chance to get acquainted a little."

"Yes, Eminence. I will look forward to that. Nicki, if you're ready...?"

Nicki stood. "Alessandro, thank you for your thoughtfulness. I'll see you at 6:30." She leaned in and kissed him gently on his cheek. "You've been so good to us."

"It has been nothing but my pleasure. Your work is helping breath fresh air into our staid little Church. It is centuries overdue."

The two women headed through the outer office and into the hall for the five minute walk to the Cardinal's quarters. Nicki inquired as to how the Sister had made her way to Rome, and it took the entire walk to answer that single question. Nicki was immediately drawn to the nun, and felt very lucky to have her assigned to help.

✠

Cavallo arrived at his office soon after he left the Cardinal and Nicki. He closed the door and pulled his personal iPhone from his pocket, then punched in a number from memory.

"Cavallo here. I couldn't find out exactly what she's looking for. I asked, but her answer was vague, something like, 'just information on an ancient city.'" He paused. "No she didn't say what city and I didn't want to press her and seem too curious. I'll contact the Vatican librarian to see what he's been told." Another pause. "Yes. I'll be discreet. Yes, as soon as I know something, I'll call." He disconnected and put the phone away.

The priest walked behind his desk and sat down. He woke up his computer and opened the Vatican directory. Using his desk phone, he called the Secret Archives. After a couple of transfers, he was speaking to the Vatican librarian.

24

ELON ABBEY, ENGLAND

O rion and Aurélio were about ten miles from Elon Abbey when Aurélio's phone rang. He pressed the answer button on the steering wheel and Bluetooth took over so Orion could hear. "Nigel, my friend, you already have something for me don't you?"

"Yes. I'll send an email, but here's the bullet point list. Established in the twelfth century, probably 1130ish. The monks who established it seem to not have been part of an order. They kind of coalesced, decided to call themselves *In Dubiis Sectatoribus*, which roughly means Uncertain Followers. Somehow the Pope, even with that dubious name, approved them. They established an unremarkable set of rules to govern the order. They kept a low profile for centuries, but seemed to prosper. The abbey was expanded several times over the centuries and now covers about five acres with maybe ten buildings. Some acreage is given to a garden that provides some of their food.

"The order is active today; well, active in the sense it still exists. It appears that it controls a good bit of territory, including much of a nearby town. All this produces income for them. Oddly, when Henry VIII dissolved the monasteries between 1536 and 1541, this onewas untouched. I need to do more research to see why he left them alone. Maybe they converted to the Church of England; I really don't know at this point. That's what I have so far. Oh, and the name of the Abbot. It's Father Innocent."

"Good work, Nigel. That helps. Keep poking, will you? Especially their role and/or activities in the modern world," Aurélio said.

"I will. I'll be in touch."

The line went dead. "Well," said Orion, "that's quite interesting. I wonder if they are a part of The Enlightened Ones or just rent space to groups to meet? I wouldn't think TEO would want a rented space for some high level meeting, though."

"Good question. This isn't much to go on, but Nigel will amaze us with more info later."

A few minutes later, their car pulled through an open gate in a four foot high stone wall that surrounded the Norman style buildings making up the abbey compound. The buildings had massive proportions with rather simple geometry. Norman arches were everywhere, including over the gateway through which they had just driven. Walls were comprised of worked, rough-faced stone,while elaborate carvings were seen over doors, windows and on the façade of the church that seemed to be at the center of a cluster of other buildings. A small, tastefully done sign directed visitors to one of the buildings, The Parlour.

The Parlour entrance was a single large, heavy wooden door. Aurélio parked on the gravel drive in front of the building. He and Orion approached and saw a small bell hanging to the right of the door. Gabriel gave the rope a couple of tugs and the bell jangled. A moment later, a small peep door inset in the entrance door opened. A friendly face peered out, and an equally friendly voice said, "Good morning, gentlemen. May I help you?"

Aurélio took the lead. "And good morning to you, good brother. We wish to speak to the Abbot, Father Innocent."

"Just a moment." The peep door closed. A key turned in a lock and the entrance door swung back. "Please come in. I'm Brother James. And may I ask your names and the purpose of your visit?"

"Of course, Brother James. I am Salvador and this is Mr. Orion. He's with an archeological research firm and is interested in the abbey from a historical perspective. He's doing some research on ancient Norman architecture in England. I'm his local guide, as it were."

"I see. And you wish to speak to the Abbot for what purpose?"

"To explore the possibility of doing some research here," Orionadded. "It would be low-key and non-obtrusive, of course. We wouldn't want to disrupt the rhythm of the Order."

"If you'll have a seat, I'll fetch the Abbot."

Brother James walked across the room, opened an interior door and disappeared.

"Man, I'll hand it to you," Orion said, "you can make up stuff really well."

"And you sang the second verse as if we'd rehearsed." Aurélio smiled.

The two men studied the room while they waited. The flagstone floor was worn smooth from centuries of use. The roughly plastered wall were whitewashed or painted white. A crucifix adorned one of the end walls. Otherwise, there was no decoration. The ceiling had exposed, large, roughly hewn oak beams. The spaces between the beams were plastered and were the same color as the walls. Furniture was sparse and simple, consisting of a half dozen chairs and two long benches. A fireplace was situated on the center of the long wall opposite the entrance door. Logs were stacked in the firebox, but were not burning.

"Pretty simple and straight forward space, isn't it?" Orion said.

"Yeah. Not too different from other Norman rooms I've been in on the continent."

The door, through which Brother James had exited, swung open. An older man dressed in a black habit entered, followed by Brother James. "This is Father Innocent," James said. "These are the two men I mentioned, Father."

Aurélio and Orion introduced themselves and shook hands with the Abbot. Innocent was in his sixties, fit and tanned. He didn't wear a tonsure; instead carried a headful of white hair, trimmed and neatly combed. Orion guessed he was six feet or so tall, and decided he looked like a businessman in a habit, as if he were at a costume party.

"Gentlemen. I understand from Brother that you wish to do research here. Is that correct?"

"Yes, Father. We are inte..."

The priest interrupted Orion. "I'm afraid that will not be possible. We do not permit outsiders to do more than visit for a few hours at a time. We have no facilities for overnight guests, nor can we manage interruptions to our daily ritual. Several books have been published by our Order on the history of the abbey. I can have copies of each sent to you. I'm sorry we can't accommodate you." The priest smiled benevolently.

"Oh," said Aurélio, "we had heard in town that you hosted small groups for several days at a time on occasion. A shopkeeper indicated limousines fromhere and Europe were often seen coming and going from the abbey."

"I'm sure he was mistaken." The smile had vanished from the priest's lips. "We do not host gatherings of any kind. Now, if you'll give Brother your contact information, he'll send round the books I mentioned. I apologize for the inconvenience you've experienced in coming all this way only to be disappointed."

Orion spoke up. "Perhaps we can have a brief tour before we go."

"Ordinarily we would be happy to provide a tour, but we are in the midst of a special spiritual retreat for our Order. Having you wander around would be disruptive. Now, gentlemen, if you'll excuse me. I must return to my prayers." Innocent nodded slightly, and turned to leave.

Oriondecided to gamble. "Mr. Gulliver had given us reason to assume we would be accommodated. He'll be disappointed to know how this trip turned out."

The priest stopped and swung around to face the pair. "Mr. Gulliver, did you say? I'm not certain I know who that is." Not only was the smile gone, but his face was ashen. "Are you certain you've come to the correct abbey? But no matter, we must ask you to leave us to our prayers." He turned again and walked from the room.

Brother James asked for their contact information, but the men declined saying they would just check the local library or Amazon. They thanked Brother James and headed for their car. Once inside, Aurélio spoke.

"Mr. Gulliver, huh? Did you see the look on the Abbot's face?"

"Yeah. He knows we know more than we should. I hope that doesn't bite us in the butt later."

"We can handle it. I'm going to get our guys to bug the heck out of this place. If they have internet access, and I'm sure they do, we'll hack that. In fact, it wouldn't surprise me to learn Nigel's already working on that."

The phone rang. It was Nigel and he had additional information to report. "I've got more. I'm into their server and I'll be poking around in their email soon. I've got another man working on their financials. But what I know already is that their firewalls are bitches. You wouldn't think a simple abbey would need that kind of protection."

"Yeah. And I bet you find a lot of very interesting things when you breach them. We're heading back to London. I'll see you at the office."

"Righto."

Both men were quiet as they let the information they had simmer.

✠

Father Innocent practically ran to his office. Once there, he pulled a cellphone from his desk and punched in a number from his contacts. When the phone was answered, he said, "Two men were just here." He described who they were and what they wanted. "I tried to brush them off, and the Orion bloke said Gulliver had told them they'd be welcome. What the hell is going on? I thought Gulliver was out of the picture. And who the hell are these wankers? Are we in danger here?"

25

ANTAKYA, TURKEY

The Turkish morning was sunny, with the temperature in the seventies. Gabriel and the team pulled up to the St. Peter's site in their rental van and parked. They headed for the tourist building sitting across and slightly downhill from the very unassuming church. Standing just outside the main door of the reception building, they saw a man in coat and tie, smoking a cigarette. When he spotted them, he dropped the smoke, ground it out with his foot and headed toward them.

"Dr. Gabriel? I'm Ahmed Tabak, the Assistant Director of the Ministry of Culture and Tourism. Welcome to Turkey and to ancient Antioch."

"Dr. Tabak," Gabriel said, offering his right hand, which Tabak took and eagerly shook. "This is Dr. Wiley and Dr. McMurphy. Thank you so much for welcoming us. We're excited about this project and eager to begin."

Tabak nodded his greeting to the other two and then spoke again. "If you'll come with me, I'll introduce you to the custodian of the site. If you think it necessary, he's prepared to close the cave to visitors while you work." Tabak led them inside the visitor center and to the office of the site custodian. After knocking politely, Tabak opened the office door and stepped inside. "Raphael, they are here."

The four entered the modest office and found themselves faced with a small man dressed in clericals. "Welcome, gentlemen and madam. I am Father Raphael Gambini, the site custodian." He stepped from behind his desk and they shook hands all around as introductions were made.

"Please, everyone, if you will come with me, we have a conference room just down the hall that will accommodate us. I also offer it as your temporary headquarters." He led them out of his office to the conference room. In a minute or so, everyone was settled around a conference table and Turkish coffee was being offered.

"Father," Gabriel began, "may I ask if you are associated with the Roman Church?"

"I am, but I serve at the pleasure of the local Syriac bishop. He has the right to approve anyone Rome wishes to post here. My background is in historical studies, with a particular interest in the Syriac Church, so it was an easy approval. I'm permitted to continue my studies while overseeing the site."

"Cardinal Greganti is a friend of ours. Perhaps you know him?"

"We've never met, but he has the reputation as a progressive in our Church, something of which I approve. Sadly, not everyone does."

"He's been a great help to us. I'll look forward to mentioning your name to him when he and I next speak."

The priest looked a little puzzled, but simply said, "How nice of you. Now, how may I assist you in your work?"

Gabriel spoke. "I'm going to defer to Trevor and Valerie for this. They are the actual advanced team and I'm a restless interloper. I've been recovering from an accident and have gotten cabin fever. Perhaps you know the expression."

"Indeed. And I am also aware of your misadventure in Israel. The field of archeology and ancient history is grateful you were spared. Trevor, Valerie, how may I help?"

Trevor explained the current mission of initial exploration, including digital mapping of the exterior and interior of the church.

He asked the priest to consider where a temporary structure, such as a tent or a truck trailer might be located once the actual work would begin to serve as storage and office space. Valerie inquired about power and toilet facilities, and in short, the two outlined a host of matters that needed to be pinned down over the next few days. Father Gambini and Dr. Tabak made copious notes.

An hour later, most questions were answered or it was certain they soon would be. At that point Gabriel injected a thought. "The thing is Father and Dr. Tabak, we aren't certain of two things. The first is what, if anything, might be there to be discovered. We were given incomplete information by a third person that suggested there might be something of great historic value associated with this church, but we have no idea what it might be. We have some knowledge of previous work here and it causes us to wonder if that information is accurate. If something momentous hasn't already been found in two thousand years, given the amount of work that appears to have been done here, then it seems unlikely we'll find anything.

"The second thing of which we are not certain is whether or not we'll actually mount a full scale operation. If our preliminary inspection and study doesn't give us some clear sense of direction, some notion that we might actually chart new territory, we are not going to explore further. So, the next several weeks are very important for us. At least for a week, we won't need anything but this conference room. We can store our equipment in it when we're not using it and meet in it as needed."

"Thanks, Gabby. I think that needed to be said," Trevor added.

"I see," replied Tabak. "Well, we think your work will do no harm. And since you have a reputation for finding the completely unexpected, we shall keep our hopes up, or as I think you would say in the States, we will cross our fingers. Father, have you further questions?"

"No, everything seems easy to do. I will set things in motion, but we can stop the process at any time. Forgive me for bringing this up, but these things that need doing, will, how can I say this, strain our already minuscule budget. Is there anyway..." he let his voice trail off.

Trevor spoke, "I'm so sorry I didn't mention this previously. We will bear all the expense as we go. Just give me the cost numbers and I will have money transferred to wherever you say."

Both priest and assistant director beamed. "How wonderful! That is a relief. Frankly, we couldn't even have the items charged to us and then have you reimburse us. Our cash flow is only enough to keep the doors open," said the priest.

"Well then, everyone," Trevor said, "I think we can begin our tour of the site. Father, will you lead this or have you asked another?"

"I am pleased to show you around and to tell you all I know," he replied. "And I wore my walking shoes this morning."

The group headed outside to stand in front of the church façade. At that point, Tabak excused himself to return to his office, but assured the team he would be available should they need him. They had seen photographs and Google Earth shots of the façade of the church, but standing in front of it was very different.

The church is located in a natural cave on the slope of Mt. Starius. Modifications have been made several times over the centuries, including the most obvious, a large plaza and a stone façade. The plaza was constructed of tiles in a pattern of large squares and was thought to have been laid by the Crusaders in the late eleventh century. At that same time, they erected the stone façade. The front is unassuming, a simple rectangle, punctured by three doorways, three multi-pointed star shaped openings over the doors, and two circles over the two doors flanking the central entrance.

The stonework towers to a mere thirty or so feet, and spans sixty or so feet across the front. The stone is not well cut, and appears to have been erected in some haste or by some inexperienced masons. All of this sits on a thirty inch high raised platform and is accessible by a small set of three steps located opposite the central entrance. To the left of the façade and on the plaza level is a one story building of the same rough stone. It too has three entrances with the left and right ones fenced with a simple wrought iron fence. Originally this was a colonnade, which had fallen into ruin. The Capuchin Friars under the direction of Pope Pius IX rebuilt it as a building in 1863. Now it stands empty. Gabriel's team, along with the priest, walked up the simple steps and across a small stone plaza and into the church.

"I've seen the few photos available on the web," Valerie said. "It really is little more than a cave with a broken, butone time finished floor. And seeing the size is surprising. It's small, just forty or so feet by thirty or so feet, I'd guess."

"Forty two feet by thirty one feet by twenty three feet tall. It's not very imposing," Trevor said. "And look at that white material covering some of the walls, especially behind the altar. Looks like it might be plaster, maybe used to repair or stabilize the rough rock faces."

Father Gambini said, "That's exactly what it is, Trevor. The interior is continually flaking off. On occasion, a piece of rock of some size breaks loose. We have plans to do more stabilization, but money is always an issue. The stonework of the narthex is the work of crusaders.Theycreated the narthex or entry when they built the façade closing it off from the outside."

"Are the pieces of the mosaic floors from the fourth or fifth centuries?" Gabriel asked.

"Yes. We think they may cover earlier ones." The priest walked to the right corner of the church. "You can see here where the mosaics you see today have broken away. The surface below it, of course, that you can see elsewhere, might be the original finished floor level. We'd like to remove more of the current floor to determine that. But..." he let his words trail off.

"But that would cost money, right?" Gabriel asked.

"Yes. Even though we have around a quarter of million visitors a year, we rely on gifts and not an entrance fee. And the gifts don't amount to much and neither do the sales of photos and the like in the visitors' center."

The priest continued, "You can see how the Roman arch shapes built into the façade extend inside in what is essentially a narthex. These three columns support the narthex arches inside, but otherwise the ceiling of the cave, and the walls, are the unfinished stone of the cave."

"Is this all there is to the inside?" Valerie asked.

"There is the stone altar, of course, sitting on that raised platform and the statue of St. Peter high on the rear wall. We have no record of when the platform was erected. The altar is not as old, but the records aren't clear as to when it was installed. It might have happened in the 1930s when some renovations ordered by the Pope were carried out. That may have been when the statue was installed, though it looks older. As you can see, he lost his head at some point.

"If you'll look carefully over on the right side of the nave, you can see the plaster that starts at the floor and reaches about five feet high. There is a cave behind it. We're not sure when it was plastered over, perhaps in the 30s as well. It has not been explored, or if it has, we have no record of what was found. Some have speculated that it was an escape route to be used by worshippers during the first three centuries of persecution. But we don't know. I hope exploring that will be a part of your plan."

"We may remove the plaster, then and reopen whatever it is?" Trevor asked.

"Yes. It might even be desirable to leave the opening unsealed. I suppose it depends on what you find."

"Sounds good," Gabriel said. "There's not really much to see in here is there? Trevor, ready to head outside and walk around?"

"Sure. Father, we've looked at Google Earth and noticed there are apparent tombs or sealed caves on the mountain around this cave. What can you tell us about those?"

"Let's head outside and I'll point out several and tell you what I know."

The group left the nave and headed to the hillside. Basically, the priest could say only that the tombs were empty and had been for centuries. He had no information about what might be in the sealed caves, those he suspected those had been cave tombs as well. "We have long wished to explore them, but again, the cost has prevented that. What records we have from previous archeological work are spotty, since most of it was done before archeology had gained its status as a profession. Essentially, we had gentlemen tomb robbers."

"I know. Those were sad days for our profession," Gabriel said, "but if it hadn't been for some of those pioneers, we might never have seen the necessity to regulate exploration of ancient sites. But clearly so much was lost as these 'gentlemen' scoured the world for things to put in museums and in the collections of wealthy individuals with no appreciation for what they had."

The walk around continued for another hour or so, and then the group headed back to the visitors' center. Once they arrived, Gabriel said, "Thank you, Father. We'll have some discussion about what we do next and come back tomorrow ready to go to work. I think Trevor and Valerie plan do some 3-D digital imaging of the church to give us reference. Is that the plan, Trevor?"

"Right. We do that while we wait for other equipment we'll need to arrive from the states. We'll have a twenty-four hour or so wait before any equipment arrives. But, this is all assuming that after our planning meeting today, we want to go ahead."

"I surely hope you do. As I'm sure Dr. Tabak has mentioned, Turkey is in some turmoil internally and with some of our neighbors. If we can emphasize what is positive and attract tourists, we can begin to raise money for more work on sites such as this one."

"Yes, he mentioned that. And," Gabriel added, "while we want to take that into account, we can't let that drive our decision."

"I understand, but I will be praying that it will nudge you if you are on the fence," the priest replied, a warm smile on his lips.

"I've been nudged before by less."

The team decided to use the conference room for their preliminary discussion. Each had been making notes on their iPads as they walked the site, and Trevor thought it would be helpful to review those and consolidate them into one document. They sat, and under Trevor's leadership began to discuss their impressions and implications. As the discussion continued, Valerie was aware her mind lost focus for a moment. She found herself thinking, *we're probably going to do this project, and I'm not sure it's a good idea. Something is off.*

26

ROME

THE SECRET ARCHIVES

D inner had ended in the Cardinal's quarters and he had returned to his office for an hour or so "to wrap up a few things," he had said. That left Nicki in the capable hands of Sister Mary Bernice.

"Would you like to go to the Archives now," the Sister asked, "or perhaps wait until you've rested and head there tomorrow?"

"If it is still open, let's go now. Getting the information I need is a little time sensitive. And that's odd, considering I'm interested in two thousand year old history."

"It is officially closed, but some staff will still be around and I have a key card. May I ask what you seek? It might help me help you."

Nicki hesitated for a moment. Taking this as unwillingness on her part, Sister Mary Bernice said, "That's okay. It's not necessary that I know."

"I'm sorry. We've been through so much and there have been some odd events in the last few days. I'm comfortable telling you. I've just become reflexively cautious."

Nicki spent the remainder of the walk to the Archives in filling in the nun. Wrapping up the narrative, she said, "So I need to find reliable, early documents, for say the first couple of centuries that shed light on ancient Antioch and the Cave Church of St. Peter. We hope it will give us a clue as to how to direct our attentions at the site. We don't know if the legend is true about it being an early meeting site of Christians. We don't know if the area was used for anything other than worship. We just don't know much of anything."

"How very interesting, Nicki. I understand why His Eminence chose me to assist you. I read ancient Greek very comfortably, and I have studied the religious history of the region in which Antioch is located, at least what there is to study. I may have access to information that will be helpful no matter what, but if we locate documents, I'm sure I can help. This is so exciting! It is seldom we academics get to use our knowledge in the real world!"

"You're an academic?"

"Yes. I have a Ph.D. from Sapienza, the University of Rome, in anthropology and religion. I was teaching there when the studies were conducted of the shroud and the facial cloth you and your husband found. We were all so excited."

"And now?"

"I'm on sabbatical this year and have chosen to do some research in the Secret Archives. This is a perfect fit. Here we are," she said, and indicated they had arrived at the entrance to the Library or the Secret Archives. The nun took Nicki directly to the chief librarian's office and introduced her to Father Arturo who seemed about to leave for the day.

"Mrs. Gabriel, welcome to our archives. His Eminence told me you were interested in first century documents we might have pertaining to Antioch in general and the Cave Church in particular. I immediately dispatched two of our staff to the area of the Archives in which we think such things may be found. But, Mrs. Gabriel, the older sections are the least well organized and least well known. At this point, I don't think we've found anything that might help you."

"I appreciate your efforts, Father. And, by the way, please call me Nicki. Perhaps Sister and I can join your staff in that area?"

"Yes. Yes, of course. Actually, they have probably left for the day, but that should not deter you. Sister, I think you may know the

115

way. It's on Lower Level 4. You see, Mrs.—I mean, Nicki—most of our Archives are actually below ground. LL4 is our lowest level and where the most ancient materials are stored."

"I do know the way Father. Thank you," the sister replied. "We'll just see ourselves to the elevator. Thank you."

"If there is anything else I can do, please don't hesitate to ask."

The women left the priest's office and Nicki followed the nun through the library's lobby. Sister Mary Bernice used a swipe card to open a door marked "Staff Only". "The elevator we need in just down this hall."

"Is the area where we're headedwhere you've been working?" Nicki asked.

"The same general area. But not precisely where the staff have been searching." The nun used her swipe card again to call the elevator. "I'm probably twenty or so feet from where they are and that could be several centuries from the time you want to study. But it could also be exactly what you want. These older areas are so disorganized."

The elevator door opened and the women stepped in. Nicki asked, "So why haven't they been organized?"

"There isn't a simple answer to that. One contributing factor was when the lower levels were built in the sixties, and materials from the existing Archives were moved, it wasn't done very systematically. You would have thought that would be a perfect time, but Nicki, bureaucracies are, by their very nature, not very rational. The emphasis was on getting the move done quickly so the vacated areas could be renovated, rather than doing it well. Plus, as well as I can determine, there just hasn't been an emphasis on the earlier centuries.

"Most people don't know this, but the Secret Archives are primarily the repository for all official papal documents. Keeping them organized and in good order is a high priority because any current theological conversation has to take into account what previous popes have said about the issue. Contradicting a former pope is something done only very reluctantly and very seldom."

"I get it. A matter of priorities driven by trying to be consistent."

"More or less. Here we are," the nun said as the elevator doors slid open. "Let's go introduce ourselves and see what's what."

✠

"Father Arturo, this is Father Paul Cavallo with Cardinal Greganti's office. How are you coming with Nicki Gabriel's request?"

"We are working on it. She's just left my office, in fact, with a nun who will be assisting her, to go make a preliminary inspection of what's going on there on LL4."

"And what in particular is she hoping to find? If the Cardinal mentioned it to me, I've misplaced that little bit of information."

"Oh. Well, she wants to look at whatever we have about ancient Antioch and the Cave Church of St. Peter that's located there."

"Right! I remember now. Anything in particular turn up yet?"

"I don't know, Father. I haven't asked the staff to keep me updated."

"Father Arturo, the Cardinal—and by the way, the Holy Father—have a keen interest in this project. Please stay updated and keep me informed. I'll past along the information to His Eminence who will relay it to the Holy Father."

"I wish I'd known that. Cardinal Greganti didn't seem to need updates when we originally talked. Perhaps I missed that in the conversation."

"Well, yes, you may have. But I think it's more a matter of his growing interest in the project. So, don't be alarmed, just keep me updated."

Cavallo ended the call and immediately placed another. When the line was answered, he said, "This is Father Cavallo for His Eminence."

"Hold please."

A moment later, Cavallo heard, "Father?"

"Eminence. I wonder if we might meet soon. I have some information in which you'll be interested and I prefer telling you rather than writing it down."

His Eminence, in this case, wasn't Alessandro Cardinal Greganti, but Raymond Cardinal Burrage, Prefect of The Congregation for Institutes of Consecrated Life and Societies of Apostolic Life. The mission of this department of the Curia was to provide general oversight of any aspect of the Church that was involved in the life of those whom the Church identifies as "religious", such as nuns and brothers. The Congregation concerns itself with every aspect of lives of these men and women, including their government, discipline, studies, goods, rights, and privileges. The seventy-year old Cardinal had served as Prefect of this Congregation for twenty-years, a record. He'd been offered opportunities elsewhere in the Curia, but he preferred to stay where he was.

"Has this something to do with our area of work, Father?"

"There is an abbey in particular that might be impacted, yes."

"Is this the abbey about which we've spoken previously?"

"It is Eminence."

"Come right over, in that case. My private quarters."

Ten minutes later the two men were sitting in the living room of the Cardinal's quarters, each with a drink in hand.

"Tell me Paul, what is it I should know?" the Cardinal asked.

"Nicki Gabriel, Stephen Gabriel's wife, is searching the Secret Archives for any material that might be there regarding ancient Antioch and the Cave Church. As I think you know, one of TEO's men, Jon Gulliver went rogue and tipped Gabriel to artifacts that might be hidden in Turkey. Apparently Gabriel has narrowed it down to Antioch and the church. This doesn't seem good to me."

"But how does this impact Elon?"

"I don't know, but I thought perhaps you can call some of our leaders and see if they see a connection. If there is one, we don't need people snooping around our business."

"I can do that. I doubt if there is any reason for alarm, but I appreciate you bringing this to my attention. Do you know if she has found anything?"

"I just learned two staff people have spent a few days looking and that the woman and a nun will join them tomorrow."

"I assume you will be kept informed."

"Yes. I've made it clear that I am to know what she knows."

"Very well. You follow that line of observation and I'll make a few calls. I think there is no danger, but we must be careful. Too much is at stake."

27

ROME

THE SECRET ARCHIVES

The day after her arrival in Rome, Nicki and Sister Mary Bernice ate breakfast together and used the time to plan their approach to the research. Sister suggested they begin by interviewing the staff who had a head start. Not only could they learn what, if anything had been found, but they could potentially narrow down the physical search area. Nicki thought the plan was splendid and they headed to the Archives to get to work.

Neither of the staff members had English as a second language, so the nun carried on the interview, stopping every few sentences to paraphrase for Nicki. Nicki's second language was French, since a lot of documents pertaining to Egyptian archeology, her area of focus, were in French. However, in working with Gabriel, she had developed a working knowledge of Greek, though far from what was needed to fully understand what she was reading.

The process the staff used was slow, and the net result was disappointing. The area of the shelves that were being searched seemed to offer little that might be helpful. The documents were collected in bundles and then secured with soft leather wrapping, tied either with leather straps or rotting strings. The process involved opening a bundle and then looking at each document inside to see if it had anything to do with Antioch or the Cave Church. That didn't require reading each document because it usually became apparent quickly what the content of the material was. When they found a document that might be useful, they slipped a place marker in the stack and kept reading. Any stack that had a place marker was then rebound and placed aside. Nicki noted there were only four or five bundles on the rolling cart the staff was using for items to be looked at more closely. She didn't feel hopeful.

Sister Mary Bernice suggested that she help the staff in scanning the bundles for useful documents, and that Nicki look more carefully at those that had been flagged. Nicki suggested a system for pulling anything useful and then marking the bundle so the document could later be returned to exactly where it had been removed. She set about trying her rudimentary Greek reading skills. The morning passed quickly. By noon, Nicki had read everything that had been flagged and concluded nothing she had read was helpful.

Most of what she had seen consisted of letters from leaders of groups of Christians in Antioch, but not one identifiable as the Cave Church. They were written to individuals in other groups of Christians, so these were apparently copies of correspondence. What couldn't easily be determined was where these other groups might have been located. The content tended to have to do with matters of order. One representative sample read in part: *Therefore, brother, if you have encountered the problem of your fellows wanting to change the manner of sharing the Supper of our Lord, please advise me as to how this was handled. The dissension is disruptive to the peace of our assembly.*

Sadly, there was no description of how the problem was manifesting itself in the Antioch community, nor was there a reply appended to the copy of the letter. All any historian could determine was that some Christians, at what *could* have been an early stage of development, were facing organizational and liturgical problems. While historically interesting, the information was, otherwise, not useful.

During the morning, no new bundles were found to have anything for her to review. At lunch, she said to Sister Mary Bernice, "This is worse than looking for a needle in a haystack. We don't even know if there is a needle, and if there is one, if it's in the haystack we're searching."

"If I may take a moment to speak to you as if I were your friend? Think of it like this: you have a tiny brush and you are carefully brushing dirt away from what you hope might be an artifact. It could also be an oddly shaped rock, but you can't tell because you haven't brushed away enough dirt. You have patience for that, do you not?"

"*Touché*, Sister. Good analogy. I need to calm down. I'm worried about Gabby over there in Turkey, so I want answers and I want them immediately. That attitude isn't good for anyone."

"No, it isn't. I understand it, though. But let's come to terms with the reality that we may find not one single, helpful clue. On the other hand, who knows, maybe this afternoon we find what you need."

"I can't let myself think that. I need to just hunker down and not set a time limit. Thanks for talking some sense into my muddled head."

"Glad I could help. Now that we're caught up on possible useful information, you want to start searching bundles?"

"Yes. Anything to help."

Late in the afternoon, just a few minutes before the staff people had indicated they were stopping for the day, a single document in each of two different bundles was flagged as potentially useful. That was the output of the entire afternoon. Nicki decided to wait until more had turned up before switching back to her original job.

"If no more turn up by lunch tomorrow," she told the nun, "I'll look at those. For now, let's keep focused on plowing through as much of this stuff as we can."

"However you want to handle it is fine with me, Nicki."

Twenty minutes later the staff members announced they were leaving. Nicki asked the Sister if she was ready to knock off, too. They decided it would be better to not tax themselves by continuing to work and left with the staff. Goodbyes were said in the lobby and the two women headed toward the Cardinal's quarters. Nicki wasn't sure she could find her way, and the nun was happy to walk with her.

As they walked away, one of the staffers pulled his cellphone from his pocket and punched in a number from his contacts.

"We found nothing the American thought was useful, Father."

"Thank you. Call again tomorrow."

"As you wish, sir. May I ask a question?"

"Go ahead."

"If we find something as we preview the documents that might be what she's looking for, we are to give it to her, aren't we?"

"Yes. What made you think otherwise?"

"Well, sometimes politics impedes pursuit of truth and, please don't think me impertinent, but since you've taken an interest in what's being found, I wondered exactly how much help we should be to her." There was a long pause. "Father? Are you still there?"

"Yes. I was thinking. For now, show her everything. I need to do a little checking on this. I may have to change that instruction. Thank you for asking. I'm afraid I'm still too naïve about some of the implications of being the Librarian."

"Yes, sir. I understand. Until tomorrow."

They ended the call, each feeling a little unsettled.

ROME

THE NIGHT BEFORE

Cavallo left Cardinal Burrage's quarters and returned to his own. The Cardinal took his drink to his desk, pulled a cellphone from a locked drawer, and punched in a number.

"Hello."

"Jack, this is Cardinal Burrage. Have you a moment to talk?"

"Sure. What about?"

The Cardinal told him of Nicki's mission and the background Cavallo had given him, then asked, "Is this anything to be concerned about?"

"Perhaps. There are other things happening, too. Gabriel and an advanced team is at the Cave Church. They have just arrived and have done nothing more than walk the site. However, a private detective Gabriel has hired is poking around England. He and another man, who we have yet to identify, visited the Abbey yesterday and indicated Gulliver had been in touch with them. The Abbot called me immediately. He said he told them nothing, but was very disturbed that they showed up. If Gulliver didn't tell them about the Abbey, who did, he demanded to know. I don't know. If the American investigator is doing this on his own, I think we can handle this if he becomes too inquisitive. The other man was introduced as his local guide, but as I said, we don't know who he is. That's our current line of inquiry."

"I don't like this, Jack. Our little enterprise doesn't need this kind of attention. May I assume you'll take whatever steps necessary to stop it?"

"Only if it seems to be more than it is now. We don't want to draw any additional attention to ourselves."

"My vote would be to act now. Maybe we need to convene the Council to discuss this."

"I think that is premature. I'm assuming you're monitoring what's going on there. If something troublesome comes up, let me know. I will keep pursuing this investigator person and his companion. When I know more, we may take action."

"Jack, I always prefer to err on the side of caution; you know that."

"Yes, Cardinal, I do. We have some time, however. Let's stay in touch."

28

LONDON

AFTER THE VISIT TO THE ABBEY

O rion and Aurélio arrived at the Worldwide Strategics London headquarters, also the headquarters of the English office of the Order of Christ. The two entered the gleaming lobby of the enterprise located in a five story building in the business district. There was a bank of three elevators directly across from the entry doors. The left most elevator had no call buttons, only a keypad. Aurélio keyed in a number and the elevator doors opened. The men entered and Aurélio punched LL2.

"Lower Level 1 is the basement level for the rest of the building. If we had gotten into either of the other two elevators, LL1 is the lowest level those elevators descend to. LL2 through LL4,served only by this elevator, are the Order's offices in England. We don't admit many non-members of the Order to these floors. You've been given special status because of your relationship with Gabriel."

The elevator stopped and as the men exited, Orion said, "I feel privileged."

"Let's go see what Nigel has for us," Aurélio said, ignoring Orion's comment.

A short walk down the wide and brightly lit hallway brought them to a glass door marked with the word Research. "Here we are," Aurélio said, pushing open the heavy door. The weight of the door was due almost entirely to the bullet resistant glass that comprised the door.

Orion looked around as they entered the area. He saw what is sometimes called a cubicle farm; a number of work cubicles filling the space. However, it was unusually quiet with no hubbub of sound filling the room. "Quiet in here," he said.

"Yeah. Sound dampening technology at work. See the strange looking ceiling tiles. They absorb about seventy-percent of the ambient sound. The lads can work in relative quiet even though they are essentially back to back in each cubicle in a kind of team." As he talked, they moved up an aisle to a cubicle with a nameplate: Nigel Poole.

"Nigel, lad, this is Paddy Orion from the States. He's our mate on this project."

The two men shook hands and Aurélio asked, "What have you learned about the Abbey?"

"Nice to meet you, Paddy. Let's go to one of our conference rooms. I've got everything so far on the flash drive."

The three men moved to a glass walled room with a table for six. On one of the four walls was a large screen that soon became alive with a display as Nigel inserted his flash drive in a laptop and opened the file marked "Abbey."

Poole started his narrative. "I won't repeat what I've already sent you. Here's what's new. There are about fifty or so residents at the Abbey. Every indication is they are working monks, with their work being prayer. A few tend a garden that supplies some of the food they eat. A late model Mercedes is registered to the Abbot, but it isn't on site. What is on site is a ten-year old Ford. I'm guessing he leaves the Abbey in the junker, and goes to where the Mercedes is parked and switches cars.

"We've not been able to hack their email server. It seems odd that an Abbey would need such a sophisticated firewall, but they have it. We'll get through it, but we need more time. Signals we've intercepted suggest they have two landlines, one of which is common and another that is heavily encrypted. There are also a number of cellphone signals emanating from the place. Again, heavily encrypted. We're not yet able to pierce their LAN—that's local area network to you—so we can look at their financials. Bottom line, something fishy is going on there. Give us a few more days and we may be able to tell you what."

"Brilliant, Nigel. Keep at it," Aurélio said.

"There's a little more."

"Oh?"

"Yep. Turns out we were able to hack the Highways England camera network, including their archives."

Orion asked, "What is Highways England?"

"They administer the roads in England. A part of their work in recent years has been installing cameras in various locations to monitor traffic for public safety and for public information purposes. You know, if you are heading into London from an outlying area, you can check with them on the web to see what the road conditions are."

"Got it."

"So, surprise, surprise, we were able to obtain videos for the last quarter for the road that runs by the Abbey. One of the lads is writing a program that will allow us to sort through all the material looking for any vehicle that has entered or left the Abbey. If he's successful, and we can get their number plates, we can figure out who has been visiting."

"Well done, lad!" Aurélio said with genuine appreciation.

"I second that," Orion added. "That would tell us so much."

"Now if you blokes will get lost, I'll get back to work," Nigel said, not acknowledging the praise, but blushing slightly.

29

ROME

THE SECRET ARCHIVES

"Another day in the dusty salt mines," Sister Mary Bernice said, as she and Nicki exited the elevator to the lower level.

"Yeah. I prayed for patience last night. I've got to come to terms with both not finding anything and with it taking days or weeks to find out there is nothing to find down here."

"You're willing to spend weeks?"

"Well, maybe. I don't want to be down here sorting dust binders while Gabby and the others are actually finding interesting things at the site. Remember, the purpose of this venture is to give them some direction."

"And if they don't find things for weeks?"

"That wouldn't be unusual at a normal dig done ten or fifteen years ago. Today, with all the technology we have we can narrow our focus more quickly. That's what we did in Nazareth that led us to Mary's family tomb. Scans made by helicopter borne equipment cut weeks or months off the search for where to begin."

"And you have access to all that new technology?"

"Sister, let's keep this my secret, but thanks to my deceased husband's good investments and generosity toward me, I have more money than I can ever spend and more coming in all the time."

"Really?"

"Yep. Even giving away millions every year through our Foundation doesn't make much of a dent. So, yes, we have access to the technology we need."

The two women arrived at the area for the day's work and were greeted by the two staff people assigned by the Cardinal. One leather wrapped bundle lay on the cart to be examined. As before, the women chose to search for several hours and then Nicki would work on whatever bundles they had pulled for examination. They decided to work on the same section of shelves, each taking an alternate bundle or codex to work through. By lunchtime, there were two bundles on the cart for later perusal. Nicki felt her resolve to be patient beginning to slip. This was just not a pace she could sustain. But, she thought, *what real choice do I have if I want to support Gabby in this project?*

Nicki thought back to the brief phone conversation between Gabriel and her the previous night. He reported on their walking survey of the site and a plan to begin digital imaging and measuring the following day. She reported on dusty bundles with no useful information. He tried to apologize, but she cut him off.

"Gabby, you've done what you had to do. I understand; I truly do. It's okay. We're fine. Please, just work the site and keep me informed."

"Okay, honey. I'll learn from this, I promise. How long do you think you'll be in Rome?"

"I think I can take several weeks of this. I'm afraid the tedium is going to be the first thing that gets to me; that or the dust."

"Just drop it, Nicki. I want you here. We'll just use brute force and check everything."

"I'm tempted, but let me try to help this way first."

There was more, but the net result was that she was stuck in the smelly basement and not with him. She hoped that decision was representative of her original pique. She really believed she had moved on. But had she? It took a while for sleep to come after that thought.

✠

ENGLAND, NORTH OF LONDON

Reynolds-Smythe was sitting in his private conference room just off his office. Projected on the large screen TV at one end of the room were the faces of the six other TEO council members. He had just completed his brief summary of what had been learned about Orion and the Gabriels.

"Jack," asked George Rutherford, the US TEO head and Council member. "what's your recommendation? Surely you wouldn't have called this conference without one."

"You know me well, George. My inclination is often to use force to protect our mission. In this case, we have no reason to believe Gabriel will actually find anything because we don't know if there is anything to be found. All we have is the flimsy information from our archivists. So I recommend we continue our surveillance of the operation. Part two of that recommendation is that the minute I think harm may be done, we act by neutralizing everyone who is a party to this intrusion."

"When you say, 'everybody', to whom do you refer, I mean, can you be more precise?"

"Certainly. Gabriel, his wife, his two principal team members, Orion, and if we can determine who his 'guide' in England is, him as well."

"We don't know who he is?" asked the head of the European office, Oliver Fletcher.

"No. I have a man working on that, but we have little more than the Abbot's description of him. The clumsy fool couldn't even remember the name he used when he and Orion showed up."

"Well," Rutherford said, "we don't have to know his name to remove him."

There were nods of assent from every head on Reynolds-Smythe's TV screen.

30

TURKEY

G abriel and the others had met for a quick breakfast and then headed to the church to begin their digital imaging. They brought two LiDar scanners to the site. Trevor had set up one LiDar, or Light Detecting and Ranging, scanner in the center of the nave. The other would be used outside to map the façade and contiguous area. When a scanner is running, it creates an electronic "point cloud" of measurements of the space it scans. However, creating an accurate cloud requires moving the scanner and running multiple scans in order to increase the accuracy of the cloud's data points. Trevor had told the others that because the cave was relatively small, he would likely have to run only three different scans. Since he was using high resolution equipment, he estimated this would be an all day project because the scanner would be running more slowly than it might for a normal scan.

"Tell me again," Gabby said, "what happens next?"

"We have software that will 'stitch' together all the data points and produce a detailed scan of the interior. We will first see a low-resolution image emerge, and I'll keep increasing the detail until we end up with a near photographic 3-D image of the interior, kind of like virtual reality. We'll then be able to 'fly' or 'walk' through the space back in our hotel or anywhere else we want to do it. We can zoom in and out, we can see measurements of distances from one point to another, or the sizes of objects, such as the altar and the St. Peter statue to a very precise level of accuracy."

"How long does all this take?"

Valerie spoke up. "We should have usable images in a day or so. We will be able to check for discrepancies in measurements, for example, that in a house image might suggest a hidden room or passage. With the surface of the cave so rough, this might not be a helpful feature, but it could. We'll be able to see things from perspectives we couldn't really create in real life. I used these on digs I was on before I joined you guys and the images are amazingly helpful."

"Okay, then. Let's get to it. Trevor, I'm assuming we need to be out of the nave while the scanner is running," Gabby said.

"Not really. You just can't be in the scanner's line of sight."

"That makes sense. I think I'll examine the altar the old-fashioned way with eyeballs, photos and drawings."

"Sounds good. Valerie will be running the exterior scanner, so we all have a task. Let's go," Trevor said.

Gabriel walked to the large stone altar and pulled the things he needed from his backpack: a field notebook, mechanical pencil, tape measure, and a digital camera. Except for the camera, he set them on the altar and began a slow walk around the altar snapping images as he went. He began with long shots that would show an entire side of the altar, and then moved in to shoot closeups of smaller portions. He also focused on the base of the altar where it sat on the stone platform and each level of the dais as well. He snapped a few pictures of the statue, but it was at least fifteen feet higher than the altar with no handy way to access it. When he finished, he had dozens of photos.

With those done, he began making measurements of the altar and recording them in his field notebook. He used those to draw a scaledimage that showed as much detail as he could. *I haven't done one of these since my days with Marty when he was a dig director and I was his assistant,* he thought. Remembering MartyFratinibrought a pang of sadness. Marty was murdered during the theft of *Mary's*

Gospel while Gabriel's team was photographing it. He sometimes still missed his close friend and mentor.

After Marty's murder, Gabriel had discovered that Marty had hidden a box in the dig warehouse.Marty had apparently discovered the contents while working on what would later be determined was the home of St. James, Jesus' brother and leader in Jerusalem after Jesus' resurrection. The documents inside were later found to be short eyewitness accounts from various followers of Jesus about their memories of him. When it became apparent that Rome was going to attack Israel, James insistedthat as many living witnesses as couldshould either write down their memories or have someone do it for them. James wanted these accounts saved for later generations. Gabriel insisted the find be called *Fratini's Cache*. As Gabriel thought at the time, Marty may have intended to steal them and sell them to ease his financial problems, but he also could have just misplaced them, intending to tell Gabriel later.

The documents were still being studied, but early work indicated many similarities between these memories and stories in both *Mary's Gospel* and in the canonical Gospels. There were also some important differences both in stories that seemed similar and in the telling of incidents that weren't recorded in the Gospels. Scholars had begun their arguments about the materials as soon as they began to emerge. Gabriel sometimes thought he might not have done the world a favor in releasing them.

Which makes me wonder, he thought, *is poking around here really a good idea?*Even as he had that thought, he continued his work. *This is what I do; this is my calling. If others misuse what I find, I'm not responsible for that. Am I?*

He refocused his attention back to the altar. The altar proved to be six feet two inches by twenty-three inches. It stood thirty-six inches high. It was composed of cut stone that had been used as building blocks held in place by mortar. The top was a single slab of limestone that overhung the altar on each side by one and a half inches, with three inch thick edges worked in an ogee shape. On the front of the altar in the center, just slightly above vertical center was a carved empty cross on the field of what appeared to be a multi-pedaled flower. Flanking the cross on the left was the Greek symbol Alpha, and on the right, the symbol Omega. They signified Christ as the beginning and end. There were no other decorations on the altar.

It was clear the altar was a relatively modern addition to the church. The wear on the stone was relatively light indicating it wasn't in use for centuries. There were a few nicks in the altar stone edges, but that was to be expected. Father Gambini had told him there was no record of when the platform or dais was installed.

That night, as Gabriel studied his photographs more closely, he would see something that would pique his interest. The wear patterns on the platform on which the altar stood indicated considerable wear, perhaps even centuries of use. It would be impossible to know exactly, but clearly the platform was ancient. Looking more closely he noticed something about the platform he wanted to study more. The bits of what might be original floor and its patterns didn't line up parallel with the base of the dais. *These old structures were often out of square. Even in the Middle Ages, great cathedrals and their attached ancillary wings were often catawampus. It's probably nothing.*

With that thought, he called Nicki to check with her on her day. She had nothing to report except that she missed him and told him she was thinking about visiting him on the weekend.

"I'll desperately need a break by then. If you take Saturday and Sunday off, we can see some sights. And...uh...make up for lost time—if you're up to it," she teased.

"I can be up to it by then," the smile on his face apparent in his voice. "I guarantee that. Let me know your plans and I'll pick you up at the airport."

"I'll get Mandy to set up something with a charter and she'll let you know."

"I'm so glad you had this idea, honey," Gabriel said. "I've been really missing you."

"Me too," she said. "Me too."

31

LONDON

The next day, Orion and Aurélio met for breakfast and to plan the day's activities. After a few pleasantries, Aurélio announced he'd received a call from Nigel.

"He says he's got some new information for us."

"Any hint as to what it might be," Orion asked.

"He's being very mysterious. All he would say is that some of it overturns much of what we've been thinking about the Illuminati." Says we should come see him as soon as we've eaten.

"Well, let's then. I don't have an idea what to do next. I reached out to a friend at Scotland Yard so see if he had a line on the Abbey. He called this morning and told me he'd drawn a blank. Well, that's not exactly true. He says, and I quote, 'the Abbey is old and does religious shit; harms no one as far as the Yard is aware.'"

"In other words, the Abbey does a good job of covering whatever they're up to."

"You know, Sal, they may be up to nothing except providing a place for some group to meet."

"Yeah. Could be. But I doubt it. Something's going on out there and I want to know what."

They men finished their breakfast, returned to their rooms to grab their gear, and met in the lobby twenty minutes later. Fifteen minutes after that, after what Orion experienced as a harrowing ride on the wrong side of the streets, they were walking into Worldwide Strategics' London office and then to Nigel's cubicle.

"Good morning, Nigel," Aurélio said, as did Orion. "What do you have for us?"

"Let's step over to the conference room. I've got a presentation ready."

A few moments later, everyone was settled into the conference room. Nigel pressed a few keys on the laptop sitting at one end of the table and the large TV on the wall came to life.

"We now know of seven visitors to the Abbey who arrived on the same day, and four days later departed on the same day. We got number plates from four. As you can see," he clicked a new slide, "they are from France, Germany, Spain, and, of course, your Mr. Hightower's company in London."

"And they belong to..."

Another slide flashed on the screen. "The French plate traces to *Banque de Paribas*."

"The French multinational bank?" Orion asked.

"The same; one of the largest banks in the world. The German plate traced to Oranstein and Kallmen, a German arms manufacturing company located in Berlin. It is one of the oldest and largest." A new slide appeared. "The Spanish plate traces to *Esperanza y Unceta*, a weapons manufacturer."

"My God. A huge bank and two arms dealers," said Aurélio. "This can't be good."

"True," said Nigel, "and if the Abbot is involved as well, that is a truly unholy quartet."

"Don't forget Gulliver. He represents the law," Orion added.

"Do we know who came in those cars?"

"Not yet. Oh, and I didn't mention, there are three more cars we couldn't trace because the plates were obscured. Our digital tech guy thinks they were obscured deliberately in some way. But if the occupants of those are on par with the likely occupants of the others, this is a high powered group."

"A group that likely has an agenda that isn't much interested in the general good," Orion suggested.

"Nigel, this is good stuff," Aurélio offered.

"Thanks. I've got a little more. I pulled together what we think we know about The Enlightened Ones, partly because I was just curious, and partly to see how these companies could fit in. Want to hear it?"

"Absolutely."

"Okay. Here we go."

Nigel began to advance slides and offer commentary. The presentation boiled down to a few simple points when all was said and done. Just as the Illuminati had been believed to control both macro and micro events throughout history, so it seemed TEO was very likely actually doing it.

"First, a common belief among Illuminati 'researchers' is that the members of the G20 nations are actually the modern expression of this group. Unlikely according to our research. Conspiracy theorists have tried to link the Illuminati to such events as the French Revolution, JFK's assassination, and Reagan's assassination attempt. The latest one I could find builds a case for finding Bin Laden and feeding the intel to the US."

"But there is evidence for some of these, like JFK's murder. The evidence is very flimsy for Reagan's shooting, but there is some. Trust me on this, I can back up these ideas, but also understand that evidence isn't proof. The overall theory is that this group is controlling world events, or attempting to control the direction of the future."

"So," Orion offered, "theorists might say Putin's resurgence and Brexit could be Illuminati meddling?"

"That's the thing, Paddy," Nigel replied. "The Illuminati may get credit for these things, but the evidence for their *actual* existence as a nefarious society or group is flimsy. I personally think they are just the fall guys for TEO. If the Illuminati actually exist, I think they are composed of wannabes and not the real deal. They have no central organization that can fight back when they are accused of something, and some lone guy who speaks out because he knows they are pretenders is discounted."

"So the Illuminati is a sham; that's a big change in our doctrine. What about our bunch?" asked Aurélio?"

"Right. Our bunch, as you put it, seem to be the actual bad guys. They exist in virtual darkness. We're pretty certain they blame things on the Illuminati to cover their own tracks. So far, we have no reason to believe the entire G20 group is TEO, but there may be enough of them to influence actions.Additionally, we've run across a few things that might cause one to believe that some very influential people, working well behind the scenes, pushed Donald Trump to victory in the US."

"What?" exclaimed Orion.

"Sounds far fetched doesn't it? Let's say I'm right. Who would stand to gain by that?"

"Good God! Trump has done as much sabre rattling as Russian and North Korea. And I happened to have read something a few days after the election that pointed out the economic sectors that benefit from armed conflict had the largest rise in stock prices," Orion said.

"Yeah. And why the sudden rise in radical Islam action in the last fifteen years? We know Bin Laden financed, or his family, financed a lot of Al Qaeda operations. What prompted that? You know one of the dictums of investigation is 'follow the money.' Who benefits? Arms manufacturers and the industries that support them, that's who."

Aurélio joined in. "So you're suggesting that TEO has an agenda similar to the supposed Illuminati, that is, influence world events, and right now, they want war?"

"It could be," Nigel continued."There's another point of view here, too. Trump has been accused of legitimatizing racism, sexism, militarism, and a host of other bad –isms. The US is in a kind of open turmoil like we haven't seen since the 60s. The country seems to be sharply divided with a lot of progressive programs on the line."

"Okay, look," Orion said, "say you're right. Somebody wants to create all kinds of chaos. Then let's ask the question, why oppose

Gabriel's work? What do the two things have in common? We know there has been a general rise in religion and a renewed interest in spirituality among Christians following Gabriel's finds. Right? And the full impact of those finds is still to come. If that trend continues and is fueled by new discoveries, this spiritual/religious revival could put greater pressure on leaders to move away from warlike and divisive talk and action. So, in a way, Gabriel's work threatens the TEO's primary agenda. I know that's a stretch, but it could happen, so if you're TEO, why take the chance?"

"Guys, this makes perfect sense. But it is still a lot of speculation," Aurélio said. "I'd like more facts."

"My lads are working their little fingers to the bones to find something more substantial. I'm putting more of our blokes into the field. These guys can go where we can't go electronically. It will take time, but I think we'll find something. That is, if there is something to be found," Nigel promised.

"Brilliant work, Nigel. Stay on it."

"I've got to talk to Gabby," Orion said. "And I'm not trusting any kind of electronic communication. I don't care how safe we think it might be. I'm going to Turkey."

32

TURKEY

A dditional equipment had arrived in the dark hours of the morning, and Trevor was busy supervising the loading of the equipment onto a helicopter. Gabriel received a phone call from Orion late the day before indicating he needed to come to Turkey. He was closed lipped about this reason, but Gabriel was certain this meant he had news of Gulliver's disappearance. His arrival was expected mid-day. Valerie was busy processing the cloud data into usable images back at the hotel. Action seemed to be picking up on the project and Gabriel was pleased. Soon they should be able to determine if there is anything worth exploring.

Trevor planned to use the same portable infrared and thermal imaging equipment on this site that had been used in Nazareth. In addition, he had ground penetrating radar, too. The plan was simple. Trevor reasoned that any additional sites related to the Cave Church would likely be on approximately the same elevation as the church on the same side of the mountain.

The initial walking study they'd done showed that most of the identified tombs were no higher than fifty or so feet from the floor level of the church. The helicopter would focus its flights on an area about one hundred feet from the floor level and extending about a quarter of a mile in each direction from the entrance. That would generate a manageable amount of data and give them a sense of what was what. He suspected if there were anything to find, it would be in that area. If not, they could extend the area searched. Or go home.

The data from the imaging equipment could indicate hidden areas of use, for example, ancient walking paths from the church to certain areas. Today's ground looks uniform to the naked eye, but the imaging equipment can pick up changes in the soil not visible with unaided vision. If large or well used paths showed up from the church to particular areas, the implication was that something was frequently visited at some time in the past. The GPR could look below ground to depths up to several dozen feet to show hidden caves, structures, or ruins. The net effect of this data generation would be to dramatically narrow down areas for greater scrutiny. Trevor hoped to be over the site by mid-morning.

The morning was warm and sunny so Gabriel had walked to the church to take a closer look at the altar area while waiting for Trevor and Valerie to do their thing. He liked using all this high tech stuff, but he was also was trained to rely on his eyes and his instincts. They weren't necessarily better than the other but he it was what he knew. Plus, he thought a little exercise would help build his stamina. He'd never tell Nicki, but he still didn't feel he was his old self.

When he arrived at the visitor's center, Gabriel checked in with Father Gambini. He refused the offered tea, and headed to the church. The moment he entered, he felt the cool of the nave envelop him. *Must be twenty degrees cooler in here than outside,* he thought. *Wonder if it's warmer in the winter or just pretty constant year round.*He walked to the altar and bent to inspect the area where the lower level of the dais met the floor, beginning at the left front corner and continuing the entire perimeter. What he saw was no different from the digital images he'd studied the night before. The pattern on the portions of the floor that remained did not run parallel to the sides of the dais. He wanted to know why.

Gabriel knelt at the rear of the altar and pulled several picks and a paintbrush from his backpack. He began to pick at the intersection of the floor and the dais, brushing away the debris he was dislodging. After clearing an area about a foot long, he removed a small hammer and a chisel from the backpack. He began to undercut the dais edge so he could see if the floor extended under the platform or stopped at the intersection. Careful to remove only a small bit of stone, he soon had his answer. The floor extended under the altar. *So, the floor was installed, and then the platform was added,* he reasoned. *That makes sense.*

Gabriel stood and walked around the platform again. *Okay,* he thought, *the floor was installed first. In the mosaic pattern around the altar, there is a four inch wide strip of black mosaic as if it is outlining where the altar platform is to go, or so it seems. But then why is the platform a little bit off kilter? Is the mosaic not square? The platform is square; I measured it. So what happened? I wonder if I can get permission to disassemble the platform to see what's going on in the mosaic?*

He concluded that would be a major undertaking. It would likely mean disassembling the altar rather than just lifting it in one piece, followed by disassembling the stones that make up the two levels of the dais. Heavy equipment was clearly going to be needed. He bent and dusted off the knees of his khakis. *They'll never let me do that.*

Through the open doors of the church the thump, thump, thump of a helicopter broke the silence in the nave. Gabriel walked outside and looked up. Swooping low over the hillside was a mid-sized helicopter. It flew parallel to the façade of the church, then turned and flew back, just slightly more uphill. It wouldn't be long until Trevor could begin crunching the data. Gabriel noticed his heart rate was up just slightly. *That's adrenaline. I'm ready to know more,* he thought. *More than ready.* The morning had gone by quickly and it was time to pack up and head to the airport to collect Orion.

33

HATAY AIRPORT

HATAY PROVINCE, TURKEY

O rion looked out the window of the airplane as it made its final approach to Hatay Airport. The modern international airport that opened in 2007 is about fifteen or sixteen miles by road from Antakya. Though on the small side for international airports, it is more than adequate for the air traffic using it. Orion felt the landing bump and heard the thrust reversers activate. He was pushed forward against his seat beat as the craft rapidly slowed.After only a moment,the plane was taxiing toward its gate. Gabriel waited for Orion in the terminal, since meeting deplaning passengers at the gate had never been allowed. The events of 9/11 changed a lot about airports all over the world and Turkey was no exception. The country had excellent reasons to be cautious, given the almost constant turmoil with its neighbors, as well as the recent coup attempt to unseat the Turkish president.

Orion only had a carryon bag, so when he and Gabriel met, they were ready to head to Antakya without any delay for baggage. After exchanging initial greetings and pleasantries as they walked to the car, Gabriel asked,

"Now that we're through being nice," he smiled, "what's the big mystery that brings you here?"

"You may be up against something far bigger and sinister than you imagined."

"Well, that doesn't sound good. What's going on?"

As the men drove the few miles to the visitors' center of the church, Orion laid out everything he'd learned. Aside from asking a few clarifying questions, Gabriel just listened. Finally when Orion indicated he had no more to tell, it was Gabriel's turn.

"I'm not ready to deal with a bunch of bad guys who don't want me to find something, particularly a something we're not even sure exists. I don't mean to whine, but I've had enough of this shit."

"I'm not surprised. That's why I wanted to let you know what we learned as soon as I could."

"Nicki's coming for the weekend, in fact she's coming in the day after tomorrow. After she arrives, we'll get everybody together and you can retell this story. I promised I wouldn't make decisions on my own any more, so they need to be in on it."

"I'm sure you don't relish that conversation."

"I don't. I love my work. These last years have been exhilarating. Any one of the finds we've discovered would make an entire career for any archeologist, and I've been lucky enough to have a bunch. I think it's time we all shifted—actually, let me speak for myself—I shifted to projects much less likely to be controversial."

"And much less likely to get you killed."

Gabriel laughed, "Yeah, that too. Here we are. The visitors' center is our temporary office. I imagine Trevor's in there crunching data we collected this morning. Let's go see."

Gabriel parked and the two men made their way to the conference room now turned office. And, as he expected, Trevor and Valerie were sitting in front of a computer connected to a several monitors. "Guys, have you met Paddy Orion? I can't remember?" Gabriel said.

Greetingswere exchanged all around and Valerie asked, "What brings you to Turkey?"

"Just needed to give my client an update on our research. I prefer face-to-face rather than electronic, plus I'd had enough of

London for a few days. They drive on the wrong side of the road and I can't get used to it."

Friendly chuckles bounced around the room, as they showed sympathy for his discomfort. "As you noticed, Turkey gets it right," Valerie said. "Of course, there is a certain amount of anarchy on the roads sometimes, but maybe that's no different from Memphis. I'm still scared to death to drive there."

"You guys find anything," Gabriel asked.

Valerie started. "The imaging of the church is complete. We have another couple of hours of data from the morning's flyover churning through this computer, but I can show you the church images on my iPad."

"Great! I'd love to see it. First, though, anything interesting from this morning? Tell me 'no' so we can all go back home. I'm tired," Gabriel said.

"There is a little bit of the picture from this morning that might be worth a second look, but we've still got quite a lot to go, as Valerie mentioned," Trevor said. "You really want to go home?" A look of concern spread across his face.

"Nicki and I are going to talk about it when she arrives, then I'd like us all to discuss it. More and more, I'm thinking this whole idea was nuts. We still have no clue what we're looking for, or if there is anything to be found. Plus, even if we find something, it may have no historic value. So, yeah, I'm inclined to hang it up."

"You're the boss," Trevor said, looking back at his monitor.

"I'm not saying that's what we're going to do. We're all going to be involved in deciding."

"Okay." Trevor looked at Valerie and she returned what was clearly a look of skepticism and concern.

"Valerie, let's see the church," Gabriel said, more sharply than he intended.

"Gimme a minute to get it booted up." Valerie tapped the screen a few times and said,"Here we go."

The view on the screen was of the façade from about fifty feet away. "We'll do a virtual walk through the center doors," she said, manipulating the image. "We're in the narthex. Let's do a quick look around." She moved her finger across an icon in the upper right of the screen, and the scene began to rotate allowing a view of the entire space. "Now we'll move into the nave itself." Again she used her finger to move them forward. Without comment, she began to track three hundred and sixty degrees. Finished with that, she shifted the view to the ceiling of the cave. "That's the overview. Want to see any part of it in more detail?"

Gabriel replied, "Yeah. Can you fly up over the altar and look down?"

"Yep." She manipulated the movement icon and the view shifted to an overhead view of the altar and its platform.

"Okay. See how there is a dark band in what's left of the floor mosaic that butts into the altar?"

"Yes."

"I think it was a large rectangle, setting off an important space. Maybe for the original altar. I don't know. Can you show that in more detail, maybe with some measurements?"

"Sure." She did as he asked. "I can do an interpolation from the existing floor pattern to show what the whole might have looked like." She did so.

"Okay. That rectangle is within fractions of an inch in being perfect. But look how the platform is slightly off center."

"I see that," she said. "What do you think it means?"

"I don't know. Sloppy workmanship? Haste? It just makes me wonder what is under that platform," Gabriel answered.

"You want to move it?" Trevor asked.

"I don't think we'll be allowed to, but that's something I want to put on our list of things to do."

"Never hurts to ask, does it?" Valerie asked.

"I suppose not," Gabriel replied. "But I'm getting ahead of myself. We're probably not even gonna stay."

"While we're speculating on things to do if we stay, take a look at this." Valerie shifted the view to the side wall of the nave where Father Gambini had said there was a tunnel plastered over. "I was just playing around with the images last night. One of the things I did was to draw a line from the approximate center of the tunnel, across the nave, and to the opposite wall. The first thing I noticed was how it lined up almost perfectly with the centerline of the altar along its long axis. Then I noticed where it intersected the opposite wall. I actually walked over this morning and took a closer look."

"And...?" Gabriel asked.

"And the surface looks as rough as the rest of the cave walls, but as I looked more closely, what I saw wasn't the natural surface of the rest of the walls. It looks as if stones have been worked to mimic the rest of the surface. With a magnifier, I was able to see a slight space around the perimeter of the worked stones. My best guess is that someone has filled a niche or another tunnel with stones rather than plastering over it."

Trevor jumped in. "We think the location on the axis that centers on the altar suggests this is an important finding. If we stay, we need to get permission to remove those stones and see what we find."

"Good work, Valerie. May be nothing, of course, but then again..." Gabriel said.

"Look," Trevor said, "we're getting images from the flyover data." Everyone's attention shifted to Trevor's monitors. "We expected to see paths to the obvious caves and bas-reliefs, but I'm seeing paths to other spots that are just grass covered hillside. Pointing to a screen that showed the topography of the site, he said, "Based on what I'm seeing on this monitor," he pointed to a different one that showed faint images superimposed on the topo, "there is something here and here. Ancient pathways point to those places more so than anywhere else. And look, the GPS overlay on this other monitor shows disturbance where those paths seem to lead. Something may be there. Caves, tombs, ruins, hard to say, but if we were going to dig, these would be the places to start."

"Is the data complete?" Gabriel asked.

"No. This is preliminary, but it's pretty interesting."

"Let's get it all done before we make any assumptions about where to do what. This is exciting stuff. Even if there are no artifacts anywhere, new finds may help tell a more complete story about the church. And if I thought we'd be left alone, I'd say we go for it."

Orion spoke up. "I know I'm an outsider here, but one option you have is to give your completed data sets to someone else, some other archeologist and let them have a go. That protects you and might still get new insight into the area surrounding the church."

"True. It could also get them killed," Valerie said. "I'd rather go for ourselves. Maybe the Templars could provide the security we need while we work. Or we could hire our own private army."

"That's our dilemma, Paddy. Anyone who works here may be in danger. So I think it's us or walk away and take the data with us."

"Glad I don't have to decide," Orion replied.

"You two keep working. Nicki will be here soon and we'll all sit down and talk. Until then, stay busy."

Valerie and Trevor both nodded their agreement, and then each turned their attention back to their computers. Gabriel asked Orion to join him. The two men walked the short distance to the church and went inside. Gabriel led Orion to the spot Valerie had said looked as if something had been filled in. A close look confirmed what Valerie had seen.

"This is interesting," Gabriel said. "The site manager told us the tunnel on the opposite wall was thought to be used to allow worshippers to escape during periods of persecution. If that's true, what was this one all about?"

"Looks like the stones need to be removed to see what's there," Orion suggested.

"Yeah. And I'm very curious."

34

ROME

THE VATICAN ARCHIVES

"H ey, Nicki. Look at this," Sister Mary Bernice said.
Nicki stopped her scan of a folder of material and
stepped over to the work area where the nun had placed a
sheet of what appeared to be vellum. "What's up?" she asked.

"You're going to love this!It appears to be a copy ofa letter from
someone named Sara addressed to...let me just read it to you. It's in
amazing condition."The sister began reading.

*Sara, servant of Jesus Christ, president of the community of
believers in Antioch, to the beloved of Jesus in Aleppo, and to its
leader, Moshe: Peace be upon you in the Lord's name.*

*Please accept a copy of the memoirs of one who walked with
the Lord before his glorious resurrection. Receive it as a gift from
the many who worship him here in Antioch. We venerate this
work and read a portion from it when we gather on the first day of
the week. Your brother, Elias, who stopped among us in his travels,
was much moved upon hearing us read this memoir in our
worship. He implored us to send a copy to you for yourwelfare and
edification. If you find these memories to be instructive for your
faith in our Lord, we ask only that your scribes create a copy and
send it to another community you believe would wish to know
about our Lord's words and deeds.*

Elias has told us much about your faith in our Lord Jesus, and about how you never cease to care for the poor and the widowed among you, and how you preach the Lord to all who will receive him. May our Lord continue to bless you until he comes again.

"Oh, my God!" Nicki exclaimed. "She's sending a copy of a Gospel to them!"

"I know! Do you know what it could mean if we found the Gospel they used? It would be revolutionary. Maybe bigger than *Mary's Gospel*!" the nun replied, every bit as excited as Nicki.

The two staff members working near them stopped and looked their way. "Did you find something?" one of them asked in English.

"Oh, probably not anything important. We got a little too excited," Sister Mary Bernice answered. The two staff members mumbled something to each other and resumed their work.

"Aren't we going to tell them?" Nicki asked in a near whisper.

"Let's keep it between us for now. The Vatican is a gossipy little town," the nun answered.

"Can you tell when the letter was written?" Nicki asked.

"Not from this. Maybe we can have the vellum Carbon14 dated. Or the ink. Or maybe paleography can give us a clue. We'd need an expert for that, of course," the nun answered.

"I can get all that done. We have a lab that does all our C14 dating and we've used a paleographer at Vanderbilt to help with the Mary Codex dating. Will the Archives let us take this for those purposes?"

"We can only ask. But we'd have better luck if you asked Cardinal Greganti. He's got pull."

"Let me call him right now." Nicki pulled her cellphone out only to discover she had no signal. "Oops. No signal. Think I should just go see him?"

"Let's wait until you return to his quarters tonight. That will keep this from looking like a big deal. Plus, we might find something else."

"You know, it just hit me. The big deal we know for sure is that the leader of the Antioch community when the letter was written was a woman. A woman!" Nicki said.

"If the letter is early, that would fit with some of St. Paul's letters. He often mentions women as a part of the leadership in the communities he writes to. For example, Acts mentions a woman named Mary, the mother of a man named John Mark, as a leader of a congregation. Some early evidence exists of the use of a Greek word *presbytis*to describe certain Christian women. It's the feminine form of the word *presbyter* that is variously translated as elder or overseer. It's the word from which priest is derived. This is independent verification of women leaders or priests. Very cool," Sister Mary Bernice replied.

"That reminds me," she continued. "The newly restored Catacombs of Priscilla right here in Rome shows a fresco of a woman many think is a priest, and another fresco show three women who seem to be presiding at the Lord's Supper. The Vatican officially denies this interpretation, but many scholars support it."

"Let's keep looking," Nicki said. "I'm really psyched now."

The women turned back to their tasks without noticing one of the staff members who wandered away. Even had they noticed, they might well have assumed it was for a restroom break, certainly nothing nefarious. But then, they didn't overhear the phone call he made once he had a signal.

"Father Arturo, they found something that excited them. They said it was nothing, but they seemed awfully pumped up."

"What is it?" the Librarian asked.

"All I could see was a single document. One page. The nun read it to the Gabriel woman and they both became very animated, and then they lowered their voices to almost a whisper."

"Good. See if you can find out what the document was. Try not to be too obvious."

After the call ended, Father Arturo made a call himself.

"They found something they became excited about. I'm trying to determine what it was."

"What did they do next?" Father Cavallo wanted to know.

"Apparently they just went back to work."

"As soon as you know more, contact me. Thank you, Father. The Cardinal will be pleased." Cavallo just didn't say which Cardinal.

✠

"Sister," Nicki said in a calm voice, "please come look at this."

The sister walked to the work area and bent over to allow the worklight to illuminate the document in bright LED lighting. She began to silently read the vellum. "This looks like a report or record of some kind."

"That's what I thought, too."

"It seems to kind of pick up in mid-sentence."

"I think there is a least one page before this one that is missing," Nicki said.

Though the ink was quite faded and she was unfamiliar with some of the words, plus there were holes in the document here and there, Sister Mary Bernice began to read what she could in a soft voice.

...broken when she [?] of her beloved husband's death in Rome at the hands of the [Emperor? Leader?]. Long ago, he went about the region [preaching?] and healing as the Lord [instructed? taught?], while she stayed behind to [lead? guide? direct?] us.He told her stories of things he [saw?] the Lord do and things he heard the Lord say.As long as she was our [?], she never tired of telling us those stories. She told themwhenever [?] gathered to eat his [flesh? body?] and [?] his blood [?] first day of the [?]. The nun turned the page. "Uh oh. The ink is so faded I can't be sure what I'm seeing. I can make out the last line, though." She picked up her reading aloud.

The Council [suggested? ordered?] we send word to those [groups? communities?] with whom we shared the memoirs we cherish, The nun turned the page and continued.*to ask them for a small [gift? offering?]. Our deaconsundertook the journeys needed, men with men and [?] with women. They have returned from the [mission? task?], which was a [?] [?].*

"I can't make out the last few words.Nicki, this is enlightening and enigmatic all at once," the nun said in a quiet voice. "Could this be Sara they're talking about?"

"I think it is. I think what was on the first page is that Sara's heart was what was broken when her husband was executed. I also think her husband was an eyewitness to Jesus's life and he shared stories with her and those stories became the heart of her sharing—or more likely—preaching."

Sister Mary Bernice crossed herself. "I think all that is very plausible."

"Sister, we're taking today's finds with us when we walk out of the Archives this afternoon. I don't think we can risk leaving them here overnight. Have you noticed how often the staff, well, one of them anyway, has been looking at us today? Every time I look up, he's turning his head quickly away from looking toward us. It may be nothing, but we can't chance it."

"I'm game."

"Okay, then. We just wait until they quit at their usual time, and we pack up and head to the Cardinal's quarters."

Speaking more conversationally, Sister Mary Bernice said, "Nicki, I don't think this is anything we can use. Just stick it back and let's move on." She winked.

Nicki caught on. "Too bad. More digging, I guess."

The next few hours seemed to drag by, but finally, the staff said *buona notte* and left. "Sister, I'm going to make a quick trip to the restroom. Can you get our stuff together?"

"Yes. I can't wait to get to a lab where I can use an alternate light source on the parts we can't read."

"I'll be quick," Nicki said. True to her word, she was back quickly and the two women headed to the Cardinal's quarters. Nicki said, "We've got to come clean to the Cardinal about the documents we took."

"He'll understand. I hope." The nun crossed herself. "And pray."

✠

"Father Cavallo, this is Father Arturo. One of my men thinks the women found something important today in the Archives. I had him go back after they left to see what they might have found. He said he could find nothing. Whatever they were talking about, they either put back or took with them."

"Could they have just walked out with something?"

"When we started our search, Cardinal Greganti made it clear they were VIPs. Consequently, I have extended them every courtesy, including not searching their belongings when they come and go."

"So they could have removed something?"

"Yes. I'm afraid so."

"Very well. Keep watching. Call every day they are there. Wait. One more thing. Tomorrow when they leave, have their bags searched. Put someone new at the exit and don't tell him to give them special treatment."

"Yes, Father."

35

ROME

CARDINAL GREGANTI'S APARTMENT

Sister, thanks for walking me to the apartment. I think I can probably find my way from here myself from now on. I enjoy your company, don't misunderstand, but I know it's well out of your way," Nicki said.

"And I yours. Do you think you can tell His Eminence what we found, including the letter we removed? I think you have more pull than I do." The nun smiled good-naturedly.

"I'll be happy to."

"It might ease the blow of our little, hmm, indiscretion if you tell him without me."

"I'm not worried. I'll see you in the morning. You have a standing invitation from him to join us for breakfast. You will, won't you?"

"I will. But will you call me if he doesn't take this well. I'll need to prepare myself for being chastised." Sister smiled again, but there was a lot of truth behind her remark as well.

"Certainly. Good night, Sister. Remember, we are on the side of the angels," Nicki said as she leaned forward and kissed the nun softly on her cheek.

"And you, too, Nicki," she said, moved by the show of affection.

Nicki knocked on the door and it was quickly opened by one of Cardinal's assistants. She greeted him and remarked about how good the cooking smelled. He replied that he would tell the cook.

The Cardinal seldom arrived home before 6:00 or 6:30. It was 5:15 now, giving her time for a shower and a change of clothes before dinner. And time to decide how to break the news to her friend. She considered calling Gabby, but decided to wait until closer to bedtime. That way she could report Greganti's reaction to the discovery, too.

✠

Sister Mary Bernice made her way to her quarters.Once inside, she placed her backpack on the small bed in the uncluttered and simple room. From it she pulled, the vellum sheets that reported about Sara that she needed to view under an alternative light source. Then, she removed an entire bundle of documents, still encased in its leather folder from her bag. It was the bundle from which Nicki had found the report mentioning Sara's wish. Convinced there had to be more, she was leaving nothing to chance. If she had the documents in her possession, she didn't need to worry what might happen to them.

Stepping over to the simple desk near the bed, she laid down the bundle, switched on the desk lamp, and sat down to begin to flip through the four or five inches of vellum in the bundle. A review now, she thought, might reveal more documents, and, if it did, they might need to be viewed in the lab, too. It wasn't long until she stopped her quick scans of each page, and began to study something more carefully.

✠

TURKEY
THE VISITORS' CENTER

Orion and Gabriel walked back to the conference room. As they walked, Gabriel said, "Here's why I'm an archeologist in one word: curiosity. I want to know what is walled up in that nave. Not the tunnel; I'm betting we'll find nothing there. But, I want to know what's behind door number two."

"You mean the one opposite; the one we just examined?"

"Yep. It could be nothing. It could be the most important find I've ever made. Likely, it's somewhere in between. I just want to know. That's all. I will wonder the rest of my life if we don't look."

"So you're staying?"

"I want to, but I've promised. It's not my decision. Nicki will be here late tomorrow. We'll decide the next day, in all likelihood."

Just as they entered the visitor's center, Orion's cellphone buzzed in his shirt pocket. "Excuse me," he said to Gabriel, taking the phone from his shirt and looking at it. "Oh! It's Aurélio. Sal? How are you?"

Orion put his phone on speaker so Gabriel could hear. The two men stopped in the entrance area. "I'm well, Paddy. I've got some news."

"I'm all ears. Gabby's listening, too."

"Gabby! How're you doing, my friend? All healed?"

"Practically. In body if not in spirit."

"I understand. Close brushes with the Reaper can slow you down."

"Doesn't seem to have that effect on you."

"Oh, but I'm a professional idiot. I thrive on danger. Hey, listen you two, is this a good time?"

"Sure. Nobody around but us and a handful of tourists who seem completely uninterested in what we're doing."

"Okay. Here's what's come up. Paddy, our Mr. Hightower was found dead this morning in his flat. It's an apparent heart attack, and I emphasize the word 'apparent.' A quick surreptitious check of his National Health Service records by Nigel shows the man is, or was, in excellent health in spite of a bunch of working class bad habits associated with the local pub."

"Who's Hightower," Gabby asked.

"Gulliver's driver. Paddy and I had a little *tête-à-tête* with him a couple of days ago."

"Oh."

"So he wasn't at risk?" Orion asked. "But that doesn't mean it couldn't have happened, right?"

"A few queries to our resident medical experts suggest the odds are heavily against it. We'll be very interested in the autopsy."

"There'll be one for an apparent natural death?" Orion asked.

"He died alone. His wife had gone to the market and when she returned, she found him in their living room. So, yes. And, just to sweeten the chance even more, we know somebody with pull who'll see to it."

"You guys are as powerful as TEO," Orion said with a chuckle.

"I doubt it, but we ain't no slouches. And on the plus side, we're the good guys."

"You're thinking foul play, then," Gabriel said.

"Yep. And as it happens, there are a couple of cameras mounted on the block of flats opposite his. I've got somebody poking around the Metropolitan Police Service to see if we can get a peek. I want to know who showed up at his door after his wife left."

"Here's hoping you guys find something useful. My fear is that even if you got a full head on face shot, along with a picture of his ID hanging around his neck, it won't trace back to TEO. They're pros. They cover their asses," Orion offered.

"Yeah, but we're pros, too. And now and then, we walk very closely to the line between good and evil, but all for goodness' sake," Aurélio replied. "But, of course, we never want to do that. What's going on there? I'll keep you posted."

Gabriel took the lead and sketched out the meager findings so far. "I'm not sure we're staying, Salvador. Lots of heat being brought to bear. Now there's a dead guy that linked to this thing. I'm thinking we may pick up our toys and go dig in a safe place."

"Given your history of discovery, that'd be a shame, but I can't say I blame you," Aurélio said. "Do what you think best, Gabby. As an organization we're going full tilt after the TEO evildoers, to quote one of your former presidents, no matter what you do. I just got that word from on high this morning."

"That's good news and bad news, Sal. I feel responsible for dragging you guys into to this. I don't really like that."

"Oh, they've been on our radar screen for more years that I've been with the Templars. The thinking is that now is the time for a full push; we've got leads we've never had. At the very least, we want to disrupt them."

"Then, God bless you and the others, Sal."

"Thanks, Gabby. Paddy, when do you plan to return?"

"I'm briefing the crew tomorrow or the next day when Nicki gets here, then I'll head back. I need to talk to Gabby and Nicki about continuing to be in their employ. I think maybe I'm not needed with you guys on the scene."

"I understand. Take your time to decide. I'll tell you straight away, though, I'd love to have you by my side as we press on. But, it's our fight, not yours, Paddy. We can keep Gabby informed if he wishes."

"When bad guys need to get theirs, it might be my fight, too. Let us talk it over," Orion said.

Goodbyes were said, and Gabriel and Orion headed to the conference room to see if anything more was showing up on the data crunching. It was.

36

TURKEY

VISITORS' CENTER CONFERENCE ROOM

As Gabriel and Orion entered the conference room, Gabriel asked, "Anything more guys?"

"It's coming along. We think those sites I pointed out to you are worth physical examination," Trevor said. "I've got some ideas about how to proceed and it won't require digging a shovel full of dirt."

"Sounds intriguing. Go for it and tell me about it later," Gabby said. "I've got to depend on you guys more for ideas."

"I had a thought while you were in the church," Valerie said. "We may not need to move the altar and platform to see if there is something under it. Our GPR might do the trick. I could run it around the altar and see if we pick up anything. At the worst, we could move the altar and use the GPR where it sat."

"That would simplify things," Gabriel replied. "See what I mean about depending on you for ideas?"

"Or," Valerie said, "If they will let us, we could try to penetrate the altar with it. That would mean standing on top of it, though. They might take offense at that."

"I think we can sell on the idea. If they don't want us to stand on it, we could build scaffolding that would allow us to be off of it and only have the GPR unit touching it," Gabriel said.

"That would work," Valerie said. "I'll get to work on figuring out exactly what we need."

"Okay, but don't order anything. We're not deciding to proceed until Nicki can be a part of the conversation—in person. I don't want to make this decision with a Skype meeting."

"That's fair. Another couple of days isn't going to change anything," Trevor offered. "Gabby, if we do decide to go forward, it might be worth the expense to do several things at once. We could have a team working on that walled up area we found and the original tunnel. Let's say we find something associated with the altar; I'd like a team to have a go at that. And we could do one or more of the sites near the church that GPR and infrared picked up."

"All that makes sense"said Gabriel. "I'd want to prioritize the sites the GPR picked up and start a team on the best candidate. But, I hate to sound like a broken record—nothing until we have Nicki here and have a discussion,"

✠

ROME

Sister Mary Bernice pulled a magnifier from her backpack and moved the light closer to the document she was trying to read. She was looking at another report. The ink was faded and there were a few holes, but she thought she could make it out. Again, the document she was looking at seemed to be a second or third page of something.

laid out their arguments before the Council. Our [brother?] Paul was [?] in opposing Peter because Peter had changed. Previously Peter [had?] eaten with the uncircumcised among us, but when Jesus' [?] James, learned of it, he [?] a delegation to [chastise? chasten?] Peter. She turned the page.

Paul believed that Peter was [wrong?] to end table fellowship with those in our [group? city?] who [?] Jesus but are not also Jewish. Peter agreed with him, but for the sake of [peace?] with James in Jerusalem, believed he must follow James' wishes. He again[refused?] to eat with uncircumcised followers.

Sister Mary Bernice pulled a New Testament from the small shelf in her room and turned to Paul's Letter to the Galatians. She flipped a few pages until she came to the verses she was seeking. The nun began to read aloud.

"When Peter came to Antioch, I opposed him to his face, because he was clearly in the wrong. Before certain men came from James, he used to eat with the Gentiles. But when they arrived, he began to draw back and separate himself from the Gentiles because he was afraid of those who belonged to the circumcision group."

Sister Mary Bernice sat back in her chair. She turned to the book of Acts and read aloud,

"And the apostles and brothers, who were in Judea, heard that the Gentiles also had received the word of God in Antioch. When Peter came up to Jerusalem, those who were circumcised contended with him, saying: Why did you eat with those in Antioch who are uncircumcised?

She continued reading and found what she remembered. Peter defends himself with the report of a long vision from God. The upshot of which was the Jerusalem followers moderated their position. According to Acts, the believers in Antioch would only have to minimally obey the Torah, specifically, eat no food offered to idols, avoid sexual immorality, refrain from eating the meat of strangled animals, and from eating meat with blood. This account indicates that Paul was in Jerusalem, and he and Barnabas were sent to Antioch to continue converting gentiles. It was obvious the two accounts clashed, and now there was independent evidence that Acts was just wrong!

The nun returned to her documents and turned another page, but this page was too faded to read. She laid it aside for her trip to the lab the next day, and returned to the other pages remaining in her bundle.

✠

LONDON
TEO HEADQUARTERS

"What do we know?" Jack asked of his chief investigator, Jemison Thorsby.

"Only that they are scanning the cave and the surrounding area with electronic equipment of some kind. They did what sounds like a helicopter flyover. We don't have anyone inside yet, so we don't know what they may be finding. They haven't started expanding their team; when they do, I'll have someone inside."

"What about the Gabriel woman and the nun?"

"They found something, but we don't know what, or if, it's important."

"This isn't acceptable, you know. I want information. I don't want them to announce a discovery and that is the first we know of it."

Properly stung, Thorsby replied, "I'll figure out something. I've got a contact at the Vatican. I'll see what I can find out."

✠

ROME

THE VATICAN

"Father, this is Carlo Ricci at the Documents Lab. I've just received a call from a Sister Mary Bernice. She wants to use our documents lab tomorrow, specifically to use some alternate light source on something. I told her it would be fine."

"Good," Cavallo said. "It's coming together. They removed something from the Archives and now they need to study it. When she arrives, you need to stipulate that you have to be with her when she uses the equipment. I want to know what she finds."

"Won't she be suspicious? We don't usually monitor someone's use when they have the proper credentials, as she claims to have."

"I don't care if she's suspicious. Come up with a good story to justify it."

"Such as?"

Cavallo raised his voice. "I don't give a shit what you tell her! Take care of it or you'll be looking for a new position!"

37

THE VATICAN

*D*uring dinner with Nicki, the Cardinal asked, "How is your search going in the Archives?"

"Alessandro, I'm afraid I may need special absolution from you." Nicki smiled. "The Sister and I found something today. It's not much, but it's intriguing."

"So far, my dear, it doesn't sound like absolution is in order. Congratulations, perhaps, but not absolution."

"I removed it without permission. Let me explain. The two staffers who are working with us have been acting especially interested in what Mary Bernice and I are finding. We felt unsettled by it. They may be too interested, if you get my drift."

"Oh, no. You suspect them of spying more than helping, don't you?"

"Perhaps we're paranoid, but given other things Gabby and I have dealt with, paranoia seems to come unbidden. My first impulse was to protect what we found."

"Yes. Yes, I can understand that. I hope you're wrong, but I'm well aware that many in the Vatican, and especially in the Curia do not approve of the direction the Holy Father is trying to take the Church. They may well be snooping on you. I'll need to do a little snooping of my own and see how they were chosen. But now, tell me more of your find."

Nicki told him about Sara and her wish, at least as much as she knew. "Sister is going to take it to the lab tomorrow and try to view it under better conditions. She's eager to see what we might have."

"Should anyone question you about this, tell them I've given you permission to remove what you need. Whether or not I actually have that authority is another matter, but until someone says I don't, I'm assuming I do."

"Thank you, Alessandro. Again, you've protected us. We both, actually, we three, will always be grateful."

"Just be very careful, Nicki. And, of course, I'll be interested in what you find."

"You'll know as soon as we do, Alessandro. And thank you for your understanding. By the way, I'm leaving tomorrow afternoon to fly to Turkey. Gabby and I have been away from each other too long. I was very distressed over his going to Turkey in the first place and I've been a bit cool toward him about his decision. I'm over it and I want to tell him face to face."

"Will you be gone long?"

"I plan to come back Sunday evening so Mary Bernice and I can get back to work. If there is anything to be found, the sooner we find it the easier it will be on the team in Turkey."

"Let me know when you return and I'll have you met at the airport. No sense in you having to deal with customs officials and such there."

"Thank you, dear friend. And thank you for a wonderful meal. If you'll excuse me, I'm going to call Sister and let her know we're forgiven for our little 'borrowing' activity and to coordinate our start time tomorrow."

"Of course. I have some things to which I need to attend, anyway. Perhaps we can have a small drink before we retire tonight?"

"That would be lovely."

✠

Turkey
Liwan Hotel Dining Room

The dining room in the Liwan Hotel was of modest size. The white marble floor had a simple design of black tile diamonds running around the perimeter of the room, and another defining the few round tables in the center of the room. The room had a thirty foot high ceiling and was framed by three walls of painted stone, and one of shuttered windows. Dominating one of the end walls was a large brick fireplace, which was not lit.

Gabby and the others sat in one corner of the room, well away from the few other diners. Their evening meal began with *anali kizli* soup made of small meatballs, *bulgura* cereal, usually wheat—tomatoes and chickpeas, all in a soup like a yogurt sauce. The name of the soup means "daughters and mothers" with the chickpeas being the daughters and the *bulgur* balls the mothers. The main course was lamb shanks, eggplant, and green peppers. They had forgone dessert for coffee.

As they waited for the grounds to settle in their unfiltered coffee before drinking it—something they had learned the hard way on their first day—Trevor said, "I think I have a site to suggest for further exploration if we stay. The scans show what appear to be the remains of three walls outside a cave that kind of frame the cave opening, or at least what I think is a cave opening. The cave itself seems to be quite large and is divided into several areas. My working hypothesis is that the cave was probably used first, and then enlarged into several other spaces, and finally the whole thing was expanded outside.

"My reasoning is that it would be easier to build walls than to dig into the stone of the cave. Plus, the original excavations probably provided a good bit of stone that could be used for the walls. If they needed more, more could be quarried from the site." He pulled a print out from his bag and laid it on the table. "You can see the outer construction was divided into several smaller rooms along one side of the building, and the rest was one large room."

"I can see that," Gabriel said. "Either those smaller rooms were some kind of storage areas," Valerie interrupted, "or maybe sleeping spaces, small bedrooms."

"Yeah, it could be," Gabriel agreed. "If we let our imagination run away with us, we could call this thing The Monastery, though if it was built early, that would be an anachronism. But maybe it was some kind of community center. Let say it was really early; the little bedrooms or cells, if you will, could have housed widows. Widows were very important to the Early Church. In fact, there is a lot of written evidence that they were sometimes or in some places, anyway, a kind of religious order, like deacon or priest."

"Sure," Valerie added. "First Timothy, which was written around120 to 150 CE seems to indicate that widows of a certain age and reputation had a spiritual ministry to the woman and children of a congregation or church. And I've read where they helped prepare for the baptism of women, visited women who were ill, and things like that. In those days, it was unseemly for a man to do some of those things."

"All that's true. But, gang; let's not get ahead of ourselves. We don't know what we have until we move some dirt and see actual walls or foundations. And, Trevor, I'm assuming the cave entrance is blocked."

"Right," Trevor said,"it looks as if the mouth of the cave was filled in at some point. Again, to get way ahead of the evidence, it could have been done during a local persecution of Christians. But it also could have just been a natural collapse. Today, the opening isn't even obvious. Had we not done the scan, I wouldn't have given the site a second look. The interior of the cave appears to be open, according to the readings we got. Before we open the thing, we could do some borings and see if we hit open air or more rock."

Orion had been listening attentively. "Is this a common conversation you guys have about a project?"

Gabriel answered him. "It depends. When we found the Mary Codex, we knew from ground scans we were dealing with a residence. From the location in the Old City, we could determine it was someone of importance because it was not far from the larger residences that had already been found there archeologists are pretty sure belonged to Temple priests. Beyond that, we didn't speculate about its age or its owner, except that it was someone of some means or importance because of the size. Had we not found the codex in a niche in the wall, we would likely never have known that Mary Magdalene lived there.

"Other times we are pretty sure going in what we're likely to find. Most of the work will be on dating objects found there, the style of architecture, or other clues we unearth. From all that, we end up years later coming up with a plausible or defensible idea of exactly what we found. The truth is, the ideas in some cases are defensible, but not necessarily true." Gabriel laughed. "Then scholars get to argue about it for decades and graduate students get to write dissertations on the finds."

"So, while science is involved, so is guesswork—educated guesswork—but guesswork," Orion said.

"Yep. Okay, Nicki will be arriving tomorrow evening. I'll go get her. We'll gather for dinner as we did tonight and lay everything out. After that, we can decide right away, or sleep on it. So, until then we work tomorrow and increase our tiny store of info, and go from there."

"Oh, Gabby!" Valerie exclaimed. "There's one thing I forgot to mention.Father Gambini said we could build a scaffold around the altar and use our GPR to see beneath it."

"That's good news, Valerie. One more thing to share with Nicki. With that, my friends, I'm going to head to my room. I'm tired. I'll see you at breakfast, say 7:30 a.m.?"

✠

ROME
THE VATICAN

As she was preparing for bed, Nicki's cellphone rang. It was the nun.

"Sister. I didn't expect to be hearing from you," she said.

"Are we in trouble with His Eminence?"

"No. He understood. He said we should tell anyone who asks that he has cleared it."

"Great! Because I took more than the page or two we were trying to protect; I took the whole volume."

"Really?"

"It was an impulse. I'm glad, too. I found more things I believe are important along with a bunch I can't read yet. I'm going to the lab tomorrow to examine them. I wanted to go tonight, but as I began to find more, I decided to finish with this folder before going. Want to join me there in the morning?"

"I'd just be in the way. You go ahead, but stay in touch. I'll go back to the archives and see what else I can find."

"Nicki, one of the documents seems to mention a cache of tablets. It's very hard to read, but it I think it says there is a *topos* that I think means room with tablets in it. If I'm right about the word, it means more than just room, but a special place, marked off from others. That seems to make it important. The document seems to describe a discussion of whether or not to keep the tablets or dispose of them, but I can't find anything that resolves the matter."

"What kind of tablets?"

"I don't know for sure. The word is *cerae* and I think it refers to a kind of writing tablet. I'm so tired, I'm not thinking straight. I'm going to try to sleep on it and start with fresh eyes and clear head tomorrow."

"Mary Bernice, you've been a godsend. This may give us an actual target in our work at the church."

"I hope so. Who knows what may turn up?"

✠

THE VATICAN
FATHER CAVALLO'S QUARTERS

Cavallo had retired for the evening, but found sleep wasn't coming. He was playing different scenarios in his head that featured TEO, the Cave Church in Turkey, and his own comfort and security. Near mid-night, he rose, switched on his bedside lamp, and slipped on his robe. The priest rummaged in the nightstand drawer and removed a pack of cigarettes. Certain they were stale since he seldom smoked, he lit one anyway. The smoke he inhaled was acrid and hot; a coughing fit ensued. It didn't deter him from taking another deep drag. Sitting on the side of his bed, he reached for his cellphone and keyed in a number that would ring elsewhere in the Vatican.

After ten or so rings, he heard, "Paul. What the hell?"

"Sorry to be calling so late, Saverio. I need a favor. There is a nun staying in the Vatican somewhere. Her name is Mary Bernice Armistead. Tomorrow she will be out of her quarters all day, beginning, I would guess, about 7:00 a.m. I want an unofficial search made. Confiscate anything that looks out of the ordinary and bring it to me."

"Can you be more precise about what we're to look for?"

"I believe she's taken something from the Archives."

"Why not call the desk at the Gendarmerie Corps? Theft from the Archives is a serious crime."

"I have my reasons, including the apprehension and interrogation not being official. Can you do this for me?"

"Yes. I will personally do the search."

"Good. A lot may be riding on this."

"Including something about our Little Thing?"

"Yes. Maybe. I don't want to chance it."

"I'll definitely take care of it. What about her?"

"She may need to disappear."

"I'll set something in place just in case."

"Thank you Saverio. Maybe I can get some sleep now."

38

TURKEY

THE NEXT DAY

"G abby," Trevor said at breakfast, "Remember how I said we could do some investigating without any digging? Late yesterday I ordered some drilling equipment and a small crew to run it. I want to do some bore holes at the site of the 'monastery' and take a look. I've got an endoscope with a long cable coming, too, so once the holes are bored, we can scope it out in safety. If you don't object, I'd like to get on that today."

"I guess that's okay. Do we need Father Gambini's permission?" Gabriel said hesitantly.

"I called this morning. Turns out he's an early riser, too. He said we could do it. Apparently word from the Vatican and the Turkey culture guys is we can do what we want—well, within reason."

"Go ahead then. Maybe by the time Nicki is here we'll know something useful to add to our meager store of facts."

Orion spoke up. "Trevor, if you need another hand, I'm going nuts doing nothing. I'll pitch in."

"That'd be great." Turning to Gabby and concerned he might have overstepped his authority, he added, "I ordered the equipment just in case. If you'd said no, that would have been okay."

"I get it, Trevor. Don't worry about it," Gabriel said.

"What do you need from me?" Orion asked.

"Got some clothes you don't mind getting dirty? Put 'em on and let's head to the site as soon as breakfast is over."

"Gabby," Valerie said, "I'm going to be arranging for a scaffold over the altar to be set up."

"You already have one?" Gabriel asked.

"I ordered it yesterday. I thought no matter what we might decide when Nicki arrives, we could do this little survey of the altar area anyway. It will take longer to assemble the scaffold than to do the survey. By late afternoon, I should have some preliminary scan data ready to assess."

"Well, guys, you two are moving at quite a clip, aren't you?" Gabriel said with a smile.

"Is that okay, Gabby?" she asked.

"Yeah, sure. Don't take this the wrong way, but I'm not used to having others make those kinds of decisions. It's good that you did; it's just an adjustment for me, is all."

"Thanks, Gabby. You're still the boss, but we're just awfully eager," Trevor said.

"Good. Eager is good. Well, let's get to work. Valerie, I'll help you, okay."

"I'd love that."

✠

ROME

THE VATICAN DOCUMENTS LABORATORY

"Good morning. I'm Sister Mary Bernice. I spoke with Dr. Ricci about using some equipment in the lab today."

The receptionist in the Document Laboratory office area, smiled and said, "Yes, Sister. Dr. Ricci is expecting you. If you'll wait just a moment, I'll let him know you're here." The woman pointed to a sitting area just across from her almost pristine desk. Just as the nun had barely taken her seat, the receptionist returned with a man in a white lab coat. "Dr. Ricci," she said, "this is Sister Mary Bernice."

"Sister, it's nice to meet you and connect a face with a voice."

"Doctor. Thank you for letting me have access to your lab."

"I'm happy to do it, especially if Cardinal Greganti makes the request," he said, smiling. Ricci had a very round head, almost Charlie Brownian with brown hair cut close to the scalp. He wore rimless eyeglasses on his friendly, largely unwrinkled face. His lab coat was starched and glowing white. Mary Bernice guessed him to be in his late forties. "If you'll come into my office just a moment, we'll sort out what you need and then I'll take you back."

"Thank you." He gestured for her to step into the open doorway from which he'd emerged a moment before. She did so and quickly took in his modestly sized office. An L-shaped desk faced the door with a monitor on the return. Two chairs faced the desk. The walls on the left and right were lined with lateral file cabinets. A tall safe stood in the corner. The wall behind the chairs wasall bookcases, neatly arranged with technical books.

"Please have a seat." He stepped around behind the desk and sat in a swivel chair that he immediately began to gently swing from right to left and back again. "Now then, I believe you mentioned you had need of viewing some documents under alternate light sources, is that right?"

"Yes." The nun tapped a briefcase she was holding in her lap. "I have them right here."

"And what might I ask is it you have?" His voice was friendly, and his smile included his eyes.

"I have several old documents with faded ink. I'd like to see if I can read them."

"By old, you mean..."

"I don't mean to be rude to my host, Doctor, but does it matter? I've often used alternate light sources to read ancient documents. I have access to the equipment at the University, but I'm on sabbatical right now, and more important, I'm in residence here in the Vatican at the moment."

"I see. Did you bring these with you to study?"

"What do you mean, 'bring them with me'? They're here in the briefcase as I said."

"I meant, did you bring them from the University?"

"Dr. Ricci, does it really matter?"

"I'm sorry, Sister. Just being nosey. An occupational hazard of sorts. Of course it doesn't matter. If the Cardinal says you are to use our equipment, then of course you may. I didn't mean to offend."

"It's nothing, Doctor. I'm sorry I was a little snappy." Sister Mary Bernice's defensive radar had already kicked in. She thought the good director was more than just curious.

"Let's head to the lab and get you set up."

The two walked into the reception area and through the door leading to the lab proper. There were perhaps a dozen workstations visible in the lab. Sister could see at the far end a door with a sign that read "Authorized Personnel Only" that likely led to other workstations. "Sister, I've arranged for you to have this one at the far end so we won't be disturbed as you work."

"We?" she asked.

"Yes. I'm afraid I must remain with you as you work. Technically, you don't have clearance to be in the lab, so someone must accompany you at all times. We have a lot of sensitive work going on, and while I doubt you'd be interested in any of it, following procedures is very important. I'll stay out of your way."

"I wasn't expecting that. But I guess you have to follow procedures." The nun paused. "You know, on second thought, I'm not terribly comfortable with an on-looker. Perhaps I can find another lab somewhere else."

"Now, Sister, I don't see the need for that. I won't be in your way. Forgive me for saying so, but for a woman under vows, I'd think you'd completely understand the need to obey procedures."

"Oh, I do. Really. You have to obey your procedures. I get that. It's just that I don't have to use your lab to look at my documents. Doing it here was a matter of convenience, and now that convenience factor has disappeared. Thanks for your time, Doctor. I think I can find my way out."

"Sister, you're being rash."

"You know what, Doctor. I don't mean any disrespect here, but go screw yourself." With that, as Ricci's mouth fell open, Mary Bernice turned and headed quickly toward the door of the lab.

"Sister, you can't leave!" Ricci fairly shouted.

"Watch." By then she was out the door of the lab, and fishing her cellphone from her bag as she walked. She keyed in Nicki's number, but it went to voice mail. *No signal in the Archives,* she thought. As she was about to leave a message, she heard the door to the Documents Laboratory fly open and slam against the wall. Ricci was shouting after her.

"Sister, we can work this out! Come back!"

Without looking back, she raised her arm and shot him the bird. *I'll have to confess that, but God will understand.* She called Nicki again, and when the call went to voice mail, she left a message.

39

ENGLAND

R eynolds-Smythe's encrypted cellphone rang. It was Jemison Thorsby.

"Early in the day for a call, Jemison. Must be important," Reynolds-Smythe said by way of a greeting.

"I received a call very late yesterday from our contact in the Turkey cultural offices. Gabriel's team asked for permission to do a GPR scan of the altar area and for permission to bore some test holes in an area near the church. Since I know they surveyed that area, I'm assuming they have found something underground that they want to have a closer look at."

"Things seem to be heating up. What do we know of the women?"

"I know they've been going to the Archives every day, but I don't have a report yet on whether or not they have uncovered anything. I'll check with Cavallo there as soon as I get off the phone with you. He's not been volunteering much."

"We'll need to watch him more closely. Can't have him getting ideas. Incidentally,it occurs to me, that if Gabriel is going to be poking around in a cave, this may be the perfect way to deal with him. An 'accidental cave-in' might end the whole thing once and for all. And, frankly, the more I've thought about him, the less I care if he's on to something or not. His work has already done too much to stir up Christians in a positive way. We don't need a stronger Christianity. If we take him out, that may solve a lot of problems in the future. However, in the meantime, we need to know what, if anything, he finds. Can you take care of that?"

"I'll find a way."

"I know you will, Jemison. Call me back when you know more about the women."

✠

THE VATICAN ARCHIVES

Nicki felt a little strange without Sister Mary Bernice nearby. The two staffers who had been working a short distance away had asked about the Sister when Nicki showed up alone. The questions seemed friendly and could have been simply normal curiosity, but Nicki had grown very cautious. She had told them the nun would be along later, that she was taking care of some personal matters. The staffers seemed satisfied with her answer.

Nicki pulled a dusty slip box from the shelf she'd been searching and sat down at the temporary work desk. She slipped the cover from the box and found more of the fragile documents she was accustomed to viewing. As she glanced at the first few lines of the first several pages, she found her mind wandering. She was wondering if Mary Bernice had been able to accomplish anything in the lab. She wondered if the staffers were actually helping or just spying. She thought about her upcoming flight in a few hours. When she realized she had no idea what she was seeing, she made a decision.

Putting the documents back in the box and slipping the cover back in place, she returned the box to the shelf. She pulled her white cotton gloves from her hands and shoved them into her backpack. *I'm accomplishing nothing here today. I'm going to see if the charter is ready and go ahead and leave for Turkey as soon as I can.* She told the staffers goodbye and headed toward the elevator.

Arriving at the lobby level, she pulled her cellphone from her bag and saw she had a voice mail. As Nicki walked across the lobby, she retrieved the message. It was Mary Bernice. "Complications in the lab. I'll tell you about it later. I'm headed to the lab at Sapienza. I should probably have gone there anyway. I'll call later." The time stamp showed 8:10 a.m. It was now 10:20.

Nicki was tempted to call her back, but decided she'd do it later. Now she just wanted to get to the Cardinal's quarters, collect her belongings, and arrange for a ride to the airport. She'd call the nun on the way to the airport.

✠

The Office of the Vatican GendarmerieCorp

Ricci found the number he needed and dialed from his office phone. When the line was answered, he said, "Superintendent. My name is Dr. Carlo Ricci. I'm the Director of the Documents Laboratory. I have reason to believe that a nun, Mary Bernice Armistead has stolen documents from the Archives and may be trying to take them from the Vatican."

"Dr. Ricci, that's a serious charge against a person in religious orders. On what do you base this?"

"I saw her with them. She ran out of the lab with them in a backpack. I tried to stop her, but she was too quick for me."

"And where do you think she was taking them?"

"I don't know. Just stop her at the gate. Please."

"Thank you, Doctor. We'll take care of it."

As soon as the call ended, Ricci called Cavallo.

"The nun was here, but when I told her I'd need to stay with her, she bolted. I called the Gendarmerie and asked them to stop her."

"Damn! I didn't want this thing to become official."

"I'm sorry. I thought stopping the theft was of paramount importance."

"Forget it. I'll take care of it. Whom did you talk to?"

"I didn't get his name."

"Ricci, you may be a good scientist, but in general, you're an idiot. Don't think I will forget this."

Ricci started to defend himself, but the priest ended the call. He needed to think about how to intervene without making matters worse.

✠

Within in minutes of Ricci's call, the Sister was sitting in a small room with a large man dressed in a navy blue uniform.

"Captain, I told you," she said,"I have Cardinal Greganti's permission to have those documents in my possession. Just call him."

"Sister, please just answer my question: why were you stealing material from the Secret Archives?"

"I'm not stealing anything. I'm doing research. Call. The. Cardinal. Please."

"Sister, I don't believe the Cardinal has the authority to allow documents to be removed from the Archives. I have a call in for the Librarian. I'm assuming he knows of this 'arrangement' that you and the Cardinal have. Once I've spoken with him, we'll see about calling the Cardinal."

Almost as if it were planned, there was a tapping on the door and it opened. "Sir. The phone call you've been expecting."

"Thank you. I'll be right there. Sister, I'll return shortly." With that, he rose and left the room. No one came to monitor her wait.

The nun couldn't' believe that he hadn't confiscated her bag. She slipped her cellphone out. It showed a strong signal. She punched in Nicki's number. Three rings later Nicki answered.

"Sister, I'm so glad you called. How..." Mary Bernice interrupted.

"Nicki, I'm being detained in by the Vatican police. They're accusing me of stealing from the Archives. I've told them to call the Cardinal, but..." Before she could finish, the Captain came back into the room.

"Put that away, please. Better yet, give it to me."

Nicki overheard him, but the nun didn't immediately comply. "Help me, Nicki." Nicki heard a scuffle and some garbled speech. The phone went dead.

Nicki was already in a car headed to the airport. She quickly keyed in the Cardinal's number. After four rings, it went to voice mail. She left a message asking him to check on the Sister. Nicki thought about turning around and heading back to the Vatican. She had two of the documents with her and decided it might not be wise. Getting out of Rome might be the best course of action. She couldn't help Mary Bernice or Gabriel if she were detained, too. She had to trust Alessandro. She didn't understand how this could have happened. Unless someone in the Vatican didn't want this project to continue. She felt physically ill.

40

TURKEY

AT THE "MONASTERY" SITE

Trevor had reckoned the overburden uphill from the apparent entrance to the cave they had dubbed the monastery was about six feet. The scan suggested the first four or five feet of the cave was filled with something. He'd start just beyond the filled in entrance. Higher up the slope the dirt and rock would be as much as twenty feet deep. No point in starting that high, anyway. He had the drill crew set up to bore a series of holes beginning near the entrance and moving up the slope at eight foot intervals. The crew was just completing the first bore of about four inches in diameter and preparing to move up slope to the next bore. Because the mountain was largely limestone, the bore went quickly.

The endoscope was attached to a monitor and a light source. As soon as the drill was moved, Trevor slipped the scope into the bore. He fed it in to a depth of about eight feet, and turned his attention to the monitor. He aimed the scope toward where the presumed entrance was and saw exactly what he expected: stone. The rubble came to within a foot or so of the bore, which meant, as he'd suspected, there would be about five feet or so of rubble to remove if they wanted to enter the cave. With the proper equipment, it wouldn't take long.

Trevor rotated the scope in a slow one hundred-eight degree turn. He saw exactly what the GPR had indicated he'd see; the cave was empty beyond the entrance. There were a few loose stones scattered on the smooth floor of the space, but by and large, they would have an easy time exploring once the opening was clear.

"Is that showing the cave is clear of other debris?" Orion asked.

"Yep. Once we're inside, if the other bores show the same thing, and I think they will, we'll have a largely rubble free space to explore. The floor to ceiling looks to be maybe seven or so feet."

"So once in, we can stand. That's good. How far into the cave can you see?"

"From this bore, about eight to ten feet. The light isn't very powerful in the scope. That's why I'm having a series of holes bored."

Trevor continued to rotate the scope back and forth to try and look more closely at what was illuminated. GPR had shown a cave width at the entrance of perhaps six feet. The left and right walls of the space were roughly hewn into verticals. He manipulated the scope for a view of the ceiling. It too had been worked, but was no smoother than the walls. But that meant the space was essentially a box.

"I don't see anything on the walls that looks interesting. If this actually was used as some sort of meeting or working space, I would expect the entrance to be more inviting," Trevor said.

"On the other hand," Orion suggested, "they did build outside of the cave. Maybe this space wasn't as important as the space we've seen the foundation walls for."

"Yeah, but my theory would go like this: first they used the cave; as the need grew for more space, they built outside. So the cave would have been important for a while, at least."

"Makes sense, and I'm no archeologist or historian, but maybe they didn't have the resources to devote to 'decorating' the cave. Thinking back on my seminary days..." Trevor interrupted him, saying.

"You went to seminary?"

"Yeah. Remember I became a priest after I left NCIS." Orion reminded him.

"I knew you were a priest. I don't know why I didn't just take for granted that since you were a priest, you'd been to seminary."

"No sweat," Orion said. "As I was saying, there may have been something else at work, too. For at least sixty or seventy years after Jesus, Christians were expecting him to return at any moment. If one believes that, then making a more attractive cave isn't so important."

"True. Plus, we don't even know how the space was used. Maybe we'll find out as we look down more bore holes."

Just then the drilling crew gestured for Trevor to join them upslope. The two men quickly did so. Only the crew leader seemed to speak English, and he clearly didn't have a lot of practice. Buthe was able to make it clear that the second hole was already finished. Trevor thanked him and headed back for the equipment left at the first hole. By the time he and Orion had collected it, the crew had moved to a third spot. Trevor asked them to move laterally this time after he consulted his GPR readings again. He wanted a better sense of how wide the cave was and what the walls looked like.

"Okey dokey," Trevor said, more to himself than to Orion. "Let's see what we can see." He fed the scope into the hole. What he saw was more of the same from the first hole. It was clear that the space was larger, right to left, than the entrance area. The entrance could be thought of as a kind of foyer that opened into a larger space. The consequence of that was he couldn't see the walls very well. He'd have to wait for the next bore to be completed. Maybe things would get more interesting then, he hoped.

While Trevor and Orion labored on the gentle hillside, Gabriel was pulling into the only available parking space outside the private aviation terminal at the airport. He was eager to see Nicki. This was the longest period since they met that they had physically been apart. Phone calls and FaceTime helped, of course, but it wasn't the same. He had convinced himself that Nicki was no longer miffed about his decision to come to Turkey, but he still felt guilty about putting her in the position he did. If getting older was supposed to make you wiser, he was flunking the test. He was surprised that she had called to let him know she was arriving earlier.

At the desk inside, he was informed that her Wheels Up chartered Cessna Citation Excel/XLS was about ten minutes out. Nicki had told him that she wasn't alone. The nine-passenger jet also held three other business travelers. Because of the others, she didn't want to explain her reason for coming early. He didn't really care anyway. He was just happy to have a few extra hours with her.

As Gabriel watched from the terminal window he saw the sleek and powerful twin-engine jet descend on it final approach. Within ten minutes, Nicki had cleared customs and the two were embracing and kissing as if they were newly-weds, drawing smiles from the few others in the terminal. Smiles of which they were completely unaware.

"I have missed you so much," Gabriel said as they broke the embrace.

"I can tell," Nicki said, smiling. "That's no roll of quarters in your pocket."

Gabby blushed. "Oops. Sorry."

"Hey, I'm flattered, Big Boy. I've missed you, too. Gabby, I've got some bad news. Can we get out of here?"

"Sure. Give me your bag. My car is just outside."

Once they were outside and away from the others, Nicki began to tell him about the nun's detention. "We found some documents that shed some light on the church." She quickly summarized what they knew for certain, which wasn't much. "The upshot is the woman Sara was an important figure in the Antioch church, so important she had a final wish which the leaders of the community agreed to fulfill. We're not sure, but I think she asked to be buried in or near the Cave Church."

By now they were in the car and heading to the church. "Holy smokes, Nicki. This could be really important. On the other hand, Paul's writings mention a lot of women who are involved in his ministry, but I don't remember a Sara. He apparently spent a lot of time in Antioch, so I wonder why he didn't mention her."

"Maybe it was timing. She could have been before or after his time."

"Yeah, I guess. Let me catch you up on a few things." He shared with her the growing apprehension he felt about the danger of the work they were considering. "Frankly, I'm for going home. Trevor and Valerie are fine with me leaving, but they want to stay and continue the work. We're all agreed that we have to sit down and talk about the decision and come to some conclusion. Now that we know your friend is in trouble for helping us, I'm more inclined than ever to quit."

"I'm torn, Gabby. Let's all talk before we decide anything. But I want you to know I respect your desire to go home."

"Thanks. Here's what else we're doing." He filled her in on the boreholes and the scan of the altar. "This will give us some useful information to add to the mix. By the time we get back, they'll have completed the altar scan and some or all of the test holes."

"So, we have a lot of very preliminary data with the original scans, and we're going to soon have some follow up stuff to consider. Good. Information is always useful. I do have to say this, though. I don't like the idea of Valerie and Trevor staying here if we as a group think it's too dangerous. That's going to be tough to deal with if they are really committed."

"Yeah. Putting them in jeopardy isn't what I want to do. Here we are," Gabriel said, pulling into the Visitors' Center parking lot. Let's call everybody together and get this discussion started.

41

ROME

Now, Sister, that was very inappropriate," the Captain said. Looking at her phone, he asked, "And who is Nicki?"

"She's Nicki Gabriel. She and I have been doing research in the Archives with the knowledge and permission of His Eminence Cardinal Greganti. Please, just call him. He will clear up everything."

Again, there was a knock on the door, followed by it being opened. Another uniformed officer stepped in and said, "Sir, you have another call."

"Tell whoever it is I will call back. I'm in the middle of something."

"Sir, I think you may want to take it now."

"Very well. Stay here with the Sister. Make sure she behaves."

The interrogator was Captain Roberto Santacruz, a ranking officer in the Corp and "friend" of Cavallo's. He was nearly six feet tall, with very short grey hair, and possessed of an angular face to match his toned body. A career officer, he'd been in the Corp for more than twenty years and an associate of TEO for almost half that time.

"What makes this caller so important, Captain?"

"It's His Eminence Greganti."

"Thank you. I'll take it in my office."

Once settled in, and in no particular hurry to answer his phone, Santacruz picked up the receiver. "Eminence, this is Captain Santacruz. How may I help you?"

"I understand the Corp has detained Sister Mary Bernice. She is doing some work for me in the Archives. I would like her released."

"Eminence, that will be difficult to do. She was found trying to leave the grounds with pilfered material from the Archives. The law is very clear on this. It is forbidden."

"She is doing research for me on an important project. She has my permission to remove whatever documents she feels are germane for examination and study."

"Forgive me, Eminence, but I have checked with the Vatican Librarian, Father Arturo. He was unaware of any such arrangement, and he tells me, that furthermore, he would never have agreed to such a policy violation in the first place."

"Apparently, Father's memory is not what it once was. Additionally, His Holiness has approved this project. In his quest for greater transparency in Holy Mother Church, he has instructed me to support the work of the acclaimed archeologist, Dr. Stephen Saint Gabriel. This project is a part of that support. I'm afraid I must insist that you release Sister Mary Bernice and return the documents she's studying to her. If she was trying to leave the grounds with them, I'm sure she has a good reason. I will hold the line while you go ask her that question."

"Eminence, I'm afraid nothing she says will change things. Please forgive me, but I have only your word that the Holy Father has approved of this matter."

"That is an easy enough thing to fix, Captain. You go ask the nun why she was removing the documents, and in return, I'll arrange for you to speak directly with the Pope."

Santacruz was taken completely off guard by this move by Greganti. Though at a deep level he was committed to TEO, at an even deeper level, he was a life-long practicing Catholic. Though he'd seen the Holy Fathers at a distance many times, he'd never spoken to one. He hesitated, and then said, "I will go speak to the Sister. Rather than have you hold, I'll return your call in minutes. Perhaps we do not need to involve the Holy Father just yet."

"Thank you, Captain."

✠

FATHER PAUL CAVALLO'S OFFICE
LATE THAT MORNING

Cavallo had been out of his office most of the morning and only now had returned from a round of routine and tedious meetings with various groups working under Greganti's area of responsibility. He needed to prepare an update and present it to the Cardinal during a working lunch. As he sat down at his desk, he picked up a stack of mail and sorted it, giving some a priority over others, but putting both aside until later. He glanced at his email inbox and stopped to read several that seemed important. Finally, he picked up his small stack of phone messages. Leafing through them, he came to the bottom one, one that had arrived early in the morning. It read, *We're holding something in our office you'll be interested in.* It was from Santacruz.

Cavallo pulled his cellphone from his pocket and keyed in the number shown on the message slip. After a few rings, the call went to voice mail. Perturbed and intrigued, he decided he'd take the ten or so minute walk over to the headquarters to see what was being held. But first, he needed a bathroom break and more coffee.

✠

THE CORP HEADQUARTERS

Captain Santacruz entered the room where Sister Mary Bernice was being held. He dismissed the officer who had been with her, telling him to wait in the hallway.

"Sister, I have spoken with the Cardinal. Tell me where you were taking the documents. Please."

"I had been to the Documents Lab to study them and ran into a problem. I am on sabbatical from Sapienza University, so I was heading to their lab, where I sometimes study ancient documents."

"I see. And the nature of the problem at our lab?"

"The lab director insisted on staying with me while I worked. I'm unaccustomed to having someone hover over me, so I decided to go where I could have some privacy."

"And the reason you didn't go to Sapienza in the first place?"

"Convenience."

"Thank you. Come with me, please."

The nun reluctantly followed him from the room. He took her to his office where he returned her bundle of documents and her backpack. "Sister, I'm sorry I detained you, but it was unavoidable. You will be allowed to leave Vatican City. When you return, please check in with me to assure me all the documents have been returned. During our conversation, we made digital photos of the documents so we can make a rough comparison when you return. I'll have an officer escort you to your car."

"Thank you, Captain. I know you only did what you had to do. I will likely be gone for two or three days, and I will check in with you when I return. You can be sure you'll find everything I left with."

The nun was escorted to her car. She got in and just sat quietly for a moment or two. Then she began to shake, just slightly. *It's just adrenaline,* she told herself. She took a couple of deep breaths and started the car. Two minutes later she cleared the Vatican gate and headed toward Sapienza.

Back in the Captain's office, his cellphone rang. It was Cavallo.

"What do you have I'd be interested in?"

"I *had* a nun, Paul, but Greganti insisted I release her. He invoked the Pope as his authority."

"Was it Sister Mary Bernice?"

"Yeah. I got a call from the Documents Lab to detain her. The director said she had a cache of documents with her that he guessed was from the Archives. Somehow Greganti found out and called me."

"What about the documents? Where are they?"

"She was allowed to take them."

"Shit! Where to, do you know?"

"She's going to a lab at Sapienza to study them."

"Why didn't you call me sooner?"

"Paul, I called as soon as I detained her. I left a message. Your assistant said you were tied up somewhere in meetings."

"Okay. I'm sorry. This is not on you. I'm just frustrated. I'll take it from here. I want those documents or to at least know what they say."

"I had them photographed, but the quality is probably not good enough for serious study."

"Send the pictures. I'll have someone see what they can learn. But, I'm also going to get that nun. I don't know where she lives normally. I know while she's working on this project she's been staying in guest quarters here."

"I can find out for you and let you know."

"Thank would help. Get me that and the pictures and maybe we can salvage this mess. I may be able to intercept her at Sapienza, too. I'll try that first."

42

TURKEY

THE CAVE CHURCH OF ST. PETER

By the time Nicki and Gabriel had returned from the airport, the boring crew was completing their eighth bore. Trevor was eager to see what this hole showed, so he slipped the endoscope into the hole and into the cave. He had specifically asked for one of the holes to be bored near the right hand wall of the cave. What he'd seen in the dim light, he wanted to see up close.

"Yep, I was right. There are niches about six feet long on the side wall, with a second row above separated by about eight inches of stone. Now that I can see it closely, they appear to be about eighteen inches deep," Trevor told Orion. "Take a look," he said, moving the small monitor so Orion could view it.

"That sounds like the Roman catacombs, except they are stacked four or five high," Orion said. He studied the pictures. "Not very deep, though."

"They're not sealed, either. And they're empty. I don't see any rubble in them or any bones.I don't think they were for burial."

"Storage, maybe?"

"Yeah, could be. In fact, I'd say likely."

"How far do they reach into the space?"

"Beyond where my light can see. I want a hole on the left side of the cave to see what's over there."

Trevor pulled away from the small screen the two men had been looking at and signaled to the crew chief to join him about thirty feet away and parallel with where the last hole was bored. The crew began to set up their drill and Trevor returned to the endoscope.

"They can't be seats and they don't seem to be loculi, so I think they have to be for storage. Either nothing was ever put on them, or they were looted some time in the past."

"I'm no archeologist, but wouldn't there be some sign of looting? You know, stuff scattered around, bits left behind, things like that?"

"Probably. So I'm thinking they were never used. We'll know more in fifteen or so minutes when the next bore is done. Hey, look, there's Nicki and Gabby," Trevor said, pointing toward the visitors' center parking area.

"Want me to go tell them what you've seen while you wait for the next hole?" Orion asked.

"That'd be great." Trevor looked at his watch. "This hole will be our last one today, anyway. Tell them I'll be in as soon as I've taken a peek."

✠

ROME
SAPIENZA UNIVERSITY

"May I come in," Sister Mary Bernice asked of the older woman sitting behind an overflowing desk. The woman was Dr. Bettina Farino, chair of the Department of Anthropology and Religion at Sapienza.

"Sister! What a surprise and coincidence."

"Coincidence?"

"Yes. I just received a phone call from someone at the Vatican inquiring about you. He wanted to confirm you were on campus."

"Do you remember who it was?"

Farino paused for a moment. Her already wrinkled face screwed up a few more wrinkles as she strained to remember a name. "I don't. I'm sorry. He was a priest, I remember that much. Wait. Goodness, I'm getting so absent minded. I wrote down his name and number right here." She began shifting and sifting the small piles of paper on her desk. "Ah. Here it is. Father Cavallo."

Mary Bernice felt a chill. Cavallo was Greganti's assistant. Why would he be trying to find her? "What did you tell him?"

"The truth, of course, that you're on sabbatical and have no particular reason to be here. Oh, he did ask me to call if you showed up."

"Bettina, I need to use one of the document labs, the one with the alternate light source equipment. Can you delay calling him until later?"

"I can delay calling him until Jesus returns if you need me to."

"I've got some documents I have to look at. I'll stop back by when I've finished. You can call him then."

"Whatever you need, Sister. May I ask if you're all right? You seem nervous, jumpy."

"I'm not really okay, but it's better if you don't know what's going on. When it's all over, I'll fill you in completely."

"Oh, wonderful! Mystery! Intrigue! I love it. Our work can be so tedious, it's nice to have something exciting going on."

"Thank you, Bettina. I'm heading to the lab. Give me a few hours. I don't have many documents to look at, so it won't take long. I'm going to be making digital images of everything as well."

CAVALLO'S OFFICE

Cavallo keyed a number into his cell. When the call was answered, Cavallo said, "Saverio, I just spoke to some woman at Sapienza. She denied that the nun was there, and I suppose she may not be, but I'm convinced she's heading there. Get over there and find her. Bring her and whatever she's working on back to me."

"I'll leave now."

"And Saverio, do whatever it takes to get the documents."

"Literally?"

"Yes. A lot could be riding on what's in them and she's just another unimportant nun."

43

TURKEY

THE CAVE CHURCH VISITORS' CENTER

Nicki and Gabriel entered the visitors' center and he led her directly to the conference room. It was empty and the door was locked.

As he unlocked the door, Gabriel said, "This is our temporary office. I guess everyone's out in the field somewhere."

"I thought I saw Trevor working out there."

"Probably. He was going to be boring holes into what the scans suggest is a large cave. We're trying to take a look before, or maybe in place of, clearing debris from the mouth and going inside. The spot looks promising. Infrared showed a lot of well-worn ancient paths leading to and from it and the area of the church. Valerie is probably inside the cave doing a GPR scan of the altar. She and I spent this morning assembling scaffolding around it so we don't have to actually get on top of it."

As they talked, the pair had headed back outside and bumped into Orion in the lobby.

"Hey, Nicki! Welcome," Orion said. The two embraced and afterwards, Orion said, "Oh, and hello to you to, Gabby. Trevor's found something. He's coming down in a few minutes to tell us what it is. Looks interesting."

"You saw it, too?"

"Yeah, but let's let him explain."

"Sure. Is Valerie in the church?"

"I think so. She ran a scan after you left, but wanted to repeat it with a different unit. The stone was more dense than she expected so the scan didn't penetrate as far as she thought was needed."

"Let's walk over there," Gabriel said to Nicki. "Paddy, do you mind waiting for Trevor and telling him where we are?"

"Glad to do it."

"Gabby, I want to call Mary Bernice."

"Sure. We can walk and you can talk."

Nicki punched in the nun's cellphone number. The phone rang and she heard, "Oh, Nicki, I'm so glad you called."

"Is everything okay? Are you okay?"

"I'm at Sapienza heading to our documents lab. Nicki, Father Cavallo called here before I arrived. He talked to my department head and asked for me. When she told him I was on sabbatical, he asked her to have me call him. He's figured out this is where I headed when I 'got sprung', thanks to His Eminence."

"Do you think that's a problem?"

"I told the Captain who released me I was coming. That means he must have called Cavallo. I don't know why he would have."

"Maybe after the Captain talked to the Cardinal, the Cardinal had Cavallo try to contact you on his behalf."

"I hadn't considered that. Could be. Maybe I'm just being paranoid. Just in case, I'm going to get these documents looked at as quickly as I can and give you a call when I can read them."

"Please do. I'll be back Sunday, but I don't want to wait. Things are picking up here and we might well begin moving dirt soon."

"Can't wait to know the details, but let me get going on these documents. The equipment's ready and I'm more than ready."

"May I say one more thing? Gabby and I have learned that paranoia is a good thing. Be very careful and let me hear from you soon."

"I will, Nicki. God bless you." She disconnected.

Gabby saw the concern on Nicki's face. He hadn't heard the nun's part of the conversation, but he'd heard enough. "That didn't sound good," he offered.

Nicki quickly filled in the blanks.

"Dammit! I don't want someone else to be in danger because of us," he responded.

"I know, honey. It may be nothing. Let's wait and see."

By now they were entering the church and saw Valerie climbing down from the scaffolding. "Gabby! Nicki! There's something under the altar, about ten feet down!"

ROME
SAPIENZA DOCUMENTS LAB

Mary Bernice had a total of five documents to view with the equipment. With the uncertainty of her own safety now paramount, she had decided to view them as quickly as possible, and as soon as she had something readable, to photograph it and move on. She wanted to get away from the university as soon as possible—just in case, she told herself. She was having good success and was on the last document. It had just responded to the same wavelength as the others. She snapped the photo and turned off the equipment. The nun slipped the original back into the cracked leather folder and retied the leather thongs around it to make it secure.

With that done, she pulled the SD card from her camera and headed to her office just down the hall from the lab. She hadn't needed her office keys in weeks so they had migrated to the bottom of her purse. But she'd retrieved them to enter the lab and they were now on the top of the various items making up a woman's necessities. She slipped the key into the lock and heard the expected click. The late afternoon sun streamed through the large window in the modestly sized office so she didn't bother with turning on the lights.

Sitting down at her desk, she turned on her desktop computer. While she waited for it to boot up, she sent Nicki a quick text via phone. Seeing the monitor come to life, she logged in and slipped her SD card into the card reader attached to the laptop. She opened her email program and began typing a short email. She opened the SD file and did a drag and drop to the bottom of the email. Satisfied she'd done what needed to be done, she closed the SD file and pulled the card from the reader.

As she was about to hit the Send icon, her office door opened. "You're careless, Sister. You should have locked it. But I guess that wouldn't have mattered; I would have picked the lock anyway."

"Who the hell are you and what are you doing here?" she demanded.

"I bet you can guess." He pulled a Glock P22 from inside his jacket. A silencer extended the barrel six inches. "You've been naughty. My people don't like that." A smile appeared, but there was no friendliness or humor in it.

"I don't know what you mean?" Her hand moved toward the mouse on her desk.

"Oh, I think you do. Where are the documents you removed from the Archives?"

"In my backpack." She pointed to it lying in the single office chair she had. When her assailant looked toward it she left clicked the mouse.

"What did you just do?" Anger clouded his face. The pretense of the earlier smile disappeared.

"Nothing."

"Lying bitch! Get up! Come over here and lie down on the floor."

The nun rose slowly, and moved to the part of the office her assailant had indicated. She knelt. "All the way down, bitch." He grabbed her hair and pulled her forward. Sister Mary Bernice was able to break her fall with her hands. She began praying, "Hail, Mary, full of grace, the Lord..." He kicked her in the side. "Shut up!" She did, but she continued mouthing the prayer silently. "...is with thee; blessed art thou among women, and blessed is the fruit of thy womb, Jesus. Holy Mary, Mother of God, pray for us sinners, now and at the hour of our death. Amen." As she continued, her assailant moved around behind her desk and said,

"Shit. You sent somebody an email didn't you? You shouldn't have done that, bitch." He walked to where she lay and stepped over her so he straddled her prone body. "You really shouldn't have." He aimed at the base of her skull and pulled the trigger. A loud pop and the acrid smell of cordite filled the room. "You really shouldn't have."

44

The Cave Church of Saint Peter

As Valerie approached them, Nicki heard her phone ping. She pulled it from her pocket and saw a message from Mary Bernice. "Mary Bernice sent me a text," she told the men. "She's taken images of the documents and will email them shortly. She not going to try to read them until she leaves the school."

"I'm eager to see them," Gabriel said. "Anything that will give us direction will be helpful."

"I know one document she was able to partially read mentioned something about tablets, at least she thinks that what it said."

"Tablets? I wonder what kind." Gabriel said. At the same time, Valerie had joined them and Nicki and she exchanged a hug. Nicki quickly caught her up.

"Did she tell you the Greek word?" Orion asked.

"She wasn't sure about the word, but she thought it might be *cerae.*"

"If I remember my Greek, I think the word refers to wax tablets, you know, wooden planks, with a coating of wax, and with a hinged cover," Orion said.

"I think you're right, Paddy," Gabriel agreed. "And if I remember, a professional scribe would take dictation from someone, or make a record of a speech, or something like that. Then the scribe would let the person who did the talking read it. Corrections could be made before committing it to parchment or papyrus."

"Yeah," Orion agreed, "with the cost of writing material so high, it was easy to heat a small spatula and melt a small portion of the writing, creating a new surface to do the corrections on. When the author was satisfied, then the final copy could be created. Additional copies could be made from it or from the tablet. Once the tablet wasn't needed any more, the wax would be scrapped off, melted and reused to cover the tablet."

Valerie joined the conversation. "There are several of Paul's letters in which he says something like 'I'm writing this in my own hand.' What scholars eventually decided was that Paul used a scribe and then on some letters he added something in his own handwriting."

"Hold on a second," Nicki said. Her fingers raced over her cellphone. "I just Googled the phrase 'in my own hand.' There are four letters that have wording like that. Galatians for example says, 'See what large letters I use as I write these closing words in my own handwriting.'"

"It's a kind of personalized message to differentiate what the scribe wrote and Paul's revision or addition," Gabriel remarked.

"So one of the artifacts we could be looking for would be wax tablets from the first century?" Nicki asked. "Would they have lasted this long?"

"In this climate, they would have lasted longer than parchment or papyrus would. It's a lot wetter here than in Egypt where most of that kind of material has been found. The wax could even have preserved the wood of the tablet, or at least some of it."

"Makes sense, but it raises another question. How were the documents Mary Bernice and I found preserved?"

"That's a good question. Let's save it until later," Gabriel said. "Sorry for the distraction, Valerie. What did you find?"

✠

Saverio stepped back behind the nun's desk. He picked up a pencil from the desk and used it to move the cursor to the Sent icon. He left clicked and saw the first email on the list was to Nicki Gabriel. He clicked again and the email opened.

Attached is a file of images from the pages. I'll call you later.

MB

The look on his face made clear his displeasure. He'd need to think what to do about the email. He stepped back to the chair where the nun's backpack lay. Opening it, he immediately saw the cracked leather bundle. He pulled it out and laid it on the nun's desk. He rummaged in the backpack some more, but saw nothing that seemed interesting.

Saverio pulled out his cellphone and punched in Cavallo's number. He was greeted with, "Did you find her?"

"Yes. She won't be a problem any longer. She emailed a file of images to the Gabriel woman before I got here," he lied. "I have the originals. What should I do with about the email?"

"Nothing. There's really nothing you can do. Where are you?"

"I'm still in her office with her body."

"Try to get out without being seen. Wipe down everything you touched."

"I'm not an amateur, Paul."

"I know. I know. I'm just being cautious. I'm going to get a call from the police when they start their investigation because I called asking for her and left my name and number. I don't want to be connected to this."

"Don't worry."

"Get back here with the documents. Wait. Check her computer and see if she has a thumb drive or SD card she used to store the images. If she does, bring that. Delete the email, too. That will make it a little harder to recover if some geek starts poking around looking for clues."

"I'll take care of it. If you know who you talked to when you called, I can take care of that while I'm here."

"No. I think we'll stop with the nun. If a problem arises because of my call, you can deal with it then."

45

AT THE CAVE CHURCH

In reply to Gabriel's question about what she found, Valerie said, "There is something under the altar, well actually, under the platform. It is a rectangular shaped void."

"Any theories, Valerie?"

"Yes. Given the location and depth, I'd say it's a tomb or grave. It is below the level of the original cave floor and pretty much centered under the platform."

"Oh, my gosh!" Nicki exclaimed. Immediately she thought, *It's Sara's tomb. I'd bet anything.*She decided to wait to share with the others what she believed, but her conviction was growing by the second.

✠

ROME

FATHER PAUL CAVALLO'S OFFICE

"Here's the bundle of stuff from the Archives. I have her backpack in the car. I'm going to dump it when I leave here."

"Did anybody see you?"

"No."

"Did you check for security cameras?"

"Paul, as I said earlier, I'm not an amateur. If you don't trust me to protect us, don't send me out to do your dirty work."

"You're right, Saverio. I don't know why I'm so uptight about this particular matter. I apologize."

"No sweat. Now what?"

"I need to find out what these documents say. I don't think I can get that done here in our lab. I need to send them to Jack."

"Send, as in FedEx them? Isn't that a little risky."

"You're right. Maybe we can put them in a diplomatic courier bag and have them hand delivered."

"I can do that. I've got the credentials. Get me a bag and I'll go on the first flight out."

"Let me call Jack first. I'll get in touch as soon as he and I've talked. I can't do it right now. Greganti is expecting me for a meeting of some kind. I'll take care of it later in the day. In the meantime, the bundle goes in my safe. Dump the backpack somewhere it won't be found."

"I'll take care of it. Call me about the trip to England." Saverio returned to his car. *I know just the spot to get rid of that thing*, he thought.

✠

After Saverio left, Cavallo pulled a highly encrypted cellphone from his desk. It was pre-programmed to call only two numbers, one in the States and one north of London. He pressed the key for the second one. The phone began to ring.

"This is Jack."

"Jack, this is Paul in Rome."

"You have something for me?"

"Yes." He spent the next several minutes filling in Reynolds-Smythe and suggested having Saverio bring the documents to the TEO office.

"That's prudent. I can notify the lab in the Abbey they are coming and we can likely have the text imaged and translated within a day or two. When can you get them here?"

"Depending on flights, late today or sometime tomorrow."

"Make it tomorrow. Let me know the details when you have them. I wish the nun hadn't been killed. This could create problems."

"There's no tie between her and us. The most that is going to happen is I'm going to get a phone call from the local police asking why I called Sapienza asking for her. That's an easy enough matter to dispose of in a variety of ways. We're safe."

"I'm counting on that, Paul. I'll be expecting your call."

✠

Saverio got in the driver's seat of his car, lit a cigarette, dropped the car in drive, and drove through the gates of the Vatican. The flag on the fender of his car represented it as belonging to a Cardinal. They were rarely if ever stopped coming or going. Today was no exception. He pulled carefully into the narrow street and turned right. His destination was about thirty minutes away. He settled in, only to hear his cellphone ring.

"Saverio."

"You're going to take that trip we discussed. There's a flight to London leaving at 9:30 tonight. Can you be on it?"

"Not a problem. What about the diplomatic pouch?"

"Where are you?"

"On my way to take care of a problem."

"Come on back right now. I'll have the pouch ready for you."

"I'm about fifteen minutes away. See you soon."

Saverio looked for a convenient place to turn his car around and up ahead he saw a MacDonald's. He pulled into the drive through lane. He had planned to eat on the way back from dumping the backpack, but since dumping it was now postponed, he decided to go ahead and eat. Using the tinny speaker, he ordered a Big Mac and black coffee. A couple of minutes later, he was exchanging a few euros for his bag of food. The clerk handed the large coffee separately.

Saverio pulled his car forward and stopped. He sat the coffee in the cup holder, removed the hamburger from the bag, and peeled back the paper. Laying the sandwich down on the bag that was spread on the passenger's seat, he punched the tab on his coffee so he could drink it and took a sip. It was near boiling, and an expletive escaped his scorched lips and tongue. Ready now to eat and drive, he pulled to the curb cut and checked the traffic. It was clear. With coffee in his left hand and his fingers lightly on the steering wheel, and the Big Mac in his right, he accelerated into the right lane headed toward Vatican City.

As he took a big bite of the Big Mac, a glob of the "special sauce" dropped onto his shirtfront. Mumbling another curse, he made a move to put the sandwich on the paper bag in the passenger seat. He glanced toward it to be sure the hamburger was going to land onthe flattened bag rather than the leather seat. In that milli-second, his eyes were averted from the road. Even so, he likely couldn't have avoided the on-coming car. It wasbarreling into the intersection where Saverio'scar was. In an instant, it slammed into the driver's side of Saverio's car.

The side airbag deployed, knocking Saverio's head sideways. His head was pushed to the left and the hot coffee followed, flying up and away.The airbag immediately collapsed and the scalding coffee hit Saverio in the face.

Saverio felt another huge jolt as his now disabled car was impacted from the rear by another car following him too closely and also driving too fast. His seat back collapsed and he was thrown backward, his head slamming into the top of the headrest, forcing his head forward at an awkward angle. The trunk popped open and the gas tank pipe was severed from the gas tank. Saverio lay still. He was dazed by the blow to the back of his head. His left eye and ear felt on fire from the coffee. He tried to reach them to wipe away the hot liquid, but his arm didn't respond. Realizing what had happened, he began to feel panic and his heart began hammering. "Oh, God! Oh, God!"

46

TURKEY

THE CAVE CHURCH OF SAINT PETER

"O kay, let's head back to the conference room and share what
we have," Gabriel said. "This is a great time to catch up
Nicki, too. After we're all up to date, we can decide what
to do about this project."

Everyone voiced agreement. Talking excitedly to Nicki as they
walked to the center, they told her how much they'd missed her.

"Just not the same without you," Trevor said.

"Yeah," Valerie added, "I've felt very outnumbered by these
guys, especially with the addition of Paddy."

"They're no match for the two of us," Nicki said, laughing.

Good natured ribbing was still going on as they entered the
conference room, until Gabriel said, "Okay, everybody. Let's get
Paddy to give us a report on his sleuthing, then we'll hear from
Valerie and Trevor, and finally, Nicki can tell us the result of her
digging in the Vatican Archives. Paddy?"

Orion only took a few minutes to quickly summarize the nature
of the organization that Gulliver had been associated with. He
illustrated the seriousness of their intention by recounting the death
of Hightower, Gulliver's driver. "I spoke to Aurélio this morning for
a few minutes. At his urging, during the autopsy, the medical

examiner looked very carefully at his entire body surface to see if there had been an injection. He found what seemed to be a recent prick under Hightower's right arm. He almost missed it in the hair, but it had bled and left a tiny bit of dried blood on his skin. A tox screen would have been done anyway, but given there was no history of a heart condition, they screened for a couple of drugs they wouldn't ordinarily look for. Turns out his 'heart attack' wasn't natural. It appears he was given an injection of potassium chloride. It's a drug easily overlooked on autopsy. They screened for it and succinylcholine or SUX, which is very hard to detect. They didn't find SUX, but they did find the other."

"So," Nicki said, "even without knowing what we had found, they started killing people we talked to?"

"Looks that way."

Gabriel spoke. "I'm ready to pull the plug and I told Valerie and Trevor that already. But I want to keep faith with group decision-making on this. That's why we've waited for you, Nicki. Trevor, tell us what you've learned from the bores."

"We've bored a series of holes, both up the slope alone an approximate centerline of the cave, and both left and right of center near to what are the side walls. We haven't covered the whole of the cave, but I can tell you several things from the endoscopic views. After the first few feet, the cave is open. I'm guessing the entrance was either filled in purposely, my initial choice, or a natural collapse. I can see on both side walls a series of niches cut into the stone." He described what he'd seen and then said, "I can't say how far back they go or with any certainty what they were for. Finding them does make me want to see what else is in there, but I think the best way is to remove the rubble from the entrance and physically take a look."

"Okay. I'd agree with that," Gabriel said. "Valerie, tell us about your find."

"It appears to be a void about the size of the altar itself, but several feet below the original floor level. It's about three or so feet wide and about six or so feet long. If this were a medieval site, I'd say we're looking at a tomb or burial. If it is that, it would be of someone very important. If we stay, we need to excavate it."

"Gabby, can I break in here? Sister Mary Bernice and I discovered something that I believe relates to this find." Nicki described the document that they'd found that mentioned Sara and a wish she had that related to the church. "I think we're looking at her tomb. We have other documents we can't read that Sister is working on. As soon as she has something, she'll call. Where we found them in the Archives seems to point to an early date, maybe very early, maybe even first century."

"So Gulliver could have been talking about a tomb as an artifact," Gabriel mused. "Or maybe a body."

"That, and maybe if we get inside the 'monastery' cave, we'll find more shelves, perhaps holding something."

"Does anybody else have something to add?" Gabriel asked. He waited a moment, and then said, "Okay. Do we want to vote now or wait until we've thought about it?"

"I'm ready to vote," Trevor said.

"Me, too," added Valerie.

"I'm not," Nicki said. "I want an update from Mary Bernice. It shouldn't be long."

"I'm not either," Gabriel added. "I need to know what kind of protection the Templars will provide for us. I need to talk to Salvador."

"Two and two," Trevor said. "What about you, Paddy?"

"I don't get a vote, but I have an opinion. Wait twenty-four hours and get this new information."

As eager as Valerie and Trevor were, they also felt that Gabriel's and Nicki's votes counted for more than their own, anyway. "Okay. Twenty-four hours, or forty-eight, if we need them," Trevor said.

"I'm going to check in with Mary Bernice. Maybe she can give us an idea of when she'll have more."

Nicki keyed in the nun's number. "This is Sister Mary Bernice. Please leave a detailed message. God bless and keep you."

"Mary Bernice, it's Nicki. Call me when you can. We've found something here, but we need more information. Bye."

"Gabby," Valerie offered, "I think we need to get a photographer or maybe invite National Geographic to join us to begin keeping a record."

"Uh, excuse me, guys," Trevor said, "but I already contacted them to see if they were interested. They can have a team here within twenty-four to thirty-six hours after I give them the go ahead."

"Good move, Trevor," Gabriel replied. "Let them know we aren't yet committed to going forward, but some interesting things are happening and see what they say."

"As soon as we're finished here, Gabby."

47

Rome

An Intersection Near A MacDonald's

Lights were strobing their reflections off of every surface. A firefighter was trying to hose away leaking gasoline. Another police officer reached into the trunk and pulled out a backpack and took it to his car; he began a search of the inside. All the doors of the car were jammed because of the two impacts. A paramedic ran to the passenger side of the wrecked car and looked in. The driver wasn't moving, but his eyes were open.

"Help me! Please, Help me! I can't move!"

In a loud voice, the paramedic said, "We're here! We'll help. Close your eyes, I'm going to break a window so I can climb in."

Taking a tool from his kit, he smashed the rear window and climbed into the back seat. Speaking in Italian he told the injured man his name. "I'm Luigi and I'm a paramedic. My friend, Dom, and I are here to help. What's your name?"

"Saverio."

"Good. Are you in pain? Anything hurting?"

"I'm not sure."

"Saverio, can you move your fingers for me?"

"Yes." But his fingers didn't move.

"What about your right arm? Can you lift it a little for me?"

"Yes." But his arm didn't move.

"Okay. Good. Saverio, I'm going to put a brace on your neck. It's just a precaution."

"Can you get me out of here? I smell gasoline."

"Soon. The firefighters are washing it away. We're not in any danger. Just relax and let me get a brace on you. I'll be right back."

Dom was standing just outside the window. "How is he?"

"I need a neck brace," and in a quieter voice said, "He's paralyzed. No movement in his arms or hands. Probably not in his legs either. We need to have the doors on his side and the center post on his side cut away so we twist his body as little possible when we try to get him out."

Dom ran to the ambulance and retrieved a brace. Returning, he handed it through the window. When Luigi turned back to his patient, Saverio said, "I'm having trouble breathing."

"Not to worry, my friend. I'll get you some oxygen." The paramedic said over his shoulder to his colleague, "Get a little tank of oxygen, please, and a mask."

Turning back to his patient, he said, "Help is on the way. Let me slip this brace on you. It'll keep your head stable while we move you. First, we're going to cut away the doors and the center post, so it will get a little stinky in here if they have to use a saw. There. The brace in on." His partner tapped him on the shoulder.

"And here's the oxygen," Dom said, handing the small tank and mask in to Luigi.

"I'm going to take your blood pressure now. Just relax. This will be tight on your arm for a minute."

Dom ran to where the firefighters were congregated. "We need to cut away the doors and the center post on the driver's side. He's paralyzed. His neck may be broken. We can't risk doing more damage by twisting him this way and that to get him free."

"We'll take care of it." He called out to one of his men and gave the order to remove the doors and the post. "Anything else?"

"That's all for now. I'm eager to get him out. The fumes are bothering him and are a concern to me."

"I think we're okay."

"What about when you start cutting?"

"We won't be cutting with a torch. Too dangerous for him. We'll use the Jaws of Life and winches and steel cables. Takes a little longer, but won't cause sparking."

"Good. I've got to get back." He returned to his patient and Luigi. "How's his pressure."

"Not great. 160 over 110. He's scared to death. He wants a priest."

"I'll see if I can find one nearby."

"No. He wants a particular one; a Father Paul Cavallo at the Vatican."

"What? Okay. Give me a minute." Dom turned to a police officer standing nearby. "He wants a priest from the Vatican, a Father Paul Cavallo. Can you have somebody call him?"

"I'll phone and see what happens. Hell, they have hundreds of priests there. Hope they can find this particular one."

"Thanks." As Dom was about to turn back to the car, a priest in a black cassock and collar came running up. "Is there anything I can do?"

"Thanks, Padre. We've got someone coming. I think. Can you just sort of stand by in case?"

"Absolutely. What's the injured person's name? I'll pray for him."

Dom told him. "Stay close. It doesn't look good."

"Hey, Doc!" A police officer called to Dom. "There was a backpack in the trunk. Looks like it belonged to a nun. A Sister Mary Bernice. Can you ask him where she is? Maybe she's family or something."

"Sure." Dom headed back to the wreck. "Luigi, c'mere." Luigi swung around to the open window.

"I'm putting some salve on his face. He got scalded by hot coffee."

"Ask him who Sister Mary Bernice is. Her backpack was in the trunk."

Turning back to Saverio, Luigi asked, "Saverio, is Sister Mary Bernice someone we should call? We found her backpack in the trunk. Is she a friend? Family?"

"I need a priest! Any priest! Please! I need to make my confession!"

"Hey," a firefighter yelled to no one in particular. "I just found a Vatican flag crumpled up under the front wheel well. This is a Vatican car."

48

TURKEY

The Cave Church Visitors' Center

"I got her voice mail," Nicki said. "Let me tell you about the documents we found that we've been able to partially read."

Nicki quickly described the process they had been using to find documents from the first century hidden away in the Archives and the problems with the arrangements. Then she pulled a folder from her backpack and laid it on the conference table. Opening it revealed a parchment document. She explained that she and the nun believe they are the "minutes" from a meeting of the church leaders. She read to the group the portions she and Mary Bernice were able to read and then said,

"We, well the truth is, just I, at that point, think Sara was asking to be buried in the church. The writing is too faded to read in some places to be sure, but I think it's a safe bet. She was apparently a person of some importance to the community, because the council of elders approved her request. I think Valerie has found where she was buried."

"Holy Mother!" Valerie exclaimed. "It fits! I already said it could be a tomb, or maybe a sarcophagus at least. Wow!"

"Gang, we've moved from knowing nothing to knowing something incredible in a very short time. We still want to wait to make a decision?" Gabriel asked.

"Gabby, may I make a suggestion?" asked Trevor. "Why not let's keep boring, except the goal of the new boring will be to create a hole large enough to climb down into the cave. If the cave turns out to be really important, we can close up the borehole and excavate the cave entrance. It's not exactly 'best practices' but we don't know how long we can work here or even if we want to. While we wait for protection from the Templars—if they still want to do it—we can establish the value of the cave."

"You're right, Trevor," Nicki said, "doing that isn't the way archeologists would normally proceed. I'm a little uneasy with the idea."

"I like Trevor's idea," Valerie said. "Under other circumstances, I'd be very hesitant to use a kind of brute force approach, but this is different. We're likely in danger if we stay here. I think we need to factor that in."

"I'm not suggesting it's the best way to go," Trevor said. "I wouldn't do it if this were a normal situation."

"I know that, Trevor. You're all making good points. Let's don't try to sort out who's right. Trevor, how about if you investigate with your drilling team if they can do it? Information. We need information. We can get that while we wait for Mary Bernice to call back. Valerie, you develop a plan for excavating the altar area. It should include getting permissions the appropriate person. How many people would we need, what equipment, and most especially, how will we get everything back in place so it looks undisturbed?"

"I can do that. I may need some help from you guys since I've never done anything like this before, but now's a good time to learn."

Nicki joined in. "Trevor, while you're at it, figure out how we could repair the bore holes, including a person-sized one, and what permissions we'll need and from whom."

"I already know what we're going to do to close the smaller ones. I asked the crew when I hired them. I'll check on the rest."

"Okay, then, everybody. We have work to do that will keep us busy for the next day or two. When we've got the plans ready, we'll make a decision. Okay?"

Everyone agreed.

✠

An Intersection Near A McDonald's

Activity around the car wrecks was picking up. The driver who tee-boned Saverio had been loaded into an ambulance and was on the way to the hospital. A team of paramedics at their ambulance was treating the driver of the car that hit him from the rear. His injuries consisted of airbag contusions, a broken ankle, and a severely sprained ankle. He would need to head to the hospital soon, as well.

The "standby priest" had been brought to Saverio and had managed, with a great deal of help, to crawl through the window that had been broken to provide access. The paramedics had balked at not staying with the paralyzed man, but the priest ultimately prevailed. After all, they were good Catholics and understood the sanctity of the rite of confession. At the same time, the firefighters were busy with the task of freeing the crumpled doors and center post. While it was not chaos, things were happening at a hectic pace.

Dom and Luigi stood by, helpless. Dom said, "You know what I'm afraid of? If he's got a blowout fracture at the C3, C4 level, he's living on borrowed time. Thank God we had a priest close by."

"I know. I've seen these before. When the swelling gets bad enough around the vertebrae, he's goingto start babbling and then he's goingto die from a brain swell or asphyxiation or both. Jesus, Mary and Joseph! We'll never get him out in time!" Luigi yelled to the firefighters, "Can you guys work faster; he hasn't got much time!"

"Hey, man, they're doing what they can." Dom said."Let's see if we can hurry up the priest. Maybe we can try something else. A trach maybe? Shit, I don't know."

As they talked, one of the firefighters called to them. "Hey! The priest says the guy seems to be going fast!"

"Got it!" Dom shouted. He and Luigi ran toward the car where the rear door on the driver's side had finally been removed. "Father, what's happening?"

"He's becoming incoherent. One minute he's making perfect sense, then he starts talking about some kind of conspiracy, something about evil people of light, and now he's just kind of babbling."

"Let us in, Father. He's dying. He can't breathe anymore." The priest crawled out of the window and Dom leaned over Saverio. "Saverio, you're going to be okay. I'm going to start some chest compressions to help you breath and I'm going to turn up the oxygen pressure, too."

Saverio's eyes were unfocused, and there were tears leaking from each of them. "Luigi, we've got to get him out now! We can't wait!"

"You guys get back!" Luigi said, shouting to the firefighters. "We're going to drag him out onto the street!"

The paramedics began to try to maneuver the dead weight of the six-foot tall man through the rear door opening. "Can one of you guys, climb through the window on the other side and free his legs? Cut the seatbelt?" Dom said to a firefighter. "I can," came back the answer, and one of the smaller firefighters ran to the other side of the car and climbed in.

But their efforts were in vain. Saverio was dead and no amount of chest compressions and supplemental oxygen was going to make any difference. One of the police officers had been standing near the car while Saverio was making his confession and overheard most of it. He was one of the few non-Catholics on the force and knew nothing about the sanctity of the confessional. He only knew he wanted information. He spoke to the priest.

"What was that he said about killing a nun?"

"You must speak of that to no one!" the priest shouted. "You shouldn't have been listening. This was a sacred moment."

"Hey, if he killed somebody, I don't give a crap about 'sacred moments.' I've got a nun's backpack from his trunk. That's probably who he killed."

"Your soul is in mortal danger if you speak to anyone!"

"I'll take my chances." The officer walked over to his supervisor. "Hey, Sarge, the victim confessed to killing a nun. I bet it's the nun whose backpack we found."

"This is not good," Sarge said. "I better call it in."

50

ROME

AN INTERSECTION NEAR A MCDONALD'S

"I s her cellphone in the backpack?" the Sergeant asked.

"Yeah. I found in a side compartment. Here it is."

"She's got an unopened voice mail message." He clicked the number and opened the voice mail. He heard, "Mary Bernice, it's Nicki. Call me when you can. We've found something here, but we need more information. Bye." He pressed "Call Back." The phone began ringing.

"Sister! I've been wondering about you."

"Hello," the Sergeant said, "This is Sergeant Ronco of the Rome Police Department. To whom am I speaking?"

"I'm Nicki Gabriel. Why do you have Sister Mary Bernice's phone? Has something happened to her?"

"Ms. Gabriel, may I ask your relationship to the Sister?"

"We're colleagues working together on a project in the Vatican Archives. Currently I'm in Turkey for the weekend while she stayed in Rome. What's going on, Sergeant?"

"When was the last time you spoke with her, Ms. Gabriel?"

"Last night? Early this morning? I can't be sure. She was going to do some work and then call me with the results. Since I hadn't heard from her, I called her a few hours ago."

"When will you be returning to Rome?"

"Sunday evening."

"Ms. Gabriel, we found the Sister's backpack in the trunk of a Vatican car that was involved in wreck. I'm afraid the driver of the car was killed. His name is, hold a second please." Turning to the officer who brought him the backpack he asked. "What's the driver's name?"

"I'll go see if he's got a driver's license."

"Ms. English. We're searching for the driver's name. He's been pinned in the car and we just removed him and are just now searching his pockets."

"Sergeant, I can't think of a reason she'd be in a Vatican car. She had her own. She was driving herself to Sapienza University to do some tests on some documents."

"Sapienza? So she's not with the Vatican?"

"No. She and I are doing research there. That's our only connection. If you'd like, you can call Cardinal Greganti. We're working with him."

"Thank you, Ms. Gabriel. When you're back in Rome, please give me a call. I may have more questions." He gave her his number. "We'll contact the University and the Cardinal. I'm sure Sister will turn up."

"I hope so. I can't understand why she'd be without her phone and backpack, though. Something is off."

"May I ask what you two are working on?"

"It's a sensitive project, Sergeant. Important to the Church. The Cardinal may want to tell you more, but that's all I'm free to say."

"I understand. Well, until Monday."

After the call disconnected, Nicki shared with the team what she'd been told. "I'm really worried now. I didn't want to ask if the bundle of parchments was in the backpack, but I bet it wasn't. Something's happened to her."

"Nicki, let me call Aurélio. Maybe the Templars can get us the information. We need to find out when they can send somebody here anyway," Orion said.

"Please do, Paddy. I'm really concerned." Nicki said.

"Let me see if I can reach him." Orion pulled his cellphone out and keyed in Aurélio's number.

"Paddy! What's up?" Orion heard by way of an answer to his cell.

"Sal, we've got problems." Orion took a few minutes to summarize what had been going on and asked the important questions about protection and help with the nun.

"I'll make a few phone calls to Rome to see what our people there can find out. I think the Grand Master has already promised help for your work at the church. Get Gabby to call him and get it set up. As soon as I know anything from Rome, I'll call you. Be careful, guys. TEO is bad."

"Did you learn anything else?"

"There was a little article in the local news about a certain Abbot being killed in a car accident."

"The guy at Elon?"

"Yep. And some of our team thinks they may have a lead on Gulliver's disappearance. Too soon to be sure, but again, when I know something, I'll tell you. In the meanwhile, we're still trying to penetrate TEO's networks. Getting close Nigel tells me."

"Thanks, Sal. Talk to you later."

Orion reported what he'd learned and Gabriel made a call to the Grand Master, Desterro. Desterro listened carefully to the update.

"Gabby," the GM said, "I can have ten men at your location within twenty-four hours, maybe less. Email me the names of your team and where you're staying, as well as where you're located at the site. I'll use Google Earth to research the church. I'll take care of everything else and let you know when our guys learn who they are. Gabby, these are military trained guys. As you know, they know how to fight. Trust them. Cooperate with them in every way. That's the only way we can assure your safety."

"Can't thank you enough, James. I'll have the email to you ASAP. We'll cooperate with your guys, don't worry. We're scared and pissed off."

"Okay. Let me get to work. I'll be looking for the email." He reminded Gabriel of the secure email address and added, "God be with you, Gabby."

"And with you, James. And with you."

Turning to the team, Gabriel told them about the help to come. "I'm angry, guys. I fear the worst for the Sister who got involved to help us, but also to help Christians everywhere. Gulliver too. He's probably been involved in bad things before, but he saw a chance to shed light on matters of the faith and he went for it. That's where I am. I'm not letting some evil bastards win. I want us to get to work, and to do it as soon as we can. Thoughts, anyone?"

"I'm in. I'm definitely in," said Trevor. "And, by the way, NatGeo will have a team here tomorrow. Having them around filming may give bad guys pause. At least at little. I hope."

"I'm in, bad guys or no," added Valerie.

"Oh, Gabby honey. We have *got* to find a more boring line of work. I'm with you." Nicki added."Let's get going."

51

TURKEY

THE VISITORS' CENTER CONFERENCE ROOM

Later in the day, the team gathered again and Valerie had a report to share. "A few hours ago, I spoke with Dr. Tabak at the ministry for culture. I explained as vaguely as I could what we needed. He said he was sure Dr. Sadik, the Director General would approve it, but he was unavailable until tomorrow. Tabak said he'd call us as soon as he'd spoken with Sadik."

"Good. Go ahead as if he's going to approve it. Get whatever equipment you need here on the site ASAP. When we get the go ahead, we'll be ready. Trevor, you do the same with the bore. We'll also need some additional crew. Nicki, I've done a little research. Bilkent University is located in Ankara, which is about 420 miles away. It's the closest school with a graduate program in archeology. Can you check with them and see if we can borrow some students, all expenses paid?"

"Yes, and if they say yes, I'll arrange to fly them here. What's money for if you can't use it for the good?"

"Great!" Turning to Trevor, Gabriel said,"Trevor, we're also going to need some labor. Made any connections locally?"

"I spoke to the boring team about who we could hire if we needed some dirt movers. They gave me some tips. I'll check into that while we wait to hear back. By the way, they can start boring as soon as we get the word."

"Terrific. We'll be ready to roll in a day or so, and by then we'll have some protection, too. I can't wait."

✠

NORTH OF LONDON
THE ENLIGHTENED ONES HEADQUARTERS IN ENGLAND

"Lance," Reynolds-Smythe said, "set us up for a video conference chat with Sergei and Maria for 3:00 today. We've got a problem and they are my solution."

"I'll get right on it. What's happened?" Lance asked.

"Our guy at the Turkish culture agency just called me. He said that Gabriel and his team have informed him they intend to go forward with their work at the site. They asked for permission to move the altar and the platform on which it sits so they can excavate beneath it. He's stalling them, but they're going to get approval, he said."

"For what, may I ask?"

"According to him, they said only that there was a suspicious return on a scan they did. There appears to be some kind of structure beneath the altar, but they wouldn't speculate."

"Hmm. Could it be a sarcophagus or a covered burial of some kind. Maybe a treasure vault."

"That was my thought. Also, they found a nearby cave with an entrance that was likely deliberately filled in long ago. They have reason to believe, based on infrared scans they've done, that it was an important site at one time. Something about beaten paths to it."

"They want to excavate it?"

"Not initially. They seek permission to bore a hole through the overburden big enough to allow a person to lower himself through. Apparently, the cave is not filled. They want a preliminary look around."

"I'm as curious as they are. Is it near the church?"

"Evidently."

"And we want to stop them?"

"I want to know what's going on. Let them find something for us. Then we'll take it from them. That's the general plan. That's part of why I want Maria. She has some training in archeology and has worked a couple of digs for us. One of them turned up some items we think may have been part of the Templar treasure they were reputed to have concealed before they were disbanded and killed off."

"As our inside person, she can keep us up to date on actual work and actual findings. Brilliant."

"Let's hope so. Sergei can provide some muscle for us."

☩

By four o'clock, the conference was over with Sergei and Maria. The two had stayed on the call with each other for a while longer to develop a rough plan for how to proceed. Maria was in Ankara and could be at the Cave Church in the matter of a day or so. Sergei needed more time to assemble the right men and move them to Turkey. They agreed that wouldn't hamper the operation, since Maria could be on site and have information for him by the time he was in Turkey.

Maria knew a few archeology students at the University. She had done a few guest lectures for a class there and it resulted in a couple of new friends. The friends were planning to get together for drinks after class was finished and after Maria was free from her "job." While her actual job was as an operative for TEO, as far as her friends were concerned, she ran a small travel agency that specialized in setting up excursions for rich people who wanted to play archeologist or learn about ancient history. Staff did the actual work, and the operation was a money loser, with the exception of the contacts that were made with rich people, especially those who were rich and bored.

Drinks were being toasted for the first time that evening when one of Maria's University friends mentioned a call that had come in during the day regarding possible fieldwork in ancient Antioch at some church site. Maria was very interested and asked for details.

"I want to go, too," she told her friends. "Do you think it could be arranged? I'd like to do research on the site for a possible destination for one of my travel groups."

"Give Dr. Omar a call. He's setting it up from the school's end. I doubt if he'd care. After all, he had you in as a guest lecturer."

That wasn't the only thing that had happened between her and Dr. Omar, but it was not any of her friends' business. Anything that might help TEO was okay with her.

52

ROME

THE CENTRAL POLICE STATION

Sergeant Ronco sat down at his desk. He put Sister Mary
Bernice's backpack in the large drawer on the left side of his
desk and slipped his firearm into the top right hand drawer.
Turning to his computer, he called up the Vatican City directory.
The directory listed all Vatican personnel along with all pertinent
contact information. He scrolled down the alphabetic listing until he
saw Alessandro Cardinal Greganti's number. Ronco guessed it was
not his private number, but it was a start.

Ronco's desk was located in a large room full of cubicles that did
little to dampen the ambient sound. Phones were ringing,
conversations were being held all over the room, and the occasional
raised voice of an unhappy suspect created a background he knew as
well as the quiet of his living room at home. Ronco retrieved his
landline desk phone and punched in the number he'd just located on
his monitor.

As he expected, he had to wade through several layers of people
whose entire reason for being seemed to be to insulate His Eminence
from the ordinary person who might be calling. Each layer peeled
away when he announced he was a police sergeant and was calling on
the advice of a Ms. Nicki Gabriel. At least six or seven minutes were
used up this way until he finally heard,

"Sergeant, this is Cardinal Greganti. I understand you wish to speak to me."

"Thank you for taking my call,Eminence. As you may have been informed, Ms. Nicki Gabriel suggested I call you. I found her cellphone number on a cellphone found in a backpack at the scene of a traffic accident in which the sole occupant of the car was killed. The backpack was in the trunk. An examination of the contents led us to Ms. Gabriel. Eminence, the backpack belongs to a Sister Mary Bernice. Mr. Gabriel says that she and the nun were working on something for you. We are unable to locate the sister."

"Sergeant, that's a lot to take in at once. Let me try to respond. First, it is Doctor Gabriel. She is an archeologist and works with her husband Stephen Saint Gabriel. They are working on a project that required research in the Secret Vatican Archives. Dr. Gabriel has been staying with me as my guest while she did her work. The Sister was assigned to her to help navigate the Archives and to provide a translator. She has been staying in temporary housing in Vatican City." The Cardinal knew Nicki didn't have a doctoral degree, but he thought this little white lie would be acceptable under these circumstances.

The Cardinal went on to explain about the nun's sabbatical and the nature of her work at Sapienza University, and then added, "She seemed a perfect fit. With all this in mind, I'd suggest you contact the University. I'm sorry I don't have her local address. She may have a small flat somewhere in Rome, or may be in residence with other sisters. I gather Dr. Gabriel didn't have any ideas about the Sister's whereabouts."

"No, Eminence. Dr. Gabriel is in Turkey at the moment. She's expected back on Sunday and I will speak with her in person on Monday. Perhaps our missing sister will contact her before then."

"We can only hope, Sergeant. And pray."

The Sergeant asked a few follow up questions, and then thanked the Cardinal for taking the time to talk. Hanging up, Ronco turned back to his computer to check for numbers for Sapienza. He decided he'd make a couple of calls, and then turn this case over to Missing Persons. This wasn't his area at all, and the sooner he was rid of the case the happier he'd be. Before Ronco could punch in the number, he heard a voice shouting his name.

"Hey, Ronco! I hear you have a missing nun!"

Ronco stood up. "Who said that?"

He saw his lieutenant standing several cubicles away. "Yeah. A Sister Mary Bernice. Why?"

"Homicide found her. She's been murdered."

"Holy Jesus!" He made the sign of the cross. "Who caught the case, Lieutenant? I've got some of her stuff including her backpack and cellphone. A murdered nun! What's the world coming to?"

"The world has decided that nothing is off limits anymore, Ronco. Nun or not, if you're in the way, you're dead. White caught the case. Give him a call.He's probably still at the scene."

"Where was she found?"

"In her office at Sapienza University."

53

TURKEY

THE LIWAN HOTEL DINING ROOM

O rion, Valerie and Trevor gathered for dinner as had been prearranged. Nicki and Gabriel were expected, but late. Just as Orion was going to call their room he saw the pair enter the dining room. In only a moment, Nicki and Gabriel joined them.

Valerie said, "Nicki, you look like you've been crying. I don't mean to pry, but is something wrong?"

"I'm afraid so, Valerie," Nicki said, as she and Gabriel sat down."I spoke with the Cardinal a few minutes ago. Sister Mary Bernice was found murdered in her office at the University where she works."

"Oh, my God!" Valerie said as she crossed herself. "What happened?"

"The Cardinal didn't know any details except that she was shot."

"Why would anyone shoot her?" Trevor asked.

"Since they took her backpack, I'd say it was for the documents she'd taken from the Archives to scan," Gabriel answered.

"Does that mean the parchments are gone?" Valerie asked.

"Just before the Cardinal called, I'd booted up my laptop to check for emails. I hate doing it on my phone; just too small for my tired eyes. Mary Bernice had sent an email with an attachment of her photographs of the documents under the alternate light that showed what was written most clearly. They're in Greek, of course, and even with the light source, not easy to read. I've sent them to Marge in Washington, to see what she can do with them."

"I'd love to take a look," Trevor said. "Maybe I can read them."

"I'll forward them to you, Trevor."

"In light of this development, guys, do we want to reconsider? I mean, another death—it's almost more than I can bear," Gabriel asked.

"No!" Valerie said, louder than she intended. "More than ever I want to go ahead. I want to do it for this holy woman who may have given her life for the Faith."

Before anyone could express an opinion, Nicki said, "I agree. Let's not talk about quitting again. We're going to make discoveries of some consequence and do it in her memory."

Murmurs of approval along with head nods from around the table sealed the fate of the project. The team would go forward.

"Trevor, I want you working the cave rather than looking at the parchment photos. The cave is the first priority. Okay? We did get the approval to go ahead, right?"

"We did. Just before we came down for dinner I got an email. Dr. Tabak is coming out tomorrow with the official letter and to watch the removal of the altar. Gabby. I'll take a look tonight, but tomorrow I'm on the boring. The guy in charge of the rig says he and a couple of cousins will help with labor if we need them once we break through. They don't have anything else lined up right now and can use the money."

"I also had an email from Ankara," Nicki said. "We'll have three students here Tuesday. I'm not going back to Rome tomorrow as planned. I want to be here with all of you. When Mary Bernice's religious order decides about her funeral mass, I'll likely go back for that and bring back the rest of my things from the Cardinal's quarters. I'm finished with Rome."

"The equipment we need for the altar work is to be delivered tomorrow," Valerie said. "Finally we can do some *real* archeology. Uh, just one thing about that. For a Sunday delivery I paid a premium."

Nicki reached out to Valerie and laid her hand on the woman's arm. "Valerie, that's not a problem. This time or ever. Okay?"

"That's surreal, Nicki. Money is always so tight on digs."

"I know, but we're very blessed to not have that problem thanks to my deceased and thoughtful first husband. So let's enjoy his foresight and hard work."

"Gabby," Orion said, "I guess there's no reason for me to stay any longer. Aurélio texted me. His guys arrive tomorrow."

Nicki looked at Gabriel and then said, "Paddy, you can stay if you like. I think maybe you've got some skin in the game now."

"I'll take you up on that. And I'll stay out of everybody's way." Orion's phone pinged as he was speaking and when he checked it was a text from Aurélio. "Hey, looks as if Sal's coming with the team. Seems the gang's all here—or will be tomorrow.

ROME

FR. PAUL CAVALLO'S OFFICE

"Father Cavallo?"

Cavallo didn't recognize the number on his phone's screen, but said, "Yes. This is he."

"This is Detective Sergeant White with the Rome Police Department. Do you know a Saverio Enrica?"

"I do. He's on my staff here at the Vatican."

"Father, we found your name and number in his cellphone as the most recent person he'd called. I'm sorry to inform you that he was killed earlier today in a traffic accident. I'm hoping you can supply some information about him so help our investigation."

Cavallo crossed himself. "My God! What happened?"

White explained what he'd learned from Ronco and then added. "Do you know a Sister Mary Bernice?"

Caught off guard by the question, Cavallo hesitated just a moment too long. "No, Detective, I don't believe I do. Why do you ask?"

White noted the hesitation. It could be a sign of deceit, but it could also be nothing. He'd need to see Cavallo in person. "I wonder if it would be convenient to come speak with you about Mr. Enrica?"

"Certainly. Perhaps we can arrange something for tomorrow."

"If it isn't too inconvenient, this evening would be better. Perhaps I could come in the next hour or so?"

Again Cavallo hesitated. He didn't want to talk to this policeman, certainly not right away. "It's not really convenient, Detective. I have another obligation."

"I see. Will your obligation last long?"

"It is a dinner meeting with a Cardinal, so yes, it will last several hours," he lied.

"Surely the Cardinal will understand if you step away from the meeting for a few minutes."

"Ask me whatever you wish right now, Detective. There's no need to come to the Vatican to ask me questions." His voice had risen just slightly. His agitation was growing.

White was now sure he wanted to meet with this priest. A colleague had just died, and he was stalling about answering a few questions. And becoming pissed on top of that. "What time tomorrow may I meet with you?" he asked.

"I have quite a full schedule tomorrow."

"Father, I'm afraid I must insist. This traffic accident is a bit complicated."

"Very well, Detective. I don't want to appear unhelpful. Let me check my schedule. Please hold." Cavallo pressed the mute icon and switched to the calendar view on his phone. He only had one thing on tap and it was late in the afternoon. He took two deep breaths and returned to the call. "I can make time for a few questions at 9:45 tomorrow morning."

"That will be fine. Where do I come?"

Cavallo gave him directions and the two ended the call. At first Cavallo couldn't think what about the accident would be, to use White's words "a bit complicated." Then it hit him. The nun's backpack might have still been in the car if Saverio hadn't yet disposed of it. "Shit!" he said out loud. Now he had two problems: the backpack and no one to deliver the parchments to Reynolds-Smythe. He'd have to think about whom he could trust to do that. If nothing else, he supposed he could actually treat them as diplomatic documents and have a Vatican courier deliver them. Or he could take them himself. *I never should have let Saverio take the backpack,* he chided himself.*I've got to call Reynolds-Smythe. He needs to know what's happened.*

Cavallo did just that. Once he had him on the phone, he explained where things were and added, "So my current problem is this detective and getting you the parchments."

"I have some people in Rome, Paul. There's no need to have a Vatican person handle them. I'll have someone stop by your office at 8:00 a.m. with a diplomatic pouch from the British Embassy in Rome. Give them to him and he'll get them to me."

"That will work beautifully."

"Paul, I'm sure I don't need to tell you that it is imperative that you give this policeman no reason to be concerned. And, of course, out little enterprise must be protected at all costs. I hope you don't think me too harsh when I say that killing the nun was probably over the top. But it can't be helped. She's dead and that's that. But, Paul, don't make things worse."

"I understand, Jack. Don't worry."

"Oh, I don't worry, Paul. I solve problems that would otherwise perplex me. Don't be a problem for me." He disconnected.

54

TURKEY

VISITORS' CENTER CONFERENCE ROOM
7:30 A.M. THE NEXT DAY

he team gathered in the conference room to officially start the day. Nicki began by saying, "I've heard from the archeology students. The plane I sent for them will be landing about noon. The hotel will collect them from the airport and get them settled into their rooms, then bus them out to us. I hired a van and driver to transport them each day."

"The equipment and operators we need to move the altar will be here at 9:00 this morning. Dr. Tabak will be here late today or tomorrow. He's trying to arrive in time to 'observe' our work, but we don't have to wait for him."

Trevor joined in. "The crew to drill the man-sized hole is setting up at the location I selected for them. NatGeo has one cameraman on site already with the rest of the crew coming today. I'm suggesting he film Valerie's work and when the larger crew arrives, they can join me. I'll probably hold off on actually dropping into the cave until they arrive. I do have a GoPro I could use instead of waiting, so I'll play that decision by ear. Gabby and Nicki, I have another if either of you want to drop into the cave with me."

"I want to go, Trevor," Nicki said.

"What?" Gabriel was surprised. "I don't want you doing that. We don't know what we might find. I'll go."

"If it's dangerous, that doesn't automatically rule me out and you in. Especially not this time. You still aren't a hundred percent and I am," she replied.

"But..."

"No, Gabby. No 'buts'. I'm going and you're not. Stay here and deal with the students, NatGeo, and Tabak, and anybody else who needs supervising or chasing off."

Gabriel face betrayed his confusion. "I...I don't know what to say."

"'Yes, dear', would be right on target."

Orion knocked on the glass door of the conference room, and then opened it. "Hey, I just heard from Sal. The troops just landed. They'll be on site shortly. I'll coordinate with them."

"Great," Trevor said, "I think everything is in place. Let do this."

Nicki let the others move ahead of her and Gabriel as they all were leaving the room. She put her hand on his arm to hold him back. He didn't resist. Once the rest were out of earshot, she said, "I didn't mean to be quite so autocratic. But you know I'm right. I just can't put you in danger again, not just yet."

"Yeah, I get it. No hard feelings. Things have changed. I see that. I've got to adjust. But it's a big adjustment, Nicki. People making decisions I usually make, taking over, acting like I'm not, well, not needed."

"You are needed, though. Right now we need you in a different capacity. We're growing as a team and that makes our future even brighter. So, I know this is a tough time for you, but it's best for all of us."

"I know. I know. Anyway, let's uh, let's get going before anybody thinks I'm pouting."

✠

Moving the altar was not as difficult as feared. The top slab was lifted away in one piece by the heavy forklift that sat on rubber tank-like treads to minimize damage to the cave floor. It was hollow, and as it appeared from the outside, made up of mortared blocks of stone. Valerie previously had numbered the blocks and taken photos to assure they could be reassembled correctly. She and Gabriel began chipping away at the mortar joints. As each block was freed, it was lifted off the structure and placed nearby. Valerie supervised the placement to make reassembly easier.By 10:45 a.m., the altar was disassembled.

The Knights had appeared while the work was progressing. Gabriel stopped to greet them and go over with them their plan for the team's security. Valerie and the forklift operator were developing a strategy for removing the large slabs that made up the platform on which the altar sat. The single NatGeo photographer was trying like crazy to make a useful and credible record of the work. At one point he stopped to call the rest of the team and learned they were still hours away.

Valerie and the forklift driver managed to communicate effectively enough, given neither spoke the others' language very well, to agree on a strategy. The mortar joint under the slabs making up the uppermost layer of heavy limestone slabs would need to be weakened by chiseling. Once that had been done, the operator would slip his forks into the space chiseled out and begin to slowly lift the slab, hoping to break free the remainder of the joint. This plan required Valerie to chip away a section about four feet long to a depth of six or eight inches. She set to work on the first of several slabs making up the top of the platform on which the altar had been erected.

Standing and brushing away dust and mortar, she signaled the forklift operator to slip the forks into the space she had created and gently and slowly apply upward force. This operation needed to be delicate to avoid breaking the eight-inch thick stone slab. The forklift moved forward and slipped in the forks. Valerie heard the motor begin to strain against the weight of the stone. The operator backed off about a foot, and slowly inched forward into the joints, trying to move more deeply than previously. Valerie watched anxiously.

Suddenly, the slab lifted and just as quickly, the operator moved the forks more deeply into the joint. He exerted upward pressure, and the slab popped free from the stone platform on which it sat. Valerie and Gabriel cheered as the forklift backed slowly away with the freed slab sitting precariously on the blades. He turned and placed the slab of stone near the altar stones in a prearranged spot.

After another two hours of work, all the platform slabs were moved. Beneath where the platform sat, there was the large black border that Gabriel had seen when he examined it earlier. Inside the border was a mosaic, now only partially visible due to the residual mortar that had held the stone slabs in place.

"Thank goodness the students are here," Valerie said. "I need to get them to work chipping away the mortar so we can see the entire mosaic."

"Yeah," Gabriel agreed. "You know that finding the mosaic under the platform just made this whole project a lot more difficult, right?" he asked.

"Yep. I was hoping it would be the original floor that we could just remove. But we've got to preserve this mosaic, even if it turns out to be something mundane."

"Dr. Tabak will want to oversee this work, I'm sure," she said. "Damn. This will slow everything down."

"Yeah, just like 'real' archeology that creeps along at a glacial pace to discover an ancient latrine or well or hearth." He laughed. "Of course, those are places where we learn a ton about the people who left them there."

"No more swashbuckling for a while," she said. "Guess I better get the students to work."

The graduate students from Ankara had been watching with fascination. "Okay everybody. Gather around. You've met Dr. Gabriel, the director of this project. I'm Dr. Valerie McMurphy. Call me Valerie. Tell me your names, please."

"I'm Vlad D'gostia. I'm a second year master's student and native of Ankara. I spent last year in the States at City University of New York. I wanted to practice my English." He smiled. Vlad was of average height, dark skin and dark hair. He was dressed in jeans and a CUNY tee shirt.

"I hope you enjoyed your year in New York," Valerie said, smiling back.

Turning to one of the women, Valerie said, "And you are...?"

"My English is not so good as Vlad's. I am Nia Karga. I am first year graduate student. My home is small village in middle of nowhere." She laughed, as did her friends.

"Welcome Nia."

"I'm Maria Teke." Maria was five foot six or so. Her hair was dark and cut very short, but it was styled in a becoming way. Her dark eyes and tanned complexion, coupled with what appeared to be a buff body resulted in a very attractive look. Her jeans had leather patches at the knees. A khaki multi-pocketed shirt matched the color of her work boots. She had come to work. "I have a graduate degree in archeology from the University of Mainz in Germany. I have worked a couple of digs, but I now put together tours of archeological sites for tourists. Currently I make my home in Ankara."

"Oh, what digs have you worked?"

Maria told her of the two most recent archeological experiences she'd been on, including one in England. She didn't mention it was for The Enlightened Ones who were seeking a reported treasure of some kind. Nor did she say that whatever the treasure was, it wasn't found. "I want to return to field work, but for now, I need to be a little more settled. So I create these tours. It gives me an opportunity to travel a little and meet people interested in archeology."

"Well welcome to each of you. Are your rooms are suitable?"

All nodded in agreement.

"Excellent. I have work for you right away, so let's get to it." Valerie explained their task and showed them where they could find the tools they would need.

"May I ask a question?" Maria asked.

"Sure."

"What is the project here? Just to dismantle the altar and look at this mosaic?"

"The dismantling was the project. The mosaic was unexpected. We have to clean it, record it, and then remove it to get at what may lie under the original floor level."

"Do we know what is there?" Vlad asked.

"Not precisely. So, let's get to work. Let me show you how you can chip away the mortar without damaging the mosaic and then I'll turn you loose." Valerie began to show them how to use dental picks to tease the mortar away from the mosaic and small paintbrushes to sweep up the removed mortar. "Work carefully and slowly. We're not in a hurry. This kind of fieldwork is tedious and even sometimes boring, but very important. In this case, this mosaic has probably not been seen for nearly two thousand years and may yield important information about the cave use in the first or second century."

Valerie had dispensed with the usual grid layout over the mosaic since the physical size of the mosaic was so small, but she was going to insist on all the other protocols. A full camera crew had joined the single NatGeo photographer and they were busy setting up to follow the work. One asked the forklift operator if she could build a platform on the forklift forks and "hover" over the work to take pictures from above. A few dollars exchanged hands, and the operator called his office to have them bring a few pieces of plywood to serve as the platform.

Dr. Tabak arrived late in the day and Valerie caught him up on the find. He was distressed about the altar and platform dismantling, afraid it might not go back together easily. She offered him assurances. On the other hand, he was excited about the mosaic, even before they had an inkling of what it might show.

"Dr. Gabriel and Dr. McMurphy, we didn't expect the mosaic," he said. "You've indicated you want to remove it, but I think I'll need to get more permission for that."

"Dr. Tabak, you knew we were going to break away the original floor once the altar and platform were removed," Gabriel replied. "The mosaic is a bonus for you. We'll be able to preserve it, and you'll be able to display it either here in the nave or perhaps the Visitors' Center. I don't think additional permission should be necessary. We're under something of a time constraint, and while we don't want to take advantage of your goodwill, neither do we want to get wrapped up in bureaucratic red tape. Surely, there's no reason to not proceed."

Tabak began to defend his need to check with his boss, and Gabriel and then Valerie tried to double-team him into agreeing they could proceed. But he persisted in needing to get his boss' approval.

The day had been very busy.

55

TURKEY

AT THE MONASTERY CAVE

"They just punched through," Trevor told Nicki. During the course of the day, he and Nicki had been strategizing about how to enter the cave and what they would do once in. They needed to build a scaffold over the hole from which they could rig a block and tackle. Nicki had spent a good bit of time getting what they needed. Lumber, lag bolts, the block and tackle, stout rope, and a sling seat had arrived only minutes before Trevor's announcement. Trevor had arranged for two-way radios to assure communication with the surface while they were below ground.

The drilling equipment was moved, and the drilling crew set to work building the scaffold Trevor had sketched on his iPad during the day. The crew had brought their own drills and a circular saw. The simple frame went together quickly and within an hour, the rig was ready to lower them into the cave.

"Let me go get Gabby," Nicki suggested. "He can supervise our descent and retrieval. Plus, we can give him a running narrative of what we're seeing. It won't be the same as being there, but it will be better than him not knowing anything at all."

Moments later, Gabby and Valerie joined Orion, a couple of armed Knights, and the men from the drilling crew who would provide muscle. Nicki and Trevor slipped on hard hats which had lights attached to the sides and a GoPro on the front. Each had an additional flashlight clipped to their belts. A roll of bright orange twine hung from a carabiner attached to a belt loop.

"I think we're ready," Trevor said. "Nicki, I'll descend first and wait for you at the bottom. We'll tie one end of the twine to a stake we can drive into the floor and then start walking. I don't think we'll be dealing with twists and turns or branches off the main cave, but if we do, we won't get lost."

"Let's so, boss," Nicki said. "I'm excited."

Gabriel shook Trevor's hand and kissed Nicki. "You two be cautious. We don't have to explore this thing all at once."

"I know. That's another value of the twine. I'm leaving it behind when we come back up. That way we won't end up just covering the same territory the next time we're down there."

Trevor slipped into the sling and gave the workmen the signal to lower away. The ride was short and the people up top heard the two-way come to life. "Ready for Nicki," was the message.

✠

INSIDE THE CAVE CHURCH

The students were making progress, but it was slow. Near the end of the workday, they had cleaned about a third of the mosaic surface. One student worked on each end of the mosaic, while the third worked in the center. In total, about a third of the surface was visible. What could be seen was black tesserae shaped into Greek letters on a white background.

Maria stood up and stretched, bending her back a little to remove a kink. "Hey, Valerie, I'm going to the restroom in the Visitors' Center."

"No problem."

Valerie had watched the students for the first couple of hours and was satisfied with their technique. They were fast learners, but then, the task wasn't difficult, just tedious. She then busied herself by inspecting the two sealed up openings in the Cave Church walls.

Since the well-known tunnel cave did not need to be resealed per Tabak, she thought it would be straightforward plaster and stone removal. On the other sealed opening Gabriel had discovered, she would need to be more careful in how she removed the stones and mortar. Resealing it might be important.

When Maria was outside of the church, she pulled her cellphone from her pocket and punched in the number for Reynolds-Smythe.

"Jack."

"Jack, it's Maria. I have news."

"Good. I'm listening."

She quickly described the removal of the altar and platform and the work they were doing on the newly discovered mosaic. "I can read a little of the Greek we've uncovered. It says something about 'most worthy Sara' and 'our revered elder'. I can't tell if 'elder' refers to this 'Sara' or not. Just not enough uncovered, that and my ancient Greek isn't all I'd like it to be."

"When you can, snap photos and send them to me. I'll have our men do the translation."

"Getting pictures will be tricky."

"I'm sure you can do it."

"I'll do my best. They are also about to descend into a cave nearby they have bored a large hole into. I'm stuck inside, so I don't have details, but I'll keep my ears open."

"Sergei will be in the city soon with some other men. He'll be prepared to do whatever we need done to secure whatever is found."

"That's another thing, Jack. There are eight or ten armed guards on site. They are dressed in various forms of civilian dress, but each has a sidearm and what I think is an Uzi or similar weapon."

"Who the hell are they?"

"I don't know, but they look professional from what little I've seen."

"I'll let Sergei know. Report every day at least once. I need to know what's happening."

"Will do. I've got to go before my absence raises questions."

✠

"Sergei, it's Jack. Where are you?"

"At the moment, I'm wandering around near the Cave Church like a tourist."

"Maria tells me there are armed men at the site."

"Yes. They arrived this morning. Nothing we can't handle if it comes to that. We'll have the element of surprise."

"She thinks they are professionals."

"Probably. They aren't dressed that way, but their bearing and their surveillance procedures smacks of a military background."

"See if you can find out who they are. And, Sergei, don't underestimate them."

56

INSIDE THE "MONASTERY" CAVE

Nicki arrived at the cave floor. Trevor helped her from the sling and then spoke into his two-way, "We're heading out. I'll be checking with you periodically to make sure the two way radios are still in communication with each other."

"Okay, Trevor," Gabriel said. "Take care."

Nicki and Trevor looked around the space they were in. To their rear, they could see the piles of stones that had been used to seal the opening, probably centuries ago. They swung their lights left to right and judged the distance between the cave walls to be perhaps fifteen feet.

"If we walk with the blocked cave opening to our backs, we should begin to see this area as a kind of foyer. Then we'll move into a larger area where the walls are farther apart and niches are cut into the side walls."

"Let's go then," Nicki said.

What they saw was exactly what Trevor had told her they would see. They had now reached the limits of what he knew from his endoscopic survey. From this point forward, it would be discovery.

"Okay. When I was using the endoscope, I could see four niches on each side. Anything beyond four is new territory."

"I can see more on my side."

"Yeah, me, too. Let's keep going. Wait. There's a turn in the cave on my side. Funny. I don't remember seeing that on the scans we did. What about your side?"

"Nope. Oh, I see now. My side runs into a wall. Looks like the cave makes a turn here."

"Yeah, and it's toward the Cave Church. Let's see where this goes."

Trevor's two-way radio sprang to life. "What are you guys seeing down there?" It was Gabriel.

Trevor told him. "We've come to a turn and we're going to follow it and see where it takes us. Looks as if it's heading toward the church."

"Are you playing out the twine?" Gabriel's voice betrayed his anxiety.

"Yep. We're good. I'll do better at updating you."

"Thanks."

"Look, Trevor," Nicki said, "More niches. Whoa! There's something in the ones on my side."

"Mine, too! You check yours and I'll check mine. Gabby," she said into her radio, "we've found something. Hold on."

She heard two clicks, the signal for "received and understood".

"Trevor, I've got sealed jars on my side. There must be dozens."

"Oh, wow! C'mere, Nicki. I think I know what these are, but I'm not sure." Nicki joined him on his side of the cave.

"I think we're looking at stacks of wooden slabs, maybe ten inches by twelve inches," he said into the radio.

"Trevor, they're stacked in pairs. And look, the left edges of each pair are held together with twine or rope. I think we're looking at some kind of small book."

"Nicki, I think we're looking at tablets. I'm going to open one."

Trevor carefully lifted the topmost wooden piece on the shortest stack. It opened like a book as they expected. "Oh, my God," he declared. "That's wax! And there's writing! I bet all of these are wax tablets and that there's writing on them!"

Nicki shined her headlamps onto the surface. "It looks something like Greek letters."

"Man, I wish Greeks knew about separating their words. It's just one long line from top to bottom."

Trevor keyed his radio. "Gabby, we found wax tablets. I'm taking a picture and will try to send it. Hope the phone works through this rock." His phone camera flashed.

"Got it. It's Greek," Gabriel said. "Let me see if I can read any of this. Hmm. The first line doesn't look like words I know. Odd. I'm shooting this to Marge. Maybe she'll have better luck."

"Gabby," Nicki said, "there are stacks and stacks of these tablets down here. We've also got stoneware jars with seals, maybe wax or bitumen, hard to say."

"Ideas about what's in them?"

"Well, we know foods was stored in sealed jars, and wine, too. But also scrolls were stored in them. I'm guessing these are for scrolls or maybe small codices. The jar openings look pretty large in some cases, so a small codex could be slipped into them. Or maybe we've got a combination. You know, this could be their larder and just general storage."

"Guys. I think you need to return. Let's remove the stones and dirt from the opening and start a systematic investigation," Gabriel said.

"Gabby," Trevor said, "let us keeping going just to see what else is ahead. We won't disturb anything; just explore."

"Trevor, I think we have a major find here. I'd prefer to follow standard procedures of exploration. I think you two need to come back out."

Nicki gave Trevor a hand signal suggesting he take his finger off the contact button so they could talk. Trevor nodded his head, but before he released the button said, "You're the boss, Gabby."

"Trevor I know you want to plunge ahead. Heck, so do I. Gabby needs to be heard on this. He's feeling pretty useless. Please don't ignore him on this. Stopping now isn't going to cost a lot of time."

"Okay. I disagree with him. I don't see what a few more minutes can hurt, but I'll yield."

"Thank you."

Trevor keyed the radio. "Gabby we're heading back." After taking his finger off the send button, he said to Nicki, "Start walking back but slowly; I'll catch up. I'm going a little bit farther. I've got to know."

"Oh, Trevor, I wish you wouldn't."

"I'll meet you at the bore hole. I promise I won't be more than two minutes behind you."

"Okay. No more than two minutes."

Nicki turned and started walking toward the bore. She keyed her two-way radio. "Gabby, I just thought of something. When we were researching wax tablets, didn't we read something about the scribes using some kind of shorthand to record what was being dictated?"

"That right. I'd forgotten. Let me take another look at the first line. I imagine the shorthand would be kind of rudimentary. Maybe leaving out vowels or using a stand-in letter, you know, like we might use the letter N for the word 'and'."

"Great. Let Marge know, too."

"Will do."

Nicki heard something behind her and turned to see Trevor trotting up. "What'd you see?"

"More of the same for another twenty feet. We're going to need a ton of people to help with this. Retrieval won't be hard. The problem will come with translation and interpretation. We aren't going to know exactly what we've found for a long time."

"Could you see the end of the space?"

"Nope. There may be twists and turns or it may just go straight to the church. But thank goodness we won't have much debris to remove. We'll be a day at most cleaning up the cave entrance and the leavings from the bores." Then, "Here we are. You first, Nicki. I haven't been this excited in a long time."

57

DINNER TIME THE SAME DAY

The site was secured. Armed guards were patrolling both the church itself and the temporary bore opening. No one outside the tight inner group knew what had been found inside the "monastery" cave, not even the Turkish officials. Except, of course, that Maria had updated TEO about the mosaic. By the end of the day, it was cleared of mortar and she managed to get a photo of the inscription. The quality wasn't good, primarily because of the angle at which she had been forced to take the picture. But it was something TEO technicians could work with.

The students had been surprised, when back at the hotel, they were asked to sit apart from the core team. They were told the truth: the team needed to talk about some sensitive matters, about which they would be informed in due course. They were assured they would be allowed to continue their work on the site, but that Non-Disclosure Agreements would need to be signed and the documents weren't yet ready. They'd been promised to be allowed to join the leaders for drinks after dinner.

Maria's interest was particularly high when she heard this. She was sure something important had been found in the very short exploration underground. She had texted that much to Reynolds-Smythe, and promised details as soon as she was brought into the full confidence of the team leaders.

The team leaders had been asked to be seated in the Liwan Hotel dining room in a far corner. They needed to have a little privacy, they had said by way of explaining their request. The Hotel staff was happy to oblige, especially since they were spending so much money there and had even brought in three more long-term guests. Orders were placed, and the tired, but excited group settled in to talk.

"Gang," I began,"I assume we're staying and that we're going all in on this project."

"You bet your ass," Trevor said. Others were less graphic, but no less supportive.

"We now have a major project on our hands. We don't know what's under the altar, but I'll tell you what I think the mosaic says in a minute. We do know we have a potentially major documentary discovery in the 'monastery' cave. It's more than we can curate, so we need to develop a plan to remove everything to a secure location here in the city, and then import as many scholars as we can to assist us to begin to make sense of what we've found.

"I'm also keenly aware that we don't know what else we may find once we're inside the cave. It could be nothing more than jars and tablets, but it could also be more. We'll know soon because the first order of business in the cave is digital mapping and scanning everything *in situ*. That will give us time to find the secure location and begin to recruit scholars and other knowledgeable helpers. Once the cave is fully explored, we can begin to remove the objects. How's this sound so far?"

"About right," Nicki said. "I think it's a good plan. We'll need more security though, either the Knights or others we can trust."

"You're right," Gabriel replied."Paddy can you talk to Sal and see what else he can suggest? And I think we need to start including him in these kinds of meetings."

"Will do. He's taking a shift at the site. I'll go talk to him when we finish here."

"Anybody else?"

"When do we tell Tabak what we've found?" Valerie asked.

"How about you catch him up tomorrow?"

"I can do that. So far all he knows is we've decided to open the cave. I avoided telling him the whole truth about our reason."

"Okay. Anybody else?"

"Yeah. Go ahead and tell us what you think the mosaic says," Trevor added.

"Sure. Roughly, I think it tells us that Sara is entombed below. I think the titles used for her indicate she was held in extremely high regard. The title most surprising for me was *episkopos.* As you know that word can mean 'elder' or 'overseer' or, eventually was translated as 'bishop'. No matter how it was meant when it was used here, it suggests she was the spiritual leader or priest, perhaps bishop of this church at some very early time.But guys, here's the biggest surprise yet. The inscription suggests she was Peter's wife."

"Those are pretty much my conclusions, too," Valerie said. "My Greek isn't as good as Gabby's so I've kept those opinions to myself. But if Gabby is right, this is freaking monumental. The Catholic Church is going to have a fit of cosmic proportions. And as Desi used to tell Lucy, it will'have a lot of 'splaining to do'. I know I find the idea of a woman bishop pretty unsettling."

"I think that's probably an understatement, Valerie," Gabby said laughing. "It's no secret Peter had a wife because the Bible says Jesus healed his mother-in-law. But a woman priest and in the hotbed of Christianity that Antioch was—wow! I expect to hear from Marge soon. She'll share with us what her experts in Greek have to say, but I don't think we're far off. That reminds me. I still don't have a word from her on Mary Bernice's documents. I'll check with her tonight."

"This may be one of the biggest and most far reaching discoveries we've made," Nicki added. "I hope we find something in the tablets or jars that support this notion. We need something more than an inscription on a mosaic."

"Just occurred to me," Trevor injected, "that could be one of the reasons the raised platform was added. Rather than just destroy the inscription as things changed in early Christianity, they covered it in what they thought was a permanent way. Something culturally or maybe in their tradition kept them from rejecting it, but they couldn't publicize it."

"I say a real possibility was the tradition here in Antioch for support of female priests may have been so strong that as the Church began to argue against them, the Antioch community protected what meant so much to them. They were hiding it to protect it from early reformers, if you will." Orion looked around the group. "What'd y'all think?"

"No matter how it came to be covered over, we've got to preserve it for her sake and for the sake of the Church," Gabby replied. "And God only knows what we'll find when we remove it. Speaking of which, we need to get people on board who have experience with removing and preserving floor mosaics."

"I've got some feelers out," Valerie replied. "I should start hearing back tomorrow or the next day."

"In any case," Gabby said, "we don't need to try to do it. It's too valuable. This isn't a good one to learn on."

"I completely agree," Valerie replied. "As eager as I am to see what's under it, we can't rush this step."

Their food arrived, and as they began to eat they continued to make some strategic decisions about proceeding. They wanted to keep faith with having drinks with the students. It was agreed that Gabriel would clue the students in, but keep the specifics vague.

58

THE NEXT MORNING

Gabriel's phone on the bedside table roused him. It was 6:30 a.m. local and he would be getting up in moments anyway, but he wasn't happy about the early intrusion. He rubbed the sleep from his eyes and picked up his phone. It was Marge, his lab director in the U.S.

"Hey, Marge. You're calling kind of late." It was 10:30 p.m. in Washington where she was working on the Mary Codex.

"I wanted to clue you in with what we've been able to read on Sister Mary Bernice's documents you sent, and on the mosaic, too."

"I'm all ears. Nicki is here, too, so I'll put you on speaker." Nicki stretched and yawned. "Hey, Marge. Good to hear from you. We were just wondering about you last night."

"Good morning to you, Nicki. First, the easy one, the mosaic." Marge went on to read the preliminary translation her scholars of ancient Greek had prepared for her. Their reading confirmed what Gabriel and Valerie had thought. "That should shake up some folks," she added.

"Our thoughts exactly," Gabriel replied. "We're keeping this under a lid for now."

"Sure. Now about those documents Mary Bernice scanned. They appear to be some sort of record or report, maybe like minutes of a group."

"That fits with some others we found that we could read," Nicki injected.

"I thought it did. Anyway, these pages look to be non-sequential, just kind of random pages."

"I'm not surprised," Nicki said. "From what we were told about how the archives in that section were treated, they haven't really been curated. It's almost as if someone dropped a folder of pages, andwhen the pages scattered, no attempt was made to put them in the right order. And that goes for whole bundles as well. They were just stuck on shelves with no thought to order."

"That goes a long way toward explaining their randomness," Marge replied. "Well, let me tell you what they seem to say and then I can forward a written translation to you."

"Shoot," Gabriel said.

"One of the pages tells about a man named Marnin who had come to Antioch and to the church. He asked for protection. He'd fled from Jerusalem when the war with Rome broke out. He asked for a place where he might work. He had collected stories from people in Galilee about..."

Gabriel interrupted. "About Jesus."

"How'd you know?" Marge asked.

"An educated guess. I think you're talking about the author of the Gospel of Mark. I read something about a growing consensus among New Testament scholars that, although Rome had been assumed as the city that the Gospel was written in, now the shift was toward Syria, with Rome as the audience. If Syria is the country, Antioch is a very likely city."

"Makes sense. They agreed to provide lodging in something they simply called the 'house'. As the page ends, they seem to be spelling out conditions, including one that he must be able to support himself. What else might be required is on some other page."

"We think we know what the 'house' is. At the cave we're interested in there are ruins of an adjacent structure that backs up to the cave we're calling the 'monastery'," Nicki injected.

"Oh, wow; this is all fitting together."

"What else?" Gabriel asked.

"There was only one page about that. A second page that was written in a different hand and our paleography experts suggest, in a preliminary way, dates from late first-century to mid-second century like the first page. That page seems to suggest agreeing to allow a man named Maththaios to lodge in the 'house' without describing his reason for asking to join the community."

"Wait a second and let me check something on Google." Gabriel typed inthe name Maththaios and clicked search. "Get this. The diminutive of Maththaios is Matthaios, a word we'd translate as Matthew. And Matthew is included in the list of Jesus' inner circle."

"But wouldn't he be too old to be writing something at the end of the first-century?" Marge asked. "If he was the same age as Jesus, say thirty at Jesus' death, by the end of the century, he'd be a hundred. Pretty unlikely, don't you think?"

"Yep. But he could be a son who was given his father's name or a follower who took the name of a disciple. Or it could be a coincidence. Or Matthew, generally thought to have been written about 85 C.E. could have been written earlier when the original Matthew was still alive."

"That's a hard sell," Marge said. "I'd go with coincidence on the name thing."

"Guys," Nicki injected, "it doesn't really matter. We don't know why they let him stay in the 'house'. He might not have written anything."

"True," Gabriel agreed, "but guess what? Syria is also thought to be where the Gospel of Matthew was written. And so if Syria, probably Antioch."

"All this makes me want to get those tablets studied as soon as possible and find out what those jars contain," Nicki said. "My God, what if we find drafts of Gospels or even complete texts?"

"What else, Marge?"

"The other couple of documents mention a visit from Pétros or Peter in English. He's welcome there and invited to stay as long as he wishes. One mentions he's brought his wife, but doesn't name her."

"Our money is on her being our Sara," Nicki said.

"It's not a big leap. Here's my scenario of what could have happened. Peter and Sara show up and stay a while. Tradition says Peter ends up in Rome sometime in the late 60s C.E. Sara doesn't go with him; she stays behind in Antioch.Perhaps because of her association with Peter, she becomes more revered. Soon she's elevated to a leadership position. Or she could have stayed behind so the Antioch community would have a leader associated with the Apostles. " Gabriel summed up. "Either way, it all fits."

"Yeah. Plus, many scholars believe that Mark's Gospel shows the influence of Peter. Some scholars, mostly conservative ones, suggest that Mark actually based his Gospel on Peter's memories and preaching."

"It'd be hard to prove that Peter and Marnin were present at the same time, but they could have been. Let's say both men were about Jesus' age. If Peter is martyred in, say 65 C.E., he would have been younger when he was in Antioch. Let's say he was there five years or so before. That makes him, or them, both about sixty. That's possible," Gabriel offered.

"Yeah," Nicki added, "and since scholars almost all agree that Matthew used Mark as the framework of his Gospel, he could have had access to Mark's work fifteen or so years later when he showed up in Antioch."

"It all fits. Really good evidence. All we lack to rock the world is something more than speculation on these few little documents. We need something solid, irrefutable."

"Maybe that's what we'll discover in the monastery cave. Holy cow! I just got shivers," Nicki said.

"Marge, you think we can borrow some of the Greek scholars you're using? We need to have them here to look at what we pull out of the cave. Not study, necessarily, but help us see what we have."

"I think they'd jump at the chance. And they can suggest others to join them if you want them."

"Would you check into that? And remember, thank God and Roger English, money's no object."

"I'll get back to you as soon as I can," Marge said. "This is going to be big! I don't know how you guys get involved in all this stuff, but I'm thrilled to death to be a part of it."

"Thrilled to death", of course, is a common idiomatic expression meaning "very excited". People never actually expect to die because of some event that is captivating or sensational.

59

BALTIMORE

TEO U.S. HEADQUARTERS

G eorge Rutherford's phone call to Reynolds-Smythe in England interrupted the latter's breakfast.

"Good morning, George."

"Good morning to you, Jack. I have some information for you."

"About?"

"Gabriel."

"Proceed please."

"We have someone close to the operation of Gabriel's laboratory operation in DC. You remember that's where scholars are still working on the Mary Codex translation."

"I do."

"Our source has just reported that the lab director has asked the three ancient Greek scholars working on the Mary Codex if they would be willing to temporarily relocate to Turkey. She wants them to suggest other scholars who might be willing to do the same."

"I assume this relocation isto the site of Gabriel's work."

"Correct. Something has been found there, apparently in a cave near the Cave Church of St. Peter that Gabriel wants their advice about. The phrase our contact used was, 'to give us an idea of what we've found.'"

"But no indication of what it might actually be?"

"No, but it's obvious it is something written in ancient Greek."

"When do the scholars leave for Turkey?"

"As soon as arrangements can be made. I'm guessing several days to a week."

"Thank you, George. We know they found a mosaic containing Greek wording referring to a woman named Sara. We also know they are preparing to remove the mosaic so they can excavate beneath it. There's a cave nearby, but we don't yet know anything useful about it."

"Given Gabriel's golden touch at finding significant Christian artifacts, I suspect we might want to find out before he does, or at least as soon as he does."

"We have two people on site, but there are armed guards that are making 'research' difficult. I guess we're going to have to take some risks. Keep me posted, George, on anything else you hear."

"Absolutely. And I'd appreciate updates."

"Of course."

✠

ENGLAND
TEO HEADQUARTERS

"Get Sergei on the phone, please," ordered Reynolds-Smythe.

A few minutes later they were connected.

"Update me Sergei."

"Yes, sir. According to Maria, the students were told at breakfast this morning that something of potentially great importance has been found in the cave. Excavation of the entrance is going to begin soon and they don't expect it to take long to clear away the rubble. My men arrived last night, so I'm no longer alone. Tonight, if conditions are right, we'll create a diversion to draw the guards away from the opening they bored into the cave and I'm going in to see what they've found."

"Sergei, it's apparent that operations there are moving forward quite quickly. We can't let this work continue without our intervention much longer. When the public learns anything about what might be going on there, it will make our work more difficult. You need to think about how to create a major cave in."

"If it weren't for the guards, setting charges to collapse the roof of the cave would be easy."

"Then figure out how to take out the guards and blow the cave. And if you can eliminate Gabriel in the process, that will be that much better. With him gone, the work will stop and whatever is in the cave will stay there."

"I don't mean to be cheeky, sir, but do you not want to have what's in the cave?"

"That would be ideal, of course. Originally I'd hoped to have Gabriel retrieve whatever was important at the site, and then we would take it from him. Now I'm concerned that may be too risky. We have some idea what he's going to find under the altar. Even the text of the mosaic covering it is disturbing enough. If the material in the cave is as important, perhaps even as revolutionary as the mosaic text, the fallout will be too great to counteract. I'd rather lose it than deal with it being found."

"I'm glad I don't have to make those kinds of decisions. I'll get back to you with our plan as soon as it's formulated. I'll even come up with a way to destroy whatever is related to the altar so you can consider it."

"Good. I knew I could count on you, Sergei."

TURKEY

"Gabby," Valerie said, "we have Tabak's written permission to remove the mosaic. I've heard back from the experts I contacted about handling that for us. The lead guy is Dr. Ronald Fitzpatrick. He's formerly associated with Yale, but actually has his own private firm like yours to do projects like these. He and his team can be here in less than a week."

"Great! Have any trouble getting him on board?"

"When he heard it was you and Nicki, he said yes immediately."

"That's flattering. I'm guessing you sent him pictures, too."

"Yep. He estimates the removal work should probably take no more than a week since the mosaic is small. Plus they have developed a proprietary method of removing these things that speeds up the process and protects the work more effectively than the traditional way of removing them."

"Great. I'm ready to dig. I want to know if Sara is under the altar."

"Me, too. But even if she isn't, the mosaic alone is going to shake things up."

"True."

60

England

Sir, we have some preliminary readings on the parchments you gave us which were acquired from the nun." The head of the Document Laboratory of TEO was speaking by phone to Reynolds-Smythe. "Shall I come to your office to brief you?"

"Yes. Come immediately."

Father Paul Cavallo had done as Reynolds-Smythe had suggested and sent the documents to England via diplomatic courier several days prior. Now TEO would know what Gabriel and his team knows about them. A few minutes passed before Reynolds-Smythe heard a soft knock on his office door.

"Come in!" he said loud enough to be heard through the solid oak door.

"Good morning, sir." Arthur Higgason, the head of the Document Laboratory was a short, balding man with a bad comb-over that always annoyed Reynolds-Smythe. He was dressed in a lab coat over a wrinkled dress shirt and badly tied necktie. His glasses frequently slid down his nose and he was habitually pushing them up. His slovenly appearance was deceptive; he was a first rate expert in the study of ancient documents.

"Good morning, Arthur. Have a seat. What do you have for me?"

Higgason's report mirrored what Marge had told Gabriel. Reynolds-Smythe was leaning forward in his chair. "Wait a moment, Arthur. You're saying the documents suggest a man named Marnin was permitted to stay in Antioch to complete some writing, and that you believe Marnin is the author of Mark's Gospel?"

"Yes, sir."

"And that a man whose Greek name can be translated as Matthew was also allowed to stay there, but for reasons unknown, but you wouldn't be surprised, if that man is the author of Matthew's Gospel?"

"Yes, sir. There's more." Now Higgason moved beyond the material Marge had translatedfor Gabriel. "Another parchment makes reference to 'our archives' and orders someone to 'create more niches for our work'."

"And this would suggest, what?"

"I believe it suggests their archives exist underground somewhere and that their archived materials are growing fast enough to warrant developing more space for storage. They aren't building shelves, but cutting into rock to create a place to stack material."

"This is brilliant, Arthur. Is there more?"

"No, sir."

"Thank you, Arthur. This is splendid work. This information will help us in our plan to protect, not only our existence, but to keep peace in the world."

"I'm pleased, sir. Truly I am. The lads in the lab will be excited to hear our work is so useful."

"Do what must be done to conserve the manuscripts and have them delivered to our archives for storage."

"I'll begin immediately, sir." Higgason stood, nodded slightly to Reynolds-Smythe and left the office.

The Enlightened Ones leader leaned back in his chair. He began to summarize what he knew, collecting his thoughts to plan his next step. The mosaic translation he'd been given strongly suggested a woman had been the priest at the Cave Church at some point early in its existence. The writers of Mark and Matthew likely did their work at "The House". Scholars knew well that Matthew relied heavily on Mark for his Gospel. If they were both at the Cave Church, even if not at the same time, that explained how he might have come in contact with Mark's work. And finally, there were archives near the Cave Church. In his imagination he could see what today would be called "source material" that Mark and Matthew had used and which would be stored in the archives. Perhaps early drafts of the Gospels were there as well. And who knew what other writing.

As he mused, Reynolds-Smythe did a quick Google search on the dates of the earliest known manuscripts for the Gospels. He learned that the earliest manuscripts of Mark date from around the year 200, or some 130 years after Mark is thought to have been written. A small fragment found as part of a mummy's mask dates from around 100 C.E. The earliest manuscript of Matthew likely dates from the 300s C.E. or 220 or so years after it is believed to have been written.

Reynolds-Smythe also was reminded as he read that thousands of fragments and "complete" copies of both Gospels exist. There are also thousands of variations of different kinds between them, but scholars deem most as largely unimportant. Mark, however, has three separate endings in various manuscripts with no agreement which might be the original ending. So, if these archives contain very early copies, they will be invaluable, no matter what else might be stored in them, if they answer the question of what is the original ending of Mark's Gospel.

I don't think I can order the cave destroyed, he finally concluded. *We need to have what's in those archives. This new information complicates things.*

After more reflection, the TEO leader called Sergei.

"Don't blow the cave. I want what's inside. They will remove it and transport it to a warehouse for inventorying and study. That's when you will take it. You'll need to surveil the contents' removal, but assume whatever it is that is removed, will be a lot of material."

"Maria should be able to find out the location of their storage area. After all, she'll likely be helping move the stuff," Sergei said. "Or we can put a tail on the delivery van."

"Yes. As soon as she knows, she should tell you. That's your signal to begin to develop a plan to steal whatever they remove. You'll need a place nearly as large as their warehouse, and ideally, it will be close by to speed up the process. Once you have it stored in Turkey, we can figure out how to transport it to England. Sergei, the material in the cave is more valuable than I first thought. Do not let me down."

"Have I ever?"

"No, and I certainly don't want this to be the first time."

61

TURKEY

he ARA team, plus Orion and Aurélio, as well as the three students were gathered around several tables pulled together. Breakfast was over and the dishes were cleared except for coffee cups and carafes of thick Turkish coffee. Gabriel began the business of the gathering. He didn't like to try to discuss projects as people ate and everyone honored that. Meals were the place where informal camaraderie could hold sway, but for business he preferred everyone's attention be undivided.

"Okay, let me summarize where we are so we can all be on the same page. The mosaic removal team arrived and has begun its work. After seeing the mosaic, Dr. Fitzpatrick thinks they can have it lifted in three days. As soon as it is moved, Valerie will begin excavation. Right, Valerie?"

"On all counts. Everything we need is in place, or will be, within twenty-four hours."

"Trevor, you've secured a warehouse for us and a truck to move whatever we find. Right?"

"Right. The moving crew will be couple of the students, some muscle from the boring crew, and me. But first, we're having the experts ascertain what we have. I believe they are due here today sometime unless there has been a change. I'll check when the meeting is over." Trevor continued. "We'll let them in via the bore hole to survey what we have in a very preliminary way. While that's happening, those of us not inside the cave will begin the removal of the cave entrance rubble and dirt. We're not going to do a careful analysis of the material until we are near ground level. We'll slow down to see if we can find anything to date when the cave was filled."

"Who is going to do that?"

Nicki spoke up. "Trevor, the students and I. Laborers will do most of the work until we need to slow down and work as archeologists. By the way, the experts can exit at the cave mouth rather than be lifted out, even if we're not completely finished. We'll have a temporary walkway over the rubble and earth for them—and us for that matter."

"Sal, do we have enough Kni...," Gabriel stopped himself. "I mean, do we have enough guards to give us good protection here and at the warehouse?"

"No, but I will tomorrow. Right now we can protect the altar crew and the cave, but not the warehouse. James is sending more men today."

Gabriel beamed. "Excellent. Trevor, what about tools and equipment the experts will need? Do we have those?"

"They sent me a list of what they'd like to have based on what we might find. I'm having Mandy secure it. We'll have it by the time the cave is empty."

"And NatGeo? What's their plan?"

Nicki spoke up. "They now have two complete teams here. One assigned to each focus area. We're asking everyone to be nice to them, but direct all their archeological questions to Gabby or me, at least for the time being."

"Okay, then. Any questions anybody?" Gabriel asked.

There weren't any.

Maria carefully and surreptitiously clicked off the record function on her phone in her shirt pocket. Sending the recording to Reynolds-Smythe would save a lot of time.

"In that case, unless you're needed by Trevor or Valerie, you have the day off. Use it to relax because it's about to get very hectic."

Maria excused herself from her friends and made her way to the public restroom just off the lobby. Once in a private stall, she sent Reynolds-Smythe a text and the recording she'd made. She rejoined her friends and the three left to enjoy aday off.

✠

For his part Reynolds-Smythe listened to the recording and then forwarded it to all on his team who might need the information. Intelligence was always essential in planning an attack and he was planning exactly that. He'd also decided to ask the Council for permission to terminate Gabriel and his team when the cave material was secure. While the man had been unknowingly very useful, he was also a pain in the ass for the TEO. His remarkable discoveries over the recent years have led toward less infighting among Christians. Mary's Codex, in particular, the half or so that had been released already was being cited as the reason people were returning to churches. The first hand account of Jesus was a compelling picture of what Jesus was about. *We can't have more unity breaking out,* he thought and smiled. *We have to keep some chaos in the system in order to profit from it.* For that reason alone, Reynolds-Smythe was confident the Council would approve.

✠

"Hey, Nigel," said Barton."I just intercepted an interesting email with an attachment." Barton was one of the cyber techs The Order of Christ was using to monitor several electronic leads that had been developed through Aurélio and Orion.

"From whom to whom?"

"Well, it's on the Eton Abbey email server we hacked. It's actually a forwarded email from a 'MT' to 'Boss'. 'Boss' then forwarded it to six other people, none of whom we recognize. The text says, 'Here's the plan.' The attachment is a voice recording that sounds like a meeting of Gabriel's team in Turkey."

A look of concern crossed Nigel's face. "Any idea who MT or the Boss are?"

"Nope."

"Thanks, Barton. I think I'll contact Aurélio."

As Sal Aurélio was in his room preparing to get back into the field, his cell pinged. He saw it was Nigel and answered immediately. Nigel filled him in on Barton's intercept and Aurélio thanked him. "I know who MT is, Nigel. She's one of the students working on the site. Her name is Maria Teke. See what you can find out about her. May as well check the other students, too. They are D'gostia and Nia Karga." Aurélio provided what background information on them he had. "Something stinks here, Nigel. Stay in touch."

With that Aurélio headed off to find Gabriel and Nicki. This was very troubling news. Was Maria a TEO operative, he wondered? If so, the situation was about to get even more complicated.

62

THE CAVE CHURCH

urélio found Gabriel and Nicki in the nave of the Cave Church. They were watching the mosaic removal experts work.

"Hey, guys. I need to talk to you about something. Can we step outside?"

"Sure. What's up?" Gabriel said.

"Let's wait until we're outside."

Confused about what difference it would make, Gabriel acquiesced. As soon as they stepped into the sunshine, he said, "This seems a little cloak and daggery to me."

"'Daggery? That's not even a word, Gabby,"Aurélio said, laughing. "But you're right. It is. I tend to be cautious all the time anyway, but after what I just learned, it's more important than ever." He told the pair about the intercepted email. "So Maria is affiliated with TEO in some way. The other two students may be as well. We're doing deep background checks on them right now back in England."

"Well, we have to get her off the team," Nicki said. "Damn. I'm so disappointed with her and with myself for not checking her out more closely."

"Slip-ups happen, Nicki. I probably should have insisted on vetting them, but I guessed incorrectly that students wouldn't be our enemies. I mean what are the chances that three random students from four hundred miles away would be involved with TEO? Right?"

"Clearly I never considered it," she said. "I'd better go find her and send her packing." Nicki turned to head toward the parking area.

"Hold it, Nicki. Now that we know she's a mole, we can make use of that to get her to either feed TEO false information, or to use her to help us uncover more of their operation, or both. Now that we know she contacts TEO, we can clone her phone and monitor her calls. That will give us new leads."

"How's that work, the cloning I mean?" asked Gabriel.

"We just need to be near her phone for a couple of minutes. We have a device with a program that will pair her phone with one of ours. When she makes or receives a call or text, we get it too."

"Okay. Now what?"

"We can't change the way we treat her. If we deal with her differently from the way we've been treating her, she'll likely sense it. This is the hard part. Just act as if I never told you about the email."

Nicki spoke up. "I can try that, but I suspect it will be hard."

"Yes, it will," Aurélio replied.

"I don't want her helping move the cave materials," Gabriel said. "She can't know what's in there. I don't know how I'm going to do that."

"Can she work with Valerie on the excavation under altar?" Aurélio asked.

"I suppose. Yeah, that'll work. She has actual field experience, well according to her, anyway, so I can make a case for that."

"That keeps her out of the cave and limits what she can tell her TEO handler."

"I don't like her knowing what we find in the church either, but I suppose that's the price we pay for protecting the cave material and using her to find out more about TEO," Gabriel said.

"It's a start, anyway," Aurélio replied. "And it may be enough."

"You're the boss on this Sal. What do we need to do about the cloning?"

"Nothing. I'll handle it. Since she has the day off, we can't clone the phone until tonight or tomorrow anyway."

"I have an idea," Nicki said. "I could call her and offer her a chance to observe the mosaic removal and at the same time, tell her she'll be working on the excavation."

"Do it. I'll contact London now to get a link set up."

Nicki made a phone call to Maria as Aurélio left. Maria quickly accepted Nicki's suggestion about observing the mosaic removal and seemed genuinely pleased to be asked to work on the excavation.

"Okay, then, Maria," Nicki said. "Come on down. I'm in the church now."

"I'm on my way."

Maria thought about calling TEO, but decided to wait until later in the day. She was sure they'd be pleased she was going to be observing and working on the excavation under the altar, but there was no need to tell her boss that right away. She decided she'd wait until she had more to report, starting with the location of the warehouse. She left the hotel after telling her friends she'd been summoned to the church and after a twenty-minute walk she was in the nave.

"Hey, Nicki. Thanks for putting me on this."

"You're welcome, Maria. I thought we could use your experience here better than we could using you as labor in the cave," a smiling Nicki replied.

"I appreciate that. I hope when the cave contents get to the warehouse, you can use me there."

"Oh, probably. We'll just have to see."

"Is the warehouse far?" Maria asked.

"I'm not certain. I haven't been there. Trevor would know the specifics. In the meantime, just watch the mosaic removal experts and take some notes. Valerie stepped out just a minute, but she'll be the lead on this."

Valerie and Aurélio came walking up to the pair. "Valerie, I've recruited Maria to observe the removal and then assist you in the excavation. I know the site isn't very large, but I thought you could use some help."

"Uh, yeah, sure. That's fine."

"Nicki," Aurélio said, "may I speak with you a minute?"

"Sure."

"Right over here," he said, indicating a spot twenty or so feet away. When they got there, he said, "Slip this device in your pocket and then stand within five feet of Maria. Press this button. Keep your hand on the device. When you feel it vibrate, press the button again. It'll probably take a minute or two, so try to maintain the proximity to her. Then bring it to me. I'll be near the cave entrance."

"Got it. See you later." Nicki walked back to where Valerie and Maria were standing to get the best view of the mosaic removal team. "Valerie," Nicki said as she pressed the button on the device in her pocket, "what's the plan once the mosaic is removed?"

Valerie began answering the question while Nicki and Maria looked on intently. After a few minutes, Nicki felt the device in her pocket vibrate. She pushed the button she'd been instructed to push and said, "Sounds as if you have it all worked out. Great. If you think you need me, just let me know. I'm going to be moving back and forth between the two projects."

"Will do."

"I'm off. I need to clue Gabby in on some things that have come up back in Memphis. Got a text from Mandy this morning. See you two later."

The two women said their goodbyes to Nicki and she headed to Aurélio's location. She wanted to get this part over as quickly as possible so they could find out as much as they could about Maria's relationship to TEO. After the handoff of the device to Aurélio, Nicki walked to the conference room headquarters to meet with Gabriel. Not only was the work at the two sites beginning to heat up, but as Sherlock might have said, "The game's afoot" with engaging TEO. She wanted them to be taken down or at least dealt a severe blow. Sister Mary Bernice needed to be avenged.

$$63$$

TURKEY

THE NEXT MORNING, 7:00 A.M.

G abriel's team was gathered in the Visitors' Center conference room and he was about to get the meeting started. American coffee had been secured and was available on the conference room table, along with some fresh pastries. Three experts in ancient Greek had arrived the previous day and were present as well. Though the core team and they had met briefly after their arrival, no substantial work related conversations had been held. Gabriel had learned that two more scholars were coming later in the week to bring the total to five. Casual conversations were taking place around the room.

"Okay everybody," Gabriel said. "Thanks to our scholars for showing up so early in spite of any jet lag they may be dealing with. I think we all met last night, so we can skip the introductions. Yesterday, Trevor and I entered the cave again to do a very preliminary survey. We recorded what we saw and left. If you'll watch that screen, you'll have some idea of the task ahead."

Nicki hadn't been happy with Gabriel for entering the cave, but the truth was, he didn't ask her. He just did it. "I thought we needed more information," he said by way of excusing his actions. She was none too happy with Trevor either for allowing Gabriel to talk him into the foray. But she did finally accept it was probably the right thing to do.

The TV switched from blue to a jumpy view of the inner wall of the borehole. Quickly, the picture stabilized and she could see the same view she and Trevor had seen as they made their way from the entrance. Gabriel began to narrate.

"As you can see we have a long corridor with niches on both sides. We measured it with a laser measure and we have about thirty feet of corridor that contains material. On one side, as you can see, we have stacks and stacks of what are almost certainly wax tablets. What we don't know is whether or not they are blank or still contain the scribes' work. On the other side you see rows of jars all approximately the same size, all sealed. We are theorizing the jars contain documents of some kind, but they may be empty or contain foodstuffs. We know early Christians collected food to give to the widows and orphans who were associated with their particular community. This could be their larder.

"However, we're betting on documents. What we'd like to spend the next couple of days doing is have you gentlemen," he motioned toward the scholars "to sample the tablets and the jars. We need some idea of what we have. We think we're on to something significant, and are prepared to deal with the find as if that's true. If you tell us we're wrong, we have only lost some money. Any questions anybody?"

The scholars asked several pertinent questions that dealt largely with logistics. One asked about light. "We will be expected to work with headlamps or handheld lamps?"

"We have those for you, but we also are going to be lowering halogen work lamps into the cave. We have a generator set up to supply power. The lighting won't be as good as you'd have in a lab, but adequate for our preliminary survey. Other questions?"

After a few more, everyone was satisfied they understood the plan. "If we find we have something of significance, we'd like you gentlemen to work in our warehouse/lab long enough to give us a greater sense of what we have. I know you're working on the Mary Codex, and we thank you for breaking away for this. I firmly believe what we find in the cave could be on par with the Mary journal in its impact on Christianity. Once we know what we have, we may need to call a time out while we ascertain who can work with us on a more permanent basis. But that's in the future. So, if we're all ready, let's head out to the two sites and get cracking."

Valerie and her three helpers headed to the Cave Church nave to begin the excavation of the under altar area. As they left the conference room, Maria excused herself to make a restroom stop. "I'll catch up in a minute, but nature is being pretty insistent. I'm afraid I drank too much of that coffee." As soon as she was in a stall, she sent the recording she'd made to Reynolds-Smythe. Feeling very pleased that she'd done her part to contain the mess Gabriel was creating, she headed to the Cave Church.

Gabriel and the others were at the monastery site. Workmen had been working since daylight. The first lowered work lights into the cave and hooked them to the generator. Then they began to clear the rubble from the entrance. By the time the experts had arrived, enough work had been done so they could avoid being lowered through the borehole. The team still had to do a little crawling to enter the cave, but it was minimal. Gabriel ordered the generator to be fired up, as very quickly, a glow emanated from the cave entrance.

✠

"Robbie," Aurélio asked, "did she record the meeting?"

"Yep. And she sent it to 'boss'. I have the lads back in England working to pinpoint the physical location of the receiving phone. Should know something soon."

"Great. I want to find those bastards. There's an innocent nun who needs justice."

64

ENGLAND

TEO HEADQUARTERS

Reynolds-Smythe played the recording from Maria to a few members of the Council he had gathered for an impromptu electronic meeting. "Gentlemen, I don't want to get ahead of the archeologists, but I'm sure they are going to find significant materials in that cave. Antioch was a major center of first century Christianity. We know from the nun's recovered documents that they kept records of various decisions and that they allowed two men who were likely Gospel writers to work there. I think the cave contains their archives.I think the material the nun recovered at the Vatican Archives was copies of material in the cave. I'm more convinced than ever we must keep this material from seeing the light of day. If nothing else, it will shed light on how the early Church operated in a major center of Christianity."

"I thought we'd already decided to steal the material once it was removed from the cave and placed in a warehouse."

"That was the plan. But the more I've thought about it, the less I think that's a good idea. The experts in ancient Greek texts that they've brought in are going to read some of this material before it's moved, maybe even as it's being moved, since two more experts are supposedly on the way. If word leaks about what they find, that could be problematic. I'm afraid we not only need to deal with the material as soon as we can, but I think we need to eliminate anyone who has an idea of what's in it.

"We can't have another surge of interest in ancient Christianity," he continued."By keeping Christians split and at odds with each other about the nature of True Faith, we have the ability to have more control over various decisions that get made which impact our plans. I recognize I may be over reacting and that religion is still probably not seen as that important to millions of so-called Christians. But we know from long experience that some chaos in the system is useful to us. Look at what we accomplished in the States in their recent elections. The delicate balance that existed within the country and between the US and Europe and the US and Asia has been totally disrupted, just as we hoped it would."

"Look, Jack," said George Rutherford of the US, "we're benefiting from the chaos you just described; there's no doubt about that. But I think you over estimate the impact of any Christian unity that might emerge from some finds in an ancient cave. Christians have always been at each other's throats in one way or another. Or at the very least, can't effectively work together when they're not at odds with each other. I'm concerned that taking out an entire archeological team will draw too much attention to the matter."

"It's a risk, I know. But if we can figure out a way to make it look like Muslim terrorism, we have nothing to worry about. In fact, that would help with the present level of turmoil in the world. I think I have a way to sacrifice a few Muslims to make it looks as if they did it and never give anyone a reason to think it wasn't them."

"Really? What's the plan?"

"We recruit a few locals who are Muslim to 'help us', kill them in the attack, plant evidence that makes it looks like a Muslim attack against Christians, and that will be that. Sergei is recruiting some poor sods over there who will have no idea they're being used. We can fabricate a terrorist cell they're a part of and the outrage will draw attention to them and not us."

"The down side to all this seems to be we'll never know what's in that cave," said the representative from France.

"Does it really matter? We don't need to let more information about early Christianity become available unless it were to challenge the veracity of core doctrines, such as Jesus' resurrection. If there were evidence in the cave that he didn't really rise from the dead, that would be helpful, but I don't think there's anything like that. I think it will be enough when they release the information about Sara, Peter's wife, being an important leader in the early Church to shake things up. That's already assured with the preservation of the mosaic I briefed you about. It doesn't really matter what they find when they dig under the altar. I don't really see a downside to nipping this whole project in the bud."

"Jack, as always, you are persuasive. Still, I'd like to give them some time to look at a good sample of the material. Maria will know what they find and she can alert us. Maybe we'll want to let it become public. If not, then strike. You might have to take out the cave and the warehouse which complicates your plan some, but I'm confident you can take care of it."

"George, I think that's risky."

"What about the rest of you? What's your view?"

To Reynolds-Smythe's surprise, the group sided with Rutherford. They'd get a report from Maria before acting. He was told to develop the plan of attack but to hold off on executing it.

"Very well. I'll update you when I next hear from Maria."

Reynolds-Smythe ended the conference call and sat back in his chair. He felt a bit of a sulk coming on. He wasn't accustomed to not getting his way. But he did admit to himself that what they asked for was reasonable. He'd let Maria know what she had to learn and get a report to him as soon as possible. He hated that she would have to be terminated in the attack as well, but armies always had casualties.

Sergei needed to get to get the new wrinkle in the plan factored in. A call could take care of that. Reynolds-Smythe would get another staff member to electronically create the terrorist cell. A few well placed bits of text traffic, a rumor or two about strange meetings, a few slightly out of focus photos of the terrorists' meeting and the like, and that would take care of that. A planted cellphone on one of the Muslim casualties would be enough to get an investigation started. He loved it when they could create alternative realities like this. People were so quick to believe anything that supported their preconceived ideas, that this work didn't even have to be done as well as he was sure it would be done. *It's easy to lead the biased, uninformed, and intellectually lazy,* he thought. That philosophy was at the root of TEO's successes.

65

TURKEY

THE DIG SITE

"S al, we just read a text message from the cellphone number of Maria's boss."

"What's he telling her?" Aurélio asked.

"It's not just to her; it's to someone named Sergei. It says to 'call as soon as possible. New plan.' Then he sent one to Maria that says, 'Need to know what's found in cave ASAP. New plan.'"

"Can you intercept the call, Nigel, when Sergei calls?"

"We think so, but we're not sure. We know we can do texts and emails on the 'boss' phone, but we haven't tried a call before with his phone."

"We need it, Nigel. I don't like the sound of this. I'm going to put the lads on full alert. I'm afraid something bad is about to happen. If we can't get the call from this Sergei bloke, we can find out when Maria and 'the boss' talk."

"Stay on it, Nigel, and call me immediately when you know anything, anything at all."

"Absolutely."

✠

Aurélio began looking for Orion and Gabriel. They needed to know something was about to happen. Besides, he thought it was time to reign in Maria. Once he found them, he told them what he'd learned and what he wanted to do with Maria. "We've got to control the information flow and the only way to do that is to take her out of the equation." Both men agreed and told him to do whatever was necessary.

The Knight decided he needed Valerie in on the plan, so he headed for the Cave Church where she and the students were beginning to dig. He called her away from the work and the two of them walked outside.

"Valerie, we've got to take Maria out of circulation and I want you to be aware of what's going to happen."

"Sure, but what's up? Why the urgency?"

He explained what he'd learned. "After she makes the call to her bosslater today, I'm going to take her into custody. We're going to detain her and take her to the place we've been using as our headquarters. That will be only temporary. Exactly what we're doing with her next hasn't been determined. But we're going to tell her we know what's going on and we'll question her—extensively. From that moment on, we'll be the ones communicating with her leader as if we're her."

"What about her friends? What are we going to tell them when she suddenly disappears?"

"Tell them she's needed back in Ankara, but you don't know the particulars."

"Okay. I can do that. Holy Mother of Jesus," Valerie said, as she crossed herself."I don't like this at all."

"I understand. I don't either, but we're worried and we need to keep everybody safe."

"I'll do my part," Valerie said, "but I've gotta say that this is freaking me out."

The wait was not long. Within minutes of reading Reynolds-Smythe's text, she excused herself and walked outside.

"Sir, I haven't heard anything about the cave yet, but wondered what's changed," she said when he answered. Unknown to them, both Aurélio's team guarding the site and Knights back in London were listening to the call on the cloned phone.

"You must find out whatever the experts learn. Use any means possible. Involve Sergei if needed. As soon as they emerge from that cave, we've got to know what they learned. Maria, we're very likely to end this project very soon. A lot depends on what you tell us."

"I'm not sure Gabriel is going to be sharing that information with the students. He's been very selective as to what he's telling us."

"If he doesn't include you, then you need to get the information from someone who knows by whatever means possible. That's why you may need Sergei."

"You can count on me, Jack, you know that. I'll do whatever it takes."

"Brilliant! Call me the moment you know something."

✠

Once Aurélio heard the call, he changed the plan. He found Gabriel and Orion again and began to update them. "This Sergei bloke is near the site. I'm stepping up our surveillance to see what we can turn up. Also, I don't like the phrase 'likely to end this project very soon'. Best case, they disappear, but I expect the worse case: they cause us harm. So, here's what I want. Gabby, I need you to call the team together, including the students, after the experts knock off for the day. You're going to give them false information about what was found. Maria will then call her boss with the news. His name is Jack, by the way. After she calls, we'll take her into our custody then."

Gabriel replied, "So I'm guessing you want me to say something like 'the tablets were largely unreadable because the wax had deteriorated and the jars that were opened basically were filled with the dust of old documents'?"

"Perfect. You can add that we'll sample again tomorrow, but you aren't hopeful. You've got to sell it, Gabby. Lives are at stake."

"I can do it. I need to get back to the cave and clue in the scholars. They've got to look disappointed. I can tell you this, Sal; it's going to be a big lie. We're finding just what we hoped for."

66

THE CAVE CHURCH SITE

ust prior to the cave work being ended for the day, Orion entered the Cave Church and walked over to the excavation. "Hey, Valerie, Gabriel would like for your team to join everybody in the conference room. He wants to get an update from you and to share what his guys found in the monastery cave."

"Now?"

"Yeah. They're headed there in just a few minutes."

Valerie stood and brushed some dirt from her jeans and hands. The three students stopped what they were doing too. "Okay. Just give us a few minutes to secure this site and we'll be right there."

Maria was trying hard to contain her excitement. This was working out more beautifully than she'd hoped. She'd be able to report to Reynolds-Smythe the information he wanted without involving Sergei. Within ten minutes everyone working on both sites had gathered in the conference room. Maria secretly thumbed her record feature on her phone and took a chair along with the others.

Gabriel stood. Maria noticed he didn't look happy. In fact, he had a very worried look on his face. "Valerie, would you mind going first? I hope you have good news; mine's not so hot."

"Sure," she said. "We are about two feet down. Based on the scans, we should hit whatever is there tomorrow easily. We've been doing sifting of the removed material, but have found nothing of value."

"Okay. Thanks. Well, um," Gabriel started, "there's no easy way to say this. Our work in the cave has been very disappointing. The tablets we've checked are virtually useless. The wax has shrunken and dried obliterating any writing that may have been on them. We've also opened about fifteen of the jars. Clearly documents of some kind were stored in them, but time hasn't been kind. The contents are essentially reduced to small bits and dust. Leather covers of some codices are hard and cracked or otherwise badly compromised. And the contents of those are also virtually useless for study. We're going to sample more tablets and jars tomorrow, but I'm not hopeful."

Maria spoke up. "Excuse me Doctor, may I ask a question?"

"Sure." Gabriel's dour look didn't change.

"Nothing is useful. Is that what you're saying? Everything is lost?"

"Everything we've sampled is useless. Unless we have much better luck tomorrow, we're going to have to think about abandoning our work. If Turkey wants us to, we can remove the contents and close the cave, but there's nothing to study."

"I'm so sorry," Maria said. "I know this is a big disappointment for you."

"Yeah. At the same time, I'm kind of relieved. We've been uncomfortable with this project from the start. It'll be good to get it over with and get on to something less potentially controversial. Right now, our best hope for anything like success is in the Cave Church work. Valerie can continue that without me. I'm tired and ready to go home."

"If there's nothing else, thank you everyone. Let's go get cleaned up and get some food and rest."

The group began to disperse and head toward the parking lot where a couple of vans waited. Maria hurried from the conference room and stepped into the women's restroom. Closing the stall door, she pulled her phone from her pocket and turned off the record feature. She thumbed a few commands and sent the recording via text to Reynolds-Smythe with the message, "Straight from Gabriel's mouth."

Aurélio and several of his men milled about in the Visitors' Center lobby. He heard in his earphone, "Text gone to Jack. His reply is: 'good work. Report tomorrow'." Aurélio said to his men, "Okay, lads. Let's nab her."

At about the same time, Maria entered the lobby from the restroom. "Maria," Aurélio said, "come with us please." Two men walked up to her and each took an arm. Aurélio walked over to her and removed the phone from her pocket and quickly frisked her.

"What the hell's going on?" Maria demanded.

"Well, sweetie, we're taking you to a secure location so we can keep you from communicating with Jack. Plus we have a few questions to ask."

"Jack? Jack who? I don't know what you're talking about!"

"Can it, Maria. We know you're a spy for The Enlightened Ones. Unless you cooperate with us, you have likely forfeited you right to enjoy the rest of your life."

"Who the hell are The Enlightened Ones? What are you talking about?" she demanded.

"Enough games. Lads, get her in the van and let's go." Once they were standing outside the van, Maria was handcuffed and roughly pushed inside the van with a guard on each side of her. "I'll be along shortly, men. Get her secured, and don't mistreat her...much." He laughed. Of course his men had no intention of doing her bodily harm, but she didn't know that, and didn't need to. It was time to begin to control her and vague threats were one of the tools of that effort. Aurélio closed the van door and slapped the roof. "Off you go."

Maria shouted from the van, "You're making a bad mistake! You'll regret this! You have no authority to detain me!" At that point, one of the guards reached under the seat and removed a roll of wide tape. He pulled a strip off, and even as Maria struggled and continued to shout, he taped her mouth shut. "Finally, a little peace," he said, as Maria fell silent and quit struggling, yielding to the inevitable.

Aurélio called Gabriel. "We've got her. We'll begin the questioning in a few minutes. I have an expert interrogator at our local headquarters who'll do the honors."

"Good. I feel safer already."

"We're going to find out what we can about Sergei, but I think we may have a lead without her. One of the men saw the same guy two days in a row hanging about. At one point, he's sure the bugger was using binoculars to surveil the site. I've given orders to intercept him if he shows again. He may not be alone, but if we can cut off the head, the rest is pretty easy."

"That's good news, Sal. You and your men are top notch. Thanks for your dedication."

"We hate bad guys, Gabby. Especially these bad guys. Listen, I don't mean to pry, but you mentioned you'd found something important in the cave. Can you give me a hint?"

"At this point, it's still very premature, but you've earned an inside look. Let me just say it has something to do with St. Paul."

"Really? I expected something relating to Peter given the Cave Church's name, but not Paul."

"Oh, I'm expecting something about him, too. This could be really significant, Sal. If the other samples we take tomorrow are as promising as today's we'll be years sorting it all out and understanding the impact on Christianity."

"Wow. Sounds like something really special."

"I think it may rank with Mary's codex. Probably even more important."

67

TURKEY

THE ORDER OF CHRIST TEMPORARY HEADQUARTERS

"M"s. Teke, my name is Samuel," said her OOC interrogator, "May I call you Maria?"

Maria didn't respond.

"I take it you have no objection. Good. Maria, here's what we know. We know about Jack and we know about Sergei. We'll soon have him in custody, too, by the way. We know you were sent to Gabriel's project to disrupt it, and that you are to do so on behalf of The Enlightened Ones. We can read and listen to communication you have with Jack and Sergei, so you have no real secrets from us. Clear so far?"

Maria's face turned pale as he spoke, but still she said nothing.

"Your cooperation will save us some time and save you a lot of future difficulty. You're in a lot of trouble legally, but that's actually the least of your concern. Just as TEO operates outside the law, the organization for which I work does as well. Like TEO we can just 'disappear' people. Or, we can help you reestablish yourself with a new identity so TEO and the law can't get to you. To receive our help, we want some information about TEO and Jack. We know they are in England and in the London area. It is only a matter of a day or so before we know exactly where. Save us that time by telling us, and we'll help you."

Samuel grew quiet. He took a drink from the coffee cup in front of him and sat back in his chair. Maria tried to avoid showing how frightened she was, but she had been unprepared for what she'd been hearing. Small beads of perspiration began to form on her face, and she involuntarily began to rub her hands together. As soon as she was aware of the movement, she stopped, but she couldn't keep the sweat from forming.

"I'm afraid I can't help. I'm just a small businesswoman who arranges tours for people who want to visit archeological sites. I don't..."

Samuel interrupted. "Maria, let me show you something." He pulled her cellphone from his pocket and placed it in front of her. "This is your phone. We can read the messages. What you don't know is this." He pulled the clone from his pocket and laid it beside her phone. "We cloned your phone a few days ago. We've been reading your texts and listening to your phone calls. Please don't try to lie to us about your real vocation."

Maria's eyes widened when she saw the phones. Then a tear formed in one. She began to blink to try to keep it from rolling down her cheek. The tactic didn't work.

"I don't know where Jack works from," she said, resigned to the situation.

"I don't believe you, but we'll come back to that. Tell us about Sergei. How many men does he have with him?"

"Ten, maybe fifteen. I don't know. We haven't discussed it." She was relaxing a little. "We try to keep information compartmentalized. He doesn't know exactly what I'm doing, and I don't know exactly what he's doing."

"But you know the general plan, right? Sergei plans to disrupt the dig. Yes? Maybe kill Gabriel and others?"

"That was the plan. But now that we know nothing was found, maybe not. I don't know."

"I see. I think you know more than you're saying, but it doesn't matter. We're minutes away from capturing Sergei anyway. We used your phone to lure him into a trap. He thinks you need to meet with him. He'll show up but instead of you, it will be us."

Maria was visibly disturbed by the news she was contributing to Sergei's capture. They had worked together for many years. She was quite fond of him. "How did you clone my phone? How did you even know to try?"

"Oh. We were able to hack into an email server at Elon Abbey. From there we were able to read an email from Jack that set everything else in motion. Cyber security just isn't what it used to be," Samuel said, folding his arms over his chest. "Now, let's try again. Where is Jack located?"

"How do I know you'll protect me?" Maria asked.

At that moment, Samuel knew he'd now find out everything he needed to know from her. He felt some contempt for her giving in so quickly. Apparently not every person associated with TEO was as committed to their group as members of the Order of Christ were to their mission.

✠

By midnight, a dozenTEO operativeshad been neutralized. Some were taken into custody; others resisted more vigorously and were taken to a makeshift morgue. All were refusing to talk to the Knights. They carried no identification and were silent even when it came to providing their names. There was no way to be confident that all of them assigned to the site had been taken. Once they had come under attack, they had destroyed their phones and radios, so those devices couldn't provide clues either.Aurélio believed they might have them all, but he couldn't be sure. Continued vigilance would need to be practiced, at least for the near term. Apparently the plan to have one of the attackers seem to be a terrorist hadn't materialized because nothing was found on any of them that would indicate terrorist connections.

Before Maria gave up the location of the TEO headquarters in England, Nigel had been able to trace it to a mansion on the fringes of Elon Abbey's property. Her admission was simply a confirmation. The principal result of that intelligence was that a task force of Order of Christ men was being assembled in England to plan an assault on the Abbey and the Mansion. The goal was to eliminate the Great Britain arm of TEO and to obtain critical information about the rest of the worldwide organization. That information would be used to take apart TEO.

Nigel's cyber team had been making headway on identifying where other groups of TEO might be located, but needed the material from Elon to nail down locations. The Order of Christ likely would be stretched thin in its attempt to engage TEO alone, but contacting local or national law enforcement would alert them to the OOC's existence. That could compromise their ability to achieve their overall mission.In the same way that TEO needed to stay in the shadows, so did OOC, but for different reasons.

With the information in hand, in an ideal scenario, all known headquarters would be hit virtually simultaneously. One goal was to secure records of membership that might be held at each location. At that point, contacts the OOC had in various national law enforcement agencies would be "leaked" the information with the expectation they would act upon it in their own way. While TEO might not be eliminated, this effort would surely cripple them for decades.

At least that was the hope.

The reality might be a little different. The plan was complex, ambitious, and comprehensive, and like all large scale plans of attack, as soon as it was launched, the plan was expected to fall apart. The so-called "fog of war" effect would develop and some measure of chaos would ensue. Should the timing of execution be off in some locales, word might be sent to other TEO groups who would then take extreme measures to protect themselves. Still, it was believed, at the end of the effort the world would know more about the insidious actions of TEO than it did at the beginning and thatwould result in society being safer and freer.

Again, at least that was the hope.

James Desterro, the Grand Master of the OOC, was worried as he considered what was about to come to pass. The group had to move fast before Jack, whoever he was, knew his two agents had been compromised. Even though concerned, he had great faith in his brothers. He was also a bit amused that something with such far-reaching possibilities started with an email and phone call to the archeologist Gabriel. If this wasn't an example of the Butterfly Effect, he didn't know what would be.

68

THE MONASTERY CAVE

THE PREVIOUS DAY

After working for most of the morning, the team had learned that for the most part, the sampled wax tablets were in condition adequate for study. On some, large areas of wax had dried and pulled away from the underlying wood substrate. The wax was brittle, in some cases curled, and in a few cases useless. But on most the experts could see clear impressions in the wax. They had expected a kind of shorthand, since that was what previous research tended to point toward. Indeed, that's what they found. But some words and phrases were more easily read.

The jars that were opened yielded both rolls of documents tied with now brittle leather thongs, as well as leather codices of various sizes. The documents themselves seemed to be parchments, probably sheep or goatskins. No rolls of documents had been unrolled because of their potentially unstable condition. They felt quite brittle to the touch, as did the leather covers of the codices. Several codices had been carefully opened and the experts were pleased to find that the ink was very readable. These were not written in shorthand, but in Koine, or common first century Greek. Different hands were clearly apparent, but a preliminary examination of the letter styles pointed to what was common in the first and early second century.

The distribution of work that had been decided on was to have Gabriel and two experts carefully look at tablets and open jars and then pass the best to the third expert for a more detailed review. They were sampling at the far end of the cave, toward the middle, and at the end of the shelves nearest the cave opening. By the end of the day, all were agreed they had made a major find of ancient documents even though careful study and translation really hadn't begun. What they had found that caused the most excitement was in some of the codices farthest from the cave entrance and late in the day.

Gabriel had pulled a codex from a jar and carefully opened the brittle cover. The first few words stunned him. They read *PÁVLOSSILVANUSKAIEÍDOSCHÓRTOU*. As was common in Greek, there were no breaks between words, no punctuation, and no paragraphs—just what seemed to be one very long run-on sentence. Gabriel recognized the first six letters as the name Paul and the next eight as the name Silvanus. He was initially stumped about the remainder, but after reflection realized together the letters would be translated in English as Timothy. He read no further, but quickly took the codex to the third expert, Dr. Jim Buttross from Vanderbilt.

"Jim, take a look at this. I'm afraid to tell you what I think it is."

"Okey dokey." Buttross removed the tablet he had under his magnifier and replaced it with the codex. "Let's see. Hmm. Okay. Sure. It reads Paul, Silvanus, and Timothy. Oh, wow!"

"Yeah, that's what I thought, too. What else do you see?"

Buttross moved the magnifier a bit to get a better image. "Oh my God," he said. "It says, *Paul, Silvanus, and Timothy, to the faithful in Thessalonica, in the name of God the Father and the Lord Jesus Christ: Grace to you and peace.* Gabby, that's a typical Pauline greeting in his letters. It looks very much like the opening to what we know as 1 Thessalonians. Second Thessalonians is very much the same, except it reads 'Grace to you and peace from God our Father and the Lord Jesus Christ'. So I'm pretty sure this is the former. Plus, 2 Thessalonians isn't generally thought to have been written by Paul." Buttross moved the magnifier again. "Let me read a little more."

The scholar was quiet for a minute or two. He adjusted the codex page under the magnifier, read more, then raised his head. "Gabby, the rest of the page reads very much like Paul's first letter to Thessalonica! We'll need to do C14 testing on the material and ink, but I'd bet important parts of my body this is a very early copy. I can't wait to see what else we have! This is incredible!"

"Oh, man! This is fabulous," Gabriel exclaimed. "Hey, guys," he said to the others in the cave, "come look at what we've found!"

The men joined Gabriel and Buttross. Buttross told them what he thought, and invited them to take a look. Both men did, and quickly and enthusiastically agreed with his assessment. "Makes you wonder what else we have. This entire find could be priceless," said Dr. Garry James of Yale.

"With Antioch having the reputation it had in the first century, I could see them becoming an archive for early Christian writing." Gabriel head slapped himself. "Oh my God! What if we have all of Paul's correspondence, not just the few letters we have in the New Testament? For example, what if we have the letters to the Corinthians Paul mentions that we don't have copies of? Can you imagine what this could do? It would rewrite major portions of the New Testament!"

The excitement among the men was bordering on exuberance. That's when Gabriel had to tell them the bad news. After sharing the information he'd gotten from Aurélio, he told them it was imperative that they act as if they'd found nothing of importance.

"Gabby, I'm not sure I can do that. I'm so excited I'm about to pee myself," Buttross said giggling.

"Yeah, Gabby. We're scholars, not actors," James said.

"Guys, lives literally depend on it. We can celebrate later. For now, we have to look sad."

✠

THE CAVE
THE NEXT DAY

With the threat now reduced, the team was eager to continue their work. Two other scholars had arrived and had been set up in the warehouse with more sophisticated tools and equipment. The first item they were given was the codex Gabriel had discovered the previous day. Everybody was in place before sunrise.

Gabriel and the scholars had agreed that today would be another sampling day, but after today, everything needed to be moved to the warehouse. Nicki had been asked to develop a plan that would offer the best security during the move and in the warehouse. She and Trevor had discussed it the previous evening and had agreed on how to proceed. For today, Trevor would join Gabriel and the others in the cave and Nicki would oversee the move.

Aurélio was overseeing the installation of state of the art security measures at the warehouse, using the latest electronic equipment to protect it. The warehouse already had an extensive sprinkler system, but he was investigating replacing it with an inert gas fire suppression system. The gas wouldn't damage the delicate materials like water would should the system be activated. It could be installed later. His second in command, Sean "Pug" McDonald, was developing the most effective way to provide twenty-four/seven armed guards as an added layer of protection.

Gabriel was finally beginning to stop worrying and allow his excitement and intellectual curiosity have free rein over the project. He was also trying to not completely ignore what Valerie was doing at the Cave Church project. At lunchtime, he excused himself from the monastery cave and visited her.

"Hey, Valerie, how's it going today?"

"Oh, hey Gabby. We uncovered a large stone slab this morning and we're about to lift it. You're timing couldn't be better."

"Great! Can I help in any way?"

"I think we've got it under control. We've managed to lever up the lid enough to allow us to slip lifting bars under it. As soon as the straps are attached, we are lifting it and swinging it out of the way.

Well, we also have to wait for the NatGeo crew to get the lighting they need set up. They want to be able to light the interior as soon as the lid is moved."

"Valerie," the NatGeo crew chief yelled, "we're ready anytime you are."

Valerie signaled the lift operator and he began to take up the slack in the straps. In a moment the contents would be visible.

✠

TEO HEADQUARTERS IN ENGLAND

"Lance, something's wrong. I can't raise Sergei on the phone," Reynolds-Smythe said to his cyber expert. "Look into it, please."

"How about Maria?" Lance replied. "Have you tried her?"

"Not recently. Let me send her a text."

"Hold up on that. Let me ping Sergei's phone. Do other team members have phones as well?"

"Only the number two guy."

"Have you tried him?"

"Yes. No response."

"I'll ping his phone as well. Let me have the number."

Lance called up the program he needed and entered a command to locate Sergei's phone. After waiting a moment, he tried the other phone.

"Jack, they are both off."

"They are never supposed to be off."

"Let me ping Maria's phone." Lance repeated the process he'd just used. "It's on and is showing up near the Cave Church. Go ahead and call her."

Reynolds-Smythe punched in her number. The phone rang a few times and then a message played that the voice mailbox had not been set up.

"That's standard, Jack. She'd have voice mail on her personal phone, but not on this one. Shoot her a text."

Reynolds-Smythe typed in "Call me ASAP" and hit send. In a moment a small message appeared that verified the text had been delivered to her phone. "Okay, now we wait until she can reply without someone seeing her. Usually only takes a few minutes."

✠

Back at the OOC headquarters in England, one of Nigel's men alerted him to a text that had been intercepted from "Jack".

"He wants Maria to call him immediately, Nigel."

"I'm guessing Aurélio has her under control. Let him know I think we should allow her to make the call to keep Jack from becoming suspicious."

"On it."

✠

In Turkey, Aurélio received the message from Nigel. He'd already decided to let her call.

"Okay, Maria. Jack wants you to call. Probably wants an update. Call him and let him know everything is going well. If he asks about Sergei, just tell him you haven't been in touch, but you'll keep trying. Got it."

Maria's face was gray. She was not happy to be in this compromised situation. She had to unclench her jaw to reply, "Yes."

"No funny business, Maria. Your future depends on your cooperation with us."

"I understand."

"Okay then. Call him."

Maria picked up the phone and entered Jack's number. He answered on the first ring.

"Maria, what's going on there? Sergei's phone is off and, by the way, why the hell has yours been off?"

Maria glanced at Aurélio. She screamed into the phone. "They know, Jack! Sergei is..." Aurélio slapped the phone away from her hand. It clattered to the floor and the screen cracked.

"That was stupid, Maria. Turning to one of his men he said, 'Take her back to her cell.'"

Orion had been watching the entire episode. "You knew it was a risk, Sal. You had to give it a shot."

"I've got to call James. The on the assault on the Abbey can't wait."

Aurélio pulled his cellphone from his pocket and made the call. After telling Desterro what had happened, he heard his Grand Master say, "It was worth the risk, Sal. You could have bought us more time. We're ready to hit the Abbey even if we can't hit the other locations we've found simultaneously. I've got to go. Hold the fort there. I don't think your situation is entirely safe."

After they disconnected, Orion said to Aurélio, "Wonder what he meant by that?"

"Paddy, these guys are tricky bastards. We just have to stay on high alert instead of believing we have the situation under control. I better let the lads know."

✠

ENGLAND

Reynolds-Smythe knew they were in trouble. He called the Abbot at Elon Abbey. "Father, the worst has happened. Begin the protocol for a major breech. You need to appear as nothing more than an isolated religious institution as quickly as you can."

"I'll start the process immediately, Jack. Can you tell me what happened?"

"Gabriel and his merry little band of minions have outsmarted us for now. Get to it, Father."

Reynolds-Smythe disconnected. He turned to Lance. "Start the wipe now, Lance. As soon as you know everything is set, we've got to all get the hell out of here."

"I'll tell the lads, Jack. We'll be okay. We've been planning for a moment like this for years."

"Yes. Well let's hope our plan works the way we envisioned."

But what plan does?

69

THE CAVE CHURCH NAVE

Without knowing all the drama taking place around them, Valerie's team continued their work at the altar site. With the stone lid removed, they were able to see inside for the first time. The stone enclosure was about eighteen or so inches deep, just enough for a body. NatGeo's lighting clearly illuminated a form lying inside a space created by lining a hole with cut stones forming the sidewalls of a tomb. The form was roughly the shape of a human lying prone wrapped in cloth. The cloth was discolored from time and leakage of bodily fluids and had collapsed in on itself. The arms of the corpse had been placed beside the body and a narrow strip of cloth held them close at about the level of the wrists. Another was tied around the feet. A third was tied over a piece of what appeared to be linen that was placed on the head. That strip of cloth stretched from the top of the head to under the chin where it was tied.

"Looks exactly like a first century Jewish burial," Valerie said to the team. "Notice that there are no grave goods. That would be expected for a Christian burial. This has all the marks of a first century Christian who was also a Jew. Exactly what we would expect Peter's wife to be. I suspect the cloth is just covering bones now."

"Hey Valerie, look at the right side of the body. There's something lying next to it," said Nia.

"Yeah, I see it. Is that wood or stone; can't really tell? Let me see if I can retrieve it."

With gloved hands, and lying on her stomach, Valerie reached for the object, which was about a foot long on the side facing her. She was able to lift it, but was surprised at its weight. Once the object was clear of the tomb, it was apparent it was stone or perhaps fired clay. She laid it carefully on the floor of the nave.

"Looks like a clay tablet," Vlad offered. "Is that Greek?" Vlad was referring to incised letters in the clay tablet.

"Looks like it," Valerie replied. "I think I can read it."

She read it to herself, and then turned to Vlad. "Please go find Nicki and Gabby. They need to see this."

"Why?" asked Nia. "What does it say?"

"Let's wait for them Vlad Okay?"

"Yes. Sure. I'm on my way."

Ten minutes later Gabriel showed up with Vlad. "This better be good," he said with a big smile. "You just tore me away from our honey hole."

"Where's Nicki? I want her to hear this, too."

"She's at the warehouse. Let me call her." Gabriel quickly connected with Nicki and said, "Hey, honey. Valerie has found something important in the tomb. I'm gonna put you on speaker."

"Hey, Nicki," Valerie said. "Gabby said this better be good. If my first century Greek is any good, I think it is. Let me read it out loud."

"Gabby, check me on this. Here goes," Valerie said.

Sara, wife of Peter, chosen by our Lord Jesus to lead the followers of The Way in Antioch, bishop and priest, awaits the final Resurrection.

"Wadda you think, Gabby? Is that right?" she asked.

"I want to run it by one of our specialists, but I can't quibble with your translation, except to say 'bishop' could be translated as 'overseer'. Might be too early for *epískopos* to be translated as bishop, though it definitely was by the early second century. I think,"

Gabriel answered. "But for certain, this confirms what we saw in the mosaic."

"Wow!" Nia said, "a woman bishop in the first century! Just like the mosaic said."

"Well female priest for sure," Valerie said.

"We can nit-pick the niceties here, but there's no disputing she was an elder and overseer," said Nicki. "For all practical purposes, she functioned as a priest and bishop just as the mosaic indicated."

"And," Valerie added with a smile, "in one of the most important centers of Christianity in the world. I would love to know what it took to cover this up. And what in the Lord's name is the Church gonna do with this fact?"

Nicki replied, "Excellent questions, Valerie. Excellent questions."

Gabriel and Valerie made plans to move the tablet and the bones to the more secure warehouse. Gabriel concluded, "We need to get this done ASAP, Valerie. For some reason, I still don't feel completely safe."

Vlad and Nia were instructed once again to say nothing to anyone. Other laborers were far enough away to know something important had been found, but not what it was. The circle in the know was small.

For now.

70

NEAR THE CAVE CHURCH

Sergei had survived the Order of Christ's actions that took out all his men. When he saw what was happening, he withdrew, leaving his men to fend for themselves. In the melee, he'd lost his phone and his Glock, but saw that as a small price to pay for surviving. Over the past hours he'd been able to secure a replacement Glock as well as a Heckler & Koch MP5K from the cache he'd developed in anticipation of an attack. The MP5 is compact and deadly with its automatic fire and thirty round clip. What he needed now was a new phone and a disguise of some sort.

He'd taken care of the disguise easily. A few US dollars bought him clothes off the back of a beggar he'd encountered. A few more dollars and he had a new iPhone. He had to admit he probably should have gotten the phone before donning the disguise since the clerk at the phone store almost threw him out before he flashed his roll of bills. As soon as he had privacy, he called Reynolds-Smythe, but this time he didn't use the cellphone number he and Maria had been using. He called the landline Reynolds-Smythe's operation used.

"Sergei, I thought you were dead or captured," Jack said as soon as Sergei identified himself.

"Everyone else was either taken prisoner or killed. I withdrew when I saw how it was going. I wanted to live to fight another day. Maria was captured. Don't trust anything she says if she contacts you."

"Yes, I know. Sergei, who were these men who attacked you?"

"I don't know, Jack. They were mercenaries I suppose. We'd seen them on site almost since the beginning. But no uniforms or any obvious thing that would identify them. Jack, I've been in disguise as a beggar since this morning, and I've been close enough to the site to learn some major discoveries appear to have been made."

"Sergei, I know you're there alone, but our operation here is compromised and I don't think I can get you help. We're in the process of closing up shop. Is there anything you can do? Can you take them out or destroy whatever they've found?"

"I may be able to, Jack. I've got a contact here that may be able to supply explosives. Otherwise, I'm prepared to go in shooting and do whatever damage I can."

"If nothing else, Sergei, Molotov cocktails will work."

"I can make those easily."

"Do what you can, my friend, and as soon as you can. When all this is over, we'll reorganize. Call me everyday. Continue doing it even if I don't answer for a few days. You understand?"

"If you don't hear from me, Jack, know I died fighting for our cause. Goodbye, Jack."

AT THE MONASTERY CAVE

The survey work in the cave was continuing. Most intriguing were some of the wax tablets that Gabriel checked. While the "shorthand" hadn't yet been deciphered, a few words and phrases did seem to pop out. Several proper names had been found on one: Stephanas, Fortunatus, Achaicus, and the most revealing, Aquila and Prisca. When Gabriel noticed those two names he called Jim Buttross over.

"Jim, didn't Paul have a tendency to greet people by name at the end of his letters?"

"Yes. Why?"

"What letter contains the names Aquila and Prisca?"

"Hmm. First Corinthians, maybe Romans, yeah Romans. They're mentioned in 1 Timothy, too, but most don't think he wrote Timothy."

"Okay, here's the tough one: what letter contains their names and Fortunatus?"

"I'll bite. Which one?"

"I think it's 1 Corinthians."

"Sounds right. Why?"

"Look." Gabriel pointed out the proper names that popped out on the tablet he was checking. "I think this could be the draft of that letter."

"Oh, my God, Gabby! Don't tell me we've not only got possible drafts of the gospels in here, but Paul's letters, too!"

"We've got to get someone working on deciphering this stuff to be certain, but yeah, I think we found the mother lode of first century writing. We've just pushed New Testament studies back to original documents or something damn close."

"Gabby, if you're right and the rest of this material is like this, what we have here is going to revolutionize our study of the New Testament! I can imagine Antioch collecting stories from travelers from Jerusalem and Galilee and the surrounding areas and storing them here. When Mark and Matthew were here, they could have used that material to flesh out what they knew. Gabby, this could be the biggest thing to hit Christianity in millennia!"

With significant reluctance Gabby and the scholars emerged from the cave to eat a late lunch. He called Nicki to catch her up and her reaction was exuberance.

"And to think I didn't want you to do this project!" she said. "My Lord, what a loss it would have been."

"I know we're way ahead of ourselves on some of this, but the evidence is so strong so far. But, Nicki, we're over our heads now. We need to start thinking of how to enlarge the team and spread out the work to be done on our find."

"I agree. Let's put our heads together with the scholars tonight and start developing a plan. I'm so excited. It's like the Mary Codex to the fourth power."

71

AT THE MONASTERY CAVE

THAT EVENING

Sergei had a successful day. His local contact had come through with several pounds of C4, or plastic explosives. The amount was more than enough to blow a crater where the cave was, destroying anything in it several times over. He had several blasting caps and a burner phone. The phone would need to be placed just outside the mouth of the cave so it could receive a signal. It would bewired to fusing that connected bits of C4 he planned to place throughout the cave. Finally, he had four hand grenades. His plan now was to situate all the explosives and immediately blast the cave. When Gabriel and his crew were called to the site, he'd take them out with his Heckler & Koch and grenades. All that remained was the problem of getting past the guards around the cave opening.

For that, he'd enlisted a helper, a local insurgent who hated anything Turkish. Sergei had told him how important the Cave Church was to Turkey's place in the world and the terrorist, Oman, was ready to do anything to hurt the Turkish establishment. Now, with darkness to provide them cover, the two men were huddled about a hundred yards from the Cave Church.

"Oman," Sergei instructed,"you must be as invisible as possible and make your way up to the church entrance. There are two guards outside the door, so you must flit from shadow to shadow. I wish we didn't have a full moon, but we do. So be very careful. When you're close enough, throw these two grenades into the church doorway. Then run like hell."

"Okay. This I do. What you do?" Oman replied in his limited English.

"I expect the cave guards to come running toward the explosion. When they do, I will run like hell to the cave to do my work there. If I work quickly enough I can get out of the cave before they return. I have all my charges wired to this phone. I just have to have a two minutes or less to place them and get out of the cave."

"Okay."

"Good luck, my new friend."

Oman grunted something in Turkish that Sergei didn't get, and the two men separated. Sergei was now about forty yards from the cave entrance, squatting behind a bush. He could see the cave entrance, but not the church. It didn't matter. In a few minutes the grenades would explode and he'd begin his sprint. He didn't have to see it to know the interior of the church would be peppered and pock marked with shrapnel.

With that thought, the first grenade exploded, the flash briefly lighting the surrounding area. Then the second. Sergei saw the two guards outside the cave speak to each other then set off at a trot for the church. That was his cue. He grabbed his satchel and sprinted toward the cave entrance, plunging into it on his belly. At the same moment, he heard automatic fire and yelling. Oman may not have run like hell as he was instructed. Too bad, but he did his job.

The TEO operative needed a moment to recover, and in that moment he realized he didn't have a light. He couldn't see anything. He began to curse, then brought himself up sharply. His new iPhone. It had a flashlight app. He fumbled for the phone and pressed the Home button twice. The home screen shone and he swiped up from the bottom. There he saw the flashlight icon and touched it. He had all the light he needed.

Sergei opened his satchel and pulled out his C4. He looked around for a rock and finding one, carefully laid the fuse on the cave floor anchoring it with the rock. He then began to play out the fuses and their charges as he made his way deeper into the cave. The charges were wired in parallel so all the C4 would be ignited at once. He found the turn and followed it, soon seeing row on row of jars and stacks of something on the wall opposite. He didn't go far; he didn't need to. He laid the last charge and headed back toward the entrance.

Shielding the light from the iPhone to keep it from being seen outside the cave, he quickly connected the fuse to the small strips of wire he'd previously wired into the burner phone. When he called the burner, the battery would send a charge down the fuse to the charges and he would blow the roof off the cave—literally. He turned off his phone to kill the light. Finally, he gathered up the burner phone and crept toward the cave opening. He had been hearing shouts while he worked; now he heard the first sirens of emergency vehicles.

A quick glance was all it took for him to determine the guards had not returned. Crouching low, he sprinted away from the cave, congratulating himself on his success. When he was safely hidden behind a low wall some eighty yards from the cave, he rested. *I probably should blow it now,* he thought, *and get it over with. But the guards are probably going to call Gabriel. He and the others will come running and they'll check the cave as an added precaution. I can take them and the cave out at the same time. Anyone I miss, I can shoot.* Sergei continued to weigh pros and cons for the next ten minutes. He made his decision.

✠

The guards had hurried to the Cave Church. The fretwork windows on either side of the entrance were heavily damaged. The doors had been blown open with the first grenade and the second detonated inside. They were waiting for the smoke to clear before entering. Pug, Aurélio's second in command, called Aurélio, who called Gabriel. Gabriel roused the team and they all headed to the site just as Sergei had expected they would.

"All I know is there were two explosions at the Cave Church just minutes ago," Gabriel told everyone as they drove. Sal will know more when we get there. Thank God we got Sara moved before you shut down for the day."

"I know. Providence," Valerie suggested and crossed herself. "God wants this information made public."

"I don't know about God," Gabriel said, "but I sure as hell want it made public."

The van slid to a stop in the Visitors' Center parking lot. Aurélio was waiting.

"We've been inside. Other than damage to the floor, you'll never notice the shrapnel marks on the walls. They're already rough. What I can't figure out is why anyone would want to blow it up."

"I guess it's safe to go inside?" Gabriel asked.

"Yeah, c'mon."

Gabriel, Nicki, Valerie and Trevor followed Aurélio inside. Valerie immediately ran toward the area where the pieces of the altar and platform sections had been laid out. After a quick inspection, she said, "I don't see any damage. That's a relief."

"Oh, Gabby, by the way, I alerted Dr. Tabak. He's on his way, too."

"Good. I should have thought of that, but, you know, not as sharp as I once was."

"You're fine, friend. Quit disparaging your abilities," Aurélio said.

"Sal," Nicki asked, "if there's no obvious reason to blow up this place, what are some of the far out reasons?"

"I asked myself that. A distraction is the only thing I can come up with," he replied.

"For what purpose?" Trevor asked.

"Well, let me tell you what happened when the grenades went off. All my men came running. They saw a figure running away and fired but by then he was too far for a good shot."

"That's it!" Valerie said. "The guards from the cave came running too, didn't they?"

"You're right! Stay here, everybody, I'm going to the cave," Aurélio ordered.

72

AT THE MONASTERY CAVE

Hell with that! I'm going, too," Gabriel countered.

"No! Gabby, it could be a trap of some kind. Stay here!"

Nicki joined Aurélio. "Gabby, do as Sal says. Let him check it out, then you can go."

"Damn it! Alright, Sal, take off."

Aurélio trotted from the nave and called out to two of his men to follow him. The three of them headed toward the cave entrance. From his hiding space, Sergei watched. It was clear these weren't the archeologists. He had a decision to make. Should he blow the cave when they got there or risk them finding the detonator? He decided to blow it when they arrived, and then when the others came to see what had happened he'd use his Heckler & Koch on them. He smiled a satisfied smile and kept watching.

Ten yards from the cave, Aurélio raised his hand and he and his men stopped. "If this is a trap, we need to be very careful to not get caught in it. You men wait here. I'm going to get closer." To one of the men he said, "Give me your torch. I'm going to inch my way forward and take a closer look."

"Sal, watch out for trip wires."

"Will do."

Aurélio moved forward very slowly in a crouch. He played the flashlight's beam back and forth on the ground in front of him and then aimed it toward the cave entrance. He saw a flash that disappeared as he moved the light. He swung the light back to the same spot. Another flash. *It's a reflection,* he thought. *But off of what?*

Aurélio checked the ground around him for something he could toss toward the reflection. He picked up a small stone, shone his light back to the cave entrance, and heaved he stone. He heard a clatter, and the reflection disappeared. He took another step forward, then yelled to his men, "Get back! Run! Now!" and as he said the words, he began to run away from the cave. "It's a phone!"

Sergei saw his prey move to safety. In his frustration at their escape he thumbed in the number for the detonator. Nothing happened. Then the cave erupted with a thunderous explosion. The ground over the cave heaved up a foot or more. Smoke, rocks and dirt were raining down from ruptures in the ground over the cave, and the blow back from the cave entrance sent debris twenty yards before settling to earth. The shock wave from the explosion hit Aurélio and his men, knocking them to the ground. The cave and its contents were gone.

As Sergei had hoped, the other guards came running from their stations and most important, Gabriel's crew came running from the Cave Church. Sure it was his target this time, Sergei stood and pointed the machine gun at the figures running toward the gaping wounds in the earth. He squeezed the trigger with the rate of fire set at fully automatic. Running bodies were soon falling to the ground. When the gun stopped, he pulled out the empty clip and was shoving another into the breech of the weapon, when he grunted, dropped the clip and pitched forward over the wall behind which he had been standing.

Aurélio slowly stood from where he'd fallen. As he looked around, he heard moans and the sounds of a few people slowing trying to rise, but amidst all that he saw one figure fully upright holding a rifle. It was Valerie.

"Valerie!" he shouted. "Valerie!"She lowered the rifle. "What the hell?" Aurélio asked.

"I saw him and just grabbed the rifle one of your men dropped when he was shot."

"One shot?" Aurélio asked, unbelieving.

"I was on my high school and college rifle teams," she said, and then slumped to her knees. "I think I'm hit, Sal."

By then a few others had recovered and began to check the figures still lying on the ground. Aurélio sent one man to check on the condition of the man slumped over the wall, and he ran to Valerie. Nicki and Gabriel were already there. "Let me see," Aurélio said, gently moving them aside. Blood bloomed on Valerie's outer thigh on her left leg. He laid Valerie down, and looked at her leg. Inserting his fingers into the hole in her pants, he torethe cloth to better see the wound. After a quick look, he said, "It's a through and through, Valerie, in the fleshy part of your leg. You're going to be fine." He pulled his shirt off over his head, and pressed it on the wound. "Sit up, Val, and put your hand here and press. You're going to be fine. You're a blessed woman. Wow! What a shot!"

Valerie smiled, her eyes rolled back and she slipped backward to the ground. "She's passed out. Nicki, hold this on her leg. I hear sirens. Someone'll be here soon, but she's gonna be fine." He stood and began to take stock of his men, checking on the wounded. Several were serious, but none were dead.

Gabriel walked slowly toward the smoking rubble that was the cave entrance. Tears were flowing. He was feeling devastated and couldn't fully grasp what had happened. The find was so promising, and now they would be lucky to find anything at all among the wreckage that must be inside the cave.

Valerie regained consciousness as Trevor took over for Nicki. Nicki jogged quickly to where Gabriel was standing and slipped her arm around his waist. She said nothing, but pulled him tight. She was feeling the loss as keenly as he was, perhaps more, because she knew how excited he was and how significant he thought the find to be.

"I wonder if it's worth it to try to excavate. Maybe we would luck out and find some materials undamaged," he said.

"Honey, if you want to do that, I'm with you all the way."

The pair turned and made their way back to the others. First responders had arrived and EMTs were rushing to Valerie and the other wounded. After he saw to his men, Aurélio walked to where Sergei lay slumped over the low wall. He quickly searched him without expecting to find anything important. He found only the cellphone Sergei had used to call the burner phone detonator. He checked the call log and saw a call to England. He recognized the number as belonging to Jack.

Aurélio sent a text. "Got him and got you, too."

✠

ENGLAND

TEO HEADQUARTERS

Reynolds-Smythe heard his phone ping. It was a text message. *Got him and got you, too.* He knew immediately that Sergei was out of the picture. He had just begun the steps he needed to take to sanitize his operation when he heard the explosion. His office door flew opened, the jamb and lock shattered. "On the ground! Now!" The armed figures that burst into his office ran toward him and forced him to the ground. "The sign on your doors says you are Jack Reynolds-Smythe. So Jack, consider yourself 'detained'." He was turned on his stomach and handcuffs slapped on his wrists.

"Am I under arrest? And if so, on what charge?" he asked.

"Jack, you are not under arrest. We're not law enforcement in the usual sense, so we don't arrest people. We 'detain' bad guys when needed, and it's never been more needed than now."

"You can't do this! This is outrageous!"

"Yeah, I know. But since you and your so-called Enlightened Ones operate outside the law, you shouldn't be surprised that other groups might as well. Jack, did you ever hear of the Knights Templar?"

"You can't be!"

"I'm not saying we are. Just taking a general knowledge survey to see what you know." His captor laughed. "Get him on his feet and get him out of here," the armed figure said to the other men who'd entered the office."We have some people who want to chat with him."

As Reynolds-Smythe was lifted to his feet, his captor said, "Oh, Jack. One more thing. We hacked your server at the Abbey a while back. We have law enforcement in several major countries raiding your regional headquarters as we speak. I hate to be the bearer of bad news, but the power you've used to screw over the world just took a serious hit. I'm pretty certain that all these government agencies are going to find out a lot about your operation and take, perhaps I can call it, 'corrective action'."

Reynolds-Smythe turned to look at his tormentor. "You have no idea the hornets' nest you just poked. You'll be surprised at how soon your whole operation gets stopped by people in high government positions."

"Maybe. But in the meanwhile we are going to take as much information from you as possible, and if mainstream law enforcement is shackled by your influence, there's always more of us to keep you from continuing your shit."

"We'll see."

"No, Jack. You won't see. Your life and your power trip as you've known it is over. You're going to disappear like a man named Jonathan Gulliver, whose conscience started this whole process in motion. He believed in something greater than repressivecontrol. He believed in truth and in freedom."

13

THE LIWAN HOTEL DINING ROOM

LATER IN THE DAY

he paramedics had taken all the wounded to the hospital. Several of Aurélio's men were wounded seriously enough to require surgery and a hospital stay. Valerie's wound was treated and, though she was encouraged to stay overnight, she elected to return to the hotel. Trevor was with her the entire time. On the drive from the hospital, Trevor said,

"I learn something new about you all the time. But you knocked my socks off with this. Wow'!"

"You know, Trevor, I didn't even think. I saw him shooting. I saw the guard next to me fall and drop his rifle and I just acted."

"You saved our lives. If he'd put another clip in that thing, we might all be dead."

"I'm still kinda shaky inside, if you want the truth. I've never shot at a live target before and I've never killed anyone. I had no idea I could do anything like that. I'm gonna need some time to process this."

"I'm here for you, Val. Forever, if you'll let me."

Valerie looked at him as he stared straight ahead, intent on his driving. "What are you saying?"

"I'm saying I love you and want to be with you forever."

"It's a deal, then," she said, touching his arm and smiling.

☩

That evening, Gabriel, Nicki, Orion, Valerie, Trevor, and the two students, Vlad and Nia gathered for dinner and attempt to process the day's events. Aurélio was still at the hospital with his men. Gabriel's rule about no business during dinner was impossible to reinforce under the day's circumstances. As they ate, Trevor told them about his and Valerie's conversation in the car. "So, uh, I think you can say we're engaged or something."

"Not 'something', Trevor," Valerie said, poking him on the shoulder. "We're engaged. Details to follow."

Congratulations were expressed all around, but then the mood turned somber again.

"Nicki and I talked some since this all happened. We've decided, or maybe I should say, we're considering excavating the cave. We may find nothing useful, but I've got to do it."

Valerie spoke, "We're in." She looked at Trevor and he nodded. "Yep. We're in."

"If we can help, we would very much like to," Vlad said and Nia nodded her agreement.

"That's great, guys. And Vlad and Nia, we'd love to have you," Nicki said.

Orion spoke for the first time, smiling, "You'll understand if I go home. My work there has a lot less drama, and I'm much more suited to it than archeology, which I have to say, I now see as a lot more exciting than I ever imagined."

Everyone laughed and offered their support for his decision and their appreciation for his involvement. Then Gabriel went on.

"As you probably know, we had moved maybe two dozen wax tablets and maybe fifteen or so jars to the warehouse. We're asking our ancient Greek experts to develop a plan for their preservation and study. They've agreed to do that with Jim Buttross as project lead. Valerie, Dr. Tabak has approved a forensic study here in Turkey on the remains from the tomb. We'd like for you to be involved on our behalf. If, in your opinion, they lack for equipment, get whatever they need as our gift."

"Wonderful, Gabby. I'd love to do that."

"No decision has been made about closing the tomb. Dr. Tabak said his people are discussing whether to reinter the bones there or put them on display. The same is true for the clay tablet you found with her, though their first thought is it should be on display somewhere. Nicki and I think we have two unfinished pieces of business in the nave, namely dealing with the two sealed openings we found. I think we should open them as we'd planned. In fact, I'd like to start that work tomorrow. Trevor, if you, Valerie and Vlad would take the tunnel Tabak pointed out to us the first day, Nicki, Nia and I will work on the one opposite it that we found."

Again, the group expressed concurrence with the plan. "We'll start the excavation of the cave as soon as we have the needed equipment and people on site. I'll take care of setting that up. We aren't waiting for armed protection. I don't think we'll need it. Let me read a text I received from Sal this afternoon. He forwarded one he'd gotten from his leader."

Gabriel pulled out his phone and read, *Operation successful. Neutralized them in six major countries. More work to do, but the world is free of their evil for now. Praise God.* Gabriel looked up and smiled.

"Amen," said Valerie, and crossed herself.

EPILOGUE

THE YEAR 110 C.E.

ANTIOCH

gnatius, the community's Bishop and president of the
Council, stood at the head of the table around which sat the
eleven men and women who comprised the Council of
Elders of the Antiochene Christians. "As you all know," Ignatius
said, "local authorities have been complaining to us about our
unwillingness to make annual sacrifices to the local so-called deities.
Their insistence that we make these sacrifices has grown ever since
the ground tremors of last week. They see those small quakes as a
warning to them from their gods. I fear they are going to move
against us soon.

"At the very least we must take action to protect the writings of
those who have told us of Jesus. I want to hollow out a section of our
nave wall and secrete these manuscripts the brethren have left to us.
It will not need to be a large area. With the help of David, our Scribe,
I have gathered the stories of Jesus left by Marnin and Matthaios, as
well as the various scraps of stories they used to piece together their
accounts. It will all fit within two clay jars. Our copies of these
writings will remain in the cave behind The House, but the original
writings will be in the niche.

"Once they are in the niche, we will seal the opening in such a
way as make it appear as the rough cave wall. We should also
complete our tunnel from the nave into the cave that adjoins The
House. Should they come for us while we are at worship, we can
escape through the tunnel and into the cave, then into the
countryside. I believe it is urgent we do these things."

There was no discussion. Assignments were made as to who
would oversee the creation of the concealed niche and who would see
to the tunnel's completion. The community's Scribe was given the
responsibility to care for the precious writings until the niche was
ready. The work began the very next day and moved quickly. Within

three days the niche was prepared and the scribe brought the manuscripts to the church and placed them in it. Artisans quickly worked the stone closure to blend with the cave wall. Only a close inspection would betray it as a hiding place.

✠

In the year 110 C.E., the local authorities arrested Ignatius. He demanded his right as a Roman citizen to be tried by the Emperor in Rome and was taken there and jailed. Sometime after his arrest, Ignatius was martyred in Rome as one of the earliest Christian victims of Imperial Rome.

A CLOSING NOTE
FROM THE AUTHOR

hank you for buying and reading my book. I hope you enjoyed *Saint Gabriel's Return*. As always, I have tried to weave actual history into the story. In this case:

1. There really is a Cave Church of St. Peter's in the area of Turkey that once belonged to Syria. My description of it is pretty historically accurate. The tunnel entrance and the concealed niche are my inventions, as are the "monastery" cave and the ruins of The House.

2. New Testament scholars are in general agreement that Matthew's Gospel was likely written in Syria. Recent scholarship, as I reported in the text, is inclined to believe Mark's Gospel may have been written there, too. Marnin and Matthaios are Greek for Mark and Matthew, but we don't actually know who wrote these two books of the Christian Bible.

3. The Order of Christ actually exists, is headquartered in Portugal and, as I explained in an earlier book, can loosely trace their roots back to the Knights Templar. What the OOC actually does today has nothing to do with the mission I created for them.

4. My comments about Antioch as the "hotbed" of early Jesus followers are historically accurate. The writer of Acts says they were first called Christians in Antioch. Paul and Peter really did spend time there, and they really did have their disagreement about what was required of non-Jewish converts. Both Paul and the book of Acts describe their disagreement, though the two sources don't report it the same way. For one thing, each reports a different outcome. History indicates that Paul actually carried the day.

5. Bishop Ignatius of Antioch really was martyred in Rome in 110 C.E. He might well have worshipped in the Cave Church, since tradition says it was a meeting place for Christians from the first century onward.

6. There really is a lot of evidence for believing women were priests in the Early Church and very likely for several centuries afterwards. Scholars tend to think that the role of women in Church leadership was diminished when Christianity became less a peasant-based religion as more wealthy people became converts. This change is thought to have speeded up after the Peace of the Church in 313 promulgated by Emperor Constantine.Here's just one example among many: The Louvre has the mummy tag of an Egyptian woman named Artemidora. She was aChristian who livedsomewhere between 250 and 350 AD. The tag describes her as a "presbyter". As the novel says, this is the word usually translated as priest.

7. A 7.5 magnitude earthquake hit Antioch in 115 C.E. There was widespread devastation and great loss of life. A small tremor in 110 could have been entirely possible.Folks at the time, often saw such natural phenomenon as a sign of the various gods' displeasure. Emperor Trajan and his successor, Hadrian, happened to be in Antioch when it happened. They were only slightly injured.

On the completely fabricated front: The Enlightened Ones are just a rip off of the mythical Illuminati. Conspiracy theorists are convinced the Illuminati are real and are evil, and what's more are shaping a New World Order. I don't buy it, but it makes for a good story.

As always, I want to thank my first readers for their feedback on the book. This time around they are: Jackie Wells in England (who was very involved and helpful, especially on some English expressions); Ann Zdunczyk; Dr. John McCann, who helped with medical accuracy; and Carol, my wife, whose valuable suggestions made the work more readable. The book is better because of their comments and encouragement, but they aren't responsible for any missteps in the book. Any you find are on me.

Most of all, I want to express my great appreciation for a dear friend, Mary Catharine Nelson, of *Ideas into Books*® *Westview*, who not only offered encouragement, but who reformatted the manuscript to produce a beautiful and very readable print version of the book.

✠

Patrick Orion is a private investigator from my other shorter series. Orion and Gabriel know each other because they both attend St. Mary Magdalene Episcopal Cathedral, the fictional Church where Trevor made some amazing discoveries and Gabby almost died. If you like Paddy, the third book in the series will be available in early 2017. It's titled *The Beale Street Murders*. Like the other Orion books, it is set in Memphis, Tennessee, my hometown.

Please go to my website www.jerryharberwriter.weebly.com to read about my writing projects or to contact me. I enjoy correspondence with my readers and promise to answer any email. Also, I very much appreciate reviews on Amazon, the only place my ebooks are available.

✠

www.ingramcontent.com/pod-product-compliance
Lightning Source LLC
Chambersburg PA
CBHW020329120726
47904CB00002B/341